Liz Byrski was born and brought up in England and has lived in Western Australia since 1981. She is the author of a number of non-fiction books, and has worked as a staff and freelance journalist, a broadcaster with ABC Radio and an adviser to a minister in the WA Government. Liz now lectures in professional writing at Curtin University. She is also the author of *Gang of Four* and *Food, Sex & Money*.

www.lizbyrski.com.au

D1513846

Also by Liz Byrski

Gang of Four
Food, Sex & Money

BELLY DANCING FOR BEGINNERS

Liz Byrski

PAN
Pan Macmillan Australia

First published 2006 in Macmillan by Pan Macmillan Australia Pty Limited
This Pan edition published in 2007 by Pan Macmillan Australia Pty Limited
1 Market Street, Sydney

National Library of Australia
Cataloguing-in-Publication data:

Byrski, Liz.
Belly dancing for beginners.

ISBN 978 0 330 42345 8.

1. Belly dance – Fiction. I. Title.

A823.4

The characters and events in this book are fictitious and any resemblance to
real persons, living or dead, is purely coincidental.

Typeset in 11/14 pt Palatino by Post Pre-press Group
Printed in Australia by McPherson's Printing Group

Papers used by Pan Macmillan Australia Pty Ltd are natural, recyclable
products made from wood grown in sustainable forests. The manufacturing
processes conform to the environmental regulations of the country of origin.

Author photograph: Jacinta Innes

ONE

Sonya was feeling very Monday morning-ish, possibly because she hadn't yet had her first cup of coffee but more likely, she thought, due to yesterday evening's encounter in a coffee shop. Gazing out of her office window she reflected on whether it was similarity or difference that brought people together and hoped, not for the first time, that it was the latter. Her ability to attract losers was worrying enough without that added dimension of cause and effect. And her latest foray into the world of Internet dating had been a reminder that nothing much had changed. The previous evening she had been about ten minutes into her first face-to-face meeting with a pleasant looking man who had described himself as an entrepreneur with an active interest in the arts. They had met in an elegant but overpriced café, lined with stainless steel and stark black and white tiles, where the noise of the grinders constantly shattered conversation and left the customers blinking in shock.

'I just want to let you know,' the man had said in one of the oases of stunned silence, 'that my wife and I don't sleep together . . . so it's, well . . . you know . . . it's all right for you and me.'

Sonya, who had not even known he was married, put down her cup and stared at him.

'I think you may have mistaken me for someone who fancies you,' she said, picking up her handbag. 'And if all the men who used that as some sort of excuse to screw around were laid end to end, more than half the men in the world would be flat on their backs.'

He opened his mouth and shut it again.

'And that might not be a bad thing,' Sonya added. 'Less violence, fewer wars, less sport on weekend television,' and with that she walked out of the café and left him staring into the remains of his macchiato.

Sonya wasn't usually quite so cynical about the opposite sex; indeed, she had once succumbed to this particular line of seduction herself, but only after weeks of agonising self-restraint. Certainly not ten minutes into her first latte. Once home she put a blocker on his email address and user name; it helped but it didn't fully erase her anger, nor soothe the sore spot in her psyche that occasionally dragged her to the brink of tedious victimhood. Why should he assume she'd want to sleep with him anyway? She'd never set eyes on him until tonight.

'Men,' Sonya said aloud, 'I don't know why I bother.'

In fact, these days she rarely did bother. She wasn't much concerned about being fifty-six and single. She had a job she loved, plenty of friends, a busy social life and her own home. After two disastrous marriages and various other relationships, there was enormous satisfaction in going home at night to domestic peace instead of the emotional minefield of someone else's emotions and expectations. She was good at doing things alone – mostly she preferred it – and if she needed company she had her friends. So what was she doing on an Internet dating site anyhow? Well, the world is designed for couples, especially if one is in one's fifties, and even the single woman's closest friends who so often secretly envy her freedom, are prone to suggest, in the most unsubtle ways, that being alone is a lesser state than being partnered.

'Don't you ever get lonely?' Sonya's friends, particularly the younger ones, would ask, small furrows of concern forming between their eyebrows. And Sonya would honestly reply that she never did.

'Well, what about sex . . . don't you miss it?' they'd persist, implying that maybe her hormones were out of sync. Sonya had had a lot of sex in the past, much of it good, much of it embarrassingly bad. There had been a period in her late forties when, newly divorced, she had enjoyed a sexual roller coaster ride, which had made up for her comparatively chaste youth. But in the last couple of years it had seemed rather a waste of time and energy, and she had grown comfortable with the sense of congruence that came with long periods of celibacy.

'Hardly ever think about it these days,' she'd reply, remembering a time when she had been able to think of little else. 'One wants different things at different times of one's life. I used to surf and go to rock concerts but I've lost interest in those things too.' On occasions she might also mention that had she put as much effort in to building an investment strategy as she had put in to searching for a relationship and/or sex, she would by now have been a very rich woman.

But the Internet dating site? Sonya suspected that within everyone there burns the flame of hope that somewhere there is a soul mate; someone with whom we will connect so intimately and intensely that we can become our best selves. These days her flame flickered only occasionally, and could usually be subdued by a surf through the depressing line-up of fifty-plus caring gents, down-to-earth blokes, silver foxes and young-at-heart romantic guys, all with a good sense of humour, who dominated the website profiles. After the coffee shop encounter, six months at least was now likely to pass before she once again decided to check out the possibilities.

So here she was the following morning, staring out of the window of the huge East Perth building that housed the Department of Education, imagining she could see through the tree tops and past the sharp angles of the new ABC studios to the prestigious East Perth development along the river inlet. She was contemplating property investment and increased borrowing. Increasing the home loan was not a huge problem – it was currently comparatively small, her income good, her job secure and she had another ten years before she retired, probably more if Peter Costello had his way with her. But the prospect of sixty being the new forty filled her with frustration: surely by sixty-five she would have served her life sentence as a wage slave. Maybe she should scrap the moving idea and take early retirement instead.

'East Perth is cool,' Angie said, sticking her head around the half-open door. 'Especially if you can buy on the waterfront. Tony and I had a look at a place there but we couldn't afford it.'

'And you think I can?' Sonya asked, without turning round.

Angie joined her at the window. 'Probably. And it's very elegant.'

'Mmm. But I'm not sure I've got the wardrobe to do it justice.'

'Course you have. Anyway, I just came to invite you to my hens' night. It's the Wednesday before the wedding. You will come, won't you?'

Sonya hesitated. 'Isn't this for your girlfriends? Wouldn't I be in the way – a bit over the age limit?'

'Of course not,' Angie said. 'My mum and her best friend will be there, and Tony's mum.'

Sonya was cornered. Angie had been assigned to her section six months earlier and Sonya generally preferred to keep her social life separate from her work. But Angie, by virtue of her engaging personality, had managed to draw her into the sort of working relationship in which some social dimension was possible. Sonya had already accepted an invitation to the wedding, although the prospect of going to a wedding where she knew only the bride was not appealing. Now she was being invited to cluck with the hens.

'Okay,' she said, cautiously. 'If you're sure, then of course I'd love to.' It was, after all, rather a privilege to be invited to something as personal as a hens' night, and she supposed she'd survive it; perhaps she could just pop along for an hour and then duck away.

'Great,' Angie said. 'I really want you to meet Mum. I've told her all about you,' and she wrote the date and the address on the pad on Sonya's desk and, with a smile with which it was impossible to argue, retreated to her own office.

Sonya tried to concentrate on feeling flattered, and to remember what it was like to look forward to marriage without the hangover of previous experience, without cynicism and residual disappointment. There had been a time like that, as indeed there had been a time when hope triumphed over experience for a second chance. These days she had to struggle to comprehend why any young woman would contemplate giving up not just her independence, but her head space, to someone who would inevitably overwrite it with his own needs, desires and expectations. Cynicism was, she realised, becoming a permanent and not very attractive feature of her personality. It would do her good to be surrounded by innocence and hope. She would try to enjoy it in the right sort of spirit.

That same morning Marissa, who was long accustomed to waking alone at dawn, wandered barefoot around her garden, wearing a cotton kimono and clutching a cup of green tea. A few days earlier she had done some intensive spring gardening: pruning, planting, mulching. Now everything was sparkling from a light, pre-dawn shower, the mulch was rich and dark and the small stretch of lawn glistened in the sunlight. Marissa breathed in the fresh damp air and curled her toes in pleasure on the wet grass. But as she stopped to admire some new buds on the Iceberg rose, she noticed that alongside it there were several large footprints that began in the soft earth close to the fence and led across the lawn. And as she traced them to the opposite bed she saw, to her dismay, that not only had several of her tomato plants been crushed, but the three marijuana plants which they concealed had been ripped out.

Marissa stared down at the earthy dark holes in shock, and then noticed that the door to the disused dunny that doubled as a garden shed was half open. When she peered inside, her heart beating uncomfortably fast, she saw that the bunch of drying leaves and seeds from the plant she had harvested a few weeks earlier was also gone.

'Kids,' her neighbour, Alberto, grumbled later that morning. 'Kids, they come through the garden last night, pick all the olives, break my new vine. Teenagers, you know? What they want olives for? They no bottle them, for sure. They take anything from you?'

'Just a couple of tomato plants,' Marissa lied, 'nothing much.'

'Huh!' Alberto said, tapping his walking stick on the path. 'Kids! No good. What the parents think they doing? When I am children in Italy, we steal from the neighbours, we in big trouble.'

He shook his finger at Marissa. 'My papa very strict, don't do me no harm, I can tell you. What the world comings to I don't know. I call the police but they don't never do nothing!'

Marissa nodded in agreement; she certainly hoped the police would do nothing. The last thing she needed was for the kids to be caught with her stash and then own up to where they had found it. Marissa was not, of course, a dealer. Keeping a couple of plants for personal use was not a criminal offence, but this year she had grown extra for an acquaintance for whom a few marijuana cookies and a regular joint provided some relief from the pain of cancer.

She thought the culprits might be a couple of rangy boys who lived at the far end of the street in a house where ancient bikes and two decaying lounge chairs filled the front verandah, and the lawn was a mass of neglected brown patches. They were often seen hanging around at weekends and after school, baseball caps worn back to front, scuffed trainers, baggy shorts, kicking a ball or taking turns on a skateboard covered in stickers. She didn't think they were bad kids, just kids doing things kids do, and she hoped they had hidden her grass somewhere safe.

Marissa didn't subscribe to the popular view of teenagers as the new urban terrorists. Only the other day she'd heard some supposedly left-wing commentator whining about how much better things were when he was a kid in the fifties; how he and his brother raided gardens pinching strawberries and watermelons. Strawberries and watermelons – was there any difference between this rose-tinted nostalgia and the theft of olives and marijuana plants? It was just a sign of the times. She too had been a child in the fifties and could remember nicking raspberries and gooseberries from the neighbours as the light faded on long English summer evenings.

In this, as in other ways, Marissa differed from the majority of her neighbours. In the twenty years she had lived in Fremantle both the street and city had changed. In the early days her neighbours had largely been postwar European migrants, the men working on the wharf, the fishing boats or the railway, and the women at the biscuit factory. But in the wave of gentrification that followed Australia's winning of the America's Cup in 1983, the cottages had been renovated out of recognition by trendy politicians, minor media personalities and professional couples with a nose for real estate values. Alberto and Maria next door were the only originals from the days when Marissa had bought this small weatherboard cottage.

The scruffy house at the end of the street was a deceased estate, let to a shifting procession of tenants who were able to ignore the fact that it was falling apart. That house and Marissa's own were a source of irritation and offence to many of the new inhabitants of Violet Street. In Marissa's case the garden was too wild and unkempt, the big clumps of sunflowers leaned out over the pavement, the ancient lemon tree dropped its fruit and the sprawling clumps of white daisies that grew thicker and faster every year poked out through the slatted front fence. Everything thrived in Marissa's garden, front and back, including the marijuana. Only not now, of course.

The neighbours, with their neatly trimmed lavender, and kitsch paved paths, their trellised clematis and dwarf orange trees in expensive glazed pots sniffed at Marissa's house. And on certain days, usually at weekends when there was a lot of DIY and potting going on, Marissa could sense waves of disapproval snaking up her overgrown front path; the flash of new gardening gloves, shiny secateurs and cans of weedkiller seemed like pointed personal rebukes.

Some years earlier, Marissa had painted the house blue, a vivid sky blue, the blue that the Mexicans paint their houses to keep away evil spirits. Worse still, the window and door frames were a rich sunflower yellow – all that and the verandah hung with a variety of cane and metal wind chimes, mirrored mobiles and colourful mosaics fixed to the wall, was a bit *de trop* for the elegant minimalist renovators. Marissa was torn between scorn and empathy. Years ago, in the early days of her marriage to Roger, playing the role of the perfect wife, she too had been fanatically concerned about appearances. Now, while it seemed trivial and materialistic, she also understood the deep-seated longing to create an ideal living space.

The day of the stolen plants was a strange one for Marissa, the theft leaving her ill at ease. She paced nervously around the house in the morning and finally went out to pick up some new business cards, then to the community centre to run a couple of classes and, once home again, she took a shower. The bathroom and kitchen had been her only concessions to renovation – she preferred to wash and pee inside, and cook somewhere hygienic and easy to clean. You can take the girl out of the middle class but you can't ever quite take the middle class out of the girl, especially a girl who grew up in the fifties. And that, of course, was why she was still worried about her plants. She was still sufficiently middle class to worry about a visit from the police and a charge.

Feeling restless she contemplated walking down to the Italian deli to buy some chorizo and pancetta, perhaps have a coffee or see who was propping up the bar at the Norfolk Hotel. And that was when the phone rang. Marissa hesitated, decided to leave it, then changed her mind. That, she thought later, was how it had all begun.

Oliver Baxter had registered with the Internet dating site in the early hours of a Wednesday morning in June, having been woken by a visit from his mother. Not a visit in person, for his mother had been dead for years, but her voice would frequently echo through his sleep as clearly as if she were in the room. Oliver's eyes would fly open and he would sit bolt upright expecting to see her standing at the foot of the bed; the clarity of tone and the sense of her presence were so intense that Oliver fell for it every time.

The most annoying thing, over and above the fact of being woken and then not being able to get back to sleep, was that his mother wasn't telling him anything he didn't already know. It was the same old stuff over and over again, the stuff she'd told him when he was a teenager, the same advice unmoderated by time: 'What women appreciate in a man, Oliver,' she would say, 'is honesty, and someone who loves them for who they really are; who isn't seeking to change them into some idealised male fantasy.'

Joan Baxter had been a prominent feminist, and raised consciousness had proved to be something of a mixed blessing for Oliver. It made him an uneasy outsider among men and did not compensate him with any outstanding success with women. Time and again, Oliver had been honest and only now had he finally come to terms with the fact that the value of honesty was entirely situational. It certainly won him appreciative women friends, but it was a distinct disadvantage in the romance stakes.

Most women seemed to prefer men who lied to them. He had learned from experience that questions about whether a bum looked big in a pair of jeans – in fact, in anything at all – should always be answered in the negative. Even Oliver's thoughtful qualifiers about the attractiveness, the sexiness of the enhanced curvature created by the garment in question didn't win him credit. And to answer 'Yes' to the question 'D'you think she's attractive?' was to invoke jealousy and suspicion; it could even result in eviction from the shared sleeping arrangements. Women who were initially drawn to Oliver's honesty and feminist awareness seemed to have a very low threshold of tolerance for them once in an intimate relationship. They abandoned him with depressing regularity in favour of complete bastards who lacked all the qualities his mother had advocated.

Now, what sort of man is still haunted by his mother's voice in his late fifties? A worried man; a man who feels that somehow, somewhere, he's missed both the point and the boat. So one morning, Oliver, sleepless and infuriated, padded through to his study in those chill, depressing hours before dawn, took out his credit card and registered with the dating site, hoping he might attract the sort of thoughtful, politically left, mature woman who would appreciate the finer points of his character for more than a couple of months. He had obviously been going out with the wrong sort of women; hopefully, cyberspace might deliver someone more appropriate.

But now, several months later, not one woman had contacted him, and Oliver was far too cautious to initiate anything himself. What's more, he hadn't seen a profile that in any way matched his own. Maybe, he thought, this was only a site for people who enjoyed wining and dining, Barry Manilow, walks on the beach, and claimed to have a sense of humour. Thus far his own pleasures – reading history, politics and current affairs; good conversation; red wine; and the music of Leonard Cohen – hadn't rated a hit.

Anyway, on this particular November morning, having checked his email to see if his luck had changed and discovered it hadn't, Oliver set off for the university where he was Professor of Modern History. Fortunately, his continuing failure as a chick magnet did not stop him looking forward to the day. He was totally committed to his work despite the horrific increase in administrative responsibilities and the spectres of restructuring, legislative changes and reduced funding that haunted the corridors. And he had arranged to start the morning with breakfast in the nicest of the campus cafés, with his friend Gayle from the library. It was a longstanding friendship that had begun with her frequent phone calls asking him to return overdue books, and it had been consolidated when Oliver had been honours supervisor for Gayle's daughter, Angie. Gayle and Oliver now met regularly for breakfast, coffee or lunch, but never in their off-campus lives, where Gayle was married to Brian, an apparently very successful marketing executive, although Oliver wasn't sure what he marketed.

Oliver sat at an outside table in the early morning sunshine reading the *Australian*'s higher education supplement, sipping his first flat white of the day and waiting for Gayle, who was a little late.

'Sorry,' she said, arriving breathless and uncharacteristically flustered, 'couldn't find a parking space.'

Oliver nodded grimly. 'Gets worse, doesn't it? Shall I order? Same as usual?'

'In a minute,' Gayle said. 'I just want to give you something first,' and she rummaged in her large black leather bag.

She was a trim woman, rather conservative in style, tending towards grey or navy suits and soft tops in pastel blues or pinks, worn with a single string of pearls and matching pearl stud earrings. Oliver liked her for her calmness, her consistency and her good sense; she was a great listener and he had often confided in her about his failures with women.

Gayle had listened with respectful sympathy to the tale of his marriage to Alison, whom he'd met during the first year of his PhD. A law student battling the institutionalised sexism of the university law school, Alison was also one of his mother's acolytes. Together Oliver and Alison had struggled on student grants and part-time work, living in a tiny flat near the campus. They married when Oliver landed an academic job. Twelve years later it fell apart when Alison, having passed her bar exam and now edging her way up the legal ladder, fell in love with a partner in the law firm – the first in the succession of complete bastards for whom women would leave him.

Gayle was reassuring; it was the story of so many couples, she said, a sign of the times rather than a sign of failure. One day someone special would come along who would truly appreciate him. In fact, the idea of Internet dating had been hers, and she was delighted when he told her that he had actually parted with thirty-nine dollars and ninety-five cents for a year's membership.

Gayle was even interested in Oliver's latest area of research on the extent to which the wives of senior Nazis were complicit in the atrocities committed by their husbands. 'Women do some strange, often inexplicable things if they love a man,' she had said, and she had listened attentively as he outlined the thesis of the journal article he was writing as a precursor to a book on the same topic.

Now, retrieving a long, cream envelope from her bag, she handed it to him. 'I don't know how you'll feel about this,' she said, sounding apologetic, 'but Angie insisted. She so wants you to be at her wedding.' She hesitated awkwardly as Oliver opened the flap. 'Of course, you mustn't feel you have to come. I'm sure you've better things to do on a Saturday than go to the weddings of former students, but she . . . well, we both . . . Angie and I so much wanted to ask you.'

Oliver ran his fingertips over the embossed lettering of the invitation and felt a little frisson of pleasure, his eyes prickling in an unfamiliar way. It was a long time since he'd been invited to anything and he was genuinely touched. His emotional reaction clashed with his aversion to the idea of attending a wedding at which he would know only the bride and her mother, but emotion won.

'It's years since I've been to a wedding,' he said, examining the invitation. 'Thank you, Gayle, I'd love to come. I'd love to see Angie married. I'm very touched that you've invited me.'

'Oh good,' Gayle said in relief. 'You'll like Tony, he's a lovely young man.' She was relaxed again now and she leaned across the table, putting her hand lightly on the sleeve of Oliver's ageing corduroy jacket. 'You never know, there're lots of people coming – you might meet someone special.'

Later, as Oliver wandered back to his office, the prospect of the wedding hung over him with all the appeal of a boot camp. But he had accepted and it was too late for him to back out now.

TWO

Gayle sat on the lounge in the family room, watching Angie opening presents at the centre of a group of her girlfriends. She was
bone tired, her feet were killing her and she would have given her
right arm for an early night and a good book, but this was a once
in a lifetime occasion.

The room was filled with noise and laughter, shrieks of delight,
the clink of champagne glasses. A well of emotions threatened to
overwhelm Gayle – love, exhaustion and the melancholy that had
haunted her since she began organising the wedding. Apart from
a longish break when she went backpacking in Asia, Angie had
always lived at home. For twenty-six years she had been there,
part of every day: the adorable toddler; the joyful little girl; the
annoying, moody teenager; the warm, intelligent young woman.
As the wedding day approached, Gayle was struggling with the
knowledge that the daughter whose presence made life at home
bearable was about to leave.

'You'll be fine,' her friend Trisha had told her. 'Honestly, I
know it feels awful now, but it'll pass. It just takes time.
Remember how I was when Lindy got married? You *do* get over
it, it's just another of life's adjustments.'

'Yes,' Gayle had nodded, swallowing the lump in her throat.
'But you and Graham, it's different . . . it's . . . Oh well, you're
probably right. I'm really happy for Angie but I'll miss her so
much.' Now that the day itself was almost upon her, it was taking
some effort on Gayle's part to hide her sense of despair.

'Who's that over there in the corner talking to Tony's mum?' Trisha asked.

'That's Sonya – can't remember her other name. She's Angie's boss. She seems nice.'

'Hmm,' Trisha said, giving Sonya a critical once-over. 'I like that printed velvet jacket. Pity she's got that weird thing on underneath.'

Gayle smiled. 'Stop doing the fashion police thing. We're not all trim, taut and terrific clotheshorses like you. You'll start on me next.'

Trisha laughed. 'No way, darl, I gave up on that years ago – you're my lost cause. But I love you just the same.' She slipped her arm around Gayle's shoulders. 'When did we get old enough to have kids getting married? Next thing'll be grandchildren, and then we'll be getting our hair permed, and wearing floral cotton frocks and fluffy slippers.'

'Sounds quite comforting,' Gayle said, glancing at her watch. 'Oh lord, look at the time. It's turned seven and the belly dancer isn't here yet. Perhaps I should call and check she's on the way.'

'Maybe you told her seven-thirty?' Trisha said, following her through the throng of young women to the kitchen.

Gayle shook her head. 'No. I've got her card here somewhere,' and she was rummaging through a drawer full of lists and recipes when the doorbell rang.

She wasn't sure what she'd been expecting but it wasn't a person in a helmet and motorcycle leathers. 'I think you must have the wrong address,' she said, glancing at the gleaming black and chrome of the Harley Davidson in the driveway.

'I don't think so. Mrs Peterson? Gayle Peterson – hens' night for Miss Angie Peterson?'

Gayle nodded, speechless.

'Oh good, sorry I'm late, a last-minute crisis, but I'm here now,' and as she took off her helmet, thick dark hair streaked with grey dropped to her shoulders. 'Marissa, from Marissa's Belly Dancing?' she said. 'I hope you weren't worried. Just show me where I can put my things and I'll be ready in a few moments.'

'She must be as old as us,' Trisha whispered, checking her own face in the hall mirror as Marissa shed her leathers in the bedroom.

'At least,' Gayle said. 'Maybe more. Sixty, p'r'aps? I hope she'll be all right. The people at the Turkish restaurant said she's the best.'

Trisha shrugged and refilled her glass. 'We'll soon see. Want me to go and organise the room?'

Gayle nodded. 'Yes please, and take this too.' She handed Trisha the CD Marissa had given her. 'Stick it on the CD player but don't start it yet.' She waited outside the bedroom, wondering, not for the first time, why Angie had wanted a belly dancer. It seemed an odd choice for a hens' night, and the biker on the doorstep hadn't inspired confidence.

'Okay,' said a voice behind her. 'So sorry, Mrs Peterson, I hate being late. Hope I haven't upset anything.'

Gayle turned. 'Gayle,' she said. 'It's Gayle, and no, of course you haven't, it's fine. I'm just very twitchy what with the wedding and tonight . . . ' She paused. 'You look . . . amazing.'

Marissa adjusted the trailing veil of lime green chiffon draped over her shoulder. 'Bit of a contrast, isn't it?' she said with a smile. 'Sometimes I feel I'd be a nicer person if I wore this all the time. Now, after the first dance I usually talk about the traditions behind it, and I'll talk about the rituals around weddings, then I'll dance again and I'll encourage the women to join in. Is that all right with you?'

Gayle swallowed hard. It wasn't just the clothes – although the purple sequinned bra with its long fringe of silver glass beads, and the matching gauzy sequinned skirt over lime harem pants were stunning – it was something about the woman herself that unnerved her.

'That sounds fine,' she replied, 'just . . . well, I don't know how many of them will actually want to dance. I mean, I don't suppose any of us has actually done anything like this before. As long as you won't be offended . . . '

'Don't worry about that,' Marissa said. 'Let's just see what happens, shall we? You relax and let the dance do its job.'

Gayle nodded cautiously. 'So should I go through and start the music now?'

'Please,' Marissa said. 'And Mrs – sorry, Gayle, no need to worry. Women usually do enjoy it, especially on these sorts of occasions.'

Gayle started the music and slipped into the seat beside Trisha as a steady drumbeat signalled the start of the performance. The chattering voices faded to silence as Marissa appeared at the top of the steps.

'My god, is that our biker?' Trisha whispered, her words dissolving into a gasp as Marissa swayed gracefully towards them and the music swelled.

Brian, propped up on pillows, lay on a rumpled bed in one of Sydney's best hotels, watching the woman repairing her make-up at the dressing table mirror, and trying to remember her name. Kelly, was it, or Kerry, perhaps? She wasn't his usual girl – her name was Collette – but when he'd called to book he'd been told she was on holiday. He watched in distaste as this one began to dress, stepping into red lace knickers and then leaning forward into the matching bra. He didn't like her, she was bolshie and too fat, he thought, eying the miniscule swell of flesh where the high-cut briefs sat on her hipbone. He couldn't bear a woman who didn't look after herself. Brian scratched the broad pale mound of his belly and wished she'd hurry up. He wanted a shower before he was due to meet his broker down in the bar in twenty minutes.

The girl reached for her bag, took out a packet of Benson & Hedges and lit one, inhaling deeply as she reached for her dress.

'This is a no-smoking room,' Brian said.

Her eyes met his in the mirror. 'So what?'

'So put it out.'

'Who're you then, the clean air police?'

'I'm the customer, remember? Put it out.' She sighed, rolled her eyes and stubbed it out in a saucer. 'And get a move on, will you, I've got things to do.'

He swung his legs off the bed and stood up, pulling the hotel bathrobe around him. His wallet lay on the bedside table and he picked it up and put it in the pocket of his robe.

'Make sure you close the door when you leave,' he said. As he passed her he delivered a hard smack to her bottom and she yelped with surprise and pain. He smiled to himself – some women hated that and he hoped she was one of them. He went into the bathroom, turned on the shower and stepped into the steaming stream of water.

Despite his unsatisfactory partner, Brian was pleased with his own performance, which he rated as worthy of a man half his age. It was value for money, he thought. You didn't only get the hour of concentrated female attention in the areas that most needed it, you got the reassurance of knowing that at fifty-nine you could still go the distance. Brian liked to think of himself as a superb sexual performer. He'd been using sex workers for years, and when he found one he really liked he stuck with her. He saw Collette regularly, whenever he was in Sydney. In Melbourne it was Janine, and Lucinda back home in Perth. They always told him he was an outstanding performer, that he was so good they really enjoyed it with him, whereas other clients left them bored and unsatisfied. Brian's ego was such that he never for one moment considered this might be a standard line; he knew the truth when he heard it, and he was proud to be able to say that nobody – but nobody – pulled the wool over his eyes.

He picked up the small tablet of hotel soap, rubbed it between his hands and began to spread it over his body, massaging his genitals first and then moving up over his belly to his chest, armpits and finally his neck. Hygiene was important to Brian. He took two showers a day, sometimes three, the only exception being those days when he'd had a skinful and fell asleep before actually going to bed. He was a large man, considerably over-weight, and he sweated a lot, even in mild weather. His doctor had warned him about heart attacks and strokes, about his diet and cholesterol, about alcohol, the value of moderation and need for exercise. He did try to fit in a walk from time to time, but his regular spectacular performances in the bedroom always reassured him that there wasn't much wrong with his health.

He turned up the hot water until it was almost painful and stood under it as long as he could bear before swinging the tap to cold and gasping as the icy blast hit him, forcing himself to stay there for a count of sixty. That must be good for him, surely, and, after all, he didn't smoke. Still breathless from the icy water he climbed out and dried himself using two bath sheets – there was a lot of surface area to dry and he hated the feel of damp towels. Dropping them both on the floor he put on his robe and went back into the bedroom from which Kelly or Kerry had now departed, leaving only the traces of a perfume he didn't much like.

Brian straightened the bedspread, sat down on the edge of the bed and picked up the phone.

'Thought I'd catch my darling girl before all those hens arrive,' he said when Angie answered.

'They're here already, Dad,' she said, and he could hear the clamour of voices and laughter in the background. 'You in Sydney?'

'I am. Working myself to exhaustion to pay for this humungous wedding.'

'Oh yeah,' she laughed, 'I can imagine! Bet you're just off somewhere for dinner, with a lot of boring old blokes.'

Brian gave a theatrically loud sigh. 'How sharper than a shark's tooth it is to have a thankless child.'

'King Lear, and it's a serpent's tooth.'

'Really? Good to see all those thousands of dollars in HECS fees have paid off. Anyway, just wanted to say I hope you have a lovely party.'

'Thanks, Dad. D'you want to speak to Mum?'

'Oh well . . . not unless she does.' He waited, picturing her waving the phone at Gayle, and Gayle shaking her head.

'She's talking to my boss,' Angie said. 'So she's saying no.'

'Good then. Take care, sweetheart. See you tomorrow.'

'Yes, only three more sleeps.'

'Still time to call it off!' he joked.

Angie groaned. 'Your jokes are so predictable.' She made a kissing noise. 'Thanks for ringing, have a nice night.'

Brian hung up, found a clean pair of boxer shorts and a shirt and dressed quickly, deciding not to bother with a tie. He thought he might just have a couple of drinks and then an early night.

Standing in front of the mirror he towelled the last of the moisture from his hair, ran a comb through it, adjusted the open collar of his shirt under his jacket and, picking up his wallet, keys and mobile, made his way out of the room. He had the lift to himself, which pleased him. The lighting in it was good, flattering. He straightened his shoulders between the tenth and ninth floors, and had smoothed his hair again by the sixth.

He was looking forward to the wedding despite the fact that it was costing him several arms and legs: the marquee, the dance floor, the band, the booze, the caterers. The bloody flowers alone cost enough to buy half a car, although not the sort he'd want to drive. And neither Angie nor Gayle had yet been prepared to tell him how much the dress had cost, but he didn't care – only the best for his girl. And it was a chance to shove it up his brothers' arses.

'Yes,' Brian murmured to himself as the lift doors opened at the mezzanine level and he stepped out into the soft lights and gentle hum of voices in the cocktail bar. 'This wedding'll show 'em, this'll sort out the men from the boys.' And, spotting his broker nursing a malt whisky in a corner booth, he raised his hand in a wave and went to join him.

Gayle had cried so long and so hard that her face burned, her throat ached and her body felt drained by the intensity of her emotions. She had wept for the loss of her daughter, the yawning gap of the future, and the leaden sense of hopelessness that had overtaken her. And she had wept with anxiety over the wedding and particularly the explosive potential of the drinking that took Brian and his brothers to the edge of aggression and sometimes beyond it.

Was the dancing the catalyst for this outpouring of grief and anxiety? From the first few drumbeats the rhythmic liquidity of Marissa's movements had sent a shiver through Gayle's body. And as her eyes followed the rotating hips and shoulders, the undulating belly, the graceful snake-like arms, she too had surrendered briefly to the powerful energy of the dance. She had only seen a belly dancer once before, a pale, skinny girl whose gestures were overtly sexual and who had cavorted through a Perth restaurant targeting the best looking men with her pelvic thrusts. She had thought it tasteless and embarrassing, almost as embarrassing as if the restaurant had employed a stripper. So she'd been both surprised and a little disappointed when Angie had said she'd like a belly dancer at her hens' night. The idea seemed vaguely tacky, but Gayle had bitten back the urge to question it – after all, she knew little about what women in their twenties enjoyed these days.

At the end of the first dance there had been a brief silence, a silence as significant as the rapturous applause that followed, and Marissa had settled cross-legged on the steps and talked about the origins and traditions of the dance. Lying now with a cool, damp towel over her eyes to stop them burning, Gayle could see her there again, calm and authoritative, talking about a celebration of female sexuality, and about the sensuousness and the self-possession of the dancer being the key to its power. Once again she saw the roomful of women rise to their feet; she felt Trisha's hand on her arm pulling her up, felt the movement of the women's bodies, saw the swaying jean-clad hips, the swirl of skirts, and Tony's mother's arthritic fingers curled with unusual grace. Self-consciousness and embarrassment evaporated as they swayed and turned together in time to the music. Then Marissa had taken Angie by the hand, draped a glittering silver veil across her shoulders and shown her the steps for the bridal dance.

'It was wonderful,' Trisha said to Marissa later, watching as she rolled her costume into a soft calico bag. 'You were fabulous, magnificent . . . Honestly, I was blown away – we all were.'

Marissa grabbed her hair in her hands and pulled it through a scrunchie. 'Thanks. I'm glad you enjoyed it.' She turned to Gayle. 'They all danced. Once they see it and understand what it means, women usually do want to give it a go.'

Gayle blushed. 'I feel really stupid . . . I'd no idea.'

'Don't apologise,' Marissa said, struggling back into her leathers. 'Very few people know anything about Middle Eastern dance or its meaning. I'm glad you enjoyed it. Your daughter's gorgeous. The wedding's on Saturday?' Gayle nodded. 'Well, have a lovely day.'

She reached into a pocket inside her bag. 'I'll just give you these cards,' she said, handing a few to Gayle and Trisha, and to Sonya, who had now appeared in the bedroom doorway. 'In case you ever feel like doing some more dancing, I run classes. Beginners always on Wednesday evenings from seven to nine, and Saturday mornings. The details are on the card.' She handed over some vouchers. 'Come along and see if you like it,' she said.

Sonya looked at the voucher. 'Yes,' she said, 'I'll give it a go. You've inspired me.'

'Me too,' Trisha said. 'We'll be there sometime soon, won't we, Gayle?'

Gayle's breath seemed trapped in her throat.

'Course we will,' Trisha continued.

'Some women find it creates a bit of a change for them,' Marissa said with a smile at Gayle. 'And it's great exercise too. It was lovely to meet you. I'll get out of your way now.'

They watched her climb onto the motorbike, heard the engine kick into action, and gazed after her as she roared off down the quiet street.

'That was amazing,' Sonya murmured as the tail lights of the bike disappeared around the corner. 'What a fabulous woman . . . '

'And the mix,' Trisha agreed. 'I mean, the bike and the leathers and the dancing.' She paused. 'I'm up for it. Why don't the three of us go together?'

Gayle had bitten her lip and said nothing, slipping the card into her pocket as Trisha and Sonya swapped phone numbers. Now, hours later, she hated herself: her caution, the emotional and physical rigidity carved into her body. And she knew that, fascinated as she had been by her brief encounter with the awesome energy of Marissa's dance, she would not risk encountering it again.

Sonya sat at the top of the steps that led from her brick paved terrace down to the lawn. The night was still and clear, the garden rendered mystical in the silvery light of a full moon.

Contrary to her expectations of awkwardness and boredom, she had thoroughly enjoyed the hens' party, but now that she was alone again, she felt a web of small cracks scoring into her mood like the crazing on old china. A sudden ripple ruffled the surface of the goldfish pond – a fish, perhaps, or a frog finding shelter. The ripples sparkled like the sequins on the hem of Marissa's skirt that had floated out as she twirled to the music.

Sonya had been mesmerised by the dance: by the riot of colour, the flash of silver beads and the sensuous undulations of Marissa's body. First on her feet to join the dance and swaying rapturously with the music, she had a sense of herself lightening, shifting, and opening up to the meaning and the power that Marissa had described. She had yearned for its promise, that flash of insight into a different part of herself, but it evaporated once the party was over, to be replaced by the ennui that had entered her life by stealth in recent years, and which she had chosen to craft with threads of humour and disappointment into a veneer of worldly good humour. Was it emptiness that she was trying to mask? She did not feel lonely and yet she knew something was lacking in her life, something of which the dance had given her a fleeting glimpse.

'It's a celebration of female sexuality,' Marissa had explained. 'And quite often women find it releases something quite primal.' She'd hesitated then at the rustle of amusement and slight embarrassment in the room. 'It's about recognising a part of ourselves that our conditioning – which separates the good woman from the sensuous woman – so often suppresses.'

The idea was not new to Sonya, who had read iconic feminist texts ancient and modern. But over time she had found that while you could change the law, changing attitudes was equally if not more important, and an awful lot harder.

'Women are still "the other",' she had said to Angie only a few days earlier. 'We're still judged and still judge ourselves based on ideas that we've spent so much effort trying to change. It just seems to be a fact of life.' The words had rolled glibly off her tongue. 'We've learned to live with the contradictions, I suppose.'

Sonya broke off a stem of lavender and crushed it between her hands, holding the pieces up to her face to sniff the perfume, then rubbed her scented fingers on her neck and temples. What was the cost of learning to live with it, and to live with it in the sort of professional environment in which she had struggled to succeed? Was it this loss of some essentially female energy that had flickered briefly with the dance and then faded? She stood up, brushing the crushed lavender from her skirt, irritated by the same sense of being stuck in a rut that had led her to consider moving house.

Marissa rode home slowly and spent some time in the queue of drivers stopped for random breath testing on Canning Highway. It was her second encounter with the police that evening; the first one had been the cause of her late arrival at the Peterson house. She had been in her leathers, ready to leave, when there was a knock at the door and she had opened it to find herself faced with two officers, one in uniform who looked about twelve, and an older man in plain clothes. Beyond them, in the street, police cars stood, doors open, blue lights flashing, voices crackling over the radios. Marissa's heart missed several beats; it was three weeks since the theft of her plants and she'd been reasonably confident she was in the clear. She swallowed hard and assumed what she hoped was a surprised and guiltless expression.

'Evening, ma'am, sorry to disturb you,' the uniformed officer said. 'Constable Martino and DI Owen. Wonder if we could come in for a moment?'

Marissa raised her eyebrows. 'Well, yes, of course, although I was just off out.'

'Won't keep you long,' said the inspector, pocketing his ID.

She led them through to the sitting room, hoping that the guilty rush of heat she'd felt was not showing in her face. She gestured towards the chairs and the two men sat down.

'We're wondering if you can help us with any information on your neighbour at number twenty-three, Kelvin Sharpton. Do you know him at all?' Inspector Owen asked.

'Only vaguely,' Marissa said. 'Why? What's this about?'

'Drugs,' he said, and Marissa blanched. 'We've just arrested him in relation to international trafficking. We're trying to pin down a couple of people who were working with him.'

'Really?' said Marissa. 'How amazing, I'd no idea . . . of course, one wouldn't. I hardly knew him but if there's anything I can do . . . '

There had been little she could tell them. Sharpton drove a silver BMW, was away a lot, often out at night, but had generally been a trouble-free neighbour – no excessive noise or wild parties. She wasn't aware of anyone coming or going from the house regularly.

'Women?' Inspector Owen enquired.

'Women?'

'Yes, did you notice if he had any particular girlfriend or other women going in and out?'

Marissa hadn't noticed. 'Apart from the elderly couple next door, I don't really mix with my neighbours,' she said. 'They tend to think my house detracts from the tone of the neighbourhood.'

Owen glanced around. 'That so? Just looks like a real piece of old Fremantle to me.' He stood up. 'Well, if there's nothing more you can tell us we'll let you get on your way.' He took a card from the pocket of his jacket. 'If anything does come to mind, perhaps you'd give me a call.'

She took the card, stuck it behind a magnet on the fridge and, picking up her bag and helmet, followed them out of the door.

'I was wondering,' Owen said, turning back as the constable went on down to the car. 'You're Marissa the belly dancer, aren't you?' Marissa nodded. '*That's* where I've seen you before. You danced at a wedding at the Hyatt, a couple of months ago. The Purley family . . . remember?'

'Oh yes,' Marissa said, twisting her hair up into her helmet. 'I remember. Lovely people.'

He nodded. 'My oldest friends; the bride was my goddaughter. Nice bike,' he added, nodding towards the Harley.

'I think so. But I'm sorry to rush you, Inspector –'

'Frank,' he cut in.

'Frank . . . I've got a booking in South Perth.'

'Oh sure, sorry,' he said, glancing down at his feet and then up at her again. 'I was just wondering . . . '

'I really have to run,' Marissa said.

'Sure,' he said. 'Okay, thanks for your help.'

It was almost ten o'clock when Marissa cruised up to the lights at South Terrace and waited for a trickle of people to cross the street from the Norfolk Hotel. She wished she'd had the chance to talk to Gayle Peterson because she could tell the dance had really affected her. She had seen it before: women so confronted they looked as though they were about to fall apart. Gayle, she thought, would by now be crying her eyes out somewhere in that mausoleum of a house where everything was colour coordinated and nothing felt real; another woman ripe for change and for whom nothing would ever be quite the same again.

The lights turned to green and she slipped the bike into gear and pulled away, down the Terrace to South Fremantle, home, and the prospect of a soothing pot of chamomile tea.

In the bedroom she dumped her leathers, slipped into a cotton wrap and took her tea out onto the back verandah. It was a mild evening, and the still air was heavy with the scent of the moon-flower that sprawled luxuriantly over the fence. She always enjoyed these times after working, when she was centred and grounded by the dancing and returned to her own, very private space, her haven undisturbed by anyone. But as her eyes grew accustomed to the dim light she realised that something was different, someone *had* disturbed it.

A black plastic sack was lying on the table just beyond her cup and she tensed immediately, jumping up to put on the light. On top of the sack was a business card. Marissa held it, frozen for a moment, screwing up her eyes to read it without her glasses. Detective Inspector Frank Owen. She put the card down and reached for the bag cautiously, as though at any moment its contents might leap out and bite her. Heart beating furiously she pulled it towards her and peered inside. There were her three withered marijuana plants, parts of them dry, other parts slimy from the moisture in the bag, and the loosely tied dried bunch, still more or less intact.

THREE

Oliver was hovering, moving cautiously from one group of people to the edge of another group. He was trying not to look like the original spare prick at the wedding, and not to look as terminally bored as he felt.

The ceremony had been very nice; in fact, he had been quite affected by the sweetness, the tradition of it all – the church, the white flowers, the old-style vows – but then there had been the endless standing about outside the church while hundreds of photographs were taken of various combinations of people from every possible angle. And now, here they were back at the Petersons' place, standing about in this vast marquee, drinking champagne and waiting while more photographs were taken before the formal stuff could begin, and he still hadn't spoken to anyone.

It was almost five o'clock and Oliver reckoned that it would be at least another couple of hours before he could reasonably expect to escape without offending Gayle or Angie. The guests' tables were set for six or eight people. The bridal party's larger table was decorated with swathes of white chiffon held in place by bunches of white lilies and trailing green ivy. On a dais near the entrance a string quartet played a familiar selection of chamber music but, stacked behind the players, a set of drums, wind instruments, an amplifier and large speakers threatened dance music. Oliver hoped beyond hope that he would be able to leave before the dancing began.

He had been surprised by Gayle's home, the size of the house and the garden, the swimming pool, the general reek of money. Wandering inside he'd found himself in a marble-tiled entrance with a somewhat pretentious curving staircase. It was all so unlike Gayle, with her restrained, almost dull suits and pearls, and her unassuming manner. The house had the cold perfection of a display home, and it confused him; he wished that their friendship had remained within the familiar confines of the university campus.

She too was different in this environment. He observed her struggling with the roles of hostess and mother-of-the-bride and saw that the effort was taking its toll. She looked different too, in a full-length dress with long tight sleeves, a mandarin collar and tiny buttons that were covered with the same material. He thought of it as a dark red but he had overheard the woman next to him in the church murmuring to her companion that it was burgundy, and made of raw silk. Oliver thought she looked amazing: sophisticated, elegant, and so unlike her usual self as to be almost unrecognisable. It added to the impression that this, all of it – the house, the marquee, the wedding – was a sort of performance, that it was about something more than a family home, and a family celebration.

Oliver sighed and surveyed the crowds, wondering who he would have to sit next to for the meal. He ambled over to the table plan and pulled out his glasses, though even learning the names of his dining companions wouldn't be much help as he didn't know anyone.

'Hello, Dr Baxter,' said a voice behind him. 'Can I interest you in a champagne cocktail, glass of champagne, soft drink?'

'Simon,' Oliver said in surprise, spinning round. 'So this is why your essays are always late! I thought you worked at Mitre Ten.'

'I do,' Simon replied, 'Fridays at Mitre Ten, Sundays and Mondays at the call centre, and this whenever I get the chance. Gotta pay the rent and stuff – it just means a bit of juggling. I should warn you that the champagne cocktails are lethal.'

'Good,' Oliver said. 'I'll have one.'

Simon grinned and turned the tray so that Oliver could help himself. 'Weddings not your thing?'

'A little out of the habit, I suppose, and I don't really know anyone except Mrs Peterson and her daughter.'

'There are worse things than being a waiter at a wedding,' Simon said. 'At least I don't have to listen to the speeches. Well, I'd better get on . . . ' He turned away and was stopped in his tracks by a red-haired woman in a cream dress and jacket who looked as tense as Oliver felt.

'What's in the champagne cocktails?'

'Heaps of alcohol,' Simon said with another grin. 'They'll blow your head off.'

'Give me one,' the woman said, 'and come back soon with some more.' She glanced at Oliver's glass. 'You too?'

'Yes,' he said. 'I felt I needed something to get me going.'

'Exactly,' she said. 'Or keep me vertical and awake. How long do you think this will go on for – oops, sorry. You're not a member of the family, are you?'

Oliver shook his head. 'No, a friend of Gayle's from uni, and Angie used to be one of my students. I don't know anyone else here.'

'Really? Neither do I. Why don't we stick together? I'm Sonya, by the way. Angie works for me.'

Gayle's face ached from the effort of smiling; she felt as though she were trembling but the hand holding her glass of champagne was impressively steady. It was the tension, she supposed, and the fact that she'd had nothing to eat since a slice of toast at seven that morning.

All around her, family and friends milled happily, greeting each other, laughing, talking and shedding the odd tear of surprise or joy. Gayle longed for a comfort zone, someone with whom she could be herself. At any other time she and Angie would have been companionably spotting relatives or friends, commenting on clothes, sharing their own jokes. But today there was no comfort zone, because not even her best friend was privy to the sense of desperation Gayle felt when she stared into the black hole of the months and years ahead.

'You look fabulous,' Trisha said, slipping her arm through Gayle's. 'Even the superintendent of the fashion police is impressed.'

'You should be – after all, you helped me choose it,' Gayle replied, looking down at the burgundy silk. 'D'you think it's all going all right?'

'Absolutely, it's perfect,' Trisha said. 'Angie looks gorgeous, the ceremony was lovely . . . Just look around you – everyone's having a wonderful time.'

'But it's all so – well, so over the top. Angie and Tony didn't really want anything so big. It was Brian, really, insisting on everything.'

'And it's lovely, honestly, Gayle. Relax, enjoy yourself. It's your only daughter's wedding.'

Gayle swallowed the last of her champagne and watched Brian talking to his brother, who'd flown in from Darwin. For the moment at least, it all seemed to be going well. They were still in the stage of backslapping one-upmanship that passed for good-will, not yet at the point where family tensions and pent-up aggression strained the seams of their suits.

She looked around for Oliver and spotted him on the far side of the marquee, talking to Angie's boss. He was wearing a char-coal suit with a white shirt and a silvery blue tie. She had never seen him in formal clothes before. He seemed almost alien, at odds with what she knew of him. He was concentrating on what Sonya was saying, his rather long, beaky face turned towards her, one elbow on the table, his tortoiseshell-framed glasses dangling from his hand.

Gayle wished that she hadn't invited him, or that he'd had the foresight to refuse. If she'd left things as they had been for years, confined by unspoken agreement to meeting on the campus, she could have related it all to him later; toned down the family ten-sions and the embarrassing excess. But he had seen her here, at the heart of it, and she could not disclaim her part. She was expos-ing her other life and she feared Oliver might not like what he saw. She sighed and made her way across to his and Sonya's table, cementing the smile back onto her face and wondering how she could talk pleasantries about the ceremony, the flowers, the music and how beautiful Angie looked, with someone to whom she normally talked in such different terms, and with Sonya, who, she suspected, was feeling as out of it as Oliver must have been.

Brian was surprised by the way he felt. In the church he had thought himself dangerously close to tears, an entirely unfamiliar sensation. The pride he had felt as he and Angie walked together up the aisle had evaporated quite suddenly once the ceremony was over and she walked back down it on Tony's arm.

Since his return from Sydney two days earlier, Brian had gained considerable satisfaction from the throb of activity; the house and garden were full of people, cutting grass, setting up tables, delivering presents. The phone rang constantly and teams of workmen were erecting the marquee and laying the dance floor. He had strolled around feeling like some feudal lord, questioning Gayle, Angie and various contractors about who was doing what and why. The pleasure he derived from knowing that it was all down to him, his money, his status, proved an antidote to his unease about what was brewing at work. He watched with pride as Angie phoned bridesmaids, and hurried from the florist to the manicurist and back again, and as Gayle, with an absence of fuss and a large number of colour-coded lists, directed everything. It was women's stuff, of course, and best left to them, but Brian enjoyed his sense of ownership of it all.

But now, standing near the entrance to the marquee, the stiff white collar biting into his neck, the dove grey waistcoat uncomfortably constricting his gut and the champagne glass turning warm in his hand, Brian felt a sense of sadness, an emptiness that was totally unexpected and somewhat unnerving.

'This'll set you back a bit,' his cousin Baz said, helping himself to another drink and splashing some of it onto Brian's lapel.

Brian squared his shoulders. 'Plenty more where this came from, Baz,' he said, unable to resist rising to the same old bait.

Everyone in his family pushed his buttons with their snide comments about how well he was doing. Normally he'd really rub their noses in it, telling them he was paying for the honeymoon and about how he was giving Angie and Tony a big deposit for their house. But somehow his heart wasn't in it today. His heart, it seemed, had been left behind at the altar and now there were hours of talking and dancing and celebrating ahead and all Brian wanted to do was lie down alone in a darkened room with a bottle of scotch. He set his half-empty glass on a table and beckoned to a waiter, who rapidly materialised beside him with a tray.

'Look, son,' he said in a low voice, guiding the young man out into the garden, 'do me a favour. In through the front of the house, first door on the right, there's a bar. Pour me a very large Johnnie Walker with soda and ice, and stuff some fruit or something in it so it looks like that fruit cup. Then keep an eye on my glass for the rest of the evening and keep 'em coming.' And Simon, pocketing a generous tip, headed off towards the house.

Sonya, only slightly the worse for wear after her diet of champagne cocktails, had claimed a vantage point on a low stone wall by the marquee and watched as Angie and Tony came down the front steps of the house towards a white Rolls Royce, its bumper decked with old cans and saucepans. It was already after ten and it was clear that as soon as the bridal couple had left for the airport, the nature of the party would change.

'I'm going to get some water,' Oliver said. 'I think I've done my dash on the dance floor for tonight. Would you like to head off soon and have a coffee down by the jetty?'

Sonya smiled, watching as Angie, dressed now in comfortable clothes for the honeymoon flight to Fiji, tossed her bouquet towards a cluster of young women who leapt in unison to catch it. 'Sounds good to me,' she said. 'Let's wait for a dignified moment to thank Gayle and what's-his-name, and then do a runner.'

Catching her eye through the crowd, Angie waved and Sonya, struck suddenly by a bolt of unexpected envy, blew her a kiss. It was the excitement, the newness, the adventure that seemed, in that moment, so desirable. Marriage did not figure in Sonya's fantasies – she had already vowed not to make the same mistake again. It was the promise of change that she envied, the feeling that Angie was setting out on a different journey, an opportunity for reinvention. It surprised her that despite her own cynicism about marriage, a wedding still had the power to revive those feelings. Perhaps the champagne had got to her after all.

Near the open passenger door of the Rolls, Angie stood on tiptoe to hug her father, and then turned to Gayle. Mother and daughter clung together briefly until Gayle stepped back, holding both Angie's hands, speaking to her under the cheers and the laughter, and Angie, with a final wave, slipped into the rear seat and the door closed behind her. A cheer went up as the car moved smoothly out of the drive, pots and pans trailing noisily behind it.

At the foot of the steps to the front door, Gayle and Brian stood side by side not touching. He was rigid and red-faced with a smile so taut it was almost a grimace, and she was dwarfed by his bulk, her earlier pretence of happiness stripped away to reveal an expression that bordered on misery.

'She looks so . . . so lost – forlorn, really,' Sonya said, turning to Oliver and discovering he had gone in search of the water. 'Bereft, totally bereft.' She sighed, there was, of course, something far worse than feeling adrift in one's own life and that was to be shackled to someone for whom your feelings had become unbearable.

As the clanking of pots and pans faded into the night, Gayle bit her lip and tasted her own blood. It was over; before long the older members of the party would drift off home, while the younger generation danced on and Brian and his brothers drank even more of the night away.

'How are you feeling?' Trisha asked, slipping an arm around her shoulders.

Gayle shrugged. 'I'm trying hard to be happy for her, for them . . . '

'I know,' Trisha said. 'Letting go is a bugger, isn't it, but honestly, it gets easier in time. In a couple of weeks they'll be home from the honeymoon and you can be a fully fledged mother-in-law, and interfere to your heart's content.'

Gayle managed a smile. 'I guess so . . . ' She marshalled her energy. 'It did go well, didn't it? No dramas, not even any embarrassing moments.'

Trisha hugged her. 'Not one. It was perfect. And now it's time for you. Angie was like my Lindy, really independent, but somehow when they get married and leave it's quite liberating.'

'I suppose so,' Gayle said, hearing her own lack of conviction. Across the garden she saw Oliver clambering awkwardly onto the wall alongside Sonya. He handed her a plastic bottle of water and unscrewed his own, chatting as he did so and then taking a long drink. She was glad he'd found someone to talk to – it might have taken the edge off the tension she had felt in him earlier in the evening.

Sometimes, Gayle thought, you could make silly mistakes mixing one part of your life with another. Sometimes it was best to keep things safely separate, in neat little compartments where they couldn't contaminate each other and create a cauldron full of messy emotions to challenge the boundaries of friendship. All she hoped now was that any damage to her friendship with Oliver was minimal.

FOUR

On Saturday morning a week after the wedding, Oliver wandered down into Fremantle, bought the weekend papers and sat at a table on the cappuccino strip, sipping a flat white. The town was already busy with early morning walkers and sociable coffee drinkers. At the far end of South Terrace the market traders were unloading merchandise and uncovering their stalls, and the smell of coffee, croissants and bacon wafted from the cafés. This was one of his favourite times of the week: good coffee, the town gearing up for the day, the mildly superior sense of ownership that comes with living in a place to which people flock for its unique atmosphere.

Apart from his frustrations about his failures with women, Oliver enjoyed a relatively peaceful life free of anxiety. He owned a small, tastefully renovated stone house on high ground close to the war memorial from where he could see across the rooftops to the port. He lived simply and quietly, socialised occasionally with his friends from university, and although he reflected gloomily on issues of national and international importance, from American imperialism to the lack of a compassionate immigration policy, he generally found little to worry about in personal terms. This morning, however, his pleasant Saturday routine was overhung with mild anxiety.

Returning home the previous evening he had found a message on his answering machine from Sonya, asking him to call her. It was the second message she had left that week. Oliver liked

Sonya very much. She had rescued him from boredom and alienation at the wedding, they had laughed a lot, and she had managed to coax him onto the dance floor, where he had caught a brief glimpse of his younger self; of those days when he had enjoyed dancing for its subtle foreplay and the promise of what might lie ahead. But Sonya was not his type. She was a robust woman both physically and in her personality, and Oliver was attracted to quietly spoken, small-framed women with finer features. It must have been the excess of champagne cocktails followed by several glasses of wine that had blurred his judgement, because they had ended up at Sonya's place just before midnight and Oliver was surprised to find himself with his hand up Sonya's skirt, and her hand unzipping his fly.

'Are you sure you want to do this?' he remembered asking at one point and Sonya, kicking her shoes across the bedroom floor and throwing her skirt after them, had assured him that she was absolutely certain.

It was so long since Oliver had had sex that he suffered a moment of sheer panic as the prospect of embarrassing failure flashed before his eyes. But Sonya's ample breasts released from a cream lace bra restored his faith in himself, and despite the fact that he had always claimed to be a small-breast man, he abandoned himself to the moment. Indeed, to a considerable number of moments that lasted well into the wee small hours. It was only when he woke with a mild headache, gritty eyes and a taste like rusty nails in his mouth that Oliver cursed his own lack of self-restraint and wondered what would happen next.

Together they had sipped black coffee in Sonya's kitchen, trying to make conversation and failing miserably. Transformed by sobriety from the unexpected lust of the previous night, they seemed to Oliver to be two well-mannered but seriously mismatched middle-aged people struggling to escape from an awkward situation.

Later that day and throughout the following week, Oliver remained convinced he had made a fool of himself, and hoped he hadn't been offensive. Initially he thought he would hear nothing from Sonya, which was a relief on one level but disappointing on another, as he had really enjoyed her company. The phone calls had put him on edge. What did she want? What should he do? He clearly couldn't just ignore her messages, but if she were calling to suggest an action replay, how would he extricate himself without causing offence? He stared at the *Weekend Australian* with the discord of his uncharacteristic indiscretion disturbing his usual sense of calm.

That same morning, Brian stood by the side of the swimming pool holding a cup of tea and staring down at the pool-cleaner steadily suctioning up the debris. He was tired and headachy, having risen at five-thirty to drive his guests to the airport, and the odd start to the day had left him out of sorts. It had been a tiring seven days, various relatives hanging around after the wedding and Mal and Rita staying for the whole week. They had combined the trip west for Angie's wedding with a few days' holiday, and Brian, having previously told Mal that he and Gayle would love to have them over for a visit, had felt honour bound to invite them to stay. Having his new boss as a house guest when the situation at work was, to say the least, uneasy wasn't something he relished, but it did provide an opportunity to cement his connections with Mal, who had been transferred from the US to Sydney to revitalise the Australian operation. Shortly after Mal and Rita arrived, all the senior executives and their wives had assembled in Sydney for a weekend to meet and greet the new arrivals. Within the first hour, Gayle had commented that she hoped this would be the last she'd have to see of them.

'I don't know why you had to invite them to the wedding anyway,' she had groaned when he'd broken the news that they would be staying on for a week.

'Good political move,' Brian had said, sounding unconvincing even to himself. 'Anyway, it'll be nice to have a bit of company when Angie's gone.'

'Oh please,' she'd said with a sigh, 'just the thought of a week of Mal and Rita is enough to make me want to slit my wrists.'

But she'd come up trumps in the end, always did, of course,

and Brian was grateful. They had spent the week eating and drinking, taking their guests on a wine cruise up the river, visiting the Fremantle markets, driving out for lunch in the hills, and up to the monastery at New Norcia. The effort of being a good host, trying to suss out the best way to stay in favour with Mal and ensure that Gayle didn't get wind of the clouds that were forming at work, had worn Brian out. Mal wouldn't have said anything directly to her, but Brian had been anxious that Rita might let something slip. In the event it had all passed smoothly and now it was Saturday and he was tired and grumpy, and didn't know what to do with himself.

At times Brian felt he was sadly misunderstood, the casualty – the victim, even – of his own generous nature; misunderstood at work, where no one appreciated his efforts to come up with creative new ideas and marketing strategies. Outside the company others regarded him as the guru on product marketing; if he weren't so loyal he could've moved to the competition anytime, not that they'd ever approached him but he just knew it. And he was certainly misunderstood at home, Angie's wedding being a case in point.

'Why does it have to be so big?' Gayle had asked him when he outlined his plans. 'They want something small and simple, that's what Angie said.'

'Nah, let's give her a big sendoff,' he'd said. 'Marquee, French champagne, live music – the works. She'll love it.' He'd wanted it to be special so he could show off his daughter, his home, his generosity to his friends and colleagues, and to show Tony and his family how fortunate they were to be linked by marriage to his own. 'Besides,' he added, 'girls always want a big wedding with all the frocks and flowers, and we've only got one daughter, after all.'

Brian sighed. Perhaps he'd feel better if he had a swim. He put down his cup and walked to the shallow end to test the temperature of the water. There was an orange and white towel spread out on one of the chairs, where Gayle had left it after her swim. Gayle: most of the time she was a mystery to him. She'd been a quiet girl, always so eager to please him. That was what he'd liked about her, the way she went along with what he said, agreed with him, backed him up; it was really what had made him decide to marry her, that and the delicate prettiness that reflected her passivity, her willingness to follow his lead. He'd put it about a bit in his youth but when he was ready for something more permanent, Gayle had seemed ideal.

From the edge of the pool he could see her moving around in the kitchen and as he watched he struggled to define why, over a period of years, he had become the one who was trying to please. When had passivity and acquiescence changed to resignation and resentment? They'd had their ups and downs, of course, and there had been times when she'd tried to leave, but he'd refused to back down. He knew he was in the right, a man had to have standards, and he'd stuck to his guns. She accepted it in the end, he'd known she would. But why couldn't she be like normal women, shopping, running up the Visa card with new clothes and stuff for the house, insisting on holidays and nice hotels, throwing dinner parties? He could cope with that. But no, not Gayle. She had to insist on keeping the stupid job in the library, and on studying. What was the point of doing all that at her age? She'd be over sixty by the time she finished this thesis thing, and then what difference would it make, being a doctor of something or other? It wouldn't improve their financial situation, which he had already secured through his own hard work. Oh yes, he was misunderstood, all right. Even his daughter was always having a go at him about his job – not that she minded him spending up big for her wedding, paying for the honeymoon, and stumping up the deposit for a house.

A slight breeze ruffled the water and a couple of pink blossoms from the bougainvilleas by the fence drifted on the ripples. Brian reached irritably for the leaf catcher and skimmed them off the surface. The day after the wedding he'd found cigarette butts in the pool. Disgusting. His relatives, probably – slobs. People just didn't know how to behave anymore.

'No respect,' Brian said aloud. 'No respect for anything, that's the trouble with people these days.' He glanced across to the house again. 'No respect and no gratitude,' he said again, although it was nowhere near loud enough for Gayle to have heard. Dropping the leaf catcher he did a rather flat dive into the pool.

At the sound of Brian's body hitting the water, Gayle looked up from unloading the dishwasher and paused, her hands full of cutlery, to watch as he ploughed along the length of the pool and back again with a messy overarm. Since the wedding, Gayle had longed for time to herself. She was used to a quiet life: Angie was often out and Brian was always travelling, away for three or four nights at a time most weeks. The week with Mal and Rita had felt like an eternity. They relished each day with an almost childish enthusiasm, and maintained a nonstop stream of cosy conversation that made them tiresome company.

'You sure know how to look after us, Gayle,' Mal had said each morning as he tucked into his breakfast. 'These are the best hash browns I've had since we came to Australia – well, apart from the ones my darlin' makes me,' and he patted Rita's hand affectionately.

That was the most irritating thing about them, Gayle thought, their stifling togetherness. Holding hands, always sitting side by side, Mal's arm around Rita's shoulders, calling each other 'sweetheart' and 'honey' like characters in an American sitcom, sharing private jokes and then explaining them ad nauseum to anyone who would listen. She almost expected canned laughter and applause to accompany them everywhere.

'Thirty-five years and she's still my best gal,' Mal said, usually several times each day.

'And you're still my guy, honey,' Rita would reply with a playful punch on his arm.

Gayle sighed. How long was it since she and Brian had exchanged endearments, shared jokes, held hands? A lifetime, it seemed. Not that she wanted it now, no way, but she envied Mal and Rita the same way she envied Trisha and Graham: people who had been together for decades and who loved each other just as much, more perhaps, than they had at the start; couples who had grown closer, who had flourished through marriage rather than struggled to survive it.

Brian hauled himself out of the pool, padded dripping towards the chair where she'd left her towel, and began to dry himself. Gayle felt a flash of anger. It was her favourite towel, and she didn't want him to use it. There was a time when she would have loved the fact that they shared a towel, and more recently a time when she wouldn't have cared one way or the other. Now she hated it. She put away the last of the cutlery and went through to the laundry to load the washing machine. Earlier she had stripped the sheets from Rita and Mal's bed, and she piled them into the washer and reached for the washing powder.

Rita had shown her a photograph taken on their honeymoon. 'I always carry it,' she'd told her, 'to remind me how much in love we were then and still are. It keeps it all alive, you see?'

Gayle saw. It had made her think about her own honeymoon. Brian was different then, never the most sensitive of men but loving in his own offhand way. He made her laugh and she felt safe and protected. So how was it that all these years later they so rarely laughed together and the one person she felt she needed protection from was Brian himself?

The washing machine rumbled into action and Gayle closed the laundry door and went back to the kitchen and filled the kettle. Out by the pool, Brian had spread the orange and white towel over the sun bed and was settling down to read the paper. She watched as he pulled out the supplements looking for the sport and business sections and dumping the rest in an untidy pile on the ground. Finally he leaned back, stretching his legs out in front of him, ankles crossed, one foot characteristically jerking up and down. In a few moments he would cross them the other way and jerk the other foot. She knew he was grateful for the way she had looked after Mal and Rita, but he was unable to say so. He found her difficult these days.

'I can't make Gayle out anymore,' she'd overheard him say to his sister recently. 'She's changed, you know, not like she used to be.'

'None of us is,' his sister had replied. 'Except you, of course, Brian. You were always a Neanderthal and you still are.'

The worst part was that he really didn't understand, despite everything that had happened, despite the fact that she'd told him just how she felt about so many things. Somehow he always managed to rationalise his behaviour and his decisions while riding roughshod over her, and she always let him get away with it. She just gave up, locked it away, closed herself off to avoid the bullying arguments, the oversimplifications, the manipulative explanations, so that in the end he believed she agreed with him.

The kettle came to the boil and she got out the milk and the plunger.

'Coffee?' she called from the doorway, and he gave her a thumbs up.

Behind her the rest of the house seemed to echo with a new emptiness. A phase of their lives had ended and for Gayle the motivation to keep going seemed to have died. As she spooned coffee into the plunger she felt devoid of emotion, as though the effort of suppressing her feelings and maintaining the pretence had finally crushed her. A light had gone out and she could no longer see the way ahead.

Sonya headed down South Terrace towards Gino's, scanning the people at the pavement tables and feeling somewhat uneasy. She'd been trying to get hold of Oliver for a couple of days but he hadn't returned her calls. This morning she'd driven down to Fremantle early to get her fruit, vegetables and fish at the markets, and when she'd put it all in the car she tried calling him once again, this time on his mobile.

'Ah,' he said – somewhat evasively, she thought – when she asked him where he was. 'I'm out, you see, not at home.'

'I realise that,' Sonya replied. 'I can hear a coffee grinder in the background. I'm in Fremantle. Tell me where you are and I'll come and meet you. I want to talk to you.'

'Er . . . yes,' Oliver said, and there was a long pause. 'I'm having coffee. Well, breakfast actually.'

'Okay, where?'

With what Sonya thought was a distinct note of reluctance he admitted to being at Gino's, and she said she'd be there in minutes. He hadn't sounded thrilled about it but she wasn't going to miss this very convenient opportunity to meet up with him and set the record straight. It had been bothering her all week and she needed to get it over and done with.

'This is excellent,' she said, sinking into a chair beside him. 'I'm so glad I caught you. How are you, Oliver?'

'Oh yes, good really, I suppose,' he said, folding his newspaper and dropping it onto another chair. 'Not bad at all. Let me get you a coffee, Sonya. What would you like?'

Sonya watched him make his way to the counter to order. There was a tentativeness in his manner that she thought quite endearing. She vaguely remembered him telling her something about being brought up by his mother, but she'd had too much champagne to take in what he'd been saying.

'So . . . ' he said, returning to the table.

'Look, Oliver,' Sonya said, 'I really wanted to talk to you about last week.'

'The wedding?'

'No, not the wedding, the er . . . the rest of it.'

Oliver blushed and wrung his bony hands. 'Well . . . yes, yes, of course . . . '

'The thing is,' Sonya said, realising she too was blushing now, 'I don't usually do that sort of thing . . . hop into bed with strangers, I mean. I didn't want you to think –'

'No, no, of course not,' he cut in. 'No, me neither.'

'Really?'

He shook his head. 'Never . . . at least, hardly ever. I mean, I could count on one hand or less the number of times . . . ' He dried up suddenly.

'The thing is,' Sonya said, 'it's not that I didn't enjoy it, because I did – well, obviously you know that. But I just don't think we should make a habit of it . . . '

Oliver opened his mouth and shut it again.

'It's not that you're not attractive or anything like that,' Sonya went on quickly, not wanting to upset him. 'You're a very attractive man. I really like you and the thing is that I would like us to be friends, just friends – that's all. Real friends, I mean, not just casual acquaintances who got it together once in bed. Proper friends, not lovers. And I'm telling you this because I don't want it to be awkward. I don't like things left hanging, not knowing where one stands.'

A change had come over Oliver's face. A smile seemed to be playing around his lips and Sonya feared it was the sort of smile people use to hide the embarrassment of rejection. 'I'm sorry if this is hurtful, Oliver, but I believe in speaking my mind, getting things out into the open. Oh god, I sound like someone's mother.'

'You sound a bit like mine,' Oliver said, and he seemed to be smiling properly now. 'That's good, Sonya,' he said, and she noticed that the tentativeness had gone and he seemed more confident. 'Very good, because that's just what I was thinking.'

'Really?'

'Yes, absolutely. In fact, that was why I hadn't returned your calls. I was worried about what to say. You see, I don't usually go to bed with strangers. Not that it wasn't very nice, of course – exceptionally nice, actually – but I think the champagne must have got the better of me, and I agree entirely, we shouldn't make a habit of it. Friends is good.'

'Really?'

'Really. Not that you're not a very attractive woman, of course.'

'I thought you might be hurt.'

'Not at all,' Oliver said, his smile broadening.

'It would be nice if you tried to look as though you were.'

Oliver sighed and wondered why he hadn't seen this coming. Would he ever learn to spot the times when honesty was not the best policy? 'But you wanted it all out in the open,' he said, wondering how they would recover from this awkwardness.

There was a brief silence and Sonya scooped foam from her cappuccino.

'You're right,' she said suddenly. 'Absolutely right. Now we both know where we stand,' and she raised her cup. 'To being friends . . . '

As Oliver raised his in response, a very large woman at the next table stood up and swung her backpack onto her shoulder, sending his cup flying across the pavement.

'A very strange start to the weekend,' he said, almost grateful for the tension breaker despite his coffee-stained trousers. 'Have you seen Angie since the wedding?'

Sonya shook her head. 'Honeymoon in Fiji. What about you? Seen anything of Gayle?'

'No, she's having time off too – time to recover, I suppose – and she wanted to finish a chapter of her thesis.'

'I liked her,' Sonya said, 'but they're an odd couple, aren't they, she and Brian?'

Oliver shrugged. 'I must say he wasn't quite what I'd expected. Gayle hardly mentions him, not to me anyway. We talk about other stuff – work, you know, university politics. She's always very interested in my work.'

'Well, it's got to be a lot more interesting than Brian's,' Sonya said.

'Really? He's in marketing, I think.'

Sonya put down her cup and looked at him in amazement. 'You mean you don't know?'

'Know what?'

'He works for a tobacco company.'

Oliver stared at her. 'Tobacco? No, no, you must be wrong. Gayle hates smoking. He does too – didn't you hear him yelling at someone who was smoking out by the pool.'

Sonya nodded, her mouth full of croissant. 'Yes, but he doesn't seem to have a problem with selling the stuff. In fact, according to Angie, when he first took the job it was to develop a campaign to market cigarettes in some third-world country. Angie says Gayle was livid.'

Oliver's mouth had dropped open. 'I don't believe it.'

'It's true. That's why Angie's lived at home so long.'

'What do you mean?'

'She worries about Gayle, what would happen if she wasn't around, especially after the business with the brother.'

Oliver patted croissant crumbs from his lips with a paper serviette.

'What brother?'

'Don't tell me you don't know about that either,' Sonya said in amazement as Oliver shook his head. 'Angie's got a brother, couple of years older than her. His name's Josh and he's gay. Brian kicked him out. This was all just after the tobacco job stuff was happening. It was a huge family drama. Gayle threatened to leave, but of course she didn't. Brian banished him, you know –' she lowered her voice and put on a severe face – 'no son of mine is a poof . . . All that sort of thing. Told Gayle she was to have nothing to do with him.

'This was about ten years ago. I don't know where he went at the time but he and his partner have some sort of business up in Broome now. Brian won't have his name mentioned.' She peered at Oliver, who looked as though he'd been kicked in the stomach. 'Are you all right, Oliver? Have this glass of water, you look a bit odd. I can't believe you didn't know all this. I thought you and Gayle had been friends for years.'

FIVE

Marissa woke at five, restless but sluggish after an uncomfortably hot night. The dawn light was pearly and the smell of the sea inviting. She pulled on an old pair of bathers and a sarong and threw a towel over her shoulder. A swim was the best start to what promised to be a sweltering day.

South Beach was deserted but that wouldn't last long. The joggers, dog walkers and early swimmers would soon be trailing across the sand, ruffling the glassy water. She sat for a moment on a flat rock staring across at the distant outline of Garden Island, enjoying the stillness and the illusion that she was miles from anywhere, alone with just the sea, the sand and a few gulls strutting back and forth at the water's edge.

Eventually, she wandered to the water, plunged in, swam briskly to the rocks at the far end of the beach, and then more slowly back again, finally rolling over onto her back to float and then tread water as she watched the beach. There were people around now, a black Labrador chasing the seagulls and an elderly couple holding hands in the shallows. Marissa wandered back to her rock to sit in the sun, gazing out to the horizon. She didn't notice anyone approaching until a shadow fell across her.

'Morning,' Frank Owen said. 'I thought it was you. D'you mind if I join you?'

She did mind, but she moved slightly so he could sit down. She hadn't seen him since the night she'd found her fading marijuana plants on the back verandah. For a few weeks after that she'd had an uneasy feeling that he might just turn up at the door, but as time passed, and Christmas and New Year came and went, she thought he had probably moved on to more important things. The whole incident had shocked her. What was she supposed to do? Feel guilty? Expect a charge? Be grateful? She wasn't sure how she felt about him returning the plants. Was it some sort of power game? In her uneasiness she had destroyed the plants and dumped the bag in a roadside skip one night when she was out on the bike. Seeing him again revived her unease. She shifted her position on the rock and pulled the sarong over her legs.

'Haven't see you here before,' he said.

Marissa shook her head. 'I usually go further up, the other side of the groyne.'

'I . . . er . . . I was wanting to talk to you,' he said, looking awkwardly away from her and up the beach. 'I thought of phoning . . . '

Marissa's stomach lurched uncomfortably. Presumably he wasn't going to charge her right here on the beach, but even a friendly caution would have been embarrassing.

'Really?'

'Wondered if you'd fancy a drink one evening?'

'A drink?'

'Yes. The Norfolk, perhaps? And then maybe get something to eat down the Terrace?'

'Oh, well . . . I think –'

'Only if you'd like to,' he cut in.

'Er . . . yes, okay,' she said. Surprise was unnerving her.

'Good, excellent – Friday okay?'

'No,' she said, shaking her head. 'No, I mean yes, that's all right.'

'Seven suit you? Meet you at the Norfolk?'

'Seven,' she nodded. 'Fine.'

He got up. 'See you Friday, then.' And raising his hand in a half-wave, he walked off up the beach.

Marissa stared after him, wondering how it had happened; how, in less than a minute, she had agreed to a date with a police inspector. It was years since she'd been asked out by a man, and police were not her natural companions – although she had never known one personally, she had a basic distrust of the species. A few years earlier she'd been part of a very vocal action group protesting about police methods employed to keep young people off the streets of Fremantle in the evenings. Besides, his knowledge of her illegal crop put them on an unequal footing, so it all felt a bit uncomfortable. She had agreed because she was scared of the consequences of saying no. She hated her instinctive fear of authority, the fact that she wasn't the confident, strong-minded, no bullshit person everyone seemed to take her for. She picked up her sunglasses, wrapped the sarong around her waist and walked up to her usual part of the beach knowing that, when Friday evening came around, having a drink and a meal with Frank Owen would be the last thing she'd feel like doing.

Marissa was still pondering the situation that evening when she went to open up the hall for the beginners' class. January wasn't usually a good month for dance classes; too many people were away on holiday and the evenings were too hot, but to her surprise several regulars were waiting at the door. And as they wandered into the hall, kicking off their shoes and complaining about the heat, the three women from the hens' night arrived, pausing awkwardly in the doorway – the red-haired woman, the bride's mother and the sporty looking friend.

'Hi!' Marissa said. 'So you decided to give it a go.'

Trisha smiled. 'We said we would, but you know what it's like, Christmas and everything. Time just got away from us.'

'Gayle nearly got away from us too,' Sonya said, taking Gayle's arm. 'We almost had to apply leg irons to get her here.'

From the look on Gayle's face, Marissa realised this wasn't too much of an exaggeration. She looked even paler and more tense than she had done the last time she'd seen her. 'How did the wedding go?' she asked.

'Good, thanks,' Gayle said. 'Lovely.'

'It was fabulous,' Trisha cut in. 'Angie looked beautiful, fabulous food, heaps of champagne and we all cried our eyes out.'

Marissa put a big calico bag of veils and hip scarves on a table. 'Sounds lovely. You've never done this before?'

They shook their heads. 'We're absolute virgins,' Sonya said with a grin, 'except for that one-night stand with you.'

'And not much other dancing?'

'Not since school,' Trisha said.

'No bad habits acquired, then. Well, you'll learn a few basic steps tonight but don't overdo it. Just try to relax and enjoy yourselves, get used to the music and the feel of your body in the dance. It's more strenuous than it looks and if you feel stiff and sore tomorrow, you won't come back.' She looked at their feet. 'You might be okay in those sandals but flatter ones will be better next time, that or dance pumps. You can dance barefoot if you want, but it's dodgy: if you step on a bead or a sequin it can be quite uncomfortable.'

She switched on the music. 'Come along, everyone, in the middle of the floor, please. Let's stretch a bit to warm up, some deep breaths to relax, listen to the music, to what it's telling you. Good. So we'll begin with something really simple – remember, Gayle, Sonya and . . . er . . . '

'Trisha.'

'Yes, sorry, Trisha – the first thing to remember is that Middle Eastern dancing is very grounded, but you still need to be light on your feet. Now, watch my feet for this basic movement . . . and try to keep in time.'

Breathing deeply was always hard for Gayle. She noticed it when she was walking and swimming. She was reasonably fit but quickly grew short of breath, as though her lungs would not hold enough air to carry her through the activity. A yoga teacher had once told her that she needed to learn to breathe again, to let the breath into the upper part of her body. 'It's anxiety,' the woman had said. 'You have a lot of tension in the upper thoracic region. If you stick with yoga and meditation, you can change it. It may be quite confronting dealing with the emotional causes – sadness, fear and so on – but it'll be worth it.'

Gayle never went back. She had enough to cope with without having to confront everything she'd managed to suppress for so long; shortness of breath seemed infinitely preferable by comparison. She breathed deeply now, feeling the old constriction and trying hard to expand her chest. Trisha and Sonya seemed totally absorbed in following Marissa's instructions, expressions of rapt concentration on their faces. She sighed. She was here on sufferance, on the basis that if she gave it a try they might stop nagging her about it. They had met regularly since Angie's wedding and it was purely her own reluctance that had stopped them from coming weeks earlier.

Gayle's response to Angie's departure had been to immerse herself in her PhD, and she cursed her own decision to take some of her leave at a time when she most needed to be out of the house. She'd only been onto the campus a couple of times to pick up some books she'd ordered, and each time she'd thought about calling Oliver to see if he'd like to meet, but something had stopped her. Apart from a very short email thanking her and telling her how much he'd enjoyed the wedding, she hadn't heard from him. Sonya had apparently seen him a few times and now he was on study leave, starting with a trip to Berlin. She was beginning to feel that letting him into her personal life had been as damaging as she'd feared.

Gayle watched Marissa as she danced in front, her back to them so they could follow her moves exactly. She was wearing a sleeveless black leotard, a long gauzy skirt in deep bronze and a shiny gold-beaded scarf tied around her hips. When she danced she seemed to be an extension of the music. Her moves were fluid, sinuous, almost mesmerising, like the music on its unfamiliar Eastern scale.

Trisha and Sonya were laughing now, stopping to get themselves together after their first disastrous attempts. Gayle smiled across at them. She hadn't mentioned that she'd been quite a good dancer in her youth, but now she envied the other two their exuberance, the enthusiasm with which they both threw themselves into everything they did. Sometimes she felt as though some great ravenous creature had devoured her energy from within, leaving her bereft of spontaneity and the ability to enjoy even the simplest pleasures. It was becoming increasingly difficult for her to be with them because she felt like an outsider, like the dull, mousey girl in the playground hanging around behind the lively ringleaders.

'Hey,' Sonya cried, pointing towards her and nudging Trisha. 'Look at Gayle – she's got it, she can do it.'

Trisha spun round in amazement, and as they looked at her Gayle realised that they were right, she was actually following the moves Marissa had shown them and she was in time with the music. She was even managing to hold her arms in the correct position. Raising her eyebrows in surprise she grinned and carried on.

'You got the steps really well,' Marissa told her later, 'but you do need to loosen up. There's an awful lot of tension in your body.'

So at least she hadn't totally disgraced herself and thankfully she hadn't had to listen to Marissa talking about what it all meant. After tonight they couldn't accuse her of not trying and being a boring old fart. She had tried it and could now say definitely it was not for her and she wouldn't be going again.

Frank, nursing his third beer at a table in the courtyard of the Norfolk Hotel, rested his foot on the strut of an adjacent chair and contemplated the error of his ways. Why was he doing this again? He'd been getting a grip on things, finding ways to cope with himself, his memories, his roller coaster moods, and to make it safely from one day to the next without falling through the cracks of his own life.

As a young man, Frank's idealism about love had died a terrible death. Forced into a shotgun wedding at eighteen, neither he nor Julie thought they should be married. A couple of years later, struggling with a baby and a low income, their efforts to make the best of it simply ran out of steam and they went their separate ways. 'Never again,' Frank had told himself time and again in the ensuing years. 'Never, ever again.' But invalided home from Vietnam, wounded in body and soul, he had fallen in love with his nurse. How many wounded soldiers and their nurses have discovered, to their cost, that long after the body is healed the soul must still wrestle with its wounds? It would be a good few years before, along with others, Vietnam veterans were clinically

51

diagnosed with the post-traumatic stress disorder that would haunt them.

Frank and Anna had lasted seven years and, on reflection, he was amazed that she had put up with him for so long. Eventually she decided to save her own sanity and took a job in New Zealand, probably, he thought, with the idea of putting some distance between them. Since then it had proved safer for him to be alone, peppering his life with a series of brief encounters that began with scorching eye contact across a crowded room and ended a few days or weeks later when the sex-fuelled illusion of intimacy had burned itself out. Then the old symptoms would start again, the nightmares, the anger followed by moody ambivalence, the sudden increase in his drinking and the bouts of depression. Sometimes it took months for him to get himself back together.

Frank finished his beer and wondered if he could squeeze in another before Marissa arrived. What was it about her, anyway? Returning the plants could have been a bad move. He'd thought he was doing her a favour but she might see it as some sort of power game. It was clear she wasn't interested in him. When he'd asked her out she'd looked as though she'd rather stick pins in her eyes than have a drink with him, so why had she agreed? 'Women,' he murmured to himself, 'they always mean trouble,' but even as he said it he knew that he was the cause of the trouble, simply as a result of what had happened to him and what he had become. And as he'd grown older he had found himself yearning for something else, tenderness perhaps, affection, someone to hold him, someone to give him purpose, someone to love. But, knowing his own weaknesses, why was he pursuing this woman? The last thing he needed in his life was a dope-smoking, Harley-riding, belly dancer.

'You're interrogating me,' Marissa said later, putting down her fork and moving her empty pasta dish aside. 'Why do you want to know?'

'Because it's interesting,' Frank said, leaning back and pulling out his cigarettes. 'Do you mind if I smoke?'

'Do I mind if you smoke now, or do I mind smoking in general?'

'Either . . . both?'

They were sitting at a pavement table on South Terrace, which was noisy with Friday night diners and coffee drinkers. 'I don't mind if you smoke out here, but basically I object to smoking because it's so bad for your health. Shit, that sounded really self-righteous.'

'Yes,' he said, smiling but looking away from her, 'it did, and I assume your objection only extends to tobacco.' She had the grace to blush and Frank lit his cigarette. 'As I said, I'm not interrogating you, I'm just interested.'

'It's a job.'

He leaned forward. 'No,' he said, shaking his head. 'No, it's more than that. I've seen you dance. There's no way it's just a job. How did you get from prim young wife and secretary in the Home Counties to belly dancing in Fremantle and riding a motorbike?'

Marissa shrugged and stared past him, to the other side of the street where people were queuing for pizzas. 'You sound like you're taking a statement,' she said. 'Okay, well, I was brought up – moulded, really – for a certain kind of life: dutiful early sixties wife, destined to keep a perfect home and be a credit to a good but boring man with a future in insurance. I wasn't Marissa in those days, I was Jean Smedley. Then one day I was shopping in Sainsbury's and an Australian backpacker bumped into me and I dropped my shopping. A couple of days later I dropped everything and did a runner.'

'What, just left your husband and legged it with the Aussie?'

She nodded, and reached for the wine bottle. 'Yes, went backpacking and finally ended up here. It was an escape route and I took it.'

'You stayed with that same guy?'

'Yes . . . same group, really. You know what it was like in the sixties, everybody into everybody else.'

Frank nodded and drew on his cigarette. 'And the belly dancing?'

'That came quite a bit later. It was a way of claiming myself, I suppose. You probably don't know this but –'

'It's a women's dance, danced for women, not for sleazy blokes on buck's nights,' he cut in.

'Oh, you do know.'

'I can read.'

Marissa smiled. 'Can and obviously do, so you know about it. I've been dancing for more than twenty years now, and slowly it became a way of earning a living. Not a great one but enough for my needs.'

'And the bloke, whatever his name was?'

'Blue? His name was Blue. That's all I ever knew him as. We called him Blue Peter. You see, you *are* interrogating me.'

'Just tying up loose ends.'

'We split up after we arrived in Australia. Port Hedland,' she said, her face darkening. And Frank, trained to read the signs, saw her grip on the glass tighten and noted how she drew her other arm across her chest.

'And you never saw him again?'

'Never. He was strange, controlling, very shut off. He was travelling alone and he'd met up with all these other people on the way. I'd never heard anyone called Blue before, then I realised it was quite common in Australia.'

Frank nodded. 'I knew a good few Blues in the army. And you never married again?'

She laughed. 'No way! I'm not the sort of person who fits well into other people's lives.' She paused and looked him straight in the eye. 'I like to please myself. I don't do relationships.'

SIX

Berlin was covered in snow; it slowed the traffic, softened the city's noise and blurred its contours. The temperature had stayed at minus four degrees for the last week, rising only slightly in the middle of the day. Oliver had thought he was well prepared for the cold but the intensity of it had taken him by surprise, and on his second day there he had headed for a palatial shopping centre and bought some thermal underwear and socks.

He had been promising himself this trip to Berlin for years and now he was here he couldn't understand why he had left it so long. What had held him back? Wanting to preserve the dream, perhaps? A subconscious fear that it would not live up to expectations? He cursed the instinctive caution that had held him back from so many things in his life. Now he felt absurdly happy and wonderfully self-indulgent. He'd made the trip at the start of his six months' study leave because he had research to do here, but also his dream had always been Germany in winter. In that dream he was accompanied by a woman; no specific woman, although a few had slipped into the fantasy and out again over the years. This elusive love of his life was now the only missing factor but fortunately it didn't seem to be spoiling his enjoyment one bit.

That day he had finally met the woman with whom he'd had an email correspondence for several months. Erika, a lecturer in the Faculty of Arts at Humboldt University, was working on a topic similar to his own – Nazi wives. She had taken him on a tour of the university and then for a late lunch in a campus restaurant. While planning the trip, Oliver had daydreamed that perhaps they were destined for a romantic as well as a professional relationship. Her English was obviously good, and they shared professional interests; if she were single, perhaps they would share more – much more.

On arrival at her office he was delighted to find that she was a very attractive woman in her forties, but his fantasy evaporated when, during the campus tour, she introduced him to her husband, who was Professor of Philosophy in the same faculty. Oliver promptly relaxed the antennae that he had raised in hope and was thereafter able to concentrate on the purpose of his visit.

'I can make you the introduction to two women you will find very interesting,' Erika told him. 'They are friends from all their lives, from school, and both married to Nazi officers, very high up. Now they live together. They are ninety, I think – perhaps more. I will take you to visit with them, Oliver, they will talk very much. Sometimes it is hard to stop them. I can take you there and translate for you; it is not far, Charlottenburg only. You have the cassette recorder? I think they let you make the recording.'

By the time he left the university it was already dark, the sky turning from midnight blue to charcoal, and the light from the streetlamps glowed gold in the fine evening mist. His breath drifted in clouds on the cold air as he wandered through the grounds to the Neue Wache, melancholy against the snow and bare trees. In a side street off Unter den Linden he found a small café, cosily overheated by a glowing wood stove. The interior was lined with dark timber panelling and hung with etchings and photographs of pre-1900 Berlin.

Choosing a table near the stove, Oliver ordered coffee and Gluwein and settled down with his book. The combination of warmth and the spicy wine made him glow, and as the alcohol hit him he settled deeper into the chair, pleasantly relaxed. So relaxed that by the time he had finished the wine and coffee he couldn't concentrate on reading. Setting aside his book he took out some postcards and reached into his inside pocket for his pen. It was an elegant black and gold Parker he had used daily since Gayle had given it to him six years earlier on his fiftieth birthday. A few months later that same year, on her own fiftieth, he had bought her a Parker pen too, this one in brushed stainless steel. These were the only gifts they had ever exchanged.

As Oliver turned the pen in his hands, the urge to clear his throat turned into a cough and his eyes stung. Everyone here smoked; if he had one complaint about Germany it was that: the smoke-filled bars and restaurants. His clothes and hair smelled of it. In the past it would have been something he'd have reported to Gayle, but now? Oliver knew he had behaved badly. Apart from a brief email after the wedding he'd made no attempt to contact her, and now it was the end of January. Before Christmas, she had left a couple of messages suggesting they meet, but the sound of her voice had paralysed him. Not only had he failed to return the calls, he had deliberately stayed off campus on the days she'd said she would be there. Christmas had come and gone and he had sent a card bearing only his signature. His leave began with the New Year and then he had left for Berlin. The least he should have done was to call or email before he left, but what he had learned about Gayle's life was so much at odds with the woman he knew that Oliver could no more ignore it than he could confront it. And, after all, it was none of his business.

He selected a postcard of the Brandenburg Gate by night, addressed it to her at work, and then paused to order more coffee and wine. What should he write? Anything that might in the past have seemed normal and natural now seemed stilted and inappropriate. His knowledge and her ignorance of it hung between them. 'An iron curtain,' he mused, enjoying the irony. 'Well, I'm in the right place.'

Despite its confinement to the university campus the friendship had been precious. He noticed he was thinking of it in the past tense, as though it were over, and realised that something really was over for him. It could never be as it had been, because Gayle had become a stranger. He was shocked to discover how little he knew about her, while he had disclosed so much of himself. He had talked at length about his childhood, his father's disappearance and being raised the only child of a single mother, about Joan's influence on him, and her activism. He had confided in her about his work and his failures with women. Now his shock was twofold. Did his lack of knowledge mean that he had always dominated the conversation? Had he been boring her for years, using her as a sounding board, a confidante to boost his ego? He had heard women complain about men who mono-logued, who bored them to tears ranting on about their work or delivering their views on the state of the world. Was that what he had done with Gayle?

And then there was Brian, the wedding and the house, all incongruous enough even before Sonya's revelation. Gayle's life had unravelled before him like some horrible reality TV program. He was angry with her for changing everything. He knew, or rather he had thought he knew, how she felt about so many things. Hadn't they shared a mutual aversion to smoking? Hadn't they even discussed their distaste for the power and influence of the tobacco companies? And yet all the time she was living, and living very comfortably, on the profits of those companies.

And, worse still, the son. The Gayle he knew would not toler-ate that kind of treatment of her child. He had respected her as a person, valued her friendship, admired her integrity – now he felt robbed and he resented it.

He stared down at the card wondering where to begin. 'Berlin is beautiful in winter,' he wrote. 'Wonderful food and wine, snow and sunshine. I'm making progress with my research. Hope all is well with you. Best, Oliver.' It was impersonal, distant and all that he could manage. He held it up and read it, waiting for the ink to dry. Then he picked a shot of the Tiergarten covered in snow and began to write to Sonya, but he ran out of space and trespassed onto the area reserved for the address, so then he tore a couple of pages from the lined A4 pad in his backpack and filled them with his small slanting script. Finally, he folded the pages around the card and slipped them into an airmail envelope, feeling guilty relief that Gayle, who scarcely knew Sonya, would never know how much he had written to her.

It was cold in Chicago too. A different sort of cold: bleak and raw under a leaden sky. Icy winds tore through the streets, along the narrow alleyways and across the open spaces of squares, ripping newspapers and parking tickets from unwary hands, seeking out ill-fitting doors and loose window frames, whipping litter to head height and bearing it off across the city. People walked with their shoulders hunched, hands stuffed in their pockets, the earflaps on their fur-lined hats turned down, scarves wound around their necks, oblivious to others, anxious only to reach their destination as soon as possible to escape the biting wind.

It was weather to set the strongest nerves on edge and it reflected Brian's mood. He had flown over with Mal for the international sales conference, and delays meant that they had to show up at the pre-conference dinner with scarcely time to wash and change. As he collected his name tag and ordered his first drink, Brian felt rushed and irritable. He'd never been keen on this conference but in past years he had frequently come to it a winner. This year was different; this year there were no awards coming his way, just a large neon question mark hanging over his head.

The pre-conference dinner was the occasion for effusive greetings and backslapping; for conversations about sales figures and new initiatives; who was on the up, who had been let go. Let go. What a misnomer that was, Brian thought, the words implying a sense of purpose on the part of the victim that could not be resisted by the employer, a sense of regret. Whereas everyone knew that when your number was up they couldn't get you out fast enough. You would be given the order to pack your things immediately, hand over your staff pass and be marched out of the building with your possessions in a box.

Brian sighed and reached for his second drink. He needed to get a few under his belt to break his mood. Perhaps he was wrong, perhaps he was misreading the signs, but one thing he had learned over the years was that when things go wrong, when something big is lost or conceded, there is always a scapegoat and it's rarely the person responsible for the stuff-up but someone else a little lower down the food chain – someone exactly like him.

A meaty hand descended on Brian's shoulder, making him start suddenly and choke on his drink.

'So, Brian, old buddy, how are ya? Good to see you.' Rod

Campbell, his former boss, was wearing a very expensive charcoal suit and looking exceptionally pleased with himself. 'How're you going back home in Oz? I sure miss you guys.'

Brian allowed his free hand to be pumped in both of Rod's. 'Good, thanks, Rod. You seem to be doing well.'

'Sure am. I love this place. America is where it's at. Family love it too. Susie's in heaven – shopping, shopping, shopping. She and the girls must have added several percentage points to the GDP already. How's Gayle?'

Brian wondered why it was that in less than a year Rod had acquired an American accent. Not just a hint, not just the odd vowel here or inflection there, but a complete transformation that made him sound more American than the Americans themselves. Suddenly he hated it all: the false bonhomie, the self-aggrandising conversations, the ridiculous charade that people from company outposts around the world were working together like a great cohesive international team, when the truth was that each one of them would cut the other's throat to gain a millimetre of advantage.

'And how's that little hiccup with the regulation board moving along?' Rod asked. 'I guess you'll have a decision soon?'

Brian gritted his teeth. It was the little hiccup with the regulation board over labelling that was responsible for his current unease. The new labelling had always been risky and potentially misleading, but Rod had been right behind it until it all went pear-shaped. Then he'd taken a swift step sideways and left Brian hanging out to dry. He attempted to look confident and unconcerned but had difficulty mustering the desired expression.

'Couple of months,' he said. 'That cock-up in the early stages hasn't helped. We haven't been able to claw back the ground since then.'

Rod's eyes glazed over and he delivered an icy smile, a warning to Brian to watch his step, but Brian wasn't in the mood.

'You think you're clear of it now, I guess,' Brian said, picking up a third drink from a passing tray, 'leaving it for us poor buggers to mop up the mess.'

Rod deposited his own empty glass on the same tray and put

his hands in his trouser pockets, leaning slightly away from Brian. 'Leaving it in your capable hands, rather,' he said. 'I'm sure you and the big Texan can pull a few rabbits out of the hat. Hope you're getting along well with Mal, Brian. It pays to keep your friends close and your enemies closer.' And with a nod he turned away, edging himself into a nearby group whose members welcomed him noisily.

Brian drank his way through the dinner and the speeches, the alcohol blurring the sharp edges of his irritability and resentment, making it possible for him to survive the pleasantries until he could get away.

Back in his room at last he flung himself on the bed with a quarter bottle of Jack Daniel's and a glass of ice from the mini-bar, and flicked on the television. But as he lay there, staring unseeingly at the screen, he was struck by a sense of hopelessness and a loneliness so overpowering that he began to tremble. Getting up he paced the room several times, and flicked the remote control through old movies, ads for fitness equipment, born-again evangelists, and back-to-back reruns of *Happy Days*.

Tossing the remote onto the bed he dragged at his tie with one shaking hand and then ripped so hard at his collar that he tore off the button. Setting his glass down to take off his jacket he knocked the conference hospitality pack off the desk. Its contents spilled out onto the carpet and, still unable to control the trembling, Brian got down on his knees to pick up the brochures and postcards, the embossed pens and a prayer sheet. A business card slipped sideways and as he went to push it back into the pile he read the name. *Ecstasy Escorts*, it said, *Professional, Discreet, At Your Service 24/7*. He flicked the card between his fingers. Despite what he got up to in Australia, Brian had always been very careful to keep his nose clean at company events. The local sex trade thrived on occasions like these but he preferred to play it safe. Tonight, though . . . He stared at the card. It would relax him, get rid of all the tension. Sex always increased his confidence, made him more aggressive, and he needed that.

He quickly dialled the number on the card, but when it was answered he paused and then put the receiver down suddenly.

Too risky. His room was next door to Mal's, and Mal was a born-again Christian, guided by the Lord in everything he did. He was prone to deliver long homilies about fidelity, chastity and family values. Brian needed Mal right now, he needed his endorsement, his trust, his respect.

He wondered about calling Gayle. It would be nine-thirty in the morning in Perth. The answering machine was on at home, and when he tried her mobile it was switched off.

'Never there when I need her,' Brian said aloud, slamming down the phone. 'Doesn't give a rat's arse about me. Everything I do for her and all she cares about is that bloody job and the stupid thesis.'

Hurling himself back on the bed he undid his fly and held himself, still at first and then moving, stirring himself to an erection. She didn't even want to screw him these days. Not that she ever refused him, oh no, she wouldn't do that, she knew there was no negotiating about that. Not a refusal, no, just waiting for him to finish, to be free of him. The ice queen treatment was enough to freeze the balls off a man.

Brian rolled on his side, rocking back and forth. The trembling stopped now but the tension multiplied. 'Fuck her,' he said, 'and fuck Mal, fuck the lot of them.' And reaching out for the telephone he dialled Ecstasy Escorts again, and this time he didn't hang up.

'So what do you think?' Sonya asked, standing back. 'Is it worth another fifty thousand dollars on my mortgage?'

'It's beautiful,' Angie said, running her hand along the marble benchtop. 'I love it. You should do it, Sonya. It's an investment, and you couldn't go wrong with a place like this.'

Trisha drew in her breath and looked doubtful. 'Well . . . it's a lot of money. I mean, it's gorgeous, don't get me wrong, but if you're going to upgrade, shouldn't you be buying a house? Isn't it land that appreciates? I don't think apartments grow so quickly in value.'

'Yes, but it will still grow in value. And I've got another ten years before I retire,' Sonya said, 'maybe more. Plenty of time to pay it off.'

'Go on,' Angie said. 'Honestly, you've got nothing to lose. I'd kill for a place like this.'

Trisha shrugged. 'If you're really convinced . . . it's certainly beautiful, and a very nice location.'

'No it's not,' Gayle said, and the others turned to look at her, reminded suddenly of her presence. 'The location is elegant but it's unnatural. It's all too new, too artificial.'

'All new areas are like that, Mum,' Angie said. 'Look at your place – we lived in that house for twelve years but it's still got that new area feel. There's nothing wrong with that.'

'Yes there is,' Gayle said. 'It lacks character, not like the older areas.'

Trisha raised her eyebrows. 'But, darl, it's lovely where you are.'

Gayle shook her head, 'No, no, it's not, it's sterile. This apartment is lovely, Sonya, but would it feel like a home?'

Sonya stared at her. 'Actually, that's what I haven't been able to work out,' she said. 'I love it, but I haven't been able to picture myself living here.'

Gayle looked around the empty room and then sat down on the cream carpet, leaning back against the wall, legs in front of her. 'That's very important,' she said. 'You need to listen to that inner voice, Sonya, it's telling you something.'

'Mum,' Angie interrupted. 'For heaven's sake, it's fantastic. Look at the quality of the tiles and the kitchen fittings, the carpets . . . '

'Those things aren't so important,' Gayle said. 'It's nice to have them but they don't make a place a home.'

'They certainly look great in your place, Gayle,' Trisha said, joining her on the floor. 'And that's a home.'

'No it's not,' Gayle replied. 'It's just like a shell. It wasn't my choice, not the location nor the house. It has no heart, no texture . . . '

'Texture?' Trisha asked, looking at her in amazement.

'I know what you mean,' Sonya said, sitting down on the other side of Gayle. 'It's about how you'd feel in it when you're on your own in your old dressing gown or trackie pants.'

'Exactly. This place is beautiful but it's like our place, lacking that certain something.'

'But Sonya would bring her own touch to it,' Trisha said. 'And your house has everything, Gayle. God knows how many bedrooms and bathrooms, the family room, the ducted vacuum thing, an intercom system, the pool.'

'But it's got no soul, don't you see?' Gayle said. 'It's like a display home. It was Brian's choice. He wanted it to show off, to impress his friends and his awful brothers. It's never felt like a home.'

'Well, whose fault is that?' Angie said. She was the only one standing now. She walked over to the window and turned back to face her mother. 'It's women who make the home, isn't it? You could've done what you wanted with it, made it your own, not handed the whole thing over to an interior designer.'

'No, I couldn't,' Gayle said, looking straight at Angie. 'It was so alien to me I wouldn't have known where to begin. But your father was determined irrespective of what I wanted.'

The atmosphere was suddenly charged with tension.

'Oh yes? And you argued with him, did you? Stood up to him? I don't think so.' Angie's face was flushed, her eyes unusually bright. 'You never stand up to him about anything. Have you ever fought for anything in your life, Mum? For the house you wanted, for him not to take that vile job, for something you believed in, for a set of taps even, or a colour scheme? No, you never ever fought for anything – not even for your own son.'

The silence in the room was deafening. Outside the window on the balcony rail a crow strutted precariously back and forth, and down on the street a garbage truck made its slow and noisy progress past the building. Gayle stared up at her daughter in shock as Angie dabbed her eyes with a tissue. Sonya cleared her throat and swallowed hard. The four of them coming here to look at the place and then going for coffee together had seemed like such a lovely idea. Now it seemed they were plunged into the middle of a family crisis.

'Well,' she began, struggling to her feet, 'why don't we –'

'It's all right, Sonya,' Gayle said, putting a hand on her arm. 'I'm sorry. Angie and I need to talk about this later.'

'Yes,' Angie said, 'sorry, Sonya.' She glanced around. 'Anyway, I still think it's gorgeous, and so near work too – ten minutes' walk and you're there.'

Trisha stood up and brushed down her jeans. 'Coffee time,' she said. 'What about that place on the other side of the water? Gayle?' She reached out her hand to Gayle, who took it and got to her feet.

'It's a lovely place, Sonya, and in the end you'll do what feels right for you,' Gayle said. 'You have the freedom to please yourself. I'll just say one more thing and then I'll shut up. It's about enmeshing yourself in debt. The real price of this place is your freedom. Suppose you wake up one morning with the feeling that you want to do something totally different – retire early and settle for less; travel, perhaps? Will this have been a wise move? Suppose one morning you wake up and just want to change your life completely?'

SEVEN

Deep in the bowels of the Department of Health, a form was being processed. It had arrived months earlier and had spent a long time with other similar forms in a file awaiting the quarterly meeting of the Healthy Ageing Programs Committee. Unfortunately, the chair of the committee had suffered a heart attack, not a good advertisement for the programs, and as a couple of other members were away, the meeting was three months overdue before the executive officer could assemble a quorum. When the members finally met, the forms were stamped and the file returned to the executive officer for action.

A few weeks later she actually got around to sorting out the guidelines and acquittal forms for successful applicants, and to drafting an accompanying letter. The form was dispatched to its destination without any of the people who had handled it giving any real thought to its potential to influence the course of individual lives. Almost nine months after the funding application had been lodged, the grant letter arrived at its destination.

Marissa was sitting on the back verandah eating a piece of wholemeal toast with Vegemite and drinking a cup of herbal tea when she heard the postie's bike turn into Violet Street and begin the stop-start journey past the mailboxes. She licked the crumbs off her fingers and wandered around to the front of the house and down to the gate. There was an electricity bill, a reminder notice to make her annual appointment with the dentist, and a bulky white envelope from the Department of Health. It was so long since she had written the funding application she had forgotten all about it, and at first she thought she must have got someone else's mail. She checked again that it was addressed to her and then tore open the envelope: 'Your application for funding for a demonstration tour to introduce belly dancing as a safe, healthy and rewarding exercise program for women over the age of fifty has been approved.'

Wandering back to the verandah, Marissa stared at the letter, barely able to believe its contents. There was provision for publicity, venue hire, travel and accommodation, and miscellaneous expenses for three dancers, for between five and eight days in each location. Marissa read the letter again. It referred her to someone in the department who would provide support with publicity material and mail-outs to local councils and women's groups. Then she read the formal letter of agreement that she had to sign and the form on which she was to provide her bank details so the money could be transferred to her account.

And she sat back in her chair staring at the pile of documents, wondering how on earth she was going to do it. The two women who had volunteered to be part of it and had helped with the application were no longer around. How would she organise this alone and who could she get to dance with her? She paced up and down the verandah, wishing she had someone she could talk to about it.

Marissa occasionally experienced bleak moments of clarity in which she reminded herself that she did not have the sort of friendships in which she could share her successes and failures. Even in the informal group of Harley riders with whom she occasionally rode she remained comparatively distant. It was, she knew, largely due to her own unwillingness to become more fully involved. Not only did she not do relationships, she didn't really do friendships; she found it safer to be friendly with a number of people but close to none. If her life were the poorer because of that it was also blissfully free from other people's emotional baggage. But at times the idea of talking frankly and intimately with someone seemed very attractive.

She padded up the passage to answer the doorbell, wondering who would be calling at eight-thirty in the morning.

'I was just passing and I thought I'd drop this off,' Frank said, holding out a book. 'Thomas Merton, *The Seven Storey Mountain*. You said you'd like to read it. I hope I didn't wake you.'

Marissa shook her head and reached out for the book. 'No, no I've been up for ages. Thanks for this.' She paused, looking at the cover and then at him. 'Cup of coffee?'

He glanced at his watch. 'Yes, thanks, if it's convenient.'

She opened the door wider and led him through to the kitchen and out onto the back verandah. 'Have a look at this while I make the coffee,' she said, pushing the grant papers towards him, and she went into the kitchen, got out the plunger and watched him through the open door while she waited for the kettle to boil. He was a fairly ordinary looking man, reasonably well built, light brown hair flecked with grey, and a generally amiable expression that could change from time to time to absolute remoteness, as though he had moved to another planet. This, she assumed, was his police look – detached, chilly, impenetrable, unlike the person she was getting to know.

'Can we do this again?' he'd asked after their first dinner and, to Marissa's own surprise, she'd agreed. He was easy to talk to, and interesting as well as a good listener. She liked his self-possession with its dangerously unknowable edge.

'Congratulations,' he said as she put the coffee, some milk and a mug down beside him. 'You must be pleased.'

'Pleased and a bit panic-stricken. I planned this almost a year ago with two women who were in my classes. Now one of them has left her husband and gone off to teach English in China, and the other's gone to live in Brisbane with a man twenty years younger than her that she met on the Internet.'

Frank laughed. 'The transformative effects of belly dancing!'

'Mmm. But it leaves me wondering how I can cope with this.'

'You still want to do it, then?'

'Well, yes.'

'Aren't there any other women who'd go with you?'

She shrugged. 'I'm not sure. I seem to have a lot of women with young children at the moment, which would be difficult, because we'd be away for a couple of months. And, anyway, this is to encourage older women, so the people doing the demonstrations need to be around my age.'

'And there aren't any?'

'A few, but not ones who I think would be willing to take off on a tour like this.'

'Sounds like you need to get a couple in training.'

'There are a couple in the beginners' class who might be okay, if I could get them up to speed in time.'

'Beginners? Don't you want people who've been doing it for a while?'

'No, not really. I want them confident enough to dance in public and to be able to talk to other women about what the dancing has done for them, but I don't want them too polished. This is for women who want to get fit and feel good, so dancers who are new and not intimidatingly good would be the best way to go.'

'And these two might do?'

Marissa nodded. 'Maybe . . . ' She paused, considering it. From the first night Gayle's aptitude for the dance had surprised her. There was no doubt that she had a feel for the music and she had picked up the steps with comparative ease. At first it had seemed that Gayle was only there to please her friends, but she kept coming back, and after the first month she had also turned up alone at a Saturday class. 'I'm enjoying it,' she'd said. 'I go away feeling really good and I've been practising at home, with your video. And . . . well, I haven't mentioned it to the others, so if you don't mind . . . '

'Sure,' Marissa had said. 'Sometimes friends can be distracting. You're improving a lot, Gayle, but you're still rigid, especially around the neck and shoulders.'

'It could work, I suppose, if they were willing to have a go,' Marissa said to Frank. 'One of them, Gayle, is really quite good, and her friend Sonya could be – she's certainly got potential. Only thing is, they come with another friend who's absolutely hopeless.'

'Maybe they don't need to travel in a pack,' Frank said. 'The third one probably knows she's not any good.'

Marissa laughed. 'I wish. Sometimes the ones who are the

worst on the floor have an incredibly high opinion of their talents.'

'You won't know till you ask,' Frank said, nudging the papers towards her. 'Send back the acceptance forms now. You'll get those two organised or find someone else.'

'You think so?'

'Sure. Go on, I'll witness the signature for you.' He pulled a pen from his inside pocket and handed it to her.

Marissa hesitated. 'There's all the organising, the paperwork and so on. It looks so messy and complicated.'

Frank leaned across the table towards her. 'Marissa, you're an intelligent woman, a businesswoman. This stuff is child's play. You can do the paperwork and the organisation standing on your head if you stop panicking and just get on with it. Fill the form in and sign it and I'll post it for you on my way to work. Then you can get on the phone to those women and sweet talk them into shimmying their way from Albany to Hedland and all stops in between.'

Sonya paid her first visit to the university campus on a Friday, knowing that this was Gayle's day off and she wouldn't be likely to run into her. She knew it was silly to feel guilty – she and Oliver were simply friends – but with Oliver being such a drama queen about Gayle, Sonya felt as though she were responsible for upsetting their friendship. As she got to know Gayle better she had grown fond of her and the last thing she wanted was to hurt her feelings. She'd told Gayle that she and Oliver saw each other from time to time and that he'd written to her from Berlin; now he was back but still on leave and had wanted to show her around the campus. But somehow meeting him there made her feel she was trespassing on Gayle's territory.

'It's okay,' Oliver said as they strolled up to the restaurant for lunch. 'Gayle's never here on Fridays and, anyway, I met her last week and we talked.'

'Yes, she said she'd seen you. Have you sorted things out? Got back on track again?'

'Not exactly. I did as you said and called her and came in here to meet her – on familiar ground.'

'Excellent! And you apologised and told her . . . what did you tell her?'

He cleared his throat. 'Nothing really. I mean, I told her I was sorry I hadn't been in touch, that I'd been busy since the wedding, then Berlin and everything . . . you know.'

'But you didn't tell her how you felt? You didn't tell her you knew about Brian's job, or the son or anything?'

'No. How could I, Sonya? It's not my business. I've got no right to demand explanations – that's her family life and our friendship was outside of that.'

'Until she invited you in by asking you to the wedding. Of course you can raise it. You've been friends for a long time, there's a level of trust. If you think the trust is broken you need to talk about it, not compound it by letting her think there's nothing wrong. What's the matter with you, Oliver? You're always going on about the importance of honesty.'

'It's just too hard,' Oliver said, shaking his head. 'It's as though she's an entirely different person from the one I knew. She didn't say much and I didn't know where to begin.'

'Well, you *have* begun, and you've done it by going backwards,' Sonya said. 'You weren't straight with her and that's unfair. Gayle's not stupid, she must know something's wrong, the wedding was in November and now it's the end of April and when you finally meet up, you pretend nothing's happened. Gayle thinks the world of you and you owe it to her to get this out in the open.'

They sat down at an outside table, and Oliver pretended to study the menu although he actually knew it by heart.

'The fish of the day is usually good,' he said.

Sonya sighed loudly. 'This is unworthy of you, Oliver.' He looked up and she saw a distinct flash of 'rabbit in the headlights' cross his face and knew she'd hit the spot. 'If this is the best you can manage after years of friendship with Gayle, I'm not sure your friendship is worth anything at all.'

He was acutely embarrassed now. 'I know, I know. I'll talk to her again. I promise, it's just so . . . so . . . '

Sonya let the laminated menu drop onto the table with a slap. 'You are being a total dipstick about this. You're the one that put Gayle on some sort of pedestal and now she's toppled off and got a bit chipped and you're too damn precious to try to sort it out. She's my friend too now, Oliver, and if you don't tell her why you're behaving like a moron, then I will.'

Oliver was not the only person with whom Sonya found herself in a difficult situation with regard to Gayle. They had met through Angie but, now that age and shared interests had brought them closer, and since witnessing the spat between mother and daughter, Sonya found herself feeling protective of Gayle where Angie was concerned.

'So what did you decide to do about that place?' Angie asked as they walked together from the car park to the office.

'I'm holding off,' Sonya replied. 'What Gayle said made a lot of sense. What am I moving for, anyway? Probably because I'm bored and restless, and that's not a good reason. I'd be better to take some of my leave, get away for a while, see how I feel after that.'

'Oh, for heaven's sake, don't listen to Mum,' Angie said. 'She's never done anything of her own volition in her life. What would she know?'

Sonya sighed with irritation. 'Well, she'd know how it feels to be in her late fifties and to realise all of a sudden that time is limited and that there are all sorts of possibilities for change,' she said.

'Change? No way, not Mum. I mean, she's wonderful and I love her to bits, but change is not her thing. Dad makes the decisions, always has, and she grumbles about it but always backs down and lets him get away with it. Honestly, Sonya, you're single, you're a professional woman and you're used to doing things off your own bat. Mum's totally different, and she's not going to change at this time of life.'

'You're being a bit unfair,' Sonya said. 'I think your mother is a great deal more complex and decisive than you realise. She may well surprise you one day.'

'Look,' said Angie, pressing the lift button, 'the most contentious thing my mother has ever done is to keep up occasional secret phone contact with Josh – and years ago she used to send him money too. That's it. I tell you, Sonya, there are very few things in life over which she's exercised a choice, and those are small things, like what she wears or domestic stuff. Oh, and deciding to do this PhD on women and libraries, but she'd probably give that up if Dad really pushed her.'

Sonya shrugged. 'Of course, you know Gayle better than I do, but sometimes we don't see those close to us the way outsiders do. Now I've got to know her a bit better, the word that comes to mind is fortitude. Sometimes the greatest strength lies in inaction.'

Angie laughed as they got out at the second floor. 'You're joking. She's the ultimate pushover. The more you get to know her the more you'll see it. Anyway, she's not the one to dish out advice on changing your life, that's for sure.'

It was early morning, not yet six o'clock, but the dawn light, soft and rosy, had found its way between the bedroom curtains. Gayle stretched out enjoying, as she always did, having the bed to herself. The dancing had done wonders for her body – she felt as though it had come back to life after years of inertia. She'd been cheating with the extra classes, but going alone made it easier to immerse herself in the dance, to attend closely to the steps, the movements, the way her body responded to the music which seemed to invite her to dance. And she was practising at home too, regularly, obsessively almost, pushing through the pain of aching muscles, losing herself in the rhythm and movement.

She smiled at the memory of that first class and her conviction that she would never go back. Gayle was not a naturally competitive person but she'd been secretly delighted with her success that first night. Even so, over the next few days she had formulated the excuse she'd give to Trish and Sonya for not going again, but when the day arrived she realised she was looking forward to it. There was considerable satisfaction in discovering that she was good at something physical, and already her body felt different.

Now the rhythmic physical workout had become essential and dancing moved her into a different mental space in which nothing else mattered. She felt stronger and more confident, as though she were unfolding into someone more substantial. Even so she'd been shocked when, after class one evening, Marissa suggested that she and Sonya might like to be part of a tour.

'I've only just started,' Gayle responded. 'I couldn't get up on stage in a belly dancing costume and perform, I'd look ridiculous.'

'No,' Marissa said. 'You'd look like a woman who was having a go and doing well. And that's what I need.'

'But it's a performance,' Sonya protested. 'What about some of the women in that team you've got? They've been doing it for years.'

'Exactly. They're really good, too good for this. Sorry if that sounds a bit odd but it's true. This isn't some sort of dance festival, it's a program to show women who've never danced before that they can have a go; that it's fun, terrific exercise and they can enjoy it all; the music, the costumes, the fitness that comes from it. We strut our stuff and then run introductory classes to let people try it out. I need a couple of people who've just started but have really taken to it, women who can say, "I've only been doing this a few months and look what I can do".'

Gayle had been sceptical. 'I don't know,' she'd said. 'It's really not me – performing, I mean.'

'I think it could be fun,' Sonya had said. 'But you're much better than me, Gayle. I'll do it if you will.'

It had taken Gayle a week of arguing with herself, of deciding she'd give it a go and then being overtaken by the fear and embarrassment that had her heart racing at the mere prospect. It was Sonya's phone call that persuaded her.

'Come on, Gayle,' she'd said. 'It'll be good. Think of Marissa. Don't you just love her, the way she is, so free, so self-possessed and so much in her own body? I want some of that. And she needs us. She wouldn't be asking us if she thought we'd make fools of ourselves and her.'

And so Gayle had agreed, and as they rehearsed, her enthusiasm grew along with a determination not to let anything or anybody stand in her way.

Brian, grumpy and short-tempered before he left for the US, had returned like a bear with a sore head and had remained so ever since. Perhaps things were not going well at work but he didn't volunteer any information, and Gayle didn't ask. She sensed a growing air of resentment when he was at home – or perhaps it was all in her mind, a side-effect of her own guilty lack of interest.

And then there was Angie – Gayle was well aware of her own shortcomings but the way Angie had spoken to her on the apartment visit, the fact that it all happened in front of Trisha and Sonya had really upset her. But, as Angie had pointed out, confrontation was not part of Gayle's repertoire and rather than talking to her daughter she reverted to pretending that nothing had happened. The prospect of getting away from it all became more enticing every day.

'You can't be serious,' Trisha said. 'Have you really thought about this, Gayle? What does Brian think about you being a travelling belly dancer?'

'I've no idea,' Gayle said, pulling onto the freeway with Trisha in the front seat and Sonya in the back. 'I haven't told him yet.'

'He's not going to like it, not the dancing nor you being away for a couple of months.'

'No, he's not, but he'll just have to put up with it.'

Trisha sighed. 'You're both mad.'

Sonya leaned forward. 'C'mon, Trish, come with us. You'll enjoy it, it'll be hilarious. You don't have to dance – you can be the roadie.'

Trisha shook her head. 'No way, José, not for me. I don't even know why I'm coming with you today.'

'Because you can't resist the chance to tell us which costumes to get,' Gayle said. 'I bet you end up trying on something yourself. Stop being such a grouch.'

'The woman who owns the largest collection of grey and navy business suits in the southern hemisphere suddenly wants satin and sequins? Yes, of course you need my help. This requires some leap of the imagination, Gayle. Is there no middle road?'

'No.' Gayle shook her head. 'It seems not. I love the dancing, and I feel heaps better for it, and I want a gorgeous, spectacular costume. I know it'll help me dance better.'

'Yes,' said Sonya. 'It'll be fabulous – we can really get into the feel of it.'

'You mean you'd roll up to classes in the full regalia?'

'Why not?' Sonya asked. 'Some of the women do. I think it'd be easier to get into the mood. And Marissa says we need to rehearse in full costume because they're not exactly comfortable. All those beads make them heavy and scratchy.'

'It sounds like a nightmare,' Trisha said. 'And honestly, Gayle, do you think you're going to bare your midriff and belly dance in front of an audience? I mean, I think you'd look wonderful and I'm gobsmacked at how good you are, but this is so unlike the Gayle I know.'

Gayle negotiated a tight turn into a parking area. 'I'm changing. You said I would when Angie left, and this is part of it. It's a challenge but maybe that's what I need right now. Besides, I don't have to have a bare midriff – I've been looking at costumes on the Internet.' She switched off the engine and turned to the back seat. 'To tell the truth, my confidence only comes in short bursts, but I am woman, hear me roar, watch me shimmy – right, Sonya?'

'Right,' Sonya said. 'I guess. Although I can't help wishing that Kalgoorlie wasn't going to be the scene of our first roar and shimmy. In fact, I wish we weren't going there at all.'

'Kalgoorlie's nice,' Trisha said. 'We lived there for a while in the eighties.'

'It's not Kal that's the problem,' Sonya said. 'It's my family, there en masse, pillars of the community and just a tiny bit conservative in outlook – my parents, that is. I don't think belly dancing is going to figure highly on my list of achievements as far as they're concerned. And then there's my sister . . . ' She got out of the car and slung her bag over her shoulder. 'But that's another story.'

'We will overcome,' Gayle said, locking the car. 'Your parents, my husband, less than perfect bodies, fragile confidence, and heavy, scratchy costumes. We will prevail.'

Trisha shook her head. 'I can't believe I'm hearing this.'

'It's all an act. Bravado. I'll be a quivering mess for most of the time, but I *am* determined to do it, so let's get on with it.'

The shop that specialised in Middle Eastern and Latin American dance costumes was in an industrial unit in the northern suburbs wedged between a panel beater and a place that made surfboards. Half the warehouse was devoted to the dancewear, the remainder to a costume and fancy dress hire business, and when they arrived, four middle-aged car salesmen were noisily attempting to kit themselves out as French maids for a party. The dance costume area was mercifully free of customers, and they had full run of the changing rooms, which consisted of rickety hardboard dividers hung with skimpy curtains. Gayle trailed her fingers along the racks of fringed and beaded bras, sequinned skirts and hip belts, harem pants and boleros.

'Look at these,' she said, discovering a shelf of hairpieces. 'There's one here exactly the same red as your hair, Sonya,' and she lifted it down and took it over to her.

'It would go well with this,' Sonya said, lifting out an emerald green top with darker green sequins and a deep fringe of tiny gold beads.

'That's your colour, definitely,' Gayle said, 'try it on.'

Trisha, still not fully in the spirit of the exercise, made a slight snorting noise. 'So now you're the colour expert. I thought I was the fashion adviser.'

'You are, but I'm the dance costume expert,' Gayle said. 'Go on, Trish, look for something for yourself, and come with us.'

Trisha shook her head. 'To be honest, the dancing's not doing a lot for me. You two are so much better at it. I just don't get it and Marissa says my arms are like windmills. I've been thinking of giving up.'

'But you were the one who made us go in the first place,' Sonya protested from the changing room.

'I know. But I feel like an elephant lolloping around the room. I think I'll stick to tennis and jogging.'

'Marissa's right about the costumes being heavy,' Sonya said, emerging from the fitting room and pinching her midriff. 'And it's the rolls of fat that really set it off, I think, don't you?'

Gayle gasped. 'It's gorgeous. Really, Sonya, you look wonderful. Doesn't she, Trish?'

Trisha nodded approvingly. 'Absolutely. If you're serious about it, if you're really going on this tour, you should get that one. And stop worrying about fat. Marissa's bigger than you. She says that belly dancing celebrates all the parts of the body that aren't fashionable, and you shouldn't worry about the odd spare tyre. You need to have breasts, a belly, a bum and hips.'

'Then I'm overqualified,' Sonya said. 'But look at my arms. They're so flabby.' She twisted around in front of the mirror. 'Oh, and look at those wedges of fat between the bra and the waistband – it's gruesome.'

'No it's not,' Trisha said, straightening one of the shoulder straps. 'Anyway, the long fringe on the bra hides them. You just get the suggestion of flesh underneath. It looks great. You can always get one of those little cropped jackets with the gauzy sleeves if you want to hide your arms, but, honestly, you don't need to.'

'It *is* lovely,' Sonya said cautiously, adjusting the sequinned belt. 'But, Gayle, I'm only getting it if you're sure about this whole thing. You're not going to change your mind?'

'No way,' Gayle said. 'Belly dancing is my new religion.' She hesitated and then drew out a silver costume.

'No,' Trisha said. 'Not that one. Colour, Gayle, colour. And not that black with gold embroidery. If you're going to do this, splash out . . . something like this.'

She pulled out a satin costume in vivid cobalt blue. Coils of silver and blue sequins encrusted the bra top and the beaded fringe matched the lines of silver thread that patterned the chiffon skirt, trailing down to the sequinned hem.

'It's lovely, but it's very . . . well . . . colourful,' Gayle said, fingering the fabric.

'Yes. Try it on,' Trisha ordered.

Gayle slipped off her clothes and stood in the fitting room in her bra and knickers looking at the beautiful costume on its hanger. Her earlier bravado had plummeted. How would she ever walk out onto a stage, hips swaying and lifting, midriff undulating with the music? Even here, alone in the changing room, she was blushing crimson at the thought.

Slowly she took off her own bra and held the blue and silver one against her. The colours seemed to make her skin glow and her eyes look bluer than usual. Cautiously she slipped the straps over her shoulders and leaned forward to do it up. The uplift gave her an unfamiliar cleavage, and she stood back to admire it before stepping into the skirt and fitting the wide sequinned belt around her hips. The woman in the mirror stared back at her like a stranger.

'Oh my god, look at you,' Sonya gasped as Gayle emerged from behind the curtain.

'D'you think it's a bit much?' Gayle asked. 'A bit over the top?'

Trisha smiled and shook her head. She swallowed hard, looking a bit teary.

'What's wrong? You don't really like it, do you?'

'I love it,' Trisha said. 'It's perfect. You look gorgeous, Gayle, honestly! That's the one for you. And you should try the silver harem pants too, and the headdress.'

Gayle did a twirl in front of the mirror. 'But will I have the courage to wear it and dance in it? I mean, I hardly ever have my arms uncovered even in summer, and never –'

'And never wear shorts or a bikini – I know,' Trisha said. 'But you can do all those things. You've just lost the habit of really being in your body. Buy it, Gayle, it transforms you. You look like a completely different person.'

'That's good,' Gayle said. 'Maybe I'll *become* a completely different person, and that should please both my husband and my daughter.'

'I wouldn't count on that,' Sonya murmured, and she and Trisha exchanged a glance as Gayle disappeared back into the changing room.

EIGHT

Oliver was hiding in his office. Still on study leave he didn't want to be on campus at all but he needed something on the office computer that he hadn't saved to his thumb drive. He had chosen a time when most of his colleagues would be at the monthly staff meeting and he was aiming for a flying visit. As the weeks of his leave slipped by he had found himself clinging to the remainder of this research time with a sort of desperation. Having time to write made him increasingly aware how the rigours of teaching, and all the associated administrativia, diverted him from the work he most enjoyed.

He downloaded the files, logged off, and almost jumped out of his skin when there was a knock on his door. The last thing he needed was students asking advice about enrolments, or enquiring whether he still had the assignment they had failed to collect two years ago.

'Yep,' he called out ungraciously, standing up and grabbing his briefcase so that it was clear he was just leaving.

'I saw your car in the car park,' Gayle said, popping her head around the door. 'Have you got a minute?'

She was the last person Oliver had expected to see. The library was at the far end of the campus, and she was rarely in the vicinity of his office.

'Oh, Gayle. Hi,' he said. 'Come in.'

She gestured towards the briefcase. 'You're just leaving?'

'Well, I was, but . . . but . . . there's no rush. Sit down.' He shifted a pile of box files off the spare chair.

'I wanted to catch up with you,' Gayle said, 'because when we had lunch it felt awkward. It wasn't like it used to be, and there are things we need to sort out.'

Oliver's face flushed to what he was sure must have been fiery red. He cleared his throat. 'Yes, well . . . '

'Look, I know you didn't like being at the wedding. You probably didn't like the house much, or anything at all there, really. It was silly of me to invite you. I should've left things as they were. But there must be something else. You see, since then I've hardly seen you and I've felt as though, because you didn't like the wedding, you don't like me anymore either . . . '

She looked straight at him as her voice trailed away and, to his horror, Oliver could see that there were tears in her eyes. Nothing had prepared him for this, not Sonya's warnings, not years of advice from his mother, nor years of disastrous relationships with women.

'Tell her,' Sonya yelled in his head.

'Women appreciate honesty, Oliver,' his mother had droned, 'they want to be accepted for who they are, not as the creation of someone else's imagination.' But Oliver's chequered history of telling the truth at the wrong time was ringing bells too. Where was the guide book for the moment when someone whom he had admired and respected – cared for, even – came into his office waving an emotional hand grenade? He swallowed hard and looked down, fiddling with the handle of his briefcase.

'Of course I like you, Gayle,' he said without looking back up. 'But I suppose I did feel a bit out of my depth at the wedding, and since then I've been busy working on the book and there was Berlin and . . . ' He found himself running out of steam.

Gayle grabbed some tissues from the box on his desk and dabbed at her eyes. 'You must think I'm stupid,' she said. 'I thought I could at least rely on you to be honest with me after all you've said about that sort of thing.'

Trapped by his own words, Oliver's awkwardness turned suddenly to resentment. 'You weren't honest with me,' he said quickly, looking up at her now. 'Things have happened in your life, important things, that you didn't tell me about. I feel . . . ' He paused. How exactly did he feel? 'I feel insulted that you didn't share things with me; that I told you so much and you told me nothing. You let me believe that we agreed on issues which it now seems aren't important to you. I don't feel good about that.'

The silence seemed to throb in his ears.

'I see,' Gayle said finally. 'I guess you mean Josh?'

Oliver turned away, looking out of the window, across the lawn to the lake. 'Yes, your son. For heaven's sake, Gayle, I didn't even know he existed.'

'So it's just that, is it?'

'That and your . . . it's none of my business, anyway.'

'Brian's job?'

He nodded.

She patted her eyes again with the tissues and crumpled them into a ball in her hand. 'You're right, of course. We were friends, that was important to me and I should have told you but your friendship . . . well, it's hard to explain . . . '

He shrugged. 'You aren't obliged to explain. It's your family stuff, nothing to do with me.'

'Oh, stop being so ridiculous, Oliver,' Gayle snapped. She was angry now too. 'First you complain, quite rightly, that I never told you, and then you say it's nothing to do with you anyway. Make up your mind.'

She had taken him by surprise. He hadn't seen her angry before – in fact, they had never disagreed about anything. With a horrible flash of insight, Oliver realised that that was one of the things that he had liked so much about her: she had never been angry, never argued, never challenged him. He opened his mouth to speak but didn't know what to say.

'I don't know if you can even begin to understand this, Oliver,' Gayle said. 'My relationship with Brian is not good, it hasn't been for years, long before Josh came out, and before the tobacco job. But for a whole lot of reasons I found a way of living with it. Part of that was through my friendship with you, by keeping it separate. I can see you're now wondering if I was telling you the truth about the things I believe in. Well, I was. I didn't lie to you, not once. My sin, if that's what it is, is one of omission. I simply chose not to tell you certain things, because I wanted a space in which I could be the person I wanted to be rather than the woman I had become. And if you feel, as you seem to, that what I've said and what I've done are two very different things, then . . . I can only agree with you, and tell you that the roots of that go back a long way. You have a tendency to oversimplify things, Oliver, to think they are black or white. But relationships are fraught with grey areas. It's not always possible to do what, in other circumstances, one would feel is the right thing.'

Oliver coughed and fidgeted in his chair. 'I, er . . . '

Gayle got up. 'No,' she said, sounding more forceful than he had ever heard her. 'It's probably best not to say anything right now. I ambushed you. Anyway, you're safe for a while. I'm going away for a couple of months. Sonya may have told you – the belly dancing thing?'

He looked up suddenly. 'You're going on that too?'

She nodded. 'Surprising, isn't it? Even I'm surprised. Maybe we can talk when I get back.' She opened the door, and he heard the ring of her heels on the tiles and the clang of the outer door as she left the building.

It was something of a mystery to Frank that Marissa seemed to like him quite a lot. It went against all his previous experience, so that while he enjoyed it, he somehow didn't quite trust it. Women usually reacted to him in predictable ways: total lack of interest, or the instant sexual attraction that got him into trouble. Just being liked by a woman, having a friendship, was something new. He supposed some of his female colleagues didn't mind him too much. He got on with them okay, but it was all confined to work and the occasional drink at the pub. They fitted into the lack-of-interest category. He was always an outsider, a loner, partly from choice but also, he suspected, because a reputation for sudden outbursts of rage preceded him. Not that anyone he worked with now had experienced those rages because he'd had that under control for some time. Just the same, word got around. And so the Marissa thing was odd.

They'd been seeing each other regularly. He'd taken to calling in at her place when he was nearby – and sometimes when he wasn't – and since the arrival of the grant letter she'd been involving him in planning her tour. He enjoyed sitting on her back verandah or in her kitchen talking, drinking the dreadful coffee she made for him. Just being with her lifted his spirits. Sometimes he felt she was a little wary of him and he wondered whether he'd done the wrong thing with her plants. She never mentioned it and he'd never seen her with a joint or smelled it in the house. Had she stopped smoking weed? Maybe the fact of him being a cop might just be freaking her from time to time.

Marissa was entirely different from any other woman he'd known: self-contained, content in the little blue house with the overgrown garden and its verandah full of tinkling chimes. As he drew up outside the gate he felt a strange sinking in his gut at the prospect that in a couple of days she would be gone.

'Come in,' Marissa said, unlocking the screen door, 'you can meet the others.' She led him through into the kitchen where two women were sitting at the table, surrounded by braid and beads, stitching sequinned motifs onto things that looked like big headbands.

If Frank had gone into a room full of women aged fifty-plus and been asked to pick the two least likely to go on a belly dancing tour with Marissa, he reckoned he would have picked these two. She had told him that one had a high-level job in the Education Department, and the other was married and a part-time librarian at the university. Even so he hadn't been prepared for them to look so unlike belly dancers. One was slight and rather colourless, wearing a dull suit, the other was smarter but looked just like any other middle-aged bureaucrat, despite the spiky haircut dyed a bright and very fashionable red. For some reason he had expected them to look like versions of Marissa, with her long skirts and tops from the Indian stalls in the markets, or faded jeans and T-shirts. Everything about her seemed to fit with her dancing. Even the Harley marked her out as different, and totally unlike these two.

'Frank's been helping me with the planning,' Marissa said. 'Sonya brought some gin. Would you like one?'

'Thanks, yes –' he looked at Sonya – 'that is, if you don't mind.'

'Be my guest,' Sonya said. 'It'll save you having to drink Marissa's herbal tea or that terrible dandelion coffee.'

'So that's what it is,' he said, 'dandelion. It certainly doesn't seem to have much to do with caffeine. So, you're off the day after tomorrow – all set?'

Sonya nodded. 'We've been rehearsing really hard. My thighs may never recover.'

'Your thighs and my knees,' Gayle said. 'We may yet end up being emergency airlifted by the Flying Doctor. I'm not really sure we're ready for this public performance thing.'

'Of course you are,' Marissa said, putting a gin and tonic topped with a sprig of mint in front of Frank. 'You're both terrific. We're going to inspire all the women we meet.'

'Here's to it, then,' Frank said, raising his glass. 'Wish I could see you doing your stuff.' They clinked their glasses.

'Did you let your parents know you're coming, Sonya?' Gayle asked.

Sony nodded, swallowing her drink. 'I did, but I chickened out of telling them why. I thought I'd face it when I get there, although I must say the prospect of it makes me feel like throwing up.'

'And what about you, Gayle?' Marissa asked. 'I know I've asked you this before, and I don't want to go on about it, but what happened when you finally told your husband?'

'I haven't told him yet,' Gayle replied, taking another sip of her drink. 'I'll tell him tomorrow. No point in prolonging the argument.'

'But suppose he says no? We leave on Wednesday.'

'He *will* say no.'

'So what'll you do? You're not going to back out, are you?'

'Of course not.'

'You've left it awfully late,' Sonya said. 'D'you think that's really fair?'

'Probably not,' Gayle said, 'but that's how it is. He's away and he gets back on Tuesday evening. I'll tell him then.'

'The night before we leave?'

Gayle nodded. 'Yes. Less time to argue about it,' she said with a half-smile.

Frank watched her with interest; under the cool surface he sensed something more – fear, perhaps, a long-term fear that had suddenly crystallised into an iron will. He'd seen it before: women who, after years of abuse, suddenly called a halt.

'This makes me nervous,' Marissa said. 'You can't just mention it as you walk out the door.'

'It does sound a bit dodgy, Gayle,' Sonya said, turning to Frank. 'What do you think?'

Frank caught Marissa's eye. 'It's down to Gayle, if that's the way she wants to do it. I know a woman who told me she bumped into a backpacker in a supermarket, and a day or two later she wrote a note and walked out while her husband was at work. As far as I know, she's never looked back.'

Marissa glared at him and cleared her throat. 'Well, yes, maybe,' she said, 'but that was a long time ago and it doesn't sound like an ideal arrangement in this case.' She leaned across the table. 'Sonya, don't forget you need to line that bra with something soft or it'll scratch you to bits.'

Frank's mobile rang and he got up from the table and wandered out to take the call on the back verandah.

'He's very nice,' Sonya whispered, picking up some flannelette and scissors. 'Is he your –'

'No,' Marissa hissed. 'He's not my anything. A friend, that's all.'

'He really likes you,' Sonya said, 'don't you think so, Gayle?'

Gayle nodded. 'Definitely.'

'Don't be ridiculous,' Marissa said, pouring herself another drink.

'Seriously, he does. You can tell. And he's quite cute, really, for a man his age, and a policeman.'

'Especially for a policeman,' Gayle added. 'I think he looks a bit like Normie Rowe.'

'Oh please!' Marissa said, rolling her eyes.

'Yes, he does, only taller. And Normie Rowe is pretty fanciable,' Sonya said.

'Quite cute in a midlife sort of way,' Gayle added.

'Lord preserve us,' Marissa said. 'You could fancy someone younger – Michael Bublé or Jude Law, perhaps?'

Gayle shook her head. 'Too young. I prefer someone of substance, someone weathered a little by life.'

'Yes,' Sonya agreed. 'Like Gabriel Byrne. But Normie has that lovely crinkly smile. He looks like a genuinely nice person, like your Frank. Definitely right for the discerning older woman.'

Marissa shook her head. 'It must be the gin. You two have totally lost it. I'm starting to feel very uneasy about this tour. I'm not sure I'm in good company.'

'Well, you can always call the police if you get into trouble,' Frank said, walking back in. 'Gotta go, I'm afraid.' He looked at Marissa. 'The guys down at the port have just picked up someone who we think is involved in the same set-up as your ex-neighbour.' He pocketed his phone and took his jacket from the back of the chair. 'Do you ladies need a chauffeur for the airport?'

Brian stood alone in the kitchen staring at the list of instructions Gayle had left on the fridge door. He couldn't believe this was actually happening. The whole situation was ridiculous. She had to be completely off her head. It had started the previous evening when she'd announced she was going off belly dancing. He'd thought it was stupid when she'd first started going to the classes but he'd never expected anything like this. His wife dancing in a public place, shaking her arse, bumping and grinding in front of . . . well, in front of anyone who cared to watch?

'It's not like that . . . ' she'd begun, but he stopped her.

'Don't argue with me, Gayle,' he said, feeling his anger burning hotter than ever. 'I've seen those women. You must be stupid if you think I'm agreeing to this. It's not negotiable.'

'You know nothing about it,' she insisted. 'It's a women's heath and ageing program funded by the Health Department, and we're only dancing at special events for women. If you'd just listen for a moment –'

'No way,' he'd said. 'Absolutely no way. Are you crazy or

something? I don't care if the Pope's funding it. There is no way I'm going to have my wife prancing around half dressed all over the state. And anyway, what about me? What am I supposed to do while you're not here? Just forget it, you hear? Forget it. I don't know where you got the stupid idea anyway. Belly fucking dancing.'

The foul mood that had begun in the Sydney office was oppressing him, and his anger was ready to burst out of his body. Here he was back home after five days, tired and pissed off with Mal and the half-witted US director who had flown over after the regulation board decision. His head ached and he was worried stiff about what was in store over the next few weeks. This was the last thing he needed.

He'd poured his third drink and was on his way to the fridge to get some ice when she started to speak to him again, and that was when he lost it. He grabbed her by the wrist and twisted her arm, dragging her towards him so their noses were almost touching.

'I'll say this one last time,' he hissed into her face. 'No belly dancing tour and you can stop going to the classes too, or . . . '

She looked at him then, cold and steady. 'Or what?'

He let go of her arm and opened the fridge. He knew he'd overstepped the mark. She'd have backed down anyway, she always did. So he got his ice, stalked out to his study, slung his jacket over a chair, undid the tight waistband of his trousers and, flopping down on the couch, flicked through the TV channels until he found a Clint Eastwood movie on Foxtel.

It was morning when he woke thinking he'd heard a car in the driveway. The bottle of scotch was empty and the time panel on the DVD player was flashing 7:10. He was horribly hungover; his eyes were scratchy, his neck hurt from the awkward half-sitting position he'd slept in and his clothes felt tight and dirty. Hauling himself off the couch he padded out to the kitchen to see if Gayle had put the coffee on. She hadn't. Irritably Brian scratched his head, yawned several times and began to fill the kettle.

'Ah, you *are* awake,' Gayle said, coming into the kitchen. 'I've left some notes for you on the fridge. Just stuff about putting out the garbage and paying the lawnmower man. There's plenty of food in the freezer, and it's all labelled. I don't suppose you'll be here much anyhow. Don't forget to check the pool-cleaner, and there's a guy coming this afternoon at four-thirty to fix the problem with the automatic gate. You'll need to be here for that. My itinerary's on the fridge.' And she walked out of the kitchen, just like that.

'Hang on,' he'd said, struggling to wake up and get a grip on what was happening. 'What's going on? Where the hell d'you think you're going?'

'I told you last night where I'm going,' Gayle said, picking up the suitcase that was standing by the front door. 'I don't think we need to go through all that again.' And with that she simply walked out the door and got into the back of a car that was waiting outside with the engine running. He was left standing in the hall, his fly undone, clutching an empty coffee plunger.

NINE

Sonya's worst fears were realised the moment they set foot inside the airport building at Kalgoorlie. There, foremost among a small group of people meeting the flight, were her parents, her mother in a neat turquoise suit, white hair permed and set like the Queen's, her father in his navy blazer and Rotary Club tie. It was, as always, a mystery to her that after more than forty years living in Kalgoorlie her parents still managed to look and behave as they had in Tasmania in the fifties.

'Darling,' her mother called, waving urgently as though Sonya could conceivably miss them. 'Sonya, darling, we're over here.'

Sonya's heart sank as she raised her hand in a languid wave. She had told them not to come to the airport, told them she was travelling with colleagues and that the accommodation and transport were all organised. Why, why, why did they have to be so perverse and interfering? Every time she came to Kalgoorlie, which was as rarely as possible these days, they tried to kidnap her.

'You can't kidnap your own child even if they're adult, I don't think,' a pedantic colleague had said when they had travelled there together as advisers on a visit with the Minister for Education.

'It's kidnapping,' Sonya had groaned, 'believe me. They bear me off to the family home, treat me like a child and hold me hostage until all their friends have been invited around to inspect me and ask questions about what I'm doing and when I'm going to find a nice man to look after me.' It had been easier on that visit, of course; ministerial demands for her presence leant themselves to exaggeration, and her parents, easily impressed, had readily accepted that her responsibility was to remain with the Minister's party. But this time Sonya knew she had stuffed up.

'Do you need to tell them you're going to be there?' Oliver had asked. 'Why not do the dancing stuff and then maybe pop in to see them, surprise them on the last day?'

'No way. They know too many people and too many people know me. I promise you, if I was in Kalgoorlie, word would reach my mother within hours. She's in everything – the CWA, the historical society, the ratepayers' association, the Red Cross, and we haven't even started on Dad's connections yet. Then there's my sister. And they will all have an absolute fit when they find out about the belly dancing.'

She had lied, as one does – perhaps not really lied, simply not revealed the purpose of the visit. A working trip with a couple of colleagues, she'd said, adding that she'd explain more when she saw them and hoping that, in the meantime, she could magically come up with an explanation that would be acceptable to them. So now here they were, obviously thrilled to see her, and expecting her to arrive looking like a serious public servant, accompanied by other serious public servants. And here *she* was, in a pair of old jeans, a cotton shirt and a backpack, accompanied by a hippy looking Marissa with mirrors embroidered into her skirt, Gayle in incredibly neat jeans and a pink T-shirt, and box after box of amplifiers and speakers, a display stand for posters and cases full of costumes and practice videos. How had she ever thought she could get away with this without a full-scale family drama?

'We know you're busy, darling,' her mother said, hugging her. 'You probably have to go straight off to some meeting, but we just wanted to say hello, and let you know about tonight.'

'Tonight?' Sonya said, kissing her father. 'What about tonight?'

'Just a little welcome home. Tessa and David and the grandchildren, and I'll just do a light meal. We're so thrilled you're here.' She turned to Gayle and Marissa. 'So sorry to intrude. I'm Vera Weldon, Sonya's mother, and this is my husband, Lew.'

'You must be Sonya's colleagues,' Sonya's father said. 'You both work in the Education Department too?'

There was a moment of terrible silence in which Sonya thought she was going to throw up.

'Actually, I work in the library system,' Gayle said hesitantly, 'and Marissa is in the arts, the performing arts.'

Sonya swallowed hard.

'How wonderful,' Vera said. 'I'm dying to hear more about it.'

'Very interesting. A multi-disciplinary project, I suppose,' Lew said. 'Splendid. Well, you'll join us this evening, I hope.'

'Gayle and Marissa are going to be pretty busy –' Sonya began.

'But you have to eat, surely,' her mother cut in. 'Do say you'll come.'

'I can't believe you didn't tell them,' Gayle said when the three of them were safely packed with their equipment into the maxi-taxi and on the way to the hotel.

'Huh! Thus speaks the woman who only told her husband last night that she was leaving this morning on a belly dancing tour,' Sonya responded. 'I'm so sorry, guys. You can easily get out of tonight if you want. I'll say you're tired or something.'

'Oh no! I wouldn't miss this for the world,' Marissa said.

'Me neither,' Gayle agreed. 'But you are just going to have to own up as soon as we get there, or it'll be a complete debacle.'

'No way,' Sonya said. 'I'll wait until later, just before we leave, otherwise it'll go on all evening.'

Marissa and Gayle exchanged a look. 'No,' they said in unison.

'Straight up, when we get there,' Marissa said. 'That's the deal, or we spill the beans ourselves, right, Gayle?'

'Right.'

'Anyway, they're sweet, and obviously tremendously proud of you and think the sun shines out of your every orifice. What are you worried about?'

Each family has its own unique dynamics, its own subtleties, sensitivities, taboos, expectations and assumptions, and Sonya knew that her own family was no exception. She was familiar with her role in the complex web of relationships, but the emotional cost of maintaining it seemed to have increased substantially over the years, as she tried to appear as the person she thought her parents wanted her to be. She knew that their kidnappings were motivated by love and their pride in her professional standing. But she also believed these were conditional on her continuing to act out her role as the successful elder daughter, the one with the university degree, the high status job, the executive salary, the house in Perth, and a closeness to what they saw as the corridors of power.

The ministerial visit had been, she suspected, a high point in her parents' aspirations for her. For a while after that she had felt assured of their love and pride, about which she pretended cynicism but which she so desperately needed. Professional success had almost wiped the slate clean of the failures in her personal life: the two embarrassing marriages to totally inappropriate men, the failure to produce grandchildren, and the continuing unsatisfactory absence of a suitable and prestigious male companion.

Living at a comfortable distance, Sonya told herself that her parents did not understand her, but the truth was that she never really gave them the chance to know her. What would Vera and Lew have felt had they known of her occasional Internet dating? Or about the extraordinary series of brief liaisons and one-night stands she'd indulged in after the break-up of her second marriage, or her few half-hearted experiments with amphetamines? Even now, years later, leading a virtually blameless life by contemporary standards, she was careful to maintain the façade.

'My sister Tessa was the bad one,' she explained to Gayle and Marissa on the way to her parents' house that evening. 'Dropped out of school, got involved with drugs. Got pregnant and had an abortion. But, of course, all that was forgiven when she got married. David's a doctor, and Tessa became a perfect wife and mother and produced three beautiful children, who are now three beautiful adults, and one of them is about to produce the first beautiful great-grandchild. So now she's number one perfect daughter. Always on hand to help the parents.'

'So d'you get on okay with her?' asked Marissa.

'Don't get me started,' Sonya groaned. 'It was fine while she was in trouble and I was constantly rescuing her. Once she got off the drugs and started to get her life together it was like she just switched off.'

'Sometimes people are like that if you've seen them at their lowest point,' Gayle said. 'Each time they see you it's a reminder that you've seen their dark side.'

'It's probably all in your head,' Marissa said. 'Just tell your mum and dad the truth, and then stand back and see what happens. It's only belly dancing, for heaven's sake. What's the worst that can happen?'

'I can't imagine,' Sonya said, feeling nauseous at the thought of it. 'I simply can't imagine.'

Gayle sat in her hotel room sorting through her costumes. After their first excursion to the costume shop, she and Sonya had got together to make some more. Now she spread them out on the bed, the original blue, another in lavender trimmed with purple and silver, and one in a deep burgundy, almost the same colour as she'd worn for Angie's wedding. There were some silver harem pants, a couple of cropped jackets trimmed with glass beads, a braided tunic, several belts, and some bras she'd covered with matching materials and embroidered with butterfly motifs. She thought of the hours she and Sonya had spent stitching the strips of sequins, and pinning the fine slippery fabric. They'd both been so excited about it and now – now with the first performance just a day away – the prospect of performing in front of an audience of complete strangers seemed terrifying. She had slept badly after the argument with Brian, waking frequently, fearing that at any moment the snoring in the study would stop and he would blunder up the stairs and into the bedroom. By morning, anxiety and lack of sleep had taken their toll and she had silently packed the remainder of her things thankful that he had not yet surfaced. His appearance as she was about to leave had left her shaking and feeling sick, and she had almost fallen into the back seat of Frank's car, her heart thumping hard against her ribs, her head pounding.

The ugly bargain they had struck years earlier had been on shaky ground for a long time and it had ended the moment he twisted her arm and dragged her towards him. She knew it and she was convinced he knew it too. He had made it just that little bit easier for her to leave. Now she was haunted by two images: one of Brian, his vice-like grip on her wrist, the veins pulsing in his temples as he thrust his face, purple with anger, into hers; the other of a bewildered middle-aged man, his hair sticking up in odd places, his trousers undone, holding a coffee plunger as he stood in an empty hallway looking totally confused.

In the next room, Marissa massaged lavender oil into her temples, dabbed a little on the back of her neck and settled cross-legged on the floor to meditate. Slowing down her breathing she started to relax by concentrating on her feet and ankles, tensing then relaxing them, and doing the same with her calf muscles, knees, thighs, hips, buttocks and pelvic floor. It wasn't working. Exhaling deeply she thrust her legs out straight in front of her and leaned back against the side of the bed.

From the moment they boarded the plane in Perth she had been captive to an unfamiliar sense of responsibility. She had organised her life so that she didn't have to be involved in other people's problems nor have to rely on their trust or meet their expectations. Now she was involved with, and relying on, two women who were both struggling with emotional upheaval. And she was flying around the state, staying in hotels, renting rooms, printing up fliers and posters, sending out publicity, all on taxpayers' money. What if no women turned up? What if they couldn't inspire even one of the women who attended to get some form of dance or other esteem-building activity into her life? The project would just have been a burden on the state.

'This,' Marissa said aloud, 'is why I avoid relationships and friends, why I never wanted to have children, or a job managing other people, or any other sort of serious responsibility.' She longed to cancel everything, call a cab, go straight to the airport and get the first flight back to Perth, back to the peace, safety and comfort of her blue house. And that was when she thought about calling Frank. He'd listen, be supportive, she would barely have to explain anything. He would just know. She dialled the number and it immediately diverted to message bank and she sat for a moment listening to the sound of his recorded voice, wondering what to say, and then she hung up without leaving a message.

When Sonya's niece dropped her back at the hotel it was after eleven, and she stood outside on the street breathing in the familiar dry smell of the town, watching as the last few customers turned out of the pub and made their way along the wide pavements where the deep overhang of the shops' verandahs provided daytime shade. She had been fifteen, angry and resentful when they moved here. Her father's job transfer had robbed her of her friends, her favourite places and the school where she was about to become a house captain.

She hated the hot, isolated town where there was nothing to do and nowhere to go. And she hated her parents for agreeing to the move and her sister for pretending that she liked the stark, reddish brown landscape better than the tree-lined streets of neat little houses with fresh green lawns they had left behind. It was only a few years later, two years into her degree in Perth when, catching the train to Kalgoorlie for Christmas, she realised that it felt like home. But despite her affection for the place, she still feared its power to draw her back and cut her off from the life she had chosen.

That she had survived this evening at all seemed to Sonya something of a miracle. She had set out determined to honour her promise and come clean straight away about the purpose of her visit. But from the moment she set foot in her parents' house the forces of family and familiarity claimed her. She was kidnapped again, a child being sized up by her parents. And it wasn't only her parents. Sonya's early intimacy with her sister still taunted her and she never quite abandoned the hope that somehow, one day, they would recapture it. Tonight it was obvious from the start that nothing had changed. Tessa greeted her with a perfunctory kiss on the cheek and the smug superiority of the well married daughter, the producer of grandchildren, the one who had stayed close to home. Tessa and David's two eldest children were there with their partners; Alannah, the youngest, was expected later.

'It's seven years since we were all together,' Vera said as Lew handed out champagne. 'What with you young ones gadding off around the world, time flies. We must celebrate.' And soon she was ushering them in to the dining room. 'Now, you'll just have to help yourselves,' she said. 'Not enough room for everyone to sit around the table.'

The table was laden with salads, quiches, a home-baked leg of ham, new potatoes dripping with butter and dishes of homemade chutney and pickles.

'Gran's traditional spread,' Tessa's eldest daughter, Donna, whispered to Sonya, nudging her in the ribs. 'You could predict it, couldn't you?'

Sonya tried not to laugh. Her niece was right – beautifully prepared and presented, it was Vera's standard meal for special occasions. 'It's quite comforting really, isn't it?' she said. 'I suspect she'll still be doing this well into the next generation.' She patted Donna's pregnant belly. 'When are you due?'

'Five weeks today,' Donna said, 'and it can't come soon enough for me. This pregnancy lark is vastly overrated.'

On the other side of the room, Sonya could see her mother bearing down on Gayle with a bowl of coleslaw. 'Do try some of this, dear,' Vera was saying, 'it's quite an old recipe from the CWA cookbook, but I think it beats any other. Now, tell me about this project you're involved in with Sonya.'

'Well,' Gayle began, helping herself to the coleslaw and shooting Sonya a desperate glance, 'it's . . . it's something new to me, new to all of us, really . . . ' and a look of relief crossed her face as the doorbell rang and Vera excused herself to answer it.

Gayle grabbed Sonya's arm. 'For heaven's sake, Sonya, you've got to tell them. You promised.'

But it was Alannah who broke Sonya's cover. Always close to her aunt, having lived with her for several months while doing her journalism degree, she was back home now working for the local newspaper, and she breezed in, apologising for her lateness and handing her grandmother a large bunch of purple irises.

'Sonj, you look fabulous,' she cried, hugging Sonya and then standing back to look at her before ruffling her hair. 'I love it, the colour, it's so cool. So, what are you doing here?'

'She was just going to tell us all about it,' Vera said, 'but you must meet Gayle first, and Marissa,' and she steered Alannah across the room.

'Oh my god,' Alannah said. 'Marissa! You're the belly dancer. I've seen you in Fremantle. We ran a story on you coming to Kal for this women and ageing thing. Mum,' she turned to Tessa, 'remember I was telling you, you should go along to those belly dancing classes?' She turned back to Marissa. 'D'you actually have to be over fifty to attend, because I'd really love to. Oh, I'm Alannah, by the way, Sonya's niece.'

Every eye in the room was turned on Marissa, who was balancing a glass of mineral water on the edge of her plate.

'Nice to meet you,' she said. 'Er . . . no, the program is to encourage older women to take up dancing but anyone can come along.'

Alannah took the glass of champagne her grandfather was holding out to her. 'Thanks, Grandad. Well, cheers, this is so great. And weren't you bringing a couple of women with you to do some demonstrations?'

The silence was agonising and as far as Sonya was concerned it was all downhill from then on.

Standing on the pavement outside the hotel, listening to the late-night rumbles of the town, she relived that moment when it became clear to her mother that not only was one of her guests a belly dancer, but her own daughter was part of the team. Gayle and Marissa had made their getaway at the first opportunity, insisting they would enjoy a walk back to the hotel, but for Sonya there was no escape.

'I can't believe this, Sonya,' her mother said, drawing herself up to her full height. 'Belly dancing? I don't know about your friends, of course, that's not my business, but for someone in your position, it's hardly suitable.'

'Come on, Gran,' Alannah said. 'Don't be such an old stick-in-the-mud. It's brilliant. Dancing is great exercise and it's really beautiful. You and Mum should go along, have a go. You could take a couple of the classes, Mum, they're on every afternoon – do you good.'

Tessa bristled. 'I have far better things to do with my time than prance around dressed up in a lot of sequins, thank you, Alannah.' And Sonya thought how much nicer her sister had been in the days when she was unemployed and zonked out of her mind on drugs.

'I'm glad that at least one of my daughters has some dignity,' Vera said. 'This is a great shock to us, Sonya, isn't it, Lewis?'

Lew cleared his throat. 'Certainly is, old girl. I mean, you've got your career to think of, and then there's us – we live here, you know. The whole town'll know about it. All that . . . well, all that thrusting and shimmying, it's certainly not what I'd have expected of you, Sonya.'

Vera looked up in alarm. 'Shimmying! What do you know about shimmying?'

'I was in the Middle East in forty-one. We weren't fighting all the time, you know, m'dear.'

The tension in the room ratcheted up as the minutes ticked away. With the exception of Alannah, the grandchildren made their excuses and left, obviously heading for the pub where they would doubtless fall about in hysterical laughter. Sonya felt crushed by the weight of her parents' disapproval. Obviously this offence was casting previous misdemeanours into insignificance. There could be no excuses, no pardons.

'I'll talk to Mum,' Alannah had said as she drove Sonya back to the hotel. 'She'll be fine when she's not with the oldies.'

'I doubt it,' Sonya said, shaking her head. 'Your mother and I lost our connection years ago.'

'She's intimidated by you, that's all,' Alannah said. 'I don't understand her, really. She's lovely about you when you're not there, and a perfect bitch to you when you are. I think she's just longing to do the sister thing, but can't bring herself to make the first move.'

Sonya shrugged. 'It's too late now. I don't even know how to talk to her anymore. I didn't want to hurt them, you know. But this was something I really wanted to do. I can't imagine, now, how I thought I could . . . well . . . get away with it.'

'They'll get over it,' Alannah said as she stopped the car outside the hotel. 'Just give them time. And anyway, it's your life. You're fifty-something, you don't need their approval.'

Sonya swallowed hard. 'That's the trouble,' she said. 'I actually do, pathetic as that may seem at my age, Alannah. I do still need their approval.'

Frank was late getting home. It was after eleven when he swung the car into the drive and he'd had a difficult and frustrating day. The drugs case was proving more complex as new leads sparked and then burned out and the tendrils of the syndicate extended up the coast and into other states. A drink and bed beckoned but, despite his weariness, the feeling that something was wrong kicked in as soon as he opened the car door. And in the next second a man emerged from the shadows of the adjacent house and grabbed him by the lapels in an attempt to thrust him back against the car.

Frank's reflexes had been honed on the battlefield and were too quick and too powerful for the aggressor. Delivering a chop to the kidney area he was free, as his assailant, who was built like a commercial refrigerator, doubled up, swearing and groaning. Grasping one of his arms, Frank twisted it back into a half nelson, pulling him upright and turning him so that he was now pinned against the car.

'Fuck off,' roared the attacker. 'What the hell d'you think you're doing?'

'I could ask you the same question,' Frank said. 'You started this.'

The man, who wasn't as strong as his size suggested, struggled helplessly. 'What are you up to messing around with my wife?' he demanded, twisting his head back over his shoulder to look at Frank.

He reeked of stale alcohol, and Frank could see a trickle of blood coming from the man's nose where his face had connected with the car roof. 'No idea what you're talking about, mate,' he said, keeping him pinned there. 'Who's your wife?'

'As if you didn't know. You picked her up this morning, drove off with her right under my bloody nose.'

'Well, your nose is bleeding now,' Frank replied, 'and that won't be all unless we sort this out quick smart.'

'You know what I mean. You were waiting for her outside and now she's in Kalgoorlie.'

'Ah,' said Frank, 'the belly dancers. And you, I suspect, are Gayle's husband.' He relaxed his hold a little. 'I haven't been up to anything with your wife, I'm just the chauffeur. So, if I can trust you to keep your hands to yourself we can discuss this in a more civilised manner.'

Brian grunted something incomprehensible and Frank tightened his grip again. 'What was that?'

'Okay, okay,' Brian yelped. 'Let me go, for chrissakes.'

Frank released him and stepped back from the car. 'What's your name?'

Brian straightened up, rubbed his face with his hand and, seeing the blood, searched his pockets for a handkerchief. 'Brian Peterson, as if you didn't bloody know. What're you writing it down for?'

'So I know who to arrest for assaulting a police officer.'

'You assaulting me, more like,' Brian said, 'and entrapping my wife –'

'Look here,' Frank said, pocketing his notebook. 'This is just bloody silly. If you've got a problem with what she's doing you'd better take it up with her. And I warn you now, if you're going to have an argument with her, you'd better not start it the way you started with me, or I'll be helping her to get a restraining order.'

'Hey, hang on a minute,' Brian said, the tone of his voice – indeed, his whole demeanour – indicating that he was backing down. 'I just want to know what's happening.'

'What's happening with you and your missus is between the two of you,' Frank said. 'She's an adult and can go wherever she likes, even if she does have the misfortune to be married to you. I suggest you give her a call and talk to her about it.'

'I've done that,' Brian said, still dabbing at his nose. 'She said the same. And she doesn't want to talk to me.'

'Then take my advice and can it, mate. Give her a couple of days and call her again when you're sober, and if that's your Saab over there, don't even think of driving it home. How did you find me?'

'Car rego,' Brian mumbled. 'Got it as you pulled out of the drive.'

'And?'

'And yeah, okay, I've got a mate in the vice squad. He did a vehicle check for me.'

Frank raised his eyebrows. 'So, will I book you or won't I?'

Brian, no longer bleeding, stuffed his handkerchief away. 'No, mate, sorry. I'll, er . . . I'll get out of your way.'

Frank gave him a long hard look. Belligerent though Brian was, there was something pathetic about the man that stirred Frank's compassion. 'You just wanted someone else to blame. A punch-up to make you feel better,' he said. 'Not very smart. So, okay, Mr Peterson, take this as a warning. If I hear you flexing your muscles on this subject anywhere else, I'll book you and I'll add assaulting a police officer to the charge. Now I assume you've got a mobile phone, so you'd better call yourself a cab.'

Ten minutes later the tail lights of the taxi were disappearing around the corner of the street, and Brian's black Saab remained parked on the opposite side of the road. Inside, Frank dropped his jacket on a chair, poured himself a large whisky and stood at the lounge window staring out into the silent street. Brian Peterson was hardly what he would have imagined if he'd been speculating about Gayle's husband, but perhaps it wasn't so surprising. He was an angry man, a bully, possibly a drunk. Frank had seen enough strange partnerships to know that they sometimes worked, but he didn't think this was one of them. Gayle's decision to tell her husband about the tour less than twenty-four hours before she left would have pissed off the mildest of men. There was something pretty unhealthy happening with the Petersons, and Frank thought he'd better warn Marissa. It was almost midnight and she'd probably be asleep by now. It would have to wait until the morning. She'd been nervous at the airport, checking and double-checking everything.

'Thanks, Frank,' she'd said finally. 'For the lift and for everything else. Might not have got this far without you.'

'Course you would,' he'd said. 'Now, get out there and swing your booty in the goldfields. I'll call you.' Instinctively he had reached out to her, and for a fraction of a second thought she was going to resist, but she had hugged him briefly before moving on.

He wished she weren't so far away and, more than that, he wished he knew how she felt. But as he couldn't work out his own feelings he had no chance of divining hers. He had rapidly grown accustomed to her being around and he missed her already. He couldn't remember the last time he'd missed anyone.

TEN

'Now, we can either rehearse in costume or do a quick run-through before we change,' Marissa said when they arrived at the hall. There was more than an hour before the first performance but both Sonya and Gayle were tense and distracted.

'Let's just run through it as we are,' Sonya said. 'We'll have plenty of time to change before the real thing.'

As soon as she had agreed to it, Marissa knew it was a mistake. The combination of the music and the costumes might have lifted their spirits, shifted their focus from their own problems onto the dance itself. And it wasn't just them. Her sense of responsibility, the feeling that everything was going to fall into a very big hole, overhung her own performance. She put them through their paces a second time, watching now from the front rather than leading, and her heart sank even further.

'Look,' she said going back on the stage, 'this dance is all about female sexuality. You need to be connected to that part of your-selves, and to be responding to the music and the meaning. What's happening in your head, what you're feeling about your-selves, is crucial. I know you've both got other stuff going on and it's hard, but you just have to put that aside for the next couple of hours.'

Gayle ran her hands through her hair. 'I'm sorry,' she said. 'It's hard to concentrate. It all seemed so much easier when we were rehearsing at home.'

'It's not any harder here,' Marissa replied. 'Not if you give it your full attention, think yourself into the meaning. It's all about what you put into it.'

Sonya pulled a face. 'I keep thinking my mother's going to show up,' she said. 'Walk through that door and demand that I stop behaving badly and go home like a good girl. It's really unnerving.'

Marissa sighed. 'I know how it feels,' she said, and there was an edge to her voice, 'having to perform when you really don't feel like it, when you've got other things on your mind. But you've done harder things than this. Concentrate, give it all you've got. You both know what dancing's done for you – particularly you, Gayle. Find that for yourself now, and find it for all those other women who are going to turn up and who might just need it as much as you did. And you, Sonya, stop looking guilty. Loosen up, have fun, and get those movements flowing again.'

Sonya nodded and started to circle her shoulders. 'You're right,' she said, 'let's give it another go.'

Marissa shook her head. 'No more time. Save it for the performance. We need to unpack the gear and get changed and made up. We're at work now so get your acts together and let those women see what you can do.'

Silently they unpacked and shook out their costumes.

'I look like a spaniel in this hairpiece,' Sonya said, pulling a long face as she pinned on the fall of red hair and fixed it with a gold sequinned headpiece.

'Bloodhound, more like,' Marissa said, hooking a floating veil to one side of her skirt. 'If your mother does turn up, all she'll see is a bloodhound in sequins.'

They were laughing now, all three of them, genuinely laughing together.

'You are such a hard woman, Marissa,' Sonya said, 'utterly brutal.'

'Brutal is good,' Gayle said, her body loosening up in response to the laughter. 'We need it. She's been pussyfooting around us all day.'

'Well, there's more brutality where that came from,' Marissa said, as some of her anxiety began to dissipate.

By the time the community centre organisers arrived, the mood had changed to nervous anticipation and the tension built as the audience began to trickle in through the doors. Soon the rows of seats were filled and more chairs were being pulled out from the stacks at the back of the hall until it was standing room only. They waited behind the screens at the side of the stage, tense and poised for the start.

'Okay,' Marissa whispered, 'any minute now, when you hear that drumbeat and see me move, we're on, and we give it all we've got.'

The lights went down and the drumbeat commenced in eight-four time, then a fast and spirited chiftitelli began and they started. Marissa was in her element now, doing what she did best and knowing that on this crucial night her own performance had the power to make or break the others. There was a rustle of delight in the audience as they swept onto the small stage in a burst of brilliant colour. Marissa sensed that it infected Gayle and Sonya, lifting them out of their distractions and into the spirit of the dance. In her peripheral vision Gayle was a shimmering siren in lavender and purple, and on the other side Sonya circled perfectly, curving her back, using her arms with unusual grace, the gold and green of her costume sparkling and flashing in the lights.

They were in the swing of it now and she could feel their energy mounting as the pace of the dance increased and they circled and shimmied in figures of eight, mirroring each other's movements. Effortlessly they moved into the next two dances, adjusting to a slower, more sensuous pace and rhythm and then, in the final dance, on to the more demanding moves, the bolder steps and the fast, complex sequences, until, breathless with effort, eyes shining, they ended with a flourish and to rapturous applause.

'I did have a terrible fit of nerves at the start,' Gayle admitted later. 'I was so scared I thought I might faint, but it was about the dancing, not about all the other stuff. By that time it was only the dancing that mattered.'

'Well, you were great,' Marissa said. 'I'm so proud of you both.'

'Obviously we respond to flagellation,' Sonya laughed. 'I'm exhausted – it must be the nervous energy.'

'Even a brief performance is more exhausting than hours of rehearsal,' Marissa answered, 'so you'll need to learn to pace yourselves, rest whenever you can, try to stay cool and not get too distracted by other things. It's a big ask, I know, but if you don't, you'll burn out really fast. What about that audience, though – so many women, and didn't they love it?'

Sonya grinned. 'They really did, I couldn't believe it. They were raring to go.'

Gayle unpinned her headdress and rolled it into her bag. 'I really only understood tonight why you wanted us, as beginners, to come with you. When I spoke to the women afterwards they were surprised and quite motivated when I told them I'd only been dancing a few months.'

'Exactly,' Marissa said. 'And tonight you didn't dance like beginners anyway. Keep that up and we'll have them hammering down the doors to get in. Gayle, remember to keep working on those shoulders and, Sonya –'

'I know, I know, the jerky bits. I'll get there eventually.'

Despite the confident and successful start, though, it turned out to be a difficult week. The nervous tension of the performances and of being watched in the classes took a greater toll on Gayle and Sonya than either had expected. After that first night they had difficulty maintaining the pace and became uncharacteristically moody. Marissa, who was both irritated by and anxious about them, found herself overcompensating, trying to motivate them with humour and encouragement, which drained her own energy. They needed to work better as a team, just as they had at that first performance.

'Perhaps we could have a bit of a strategy meeting,' she suggested on the day they were due to leave Kalgoorlie. 'It's three hours before we have to go to the airport, so it's a good chance to talk about how we can improve the way we work together.'

Sonya pushed her muesli bowl aside and got up to fetch more coffee. 'I hope I'll be able to put on a better show once we're away from here. I still feel really tense.'

Gayle nodded. 'I know. I'm feeling a bit wobbly myself. I hadn't reckoned on it being so exhausting.'

Marissa gritted her teeth. 'You're not going to pull out, are you?'

'No way. It's just taking me a while to adjust, and I suppose to get over the shock of what Frank told you on the phone about Brian going after him. Even I'm amazed he'd behave like that, and I feel so guilty about poor Frank – after all, it's nothing to do with him.'

'Frank's fine, he's a policeman,' Marissa said. 'They're used to that sort of thing.'

'Just the same –'

'Marissa's right,' Sonya cut in. 'Frank'll have forgotten it by now, but I can understand how you feel. Has Brian called again this morning?'

'Yes, but he's calmer now. He's gone from wild and threatening through cold anger and now we're in hurt little boy stage.'

'How long since you left him behind to do anything of your own?' Marissa asked.

'How long? Well, never really. Angie and I went away on our own sometimes, but only when he was going to be away too. Other than that, I've always been there.'

Marissa raised her eyebrows. 'No wonder he's freaking out now. By the way, Sonya, was that your sister at the back of the hall last night?'

'Huh! I doubt it,' Sonya said. 'Alannah, maybe, she came to a couple of classes, but not last night. And there's no way Tessa would come.'

'I think she was there,' Gayle said. 'I meant to mention it yesterday evening but I forgot. It looked like her.'

Sonya shook her head. 'It couldn't have been. My sister watch me belly dance? Not in a million years.'

'Okay,' Marissa said. 'Next stop Albany. We have an hour and a half to wait in Perth for the Albany flight. Don't decide to pop home, either of you.'

'I bet Frank'll be there to meet us,' Sonya said with a grin. 'Nice man, a lot like Normie Rowe.'

'But taller,' Gayle said with a smile, 'and pretty cute.'

'Especially when he sings "It's Not Easy".'

'Don't start that again,' Marissa said, laughing.

'What have you got against Normie?' Gayle asked. 'I used to think he was gorgeous.'

'Nothing at all,' Marissa said. 'In fact, I used to have a bit of a thing for him myself. But it's not like that with Frank. And anyway, I don't do relationships.'

'Ha! I know that line,' Sonya said. 'I've used it myself quite a lot, usually just before leaping into some terrible liaison with a totally inappropriate man.'

'Not me,' Marissa said. 'The last time was so long ago I can't remember it, other than as the point at which I decided that celibacy was my new career. Now, let's think Albany. It'll be coldish, but the bed and breakfast place looks nice. Strategy? Anything we want to change?'

Sonya leaned forward and patted her arm. 'It's okay, Marissa, we're not stupid. We know it was team building we needed, not strategy, and we've just done it.'

'Really?' Marissa said, startled. 'Was that it?'

Gayle nodded.

'So team building is about getting a rise out of the team leader?'

'Of course it is,' Sonya said, rolling her eyes. 'Trust me – I'm a bureaucrat, I know about these things.'

ELEVEN

In 1956, the year Oliver turned seven, the Soviet Union invaded Hungary, Britain formed a military alliance with France and Israel to prevent General Nasser from nationalising the Suez Canal, and rock'n'roll, after a dodgy start a few years earlier, started to take a hold in the US. Not surprisingly, none of these events made much impression on Oliver at the time, although a couple of decades later he would develop an abiding interest in them all and go on to write papers about them in the course of his academic career. None, however, had the long-term impact on him that an event within his own home was to have.

In that same year Joan Baxter read Mary Wollstonecraft's *Vindication of the Rights of Woman*, closely followed by Simone de Beauvoir's *The Second Sex*. Oliver was unaware of the presence of these books in the small terraced house in Claremont, but they were to affect his life in ways rather more profound than the international events of that year. Some years later, Joan was among the first women in Perth to read Betty Friedan's *The Feminine Mystique* and by the time Germaine Greer's orifices appeared in *Suck* and *The Female Eunuch* was published, Oliver was a young man ahead of his time.

Years earlier, Joan Baxter was teaching at a local primary school when she met a merchant seaman called Bruce one night in the pub, and promptly embarked on a live-in relationship of which her mother, had she still been alive, would have seriously disapproved. Her father was otherwise occupied, with a plan to make money from a betting syndicate and barely seemed to notice Bruce's arrival, or Oliver's birth the following year. Similarly Oliver, at the age of three, barely noticed his father's failure to return from one of his trips to sea. Joan *did* notice and was, by that time, heartily relieved. She went back to teaching and, a few years later, started all that dangerous and subversive reading.

'You'll be the most aware man on the campus,' Joan had told Oliver when he began his history degree at the University of Western Australia. 'You're at the forefront of a new generation of men; men who will understand women and be able to communicate with them.'

Oliver, who was eighteen at the time and obsessively interested in sex and how to get lots of it, was optimistic. He visualised sexual conquests in the university's sunken garden, or its cool, shadowy cloisters. But his hit rate in those early years was very disappointing.

'Academic life is good, Ma, but the woman thing doesn't seem to be working for me,' he told her a year into his PhD.

'It will all happen in good time,' Joan reassured him. 'The smart young women are concentrating on studying.'

It was a year later that he ended up dancing with Alison at a campus party and she was seriously impressed to find he was Joan Baxter's son. It was the only time in Oliver's life that having a mother who was a prominent feminist seemed to have a beneficial effect on his romantic status.

Oliver had never felt that being raised by one parent was any sort of disadvantage; he was highly sceptical when bad adolescent behaviour and dysfunctional adult lives were blamed on the fact that the person was the child of a one-parent family. On several occasions he had written letters to newspapers when he read newly published studies of the disadvantage to children of sole parenting. Many people, he would point out, thrived with single parents; they became writers, plumbers, film stars, dentists and hairdressers – *and* functional parents – just like the children of two-parent families, but the one-parent status was only ever cited in association with failure and dysfunction. Various versions of this letter had been published in state and national newspapers over the years, and once, to his surprise, in the *Australian Women's Weekly*.

When Oliver was nine, Joan had moved them into a house shared with two other single mothers. There were three young girls in the house; the only male competition was William who, at seven months, was too small to count. Oliver spent his adolescence in this lively and harmonious environment, surrounded by women doing the things that women do so well: listening to him, validating his views and experiences and sharing their own, and generally being there for him.

Janet, Pam and Linda, the daughters of the shared house, were like sisters to him, and along with various friends had continued to fill his life with pleasant and supportive female company. But Pam had recently retired early and moved to the southwest, and Janet and Linda were on long service leave to walk the pilgrims' route to Santiago de Compostela. And now Sonya and Gayle were gone too. Oliver felt strangely sad and ill at ease. He missed Gayle's reassuring presence and sympathetic ear, and Sonya's lively conversation and robust good sense. Feeling abandoned, he hovered frequently near the phone on the brink of calling someone, only to remember there was no one to call.

'You're looking peaky, Oliver,' Rhonda remarked when he turned up to collect the transcripts of the interviews he had taped in Berlin. 'I thought you were supposed to be on leave.' Rhonda had been private secretary to a vice-chancellor before she took early retirement to work part-time and help out with her grandchildren.

'It's over, unfortunately,' Oliver said, 'and I'm feeling a bit sort of blue, you know, Rhonda.'

'You need to get out more,' Rhonda said. 'Take more exercise and eat more vegetables. You single men, I know what you're like. What is this problem you all seem to have with vegetables? There's no mystery to making a salad, or cooking the odd bit of broccoli.'

'I'm actually quite good with vegetables,' Oliver protested.

'Well, maybe it's not the veggies,' Rhonda continued. 'I've known you a long time, Oliver, and you're always off colour when you haven't got a few women around keeping an eye on you.'

Oliver drove home with the transcripts wondering whether Rhonda was right and, if so, whether it indicated a character defect. Like many people who have lived alone for a long time, he was prone to introspection, sometimes even to a morbid level of self-analysis. Was he reliant on the feeling that women were keeping an eye on him? Had he fallen into the habit of needing women to reflect him back to himself, just as Virginia Woolf had said, at twice his natural size?

The business with Gayle had already made him question the imbalance in the sharing of information. Had she been deliberately secretive or was it his own narcissism? Maybe he was a really poor listener. Their last encounter in his office had been excruciating and he recalled her comment, accusation almost, about him seeing things in black and white. Was he really that narrow?

He was still agonising about it when he got home, and to distract himself he decided to listen again to the tapes and then mark up the significant passages in the transcript. The ponderous and awkward conversations with the two elderly sisters recorded in Germany demanded special attention. Parking himself in his favourite chair, feet on the coffee table, Oliver switched on the tape and the women's voices filled the room.

'It is hard to explaining it,' Helga said. 'Hitler is rescuing Germany, my Manfred, he believes it and I believe him. It is not for me to question the men – my father, my husband. I am woman, *Hausfrau*, I have to care for childrens, to look after my home.'

Oliver closed his eyes. The accent and awkward English didn't make for easy listening and from time to time Erika cut in with a translation. Outside his window the next door neighbour's cat was stalking a bird, making its way cautiously along the top of the limestone wall towards its prey. The tape droned on and Oliver watched as the cat's body tensed. He could almost see the muscles tightening as it poised for the leap that would capture the prize, when a huge blackbird swooped from a nearby branch and the cat swayed to retain its balance as the small bird took off to safety. Oliver reached out to stop the tape, as he had lost concentration and had a vague feeling he had missed something important. He rewound it, setting it to play again.

'I must make the truth,' Helga was saying. 'I hear bad things are happening but Manfred, he tells me, "Helga, it is necessary". He is a good man, I love him. I do not make the trouble for my family, for the man I marry.' She lapsed into German then and Erika translated.

'She is saying that sometimes it is best to hope that things will pass. You know a side of a man that no one else knows. The good things, the person he is capable to be. His . . . I think it is vulnerability, yes? This makes it more complicated.'

Oliver stopped the tape once more and rewound it a second time. Listening again, carefully this time, he highlighted specific sections of the interview in yellow, and read it over.

Gayle stood on the flat rocks above the inlet where the waves crashed against the steep cliffs. She had always loved Albany; the ragged coastline with its islands scattered through the bays, and the stunningly pure air from the Southern Ocean. As a child she had spent time here with her grandparents – a welcome relief from life at home – watching the whales make their way south, collecting shells on Middleton Beach, and here at The Gap, clutching her grandfather's hand in order to lean over the rail and look down into the swirling water. The mix of beauty and danger was intoxicating. High winds had been known to sweep people from these rocks, hurling them mercilessly to their death.

Gayle remembered her grandfather's firm grip, her hand small and cold in his large, warm one, and the longing to be held safely combined with the almost overwhelming temptation to let go and risk what might happen. She had dreamed of being swept away from this spot, but rather than crashing downwards, in her dreams she was carried off on the high winds to the kingdoms of her imagination. She smiled, thinking how notions of adventure changed with the decades. The islands and castles, the cities and cloud havens she had envisaged in her youth had shrunk to longings within the realm of the possible. She dreamed now of a small, cosy house located on high ground on the outskirts of the town and in those dreams she was sitting at a desk by a window that looked out across the water. She would be working on her PhD or just relaxing, listening to music, reading a book or writing a letter, buying food in the Farmers' Market on Saturday mornings, collecting, once again, those shells at Middleton beach, waiting for the sun to set.

Gayle's childhood memories were of long periods of time spent in her own company. Never lonely with her books and her imagination, and always thankful to escape her father's overbearing presence, she had cherished solitude. She sighed now, turning up the collar of her jacket against the wind. If things were different this would have been the perfect place to live, to build a reflective, creative life, but there was another life to contend with, another person to accommodate, and Brian did not figure anywhere in her fantasies.

The Albany performances and classes had nourished her spirit as had the conversations with the women in the audience. Letting them see her dance, and later talking with them about how it was changing her, all worked to strengthen her own resolve.

'You look so wonderful in that costume,' a woman had said to her that morning at one of the classes in the arts centre, 'and the dancing is amazing. But I don't think I could ever do it.'

'That's what I thought,' Gayle told her. 'I went to one class to satisfy my friends, and it just sort of grabbed me. I've only been doing it about six months but it's changed my life, really it has.'

'Yes,' said the woman, her eyes bright with tears. 'I can see that it would, but that's why, you see, why I couldn't do it. I couldn't take that risk.'

The wind whipped Gayle's hair around her face and she turned into it, thankful that, in spite of the problems that lay ahead, she *had* taken that risk. She had survived the first week of the tour despite Brian's outrage and Angie's pleading.

'I'm not coming back until the end of the tour,' she had told her daughter on the phone, surprising herself with the decisiveness of her tone. 'He'll have to get used to the idea.'

'But he's really wild about you being away,' Angie protested. 'And he's being such a pain, calling all the time, yelling at everyone. Mum, *why* are you doing this? Can't you just come back?'

'Aren't you the person who thought the belly dancing was a fabulous thing for me to do?' she asked in frustration. 'Didn't you tell Sonya that you were really proud of me deciding to do the tour?'

'Yes, yes, of course I did, but it's different. I mean, it's not really fair to Dad to leave him on his own like this and –'

'Angie!' Gayle cut in, anger and injustice erupting like fire in her chest. 'For years you've urged me to take a holiday, spend time doing something I wanted to do. You attacked me in front of Trish and Sonya for never holding out for anything against your father. Well, now I'm doing it, and you don't like it because it's creating a few problems for you. I'm afraid you just have to quit moaning and get used to it.' She had hung up close to tears. She had known that going away would indicate a tectonic shift between her and Brian. Now Angie was caught in it and, like the delayed wash from a passing liner, the swell of tension between her parents was rocking her own comfortable boat.

Back at the guest house there was a text message from Trisha asking Gayle to call her.

'Of course you know all hell's broken loose here since you left?'

'So I gather,' Gayle said. 'But it must be calming down now.'

'I'm not so sure about that. Brian was here last night, turned up unexpectedly just as Graham and I were heading out for dinner.'

'And?'

'He seems to think I'm a bad influence on you. Bit late, really. I mean, I've been trying to be a bad influence on you for donkey's years. Now when you *do* go off the rails, I'm staying home knitting a shawl for my first grandchild.'

Gayle paused, staring at herself in the bedroom mirror. 'Am I really going off the rails?'

Trisha laughed. 'A figure of speech, darl. But he's in a nasty mood, and he's upsetting Angie too.'

Gayle sighed. 'I've been umpiring between the two of them for years, Trish, explaining them to each other. Maybe this is good, maybe it's time they faced each other. Angie's married, she's got

Tony and a life of her own. She has to negotiate her own way with Brian now.'

'Of course, but I guess it's all happened rather quickly –'

'Look,' Gayle cut in, 'I know I didn't give Brian enough notice, but I gave him more notice than he's often given me when he's going off somewhere or bringing home a houseful of visitors that need catering for. And I told Angie well in advance. There's more going on here than the surface stuff, Trish, you know that. For the first time ever I'm doing something for myself, and everyone else is going to have to hang on and make the best of it.'

There was a long pause at the end of the line, and Gayle glanced at the phone wondering if they'd been cut off.

'I know,' Trisha said eventually. 'And you mustn't back down, Gayle. I guess I'm just a bit pissed off with myself that after all this time I'm not there to watch what's happening to you.'

'So how do you think we're doing?' Sonya asked on their last night in Albany. They had celebrated with dinner at a local restaurant where a blazing open fire and an excellent Mount Barker Shiraz had them light-headed and relaxed.

'Brilliant,' Marissa said. 'Honestly, you've both improved dramatically this week. We're working together better now. I'm very happy and I've got some news – a bit of a change to our schedule. It's on to Bunbury tomorrow for a week as planned and then instead of having that break back home we're heading straight up to Broome.'

There was a pause, and Sonya and Gayle exchanged glances.

'I was looking forward to –' Sonya began.

'That's a good idea,' Gayle cut in. 'Best to keep going.'

Marissa nodded. 'Yes, but it's because I've had to rearrange the Broome plans. As well as the performances and classes we've been asked to do a special gig at the Cable Beach Resort.'

'What sort of *gig*?' Sonya asked.

'There's a women's health conference on up there and the organisers heard we were going to be in town so they've asked us to dance at the conference dinner on the opening night, and again at the close.'

'Sounds scary,' Gayle said.

'I don't think so. I spoke to the organiser last night. She's thrilled that we can do it, and reckons it'll set just the right tone for their conference.'

'Women's conferences are great,' Sonya said. 'They're really relaxed and informal. I was looking forward to a few days at home but I think this'll be fun.'

Marissa topped up the wine glasses. 'Tomorrow I'll reorganise the flights and the morning after the last performance in Bunbury we'll drive straight back to the airport and get the early afternoon flight to Broome. We'll need more videos, they've sold so well, so I'll ask Frank to pick some up from my place and bring them to the airport.'

Sonya grinned. 'Sounds good. Should we have some sinful dessert to celebrate?'

'Yes,' Gayle said with unusual force. 'Fortify us for Bunbury tomorrow. I'm having the steamed chocolate pudding with hot chocolate sauce, and ice cream.'

'But you don't eat desserts,' Marissa said. 'You're the virgin queen when it comes to sugar.'

Gayle shrugged, her cheeks pink from the warmth and the wine. 'So now I'm going to lose my virginity.'

Three chocolate puddings and several glasses of Baileys later, they made their way back up the hill to the guest house, three abreast across the silent street, their laughter ringing clear in the cold night air.

'I feel different,' Gayle said, stopping under a streetlamp. 'My body feels different.'

The tension had dropped from her face, and in the pool of light the fine lines around her eyes and across her forehead had disappeared. Her face looked fuller, more peaceful. She circled her head as though sensing its weight on her neck.

'It's called relaxation, and having fun,' Sonya said. 'You should try it more often.'

'This is what I want to feel always, like this. Lighter, sort of hopeful.'

'It's the dancing,' Sonya said. 'I feel it too. That and good food, good wine, the company of good women and a large helping of chocolate pudding.'

'I'm glad we're going straight on,' Gayle said. 'I didn't want to go home yet.'

'I thought so,' Marissa said. 'That's why I agreed to the conference without asking you first. I thought if you had time to consider it, the angel in the house might win the day.'

'Yes,' Gayle murmured, moving away from the streetlamp to stare straight up at the night sky. 'She might have. But what if the angel doesn't ever want to go back to the house again?'

'That,' said Marissa, 'could be a little more difficult.'

'But not impossible,' Sonya added. 'By no means impossible.'

Brian was essentially an optimistic person, a man who could push through the occasional emotional trough and thrust upward to the next peak. He had an ability to get people to see things his way, usually by overbearing argument and by withholding approval or favours. In business all was fair to Brian: you did what you had to do to achieve a result. He was smart and hard-working but insecure, and the latter quality gave him an aggressive and controlling edge. His team, particularly the women, thought him a bully and his rough edges and belligerence seemed at odds with their expectations of a senior executive; but each one knew he would not hesitate to give praise or be slow to share any rewards resulting from their joint success.

As far as his bosses were concerned, he was solid, with a ruthless competitive streak, occasional surprising bursts of creativity and, despite a lack of finesse, the ability to sweet-talk his way through difficult deals. For a long time, Brian had enjoyed a dream run. He had been in the right places at the right times and his determination and hard work had been generously rewarded. His home life was comparatively peaceful despite the cooling distance that had developed between Gayle and him over the years. His daughter rattled his cage from time to time, but kids were like that, and his own relatives were all comfortably far away in other states. As for his son, well, as far as Brian was concerned he had no son, and on the rare occasions that he felt the nudge of regret it was always alongside a strong sense of his own unquestionable rightness of judgement.

But into each life some rain must fall and Brian, in a taxi on his way from the hotel to the Sydney office, was hoping the cloudburst was about to dry out.

'You've known me a long time, Collette,' he'd said the previous night, his confidence restored by a remarkably virile performance. 'Is this the menopause or what? What do you reckon's going on with her?'

Collette was sitting on the edge of the bed pulling on her stockings, stretching out one slim leg and then the other, drawing on the sheer black nylons with the lacy tops that somehow seemed to stay up on their own without needing suspenders.

'So she was going to the classes, you said?' she asked. 'And then she just went off on the tour? Ignored what you said?' Brian nodded. 'How long has she been gone?'

'Three weeks, and she's still refusing to come home.'

'Hmm . . . ' Collette pondered. 'And you're still calling and leaving messages every day? Not nasty, threatening messages, I hope?'

Brian coloured slightly. 'Maybe a bit, but only at first. Not now. I just keep telling her she's got responsibilities and she's got no right to go off like that.'

Collette shook her head, tut-tutting loudly as she stepped into her skirt. 'Bad tactics, Brian, very bad tactics.'

'But I'm right,' Brian protested. 'She should be there.'

'You're sounding a little unreconstructed.'

'Huh?'

'Boorish. And you have to stop calling her every day. Time for a new strategy. Step number one, stop calling.'

'Stop?'

'Exactly. You stop calling. If you must do something send a nice, friendly text message, saying you hope the tour is going well and you miss her.'

'Miss her?'

'You do, don't you?'

'Well, yeah, but . . . '

'No buts. You back right off. Ideally you do nothing, but if you can't handle that then you change your tune. Give her some space. Chances are she'll be back in a few days if you stop bullying her.'

'Yeah? She's supposed to be home for a couple of days before they go off up north.'

'There you are then. Back off, send a nice message and be there when she gets home. I bet she's been missing your daughter since she got married. Get some nice flowers, chocolates maybe, take her out for dinner. I bet she'll stay right where she is and it'll all be forgotten.'

'I won't be there,' Brian said, watching his foot twitching nervously. 'Taking a couple of clients on a golfing break to the Vines Resort.'

'Cancel it, postpone it,' Collette said. 'Be there. Surprise her, make a fuss of her.' She walked across to the full-length mirror. 'I know you're a bit of a stud, Brian, but you have an awful lot to learn about women.'

For some time after Collette had left, Brian lay there contemplating her advice. Perhaps she was right, maybe he did need to try another tack. The problem with getting advice from someone else was that you could never really describe the subtleties to them. What he hadn't been able to explain to Collette was the strange nature of his and Gayle's relationship; the crises they'd weathered, the deal they'd made and the uncomfortable feeling that since Angie's wedding there had been a radical shift in the balance of power.

In his youth, Brian had been a bit too free and easy with his fists and there had been some episodes, particularly with women, that he preferred to forget. When he'd first met Gayle he'd vowed to change his ways and he'd succeeded for a while. But a few years later, lack of money and the demands of a young baby had driven out his good intentions. And then there was the big crisis and Gayle, pregnant and threatening to leave. Bad times, but Brian knew he'd done the right thing, settled it the right way – they'd lasted all this time. Even so, Collette might have a point; he needed to do it differently.

This morning, before calling his cab, he'd faxed the clients, postponed the three-day golf break and cancelled the booking at the Vines. As the taxi swung into Market Street and joined the line of traffic waiting at the lights, he felt remarkably pleased with himself. Problem number one was taken care of. Gayle was missing Angie and he probably should've spent more time with her. He'd surprise her, take her out somewhere nice, and she'd relent and cancel the rest of the trip. Outside the office, Brian signed the cab voucher and strode up the steps watching his own reflection in the smoked glass of the double doors. It had been remarkably calm since the regulation board decision. Clearly his concerns there had been unfounded – things were looking up. He straightened his shoulders and walked in through the doors, flashing his pass at the security officer in the foyer, and took the lift to the thirteenth floor.

Behind the curved blond wood reception desk, Sandy, the stick insect receptionist who wore skirts so small they could have been sleeves, was sorting through a pile of mail. She raised her eyebrows as Brian stepped out of the lift.

'Big Mal wants to see you,' she said, pulling a face, 'soon as you come in, in the boardroom. And –' she lowered her voice confidentially – 'the Chicago mafia have arrived, including our beloved former leader.'

Brian's stomach took a dive. 'Shit,' he murmured. 'Just when I thought we were in the clear.' He dumped his briefcase in the office he always used in Sydney, and stood by the window taking deep breaths to calm himself. Then, buttoning his jacket and with beads of sweat breaking out on his forehead, he headed down the passage towards the boardroom.

TWELVE

Sonya, dozing in the window seat half an hour into the flight from Perth to Broome, still wished she could have had a couple of days in her own home before taking off again. The conference thing sounded good but, just the same, after more than four weeks away it would have been nice to sleep in her own bed, check her mail, and maybe even book a massage. Most of all it would have given her time to think about what had happened with her family and what it all meant. After Marissa's suggestion that Tessa had been in the audience, Sonya had begun to wonder whether she too had seen her sister; and every time they danced in Albany and then in Bunbury, she had the eerie feeling that Tessa was there in her peripheral vision, always vanishing from sight.

Sonya was a very practical person who liked to be clear about boundaries. She tried to keep her life simple, to speak out about things that bothered her and equally to let people know it when she liked what they did. Her straightforwardness with Oliver had been characteristic of a manner that some people found confronting. She had risen to the mid-levels of the Senior Executive Service, and might have gone higher had she been more willing to compromise and play departmental politics. But Sonya preferred the truth – except, of course, when it came to her family.

She had grown up in the stifling social climate of the fifties, dominated by her parents' attempts to claw their way up the financial and social ladders. Lew's life revolved around his job with the bank, and the cricket: playing it, listening to it or watching it. And Vera was in a constant state of domestic production – lamingtons, jams, pickles or lemon butter, and crocheted squares to be joined into rugs for the people of Hungary recently invaded by the Soviet Union.

'Aren't you being a bit unkind?' Gayle had commented when Sonya described her upbringing. 'Lots of people's parents were like that. It's just that we baby boomers have such different lives and such high expectations, those times inevitably look pretty bland.'

Sonya only half agreed. 'I suppose so,' she admitted, 'but I still think mine were obsessive. We always had to pretend that everything was perfect, as though if it got out that one of us was sick or we'd had an argument, a black mark would be recorded against our name in some great public register, and if it happened often enough we would become social outcasts.'

'But it *was* like that,' Marissa said. 'At least, it certainly was in England – just like that. My parents were the same and so were their friends. I was like it myself, and that was how I ended up marrying Roger and why I was never forgiven for running away.' And she told them how she'd left that day and never looked back.

And Gayle, listening wide-eyed to the story, had leaned back with a sigh. 'Fancy just taking off like that. You've been so adventurous,' she said. 'I got married young and just relived my mother's life. I had more money, of course, more freedom and a job I liked, but I never learned another way to live or had the confidence to believe I could cope on my own.'

Sonya shifted her position and half opened her eyes to look out at the raft of white cloud beneath the aircraft wings, wondering about families, and how it seemed impossible to escape their emotional tentacles. She couldn't imagine how she would ever be able to go back to her parents' home – her pride wouldn't let her – and yet love and blood would never allow her to be free.

Gayle was only feigning sleep as she backtracked over her conversation with Angie, who had come to the airport with a gift she wanted Gayle to take to Josh.

'Dad'll have a fit at you not coming home,' she'd said, glancing nervously around the airport café as if Brian might materialise beside them at any moment.

'It won't make any difference to him,' Gayle said, watching a Virgin flight taxiing to the gate. 'He's taking clients to the Vines for a golf weekend. Our paths wouldn't have crossed anyway.'

'You can't imagine how difficult it is,' Angie said. 'Couldn't you skip the rest of the tour and come back now? You're upsetting everyone. Your mobile's switched off most of the time and that means Dad keeps calling me.'

'Angie, I'm upsetting Brian, and *he's* upsetting everyone else. Let's be clear about that. The phone's off because I need some time and space for myself but I always return your calls. This is the first time in more than thirty years that I've gone off and done something on my own. I think I deserve this without all the pressure from you and your father.'

'Okay, okay,' Angie said, 'but if you could just come back for a bit and sort things out –'

'And have you tell me again that I never hold out for anything I want?'

'I know, I know, I shouldn't have said all that. I'm sorry – really – but everything's such a mess.'

Gayle stirred her coffee and looked across to where Marissa, Sonya and Frank were sitting at a nearby table. She wanted to be with them. Much as she loved Angie, right now she was an intrusion, a reminder of the complex web of relationships and expectations from which Gayle felt so alienated, a reminder of what she would have to face when she went home. 'Don't be so selfish, Angie,' she said. 'So, you have to cope with your father for once. Be firm with him, like you told me to be.'

'You've changed,' Angie said.

'Isn't that what you wanted?'

'Yes, but not like this.'

'Like what, then? In a way that doesn't inconvenience you or upset Brian?' It was years since Gayle had felt anything but pleasure in her daughter's company, and this new irritation disturbed her. 'That's not how it works, Angie. Any sort of change affects the people closest to you. I'm sorry this is hard for you. It's not particularly easy for me either but I need to do it.' She took Angie's hand in hers. 'I've kept my eyes closed and my mouth shut for years and I can't do it anymore. This is important to me, and the things you said made a difference. You said it all in front of other people, and that meant I couldn't brush it aside or pretend it wasn't said, I have to confront it, work out what to do.'

Angie scrubbed at her tears with a tissue. 'Everything seems to be falling apart,' she said. 'That's so scary, and Tony doesn't like it either. You know how uptight and conservative his family is. His mum and dad don't approve of you belly dancing, or being away like this.'

Gayle withdrew her hand. 'And you want me to come home to keep your husband and your in-laws happy?' She stood and picked up her bag. 'That's our flight boarding now,' she said. 'I'll be back at the end of the tour, and I hope I'll feel clearer about things by then.' She put her hand on her daughter's shoulder. 'Angie, come on, darling. You know how much I love you. You have to do what I haven't done all these years. Take a stand with Tony, and with your father. And I need you to give me some space. Dry your eyes, go back to work and get on with your own life, while I sort out what's happening with mine.'

Marissa got up from her seat, stretched her legs, rotated her shoulders and sat down again. She hated flying and rarely did it: the enclosed space, the sterile air, just being in a plane distressed her. She was restless too, unusually so. Maybe the coffee had done it. Frank had fetched her one at the airport, perhaps he had forgotten to order decaf. She'd spotted him waiting for them by the car hire desk as they'd made their way in from the car park, on time just as arranged, with the boxes of videos stacked on a trolley. Her immediate reaction was delight and she wanted to hug him but, embarrassed, she held back and it was Sonya who had broken the awkwardness.

'Hey, Frank,' she said, punching him gently on the upper arm. 'Gayle and I reckon you look like Normie Rowe.'

'But taller,' he said, smiling. 'Exactly two inches taller, in fact. You're not the first to notice it.' Turning away from Sonya, he reached to take Marissa's hand. 'Hello, Marissa. You look terrific.' He turned back to Sonya. 'Nice guy, Normie Rowe. Haven't seen him for years.'

'What? You mean you *know* him?'

Frank nodded. 'Years ago. We were in Vietnam together, often mistaken for brothers. Joined up on the same day and we were in the same battalion.' He turned back to Marissa then, putting his arm casually around her shoulders, guiding the trolley with the other hand as they walked together to the check-in desk. 'If you're very nice to me, one day I'll play you my Normie Rowie collection.'

Unwrapping one of the packets of airline biscuits, more from the need to do something than the desire to eat, Marissa thought about the night she'd met them all. It seemed a bit surreal now, the police cars in the street, her fear about her plants, the crowd of women in Gayle's great big showcase house. And now these three people had become so important in her life. Across the aisle in the seat by the other window sat Gayle, eyes closed, head resting on a small pillow, the sun from the aircraft window slanting across her face. She looked so different from the woman who had opened the front door the night of Angie's hens' party.

Marissa realised how easily she too could have been living a life like Gayle's had it not been for that extraordinary encounter in Sainsbury's all those years ago. One minute he was a big, raw-boned stranger with long reddish brown hair and several days' stubble, and the next he was something more: a gift, perhaps, an adventure waiting to start.

'Sorry,' he'd said, picking up the two tins of baked beans she'd been holding when he bumped into her. 'Not looking where I was going.'

The space between them was alive with chemistry. Marissa's heartbeat quickened and her mouth went dry.

'G'day,' he said, 'I'm Blue.'

'Blue?'

'Blue, it's my name.'

'What sort of name is that?'

'An Aussie one,' he said with a grin. 'Can I buy you a beer?'

'Well,' she wavered, 'I was just . . . '

'It's a very warm day,' he persisted, 'and if you're not in a hurry . . . '

She was twenty-three and part of her longed to escape the tedium of her predictable suburban life. Her head buzzed at the prospect of risk, of adventure just within reach. She put the cans back on the shelf, abandoned the basket of shopping, and walked with him to the pub on the corner. On a wooden bench in the garden the warmth of his leg pressed against hers. He kicked off his sandals and stroked his bare foot against her ankle.

'Where do you live?' she asked, and he told her about the west coast of Australia and how the waters of the Indian Ocean crashed against the rocks and unrolled onto white sandy beaches; about the rocky red outcrops of the Pilbara, the gorges and waterfalls of the Kimberley, the moist green forests of the southwest.

'And it's hot,' he said. 'Too bloody hot in summer.' He had told her about swimming, surfing, and picnics at the beach.

It was simplicity and the smell of freedom that seduced her. It seemed to be a part of him and she wanted it for herself. The pleasant street of identical houses, the cupboards filled with wedding gifts – linen, crockery and glasses, some of them barely used – the predictable pattern of her days seemed suffocating. At the campsite on the edge of the town they lay in his tent on a sleeping bag, their bodies slick with sweat, the midges biting, the sound of his mates drinking noisily nearby. He was a selfish lover, fast and rough, but it didn't matter. She wasn't there for the sex but for what it meant: that she could never go back. In a couple of days' time he and his friends would hitchhike to the south coast to catch the ferry to France. From there they would head south to Spain, then Tunisia, Morocco and on to Turkey.

'Come with us!' he said later that day as he walked back to town with her to finish her shopping. And there, inside Sainsbury's near the counter where a man in a white apron was slicing bacon, she made up her mind.

'Okay,' she said.

Shock flickered across his face and he stepped back slightly.

'Sorry,' she said, blushing, embarrassed now by her own stupidity. 'Sorry, for a moment I thought you meant it.'

'Well . . . ' he hesitated. 'I didn't think you . . . .'

'So can I go with you, then?'

'Yeah . . . of course, if that's what you want,' Blue said, a smile spreading across his face. 'But no strings, eh, Jean? No strings attached.'

'No strings,' she nodded. 'What about your friends?'

He shrugged. 'No worries there. There's already a couple of girls in the group. They'll be right.'

She was strangely calm and orderly in what she did next. She finished the shopping, and then went to the bank and withdrew the contents of her savings account. Back home she packed a bag and hid it in the spare room and sat down at the kitchen table to wait for Roger. The least she owed him was to tell him to his face, and all through that long hot evening, with the sounds of children playing in the neighbouring gardens and the BBC news droning in the background, she tried to summon the courage and failed.

It was the same the next day. She operated on automatic, waiting for him to get home so she could break the news, dreading the encounter but never wavering in the commitment she had made to herself.

'I'm off to squash,' Roger said that evening, his back turned to her as he rummaged in the hall cupboard.

'I need to talk . . . ' she began, her voice faltering.

'Yep, okay, but d'you know where my squash racquet is?' he asked, without looking at her. 'Ah, got it! I'll be late, don't wait up.'

She didn't. Knowing she couldn't face it, she waited until he left for work the next morning, propped a note on the kitchen table, took a last look around the house and the possessions that had once seemed so important, and knew that what she was doing was unforgivable. She wondered whether she had all she needed in the bag and realised that it didn't matter. If she needed something she would get it somehow – earn it, borrow it, whatever. The thing she really needed was to leave, and leave now, before her courage evaporated and she found herself back in the mind-numbing domestic rut. She was running away and Blue was part of it but only a small part. He was simply the catalyst and, despite what happened later, the fact that he had opened the door was something she would never forget.

THIRTEEN

The room was a little too warm for Oliver's liking. Winter sun poured in through the west facing window, and in one corner a column heater seemed to be radiating more heat than was appropriate for its size. Oliver fiddled with the neck of his sweater, shifted his position in the green leather armchair, and wondered if this had been such a good idea after all.

'So, Oliver, where're we going with this?' Andrew asked. 'I have all the notes from your sessions with Elaine, but I'm not quite sure why you feel a change of therapist might help.'

Oliver hesitated. He had no idea where to start. The trouble with psychologists was that they always wanted you to sit straight down and start talking, just like that. They smiled and waited for you to kick off, but what if you couldn't kick off? What if you needed them to kick-start you? Elaine had been like that too. He wished they'd just interrogate him and then tell him what was wrong and how to fix it. But apparently that was contrary to the principles of most therapists, who insisted that the client be encouraged towards their own resolution. Oliver was dying for someone to give him the answers.

The idea of changing therapists had struck him when Elaine's receptionist told him she was on leave and he'd have to wait three weeks for another appointment. He didn't want to wait and in that instant he asked instead for an urgent appointment with a male therapist in the same practice. Now, facing a complete stranger who was waiting for him to open up, Oliver wrung his hands and wondered if he were seriously neurotic or just aver-agely so. Andrew's face was impassive; he sat with his hands clasped on Oliver's file, looking at him over his half-glasses.

'So, tell me what's troubling you,' he finally said. 'Take your time.'

'Well,' Oliver said, twitching his wrists further out of the sleeves of his sweater, 'it's complicated, and it goes back a long way. To my mother, actually, and to . . . well, to my relationships with women.'

Andrew smiled. 'Of course,' he said nodding sympathetically. 'So let's begin with your mother.'

Two and a half hours later, Oliver sat on a wooden bench in the park opposite Andrew's practice gazing at, but not actually see-ing, the silken surface of a small pond, broken only by brown and gold leaves that fluttered onto it from nearby trees. His life, it seemed, had been transformed, the scales fallen from his eyes. It had taken a while for him to warm to the telling of his tale but Andrew made it easy, helped him along, prompted him in ways that Elaine had never done. As the consultation drew to its close, Oliver was talking as he had never talked before and was close to weeping with the frustration of having to stop.

'My next appointment has been cancelled,' Andrew reassured him. 'You're welcome to the next hour if you're not too tired.'

Oliver wondered why it was only now that he had chosen to speak to a man. Whenever he talked about important things it had always been with women and he was suddenly shocked to realise that he had no male friends. Joan had insisted that women were so much better at dealing with serious issues, especially emotional ones. Why had he not understood how constrained he had always been with Elaine, and with other women, on the sub-ject of his mother? Each time he had ventured into counselling he had done so wearing Joan's politics like a banner, quoting her like some guru, but he couldn't talk about her as a person, and cer-tainly not in relation to himself. Mothers, Joan had always said, were all too easily blamed for their sons' hang ups or misde-meanours; it was a sign of weakness, a shifting of responsibility onto women.

'They always blame the woman, Oliver,' she had said. 'If the child gets into trouble it's always the mother's fault. Don't fall into the trap of blaming mothers.'

'But speaking frankly about the way your mother raised you isn't blaming her,' Andrew pointed out. 'It is not anti-woman to relate the facts, or to discuss how your upbringing might have influenced your relationships with other women. In fact, it's all part of the process of taking responsibility for your own behaviour.'

Oliver had stared at him open-mouthed and accepted the second hour. And as he spoke aloud about his mother and about the dreams in which her edicts were constantly repeated, he began to realise how the complexity of her personality had been lost in his assumption of certain maxims. She was a woman to examine every shade of grey, so why had he etched her in his memory in stark black and white? Quite suddenly he recognised that he had used it to create a blueprint for himself and his life, thinking that if he followed it word for word things would work out right, but, of course, they hadn't.

'I accepted what she said like some magic formula,' he said to Andrew, grasping at this new clarity and trying to articulate it. 'It never occurred to me to try changing the ingredients, to try interpreting it in my own way. I feel such a fool, as though all my life I've been walking around wearing a sign saying "trained by eminent feminist".'

He paused for a moment. 'It's as though I separated what my mother said from who she was. She was a passionate, eloquent and . . . sensuous woman, but somehow I've left that out of the whole equation. I listened to the words but didn't look at the woman who spoke them. I guess I didn't look at the women I was with either – I suppose I thought I had a formula that would work with any woman in any situation. But people are individuals. I've been mouthing this stuff all the time and not actually engaging with the women I was with. What's wrong with me?'

'There's nothing wrong with you, Oliver,' Andrew said. 'But these are big questions and we'll have to leave them for another day.'

Oliver made an appointment for five days later, and wandered out into the sparkling winter sunshine. He was pretty drained emotionally but the door to understanding had been opened to him. It would be onward and upward from here. As he sat in the sunlight watching the water, the simplistic way he had interpreted Joan's words, indeed her life, troubled him deeply. He had misused her – no wonder she haunted him – but now he had seen the light, and he felt quite exhausted with relief.

That night he fell into a deep and troubled sleep and woke in the cold pre-dawn darkness unable to stop shivering. It was three days before he was able to do more than stagger between bedroom, bathroom and kitchen. Three days before he could eat anything solid without throwing up, three days before the headache and the alternating hot and cold sweats abated. On the morning of the fifth day he ate some toast and drank a cup of tea, showered, dressed and drove to the psychologist's rooms as though in a dream.

'No crisis, then?' Andrew asked, opening his file.

Oliver shook his head. 'A touch of flu, I think, or something I ate,' and he described the symptoms.

Andrew took off his glasses and smiled. 'How easily we mistake emotional crises for physical illness,' he said. 'This is all part of the healing process and the beginning of change.'

The worst was indeed over, but now the hard grind began. The women who had been his friends or lovers over the years ran through his mind like actors in a speeded-up black and white movie: foolish, poorly made, jerky and simplistic. Cautiously he began to describe his marriage to Alison, recognising how he had behaved in that and subsequent relationships, wondering how any woman could ever have related to him. His past seemed to be unravelling, constantly acquiring different meanings, and this time when he left Andrew's rooms, Oliver felt profoundly sad. Now the black and white film showed him lost opportunities, chances for happiness slipping through his fingers because of his own failure to question, to learn and to grow in this aspect of his life, as he had grown in others.

'Water under the bridge,' Andrew told him as they shook hands at the door. 'You're only in your fifties – plenty of time left to do things in a different way. This is the best time of your life, Oliver, take my word for it.'

'A live band?' Sonya said, looking at Marissa in disbelief. 'You never mentioned that before.'

Marissa reached across the verandah table for the gin bottle. 'I didn't want to worry you.'

'So you're doing it today instead?'

'You're more confident now, both of you. You're dancing really well.'

'But suppose they don't play the music we know?'

Marissa held up her hand. 'They will. I know them, I've worked with them before and so have you. The CDs we always dance to are theirs. It's just that this time they'll be playing at the back of the stage while we dance.'

'But why?' Sonya asked, gulping at the fresh drink Marissa had poured for her and thinking how close the musicians would be to her wobbly bits when they were in full wobble.

'Why not?'

'Well . . . I don't know, but . . . '

'Look,' Marissa explained, 'we're part of the entertainment. There's more than a hundred women attending this conference.' She tossed each of them a copy of the conference brochure. 'It's all about older women's health, and the entertainment at the conference dinner is designed around healthy, self-esteem building activity.'

'But the band . . . ' Gayle began.

'These guys are here, on tour, so I asked them to play for us too. It adds to the whole package of the performance and we've got plenty of time to rehearse with them before the big night.'

'Suddenly it seems rather important and sort of professional,' Sonya said.

'I think it's all important and professional,' Marissa said crisply, 'otherwise I would never have applied for the grant.'

'Yes, yes, I know,' Sonya responded, flushing. 'I know that, it's just a bit scary, I suppose.'

'You'll like them,' Marissa assured her. 'They're nice guys and I can guarantee that once you dance with a live band you'll never look back. The CDs will always be second best.'

Gayle sipped her drink. 'We've come this far so I guess we'll manage this.'

'Of course you will, you'll love it,' Marissa said, getting up and unhooking her bag from the back of her chair. 'Now I'm just going down the road to see them and arrange a time to rehearse tomorrow. Stop worrying. Have a rest or a swim and then we'll go for dinner. We're in glorious Broome, the pearl of the northwest. Enjoy it!'

'Thank you, Aunty Marissa,' Sonya said. 'I'm contemplating the thought of those guys getting a close-up view of my rolls of fat shimmying across the stage.'

Marissa laughed. 'They've seen far bigger dancers than you or I, Sonya,' she said, and she made for the door. 'I'll be about an hour,' and she went out of the chalet and down the steps.

Sonya looked across at Gayle. 'You don't seem worried.'

Gayle shrugged. 'I've other things on my mind.'

'Sorry,' Sonya said, 'of course. Does your son know you're here?'

'He knows we arrive today,' Gayle said. 'I haven't seen him for eleven years.' She paused. 'It was you who told Oliver, wasn't it?'

Sonya nodded. 'I'm sorry, Gayle. Angie had told me and I just assumed Oliver knew because you'd been friends so long.'

Gayle added tonic water to her glass. 'It's okay. Best in the long run, I suppose. I'd sort of quarantined my friendship with Oliver from the rest of my life. It allowed me to feel like the person I wanted to be.'

'And now it's messed up?'

'Maybe, maybe not. We'll see. I'm sick of secrets anyway, sick of hiding things and pretending. I so much want to see Josh, to explain things to him, things I should have told him years ago.'

'And Brian?' Sonya asked.

Gayle shrugged. 'I don't know. Too hard to think about at the moment. I'll have to sort things out when I get back. Anyway, you said you'd had an email from Oliver?'

Sonya laughed and got up. 'I did. He's seeing a therapist!'

'Don't tell me,' Gayle said. 'I bet it's about his mother.'

'Right first time, but it's a new therapist, a man, and Oliver feels he has had an epiphany.'

'Dear Oliver,' Gayle said affectionately. 'He's a lovely man but he gets himself so tangled up trying to do the right thing that he does it all wrong.' She sipped her drink. 'Do you like him, Sonya? I mean, really like him . . . I mean . . . '

'You mean am I sleeping with him? No, I'm not. We did once, the night of the wedding, but then we both backed off. I like him a lot, but not in that way – at least, I don't think so.'

'You don't fancy him?'

'I did that night. But it didn't seem to work the next morning. It's odd because he's clever and funny and he's got a really sweet nature, but he's . . . well, he's just not sexy.'

'He can't be spontaneous because he's always running himself through this filter he's created about being a feminist man,' Gayle said.

'That's exactly right! I couldn't have put it into words but that's exactly what he's doing. And that was why he was such fun the night of the wedding, all those lethal champagne cocktails made him completely spontaneous. As though that filter was switched off.'

'His mother was an amazing woman,' Gayle said. 'I looked her up on the Internet: prominent feminist, human rights activist, PhD on women and the electoral system. Oliver looks just like her, that same beaky face, big glasses, rather floppy dark hair. It must be hard to step out of her shadow.'

Sonya nodded. 'I suppose so,' she said thoughtfully. 'I'd never thought of it like that.'

Frank woke suddenly, sitting bolt upright in the bed, sweat pouring off him. The clock radio said four-fifteen, and his body was burning despite the chill in the bedroom. Resting his head against the wall he waited for his heart rate to slow and for the prickling of his skin to ease. The nightmares always left him low and exhausted but tonight was worse because it was so unexpected. It was months since the last time, so long that he'd dared to hope they'd stopped. There was a time when he'd fought this battle night after night, and he'd staggered through the fatigue of the days, with no period of reprieve. But time, and careful adjustments to the way he lived, had helped.

He got up slowly, pulled on his grey towelling bathrobe and wandered in the dark to the kitchen to make some tea. There would be no more sleep now, just a tangle of horrific images: burning bodies, flesh shrinking back from the faces of the dead, the screams of children. And he would struggle through the day trying to stay in the present, battling depression and exhaustion, struggling to control his anger and to make even simple decisions. Sudden shafts of sunlight would make him flinch and each small sound startle him like gunfire.

Taking his tea he switched on a small lamp; shadows of memory crawled around the walls. He could smell burning flesh, and the acrid mix of sweat and urine that made up the scent of fear. It would have helped to have someone to talk to at times like this. In the early days of their marriage, Anna had been endlessly patient, talking him down, helping him to a point at which he could start the day. She had hung on through the mood swings, the brooding silences and those times when he had seemed suspended in another world. But he'd been so fucked up in those days that he'd driven her away.

After all this time, Frank had learned something about the external factors that would set him off – casual sex, too much alcohol, violent movies, heavy metal music. He knew he was in the wrong job, that he was always better when he wasn't confronted daily by the uglier aspects of human behaviour. He shuffled through his CDs, selected a couple and dropped them into the tray.

'So, you have *all* Normie's music?' Sonya had asked as she and Marissa sat with him in the airport café.

'All of it,' he'd said. 'And videos of some concerts.'

'Wow! That sounds a bit obsessive.'

'Probably.' He looked at Marissa. 'But we all have our weaknesses.'

Sonya flushed. 'Sorry, that was rude and thoughtless. I didn't mean . . . you seem more like an Eric Clapton or even a Pink Floyd man to me.'

He laughed. 'Not a bad guess. Eric Clapton, certainly.'

'And Normie? Sentimental reasons, I suppose.'

'Bonds forged in battle,' Marissa had said quietly, looking up at him. He had flushed and looked away, thinking that she must have known, must have understood.

He hit play and the music surged into the room. The first sound of that familiar voice was like some calming drug shot directly into a vein. Could Marissa have understood that the first step out of the darkness was triggered by the voice of someone who had also been there, someone whose arm he had gripped, whose fear he'd shared, who had seen what he had seen? This was the first time since Anna left that Frank had felt the urge to reach out to a woman for anything other than the fleeting comfort of sex. Marissa, he was sure, was also a survivor of some sort of trauma. Her apparent self-containment had a brittle, fragile edge that was familiar. The incongruence of the belly dancing and the Harley were also a part of it.

'Why the Harley?' he'd asked her. 'How does it fit with the dancing?'

'Maybe it doesn't,' she'd said. 'At first it was because I was so afraid of bikes.'

'Afraid?'

'Yes. When I drove a car I was always scared of the way motor-cyclists weave in and out of the traffic, cut across lanes. And the prospect of riding one was terrifying. That's what made me do it. I remembered my father saying that if you take the thing you fear the most and confront it, then everything else falls into place. Anything else you're scared of just seems trivial. So I learned to ride a bike.'

'And did it work?' Frank asked.

'Partly. But I cheated. I was scared of bikes but there was other stuff in my life that I couldn't face so I opted for the lesser evil.'

'Why a Harley?'

'Because it's special, full of character. It just spoke to me in a way the other bikes didn't. I learned to love the freedom, the solitariness of riding a bike, the open road, sweeping bends – a Harley is the right bike for that. Magic, really. It took forever to pay it off but I managed it eventually.'

He hadn't asked about the 'other stuff' and he knew she would not have told him anyway, but Frank suspected that the unspoken awareness of painful survival was what had drawn them together, and what had kept them walking careful circles around each other over the last few months. He was not foolish enough to think that any woman could heal him, but he did think that love, if he ever found it, might help him to heal himself. And he wondered just how long it would take before he and Marissa trusted each other enough to disclose the darkness that haunted them.

FOURTEEN

They had agreed to meet at four but Gayle was half an hour early, sitting at a café table in the shade of the palm trees, fiddling nervously with a pot of peppermint tea. She stared down the street, knowing it was premature but anxious not to miss the first sight of him.

Broome was busy with locals and tourists, a pleasant, relaxed busyness that reflected the nature of the town itself. Its charm had taken her by surprise; the picturesque streetscapes with their Chinese and Japanese influences, the wide, palm lined streets. The café hadn't been Gayle's choice; she would have preferred to meet Josh at the resort cottage, and Sonya and Marissa had offered to disappear for a couple of hours to give them some privacy. Her second choice was Josh's own place, but he was more cautious.

'Somewhere on neutral territory, I think,' he'd said. 'Let's keep it cool, low-key first off, see how we go.'

She could hardly blame him for his caution. It was so long since they had seen each other he must be as nervous as she was, and this was his town, she was the intruder. She repeated that to herself over and over again, each time the words 'cool' and 'low-key' surged into her mind and left her insides turning to jelly. Of course he must feel anger, resentment, confusion – she should expect nothing less after all this time. Their occasional telephone conversations had seemed couched in an unspoken understanding that the appalling rift could not be discussed at a distance, and as time passed it had become more and more difficult to imagine the possibility of talking face to face.

Gayle's anxiety made her weak and nauseous, her legs and hands trembling uncontrollably. It seemed impossible now that she could have done this, abandoned her son, failed to fight for him, to stand between him and Brian and hold her ground. Who had she been for all those years? How could she have done something so shameful and gutless, something so entirely at odds with everything she believed? It was a blur, but perhaps she had deliberately contrived to blur it, to take the edge off the pain and the guilt. Some moments remained with extraordinary clarity, though, especially the day Josh had brought Dan to the house for the first and only time.

'So how did you and Dan meet?' she'd asked Josh that evening.

'Connections,' he'd replied.

'What sort of connections? Friends from work or something?'

'Connections, Mum. It's a club in Northbridge.' He paused, looking straight at her. 'A gay club.'

The minute the words were out of his mouth, Gayle wondered why she hadn't realised it before, why, only a month from his twentieth birthday, she suddenly understood who her son was.

'Don't tell your father, Josh,' she begged him, 'not yet. Let's take a bit of time to think about it . . . '

'I have to tell him,' he'd said. 'I was going to tell you both together tonight but you beat me to it. It's only fair to tell him now.'

'But you don't need to tell Brian yet.'

'Yes I do,' he said. 'And I want him to meet Dan too. We're in love – he'll be part of our family.'

She had thought that Dan might just be a casual boyfriend and that somehow the truth could be kept from Brian, for a while, at least.

'Are you sure?' she asked. 'How long have you known?'

'From the moment we met, eight months ago,' Josh said, his face lighting up at the chance to talk about Dan. 'We're both –'

'No, I meant how long have you known about yourself?' Gayle asked.

Josh shrugged. 'Ages. Seven years, eight, maybe more.'

'And you didn't say anything to me?'

'I wasn't ready,' he said, 'didn't know how.'

In view of her subsequent betrayal it now seemed insane to Gayle that she could for a moment have reproached him for not telling her earlier. She had abandoned him to his father's prejudice and perhaps Josh had always known that would happen. Perhaps he had known it that day as she stood there hugging him, telling him it made no difference, that she was proud of him and loved the person she now knew him to be. Perhaps he already knew that it was the beginning of the end, that despite what she said, she didn't have the strength or resolve for the battle ahead.

Brian's outrage had been boundless; his demands that Josh never see Dan again, his threats of involving the police because the law protected men under the age of twenty-one, merged with her own protests and Angie's tears.

'Well, if that's what you want, Dad, that's what you'll get,' Josh said when his father told him to leave, told him that as far as he was concerned, Josh was no longer his son. A few hours later, his possessions in the car, he had driven off into a wintry night of torrential rain and wind that howled around the house, echoing Gayle's misery.

Back then she had believed it was temporary, that somehow in the coming weeks, when Brian realised the enormity of what he'd done, she would be able to change his mind, approach Josh, bring him back. But his intransigence continued alongside her own fearful ineffectiveness. It was so easy now to see what she should have done, and to see how 'cool' and 'low-key' might be just the sanitised tip of Josh's feelings about this meeting.

'Hi,' said a voice behind her, and Gayle jumped to her feet, shaken by his arrival, confused that he had approached her from a direction she hadn't been watching.

'Josh!'

'Yep. Hi, Mum.'

Instinctively she reached out to hug him but he stiffened, patted her shoulder awkwardly and broke away. The rejection was agonising and she steadied herself against the chair as he made his way to the other side of the table.

She had known a boy and he had become a man. A man she didn't know. A handsome man, with a deep tan and hands calloused from his job. A serious man with sad eyes, even features and light reddish hair bleached blond and coarsened by the sun. Gayle, unable to stop the tears rolling down her cheeks, watched him, trying to fit the old Josh into the one who now faced her across the table.

'I don't know what to say to you,' she said. 'How to begin.'

Josh shook his head and looked away, his jaw tightening. 'Let's begin by ordering some coffee,' he said. 'We probably need it.'

'It was fabulous,' Sonya said, hauling herself out of the pool and lying down on a towel. 'Dancing with those guys was the best thing yet.'

'We've only had one rehearsal,' Marissa pointed out.

'I know, but it was just like you said – great, totally different.'

'Yes, something happens between musicians and dancers. You'll feel the connection even more strongly when we're in costume and there's an audience.'

Sonya nodded. 'I'm looking forward to it now. I felt I was dancing better this morning.'

'You were,' Marissa said, 'both you and Gayle, much better. Hate to say I told you so.'

'But you're going to say it anyway.'

'Of course.'

'Well, I don't care, I loved it. So did Gayle – or she would've done if she hadn't been so tense about meeting her son. And those guys are so great, I really liked them.'

'Good,' Marissa said. 'Glad we've got one satisfied customer.' She smoothed her towel and lay back. 'How d'you think Gayle's getting on?'

'With difficulty, I should think,' Sonya said. 'It's going to take more than tea and sympathy under the palm trees to put this right.'

Marissa sat up again. 'I don't really understand how she could have done it. I mean, I don't have children, but I still don't see how she could have just sort of abandoned him like that. After all, it's not even as though she actually minded about him being gay, it's just the husband. I don't get it.'

'You haven't met Brian,' Sonya said. 'He's totally unlike the sort of person you'd expect Gayle to be married to. If you'd met him you'd realise how amazing it is that she's still married to him. Oliver thinks so too and he's known her for years.'

'It's odd what happens in relationships,' Marissa said. 'But Brian can't be all bad or she *would* have left him by now.'

'I've only met Brian once,' Sonya said, 'but I've heard quite a bit from Angie and from Trisha, and if Brian has any redeeming features he keeps them well hidden. And I think she *is* leaving him now. She stood her ground, didn't rush back when he demanded it, didn't give in to Angie's whining at the airport, and now she's meeting Josh. She's changed a lot just in the time I've known her. She's said herself that dancing has changed her, and this is the result. If she does go home at the end of the tour, my guess is that she won't be there long.'

'I've seen this kind of thing before,' Marissa said.

'Of course, and that surely is what this tour is all about.'

'It's not about breaking up marriages.'

'No, but it's about health, self-esteem and confidence. There are bound to be casualties – relationships, jobs, lifestyles . . . whatever.' Sonya rubbed sunscreen on her legs. 'It's the same for me, really. The dancing made me stop pretending to my parents. I kept putting it off but in the end I let them know I was doing something they'd find unacceptable. I guess I realised it would happen – maybe I even wanted it to.'

Marissa stretched her arms above her head. 'It makes me thankful I'm single, and that my family ties withered decades ago. My parents didn't want to know me after my disappearing act. I wrote to them many times but they never replied.'

'What about your husband? I s'pose you got a divorce.'

Marissa laughed. 'No. It must sound weird but we were still officially married when he died a few years ago. It didn't bother me because I knew I'd never get married again, but I kept expecting him to divorce me. He lived with a woman for about fifteen years. I suppose it must have suited him that way.'

145

'Relationships are so complicated,' Sonya said. 'I grew up thinking that it was all so straightforward: you met someone, fell in love, got married, and if you got that right everything else fell into place. And, you know, despite everything I've learned, despite the seventies and feminism and two brief but disastrous marriages and a career, that image of what women should do and be still gets to me.'

'I know what you mean,' Marissa said with another laugh. 'I love my life, wouldn't have it any other way, but a bit of me still feels I failed because I ran away from it. Someone once said "scratch any woman deep enough and you'll discover a lounge suite". I knew just what she meant.'

'Yes, me too.' Sonya stood up. 'I think I'll go back to the cottage and have a shower. It's getting a bit too warm out here. I hadn't thought about dancing in the costumes in the heat. It was so nice and cool down south.'

'They are uncomfortable,' Marissa said, 'heavier than ever when it's hot and every sequin and bead scratches. I'll come with you. Gayle will probably be back soon.'

They gathered up their things and walked back along the path to their cottage.

'So what did belly dancing do for you?' Sonya asked, turning to look at Marissa. 'Who or what was the casualty of your change?'

Marissa's face flushed. 'No casualties. It just helped me cope with . . . come to terms with . . . well, with some stuff that happened a long time ago.'

'Relationship stuff?'

'Something like that,' Marissa said, looking away and increasing her pace. 'It's a long time ago – I don't really want to get into it.'

'Sorry,' Sonya said, unlocking the door of the cottage and dropping her sunglasses onto the hall table. 'I didn't mean to intrude. I have a horrible habit of sticking my nose into things that aren't my business.'

Marissa smiled. 'It's fine. Really.' And she went to the sink and began to fill the kettle. 'You have a shower first. I'll make some tea. Gayle'll need it.'

Sonya dragged off her bathers, dropped them on the bathroom floor and stood for a moment staring at the cascade of water. Clearly her question had touched a nerve and she couldn't help feeling that while the belly dancing might well have helped Marissa, her reluctance to talk about it was probably a sign that whatever haunted her hadn't yet been laid to rest.

Brian had flown home to Perth in very good spirits. His worst fears as he walked down the passage and into the Sydney board-room had not been realised. Mal was at the head of the table and either side of him sat Rod Campbell and the US sales and market-ing director. He had expected to see them rearrange their faces into expressions of false solicitude as they heaped the responsibil-ity for the regulation board decision on him. He was tense and ready for battle but it didn't eventuate. All they wanted was an update on his latest initiative and an explanation of a paragraph in one of his recent reports. He joined them at the table, was given coffee, provided the information and left half an hour later, his heart lifting, his stomach settling as he made his way back up to his office. The danger had passed, and this weekend he would sort Gayle out and everything would be back on track.

The lunch on the flight to Perth was excellent, as was the wooded Chardonnay, of which he had several glasses. When the taxi dropped him at home he was surprised not to find Gayle there. She was due back from Bunbury by now. Brian went to the wine rack, found two bottles of the same Chardonnay he'd drunk on the flight, put them in the fridge to chill, and rifled through the mail. Then he went upstairs, had a shower, changed his clothes and considered where he should book a table for dinner. What would Collette have recommended? Somewhere really special, probably, or maybe he should ask Gayle where she'd like to go. Leaning back in his favourite chair he dialled her mobile and was diverted to the message bank.

'What's the point of a mobile phone if it's always bloody well switched off,' he demanded aloud, and dialled Angie's office number.

'Why are you at home, anyway?' Angie asked. 'Mum said you were going to the Vines with clients.'

'Came home to surprise her,' Brian said. 'Thought I'd take her out, got her some flowers at the airport. Anyhow, her phone's off so when'll she be back?'

'She won't,' Angie said, and Brian thought she sounded a bit strange. 'They changed the schedule and flew up north a couple of days ago. She's in Broome now.'

'Broome?' he said, putting on his glasses and looking again at the itinerary. 'Says here she'll be home today.'

'Yes, well, they changed their plans,' Angie repeated.

'But she's supposed to be here,' Brian stormed. 'It says so. She can't just change it like that.'

'You changed your plans,' Angie ventured. 'Anyway, you can have a rest and a nice quiet weekend.'

'A quiet weekend? What am I supposed to do here all on my own, no food in the fridge, and what about my washing?'

'There's heaps of food in the freezer,' Angie said. 'You just need to microwave something, and you must know how to use the washing machine.'

'That's not the point. She should be here. You'll come over and organise things for me, won't you, Princess? I'm going to have more than a few words to say about this when her ladyship finally decides to answer her phone.'

There was a brief silence at the other end of the line. 'Dad, I'm at work right now, and Tony and I are going down to his parents' place in Mandurah tonight for the weekend. So you'll just have to manage, and . . . and please stop going on at me. It's hard enough with Tony's family.' She slammed the phone down and Brian was left, receiver in one hand, listening to the buzz on the empty line.

FIFTEEN

On the mantelpiece of the two-storey mock Tudor house in Dorking where Marissa had spent her childhood, was a picture of her father on a camel. Colonel Bedford had been with the 8th Army when Montgomery assumed command in 1942. His part in the defeat of Rommel at El Alamein had dominated Marissa's childhood. Stories of hardship and valour in the desert, Monty living in his caravan in the grounds of a splendid Egyptian mansion, and the alternating privations and luxuries of battlefield and colonial life were Arthur Bedford's obsessions.

'For goodness sake, stop going on about the war,' his wife would beg him in increasingly hysterical stage whispers that floated up the staircase and under their daughter's bedroom door. 'It's over, Arthur. It's been over for years and, yes, the whole world is grateful that Rommel was defeated, but there has to be an end to this constant rehashing. The only stories you ever tell Jean are war stories, what sort of upbringing is that for a little girl?'

It was a confusing one, for the nuns at the small Anglican convent that young Jean attended were unimpressed by the military anecdotes recycled in her English compositions. More than a decade after peace was declared, they were preparing the girls for jobs as secretaries, teachers or nurses until the right man came along or, better still, encouraging them to consider taking the veil. Jean was not destined for the latter but she was a well-behaved, compliant child with a talent for dancing and needlework. She was an avid fan of *The Famous Five*, and revealed an unhealthy interest in the activities of the British Expeditionary Forces in Egypt in which historical fact was dangerously confused with imagination.

The nuns taught a different sort of history, beginning with the Roman occupation of Britain followed by a huge leap to the thirteenth century and King John losing his crown in the reeds at Runnymede, and on to the House of Hanover. It was a sketchy Cook's tour that depended entirely on the interests of whichever nun was teaching history at the time. The teenage Jean dreamed of luxurious palaces occupied by handsome, olive-skinned princes, courageous British officers and beautiful women in diaphanous evening gowns, waited on by white robed servants in red fezzes. It was hardly surprising, Marissa thought, sitting now on a camel on Cable Beach, that it was Blue mentioning they were heading for the Middle East that had contributed to that extraordinary decision outside the Horsham branch of Sainsbury's.

Almost a year later, in one of her many attempts to re-establish communication, she had sent her father a picture of herself on a camel along with news of the places he had described to her. But there was no response. Years later, on his death, she received a package from his younger sister, the only member of her family who had kept in touch with her. It contained her father's wartime diaries, the camel photograph taken in 1943, and her own, taken almost a quarter of a century later.

'This photograph of you was very important to Arthur,' her aunt wrote. 'But he was too proud ever to forgive you. Sad for him and most of all for your mother, they missed so much by being so unforgiving.'

Marissa had wept when the package arrived. She had long ago given up any hope of reconciliation, but somehow love had survived. Leaving her marriage had been deliberate and final, but at the time she believed that her parents would eventually come around. For more than a decade, despite the unanswered letters, she dreamed of the feasting that would take place at the return of the prodigal daughter, and she would have made a trip home had she received any encouragement, but it never came. Now, being with Gayle, hearing her story and watching the painful process of her attempts to reconnect with her son, Marissa was thinking about her own mother.

Daphne Bedford had never done a thing without her husband's approval. She had spent the war with her own parents in a small cottage at the foot of the Sussex Downs, helping the Women's Voluntary Service and waiting for Arthur's return. She was the perfect housewife: quietly spoken, submissive, running a spotless home and never taking a step out of line. Was she really like that, Marissa wondered now? A part of her had always despised her mother for colluding in Arthur's dominance. She had assumed that Daphne simply accepted his refusal to have anything to do with their errant daughter, but maybe Daphne *had* fought for her, argued, begged, even – maybe considered or attempted some secret correspondence. It no longer seemed as simple as she had imagined, and now Marissa wished she had made some attempt to contact her mother separately – a phone call, a letter through a friend, perhaps. If breaking through the barriers of upbringing and social expectation had seemed too hard to Gayle, a woman of her own generation, how insurmountable it would have been for her mother to break out of her suburban timidity.

The camel train made its way slowly along the beach as the turquoise water darkened to navy and the sun rested, a crimson orb on the horizon, turning the clouds through gold and orange to deep rose and purple. She had wanted this ride since she had known they were coming to Broome.

'No way,' Sonya had said. 'Not for me. Terrible, smelly, unpredictable creatures, camels – you won't get me near one.' And Gayle had been too absorbed in the aftermath of her meeting with Josh even to hear the invitation.

'Well, I like camels,' Marissa had said. 'I rode one in the sixties and now I'm going to try again. You know there is a school of thought that insists the camel's walk is highly relevant to belly dancing.'

Gayle and Sonya exchanged a glance but Marissa was not to be put off.

'You see, a camel walks by moving its hind leg first, followed by the front leg on the same side, unlike most other animals, which move a *front* leg first followed by the hind leg on the *opposite* side. So, for those of us with two legs the camel principle works like this . . . ' And she demonstrated the move. 'You see, it pushes the pelvis forward as the other foot catches up.' She picked up her sunglasses. 'So, really, we have quite a lot to learn from the humble camel.'

There was a pause in which Sonya blinked and took a deep breath. 'Thank you for that, Marissa,' she said. 'Now, why don't you just buzz off and commune with the camels while we inspect the insides of our eyelids.'

'You're a philistine and a wuss, Sonya.'

'Indeed I am,' Sonya replied. 'And it's not only camels. The idea of riding that horrific bike of yours would elicit the same response from me. Anyway, I'm tired. The rehearsals with the band seem very energetic. This is the time for vegging out, followed by a nice glass of wine and dinner. We'll meet you on the terrace in a couple of hours.'

And Gayle had nodded, waving a hand listlessly as Marissa went out the door.

Marissa's camel was last in the line and most of the other riders were travelling in pairs, fragments of conversation and laughter drifting back to her. She would have liked to have someone to ride with. *Someone*, not just anyone. Someone with whom she was at ease. Sonya or Gayle would have been fine, but really she wished that Frank were there.

'Take care,' he'd said as they walked to the departure gate in Perth. 'I'll be thinking of you.'

'Me too,' she said, realising in that moment how much he had occupied her thoughts recently. 'I'll call.'

'Please,' he'd said. 'And when you get back, we'll do some things . . . together, I mean.'

Part of her hoped she'd imagined the intensity of the hug they exchanged; she didn't want anything ruffling the calm waters of her emotional life.

Gazing out across the darkening sea she felt her anxiety rise at the thought of the next stop on the tour, Port Hedland – the place of her worst memories. It hadn't even been on her original plan for the tour, but somehow the project officer at the department had persuaded her: 'You really should include Hedland, Marissa,' she'd said. 'It's got a large population and there would be a lot of women there who would benefit. It makes sense to go to Port Hedland.'

So perhaps it was meant to be. Perhaps it was time to stop pretending that it was all far enough away in time and place to matter anymore. She would concentrate on surviving Hedland and then she would give herself the time and space to think about Frank.

Gayle was struggling. She was convinced that without the rehearsals to absorb her, she would not have been able to function at all. Now, standing behind the temporary stage waiting for their cue, she was longing for the music to begin, to lift her out of herself briefly. Four days had passed since her meeting with Josh and she had heard nothing more from him. Soon they would have completed not only the final conference performance but the other demonstrations and classes and they would be on their way to Port Hedland.

She had been foolish to hope for some sort of ecstatic reunion in which the past could be forgiven in the sheer joy of meeting again. She had sacrificed so much and for what? For Brian and his ignorance and prejudice, for a deal struck long ago, for Angie. Now she had come face to face with what she had lost: her integrity. Josh's hurt, his anger and intransigence were understandable but devastating.

'I hoped for too much, I suppose,' she had said wearily as they sat together at the café. 'I hoped that it would be like it used to be, that we – you and I – could go back to where we were.'

Josh had looked at her for a long time before speaking. 'How *could* you think that?' he asked. 'Too much has happened: too much time, too much everything. He . . . ' Josh seemed to be trying to say his father's name but couldn't manage it. 'He kicked me out, disowned me because of who I am. I know you didn't feel the same way, but you didn't stop it either, you didn't protect me. You let me go, and now you want to forget it happened, have it all back again . . . ?'

'It wasn't so straightforward, Josh,' she said, struggling to fight back more tears. 'I know you can't forgive me but let me explain more. It goes back a long way and your father, he's . . . he's –'

'I know what he is,' Josh cut in. 'He's an arrogant, ignorant bully. He was then and probably still is. But that's what you opted for, it was your choice. Just don't expect me to like it any better now than I did then.'

'I was trying to keep things together,' she protested. 'The family . . . your father, Angie, the commitments I'd made. I was trapped, don't you see that?'

Josh rubbed his eyes and sighed. 'But why? For some game of happy families with everyone pretending that it was all right? It hadn't been all right for ages – for years before I came out.' He leaned across the table towards her. 'For as long as I can remember, Mum, you have walked on eggshells, backed away from confronting him, appeased him, compromised on everything. He's a bully, he bullied all of us, and he still bullies you and Ange. Maybe you want that. Maybe security, the house and everything that goes with it is worth that to you, I don't know.

'All my life you've been pretending everything was all right, pretending you agreed with him, pretending you'd fix it all later. How can we put things back together, you and I? I don't even know who you are under all the appeasement, and you certainly don't know me. Oh, I love you, somehow that hasn't changed, but I can't talk to you because there is nothing to hold on to. Everything I thought I knew about my mother turned out to be wrong – most of all that you would always be there for me. But in the end you weren't. It's not that I can't forgive you, but I can't trust you. It's too dangerous to even try.'

'Let's meet again, please,' she'd begged as he finally got up to leave. 'I'll come to your place, meet Dan. I want to explain.'

'There's nothing *to* explain,' he'd said, holding both her hands. 'I understand how it's been for you, but you have to understand where I'm coming from. Being gay, it's . . . it's not always easy coping with the way other people feel. Dan and I, we look after each other, we have friends, a business, a life. Our relationship is precious and I don't want it all stirred up again.'

He had hugged her in the end, not stiffening as he did when he arrived, not holding her away from him.

'I'll call you,' he said as he walked away. 'Take care, Mum, and . . . well, thanks for coming.'

Gayle felt his words were carved into her flesh. Her body was sore, her head throbbed. One minute she wished she hadn't come and that she could run away, then she wished she could turn back time, wished she could make him listen to what she needed to tell him, wished she were still at home in her brittle, empty life, wished she had never started dancing or rocked her own boat.

'Okay?' Marissa asked, adjusting her own sequinned headdress. 'You both ready?'

Sonya nodded. 'I'm okay.'

'Me too,' Gayle said.

'So when they finish this number we're on. Remember to wait for Imran on the doumbek – it's a drumroll, just like always. Then we're out there and let's give it all we've got.' She looked anxiously at Gayle. 'You sure you're okay, Gayle?'

'I'll be better when we start,' Gayle said.

The band played a few chords, there was a pause and then the drumbeat. Tonight they were starting with a slow, sensuous chiftitelli. Marissa stepped out, gliding across the stage and taking up her position as the applause began.

'It's like magic, isn't it?' Gayle whispered as they stepped from the shadows. 'You step into the spell and it carries you away.' It felt like that first night in Kalgoorlie, as though the music and the dance possessed her, driving out anxiety and confusion. Gayle had been surprised to discover her inner performer, and she responded instinctively to the energy of the audience. When she danced, the changes within her were crystallised into a powerful sense of who and what she could be, and each time she retained more of that new self after the music stopped.

Sonya too was more in tune with her body every day, and now, on this balmy moonlit night, on the open air stage with the band in the background, she knew she could be at her best. She had always enjoyed the company of men and these musicians were easygoing, appreciative of the women and relaxed in their company. Three of them had joined them for dinner the previous night – Imran, the drummer, who was Indian by birth but had lived most of his life in Egypt; Josef, from Turkey, who played the lute-like oud; and Ali, also from Turkey, whose triangular kanoun had the haunting qualities of an autoharp. Their company was refreshing and Sonya had realised with some satisfaction that the days when she would have looked for a sexual adventure in this situation were long gone. It was good just being there, and she felt more alive than she had for a long time.

'You are very good dancer, Sonya,' Josef had told her. 'Very nice moving. You can go get a job in an Istanbul club anytime.'

'Thanks, but no thanks,' she said, smiling as she passed him the wine bottle. 'That would be too much like hard work.'

'Nonsense,' he said with a laugh. 'You have a wonderful time. Customers throw money at you, they tuck it in your belt, under the strap of your shoulder. I tell you, you be very popular and you make lots of money.'

'And what about my superannuation and my pension, and my long service leave?' she had teased.

'Pouf!' cut in Ali. 'You find some rich man to keep you in luxury – very easy, I think.'

Marissa rolled her eyes. 'Don't put ideas in her head, Josef, for heaven's sake. I only just got her trained up.'

'Ah, Marissa,' Imran said, 'you are the best of all the dancers we play for. I don't see nobody better in Marrakech.'

As they danced now on this beautiful night, the faces of well over a hundred women formed a sea of pale ovals in the half-light. Sonya's eyes roamed across the audience, flicking sideways only once when she had that recurring eerie sense of Tessa's presence. She felt good, so much herself, so much *better* than herself, and she glanced across at the others. Marissa, as always, was magnificent, sensuous, every move perfect despite the pain of her inner thighs rubbed sore by the camel ride – and despite some unspoken worry that seemed to be focused on something in Port Hedland. And Gayle, battling with a life crisis, abandoning herself to the transcendent power of the music and the dance.

This can't be bad, Sonya thought as they began the caleshmar. Whatever my family thinks of me, something this good, that gives this much pleasure to so many people, simply can't be bad. And once again she scanned the faces in the audience, wondering if some among them would recognise and accept the challenge offered by the dance.

SIXTEEN

Oliver, most of the way through a bottle of good red and feeling pleasantly relaxed, was packing Joan's books into a couple of cardboard boxes.

'I'm not cancelling it all out,' he said aloud, catching a glimpse of her looking forbiddingly at him from a silver frame. 'Just changing direction. Getting my own priorities sorted out instead of yours – should've done it years ago.'

The photograph, taken on the night she was awarded her PhD, showed Joan in an academic gown staring straight ahead at the camera, clutching her degree and looking fierce and awkward. Oliver emptied the remains of the bottle into his glass, studied the picture for a while and then took it down from the shelf.

'I think I've misrepresented you, Ma,' he said aloud in tones that were a little slurred. 'I've turned you into a harridan. You know, what I've done to you is what you always said the media did to feminism – trivialised it, stripped it of its humour, its inclusiveness. I allowed myself to forget who you really were.'

Climbing onto a chair he reached up to a high shelf and retrieved a couple of bulky photograph albums. Abandoning his packing he sat at his desk turning the pages. There was Joan, in her twenties, about the time she met his father, wearing a full skirted, sleeveless cotton dress, laughing and pointing at someone just outside the frame. And there she was in a conga line of young women, all of them wearing paper hats, streamers draping their shoulders and circling their arms.

A few pages further on, she was sitting on a staircase in a tight-fitting sweater and skirt, holding a baby above her head, gazing joyfully into its face. Oliver looked at his mother and himself, connected as they were by love and blood, a symbiotic relationship that had survived for decades on her love and generosity and what now seemed like his own spineless and unquestioning dependence. He turned another page and found his christening, his first day at school, and then high school, birthday parties, Christmases, his own graduation, and always Joan: smiling, laughing, making things happen. There were pictures taken in the shared house, messy cooking in the kitchen, makeshift barbecues in the garden, Joan on a swing, and legs crossed, in a chair eating an ice cream, and then in bathers spraying him with the hose. Oliver shook his head.

'I know you,' he said to the woman with the ice cream. 'You're my mother, the woman who laughed and cried and played terrible tennis, who was a lousy cook but always got boiled eggs just right. And you hated bananas and Brecht and you loved dancing to big band tunes and had a crush on Gregory Peck.'

In the next album he found her again, well into her forties this time, in a satin evening dress, dancing with a man whose name he couldn't remember. And then with Jackson, the Nigerian philosophy lecturer with whom she'd fallen madly in love at sixty. On the last page the two of them were together, Joan in a long purple caftan and Oliver in his best suit, dancing at her seventieth birthday party. Oliver picked up the serious graduation photograph that had stood on its shelf for longer than he could remember.

'Why this one?' he wondered aloud. 'Why did I choose this one?' And opening the catches at the back of the frame he took out the photograph. Then he removed the woman with the ice cream from her place in the album.

'I'm outing you,' he said seriously, slipping the picture between the glass and the backing board. 'Giving you a chance to see the light – or do I mean giving me a chance?' He was rather drunk by now and he fumbled as he slipped the backboard of the frame into place, snapped on the catches and put it back on the shelf.

Joan smiled down at him, traces of ice cream on her lower lip, a little running onto the back of the hand that held the cone. Her legs were crossed and her left shoe dangled from her toes. 'Nice to see you again, Ma,' Oliver said, raising his glass to her. 'I'd almost forgotten who you really were.' As he stepped back, pleased with the transformation and the way it made him feel, he tripped on the carpet and stumbled against the corner of the desk.

'Whoops!' he laughed. 'Better get something to eat, piss-head,' and, checking his pockets for money, he let himself out of the house and strolled down the hill into Fremantle.

He ordered a pizza with double anchovies and another glass of red. The pizzeria was bright and noisy and Oliver sat happily devouring his meal, feeling extraordinarily liberated and unusually benign. Then he had another glass of red, a long macchiato, and walked home contemplating what a fortunate man he was to have always been surrounded by splendid women, even though he hadn't managed to land many of them.

He thought of Gayle and suffered a fleeting stab of shame at the way he had treated her, at his own self-righteous pomposity, his insensitivity and narrow-mindedness. But nothing could mar his pleasant mood for long. And as he reached home the vision of Sonya, and particularly Sonya's breasts, engaged him. Why had he ever thought, boasted even, that he was a small-breast man? As though it were some politically correct response to a woman's body, as though to admire large breasts was somehow lascivious in a way that admiring small breasts was not.

He sank down in a chair and closed his eyes remembering Sonya shedding the cream lace, recalling the delights of burying his face in her breasts, feeling her firm thighs against him, her legs wrapped around him. He burped as the wine and the pizza tangoed noisily and decided that another drink might fix it. Getting up to fetch a second bottle he caught his foot in the phone cable and the instrument crashed to the floor.

'Phone,' he said aloud. 'Phone! Bloody good idea. Phone her.' It took him another glass of wine and a bit of a search before he could find the tour itinerary and work out where she would be. 'Broome!' he exclaimed, triumphantly, and hit her mobile number, which was on his speed dial. 'Damn,' he said getting the answering service, 'must be switched off. Never mind, I will not be defeated by technology.' And he called enquiries and got the number of the Cable Beach Resort.

Gayle, unable to sleep, was lying on the couch watching Deborah Kerr and Burt Lancaster getting it together on the beach in *From Here to Eternity*, and thinking about Josh. The shallow waves crept up the beach and over Burt and Deborah's feet. Watching them, Gayle considered how she would feel if she never had sex again and was surprised by her own sense of detachment. It had never been good with Brian always caught up in his own satisfaction, seemingly obsessed with penetration and orgasm as some sort of triumph. But there had been someone, a long time ago, a gentle, passionate man with a touch so tender and a mouth so sensuous that even now her body stirred at the memory. It wasn't so much sex but the intimacy and affection, the tenderness, that she craved. The dancing had reminded her, had brought her back to life physically, and had her reaching back in time to the feel of being held lovingly against a warm body.

The phone shattered her reverie and she picked it up quickly, her heart beating fast with the shock.

'Sonya, Sonya, issat you?'

'No,' she said. 'It's Gayle, Sonya's asleep. Is that you, Oliver?'

There was some mumbling and shuffling at the other end of the line before his voice came back again, uncharacteristically loud and cheerful. 'Gayle! Hello, Gayle, are you having a lovely time, doing all that dancing thing? I changed my mother, Gayle, she's eating ice cream in this one, wearing high heels. You'd like her, Gayle, you really would. Can I speak to Sonya?'

'Oliver,' Gayle hissed, 'it's two in the morning, Sonya's asleep. Can't it wait till morning?'

'No! No, no, no, very important to tell her. Need to talk to Sonya, s'urgent.'

Sonya appeared bleary eyed in the bedroom doorway, red hair in a spiky halo. 'Did I hear the phone? Who the hell's ringing at this time?'

Gayle held the receiver out to her. 'Oliver. He wants to talk to you. He sounds drunk.'

Sonya rubbed her eyes and padded across to the phone. 'Oliver? What's the matter? Why the hell are you ringing me at two in the morning?'

'Sonya!' Oliver exclaimed. 'Sonya, my dancing friend. Two o'clock, three o'clock, five o'clock – what does it matter?'

'It matters to me but obviously not to you, as you're clearly pissed out of your brain. What do you want?'

'Had to tell you,' Oliver slurred. 'Had to tell you that you have magnifishent breasts. Big breasts, all bouncy and creamy with gorgeous nipples –'

'Oliver!'

'Yes, it's me, Oliver the big breast man. Don't think I told you before 'cos I didn't know but I think I am definitely a big breast man. Knockers, jugs, hooters – I love 'em all, but especially yours. You are a splendid, sexy woman . . . and I am an entirely new man . . . '

'Clearly,' Sonya said. 'And an entirely drunk one. Go to bed, Oliver, go to bed and pray that you won't remember this in the morning.' She slammed down the phone and sank onto the couch alongside Gayle, laughing.

'What did he want?' Gayle asked.

Sonya shook her head. 'He wanted to tell me that I have magnificent breasts, or rather, I think the word was "magnifishent".'

Gayle's mouth fell open. 'Oliver said that?'

'Not just that, he went on to describe them and then to claim a global appreciation of not just large breasts but jugs, hooters and knockers.'

'You're joking.'

'Nope. And, just as an aside, you'll be interested to know that he is an entirely new man.'

Gayle took a deep breath. 'Obviously . . . this is clearly not the Oliver we know.'

'Therapy,' Sonya said, 'can do funny things to people.'

'Hmm,' Gayle mused, 'I'll have to try it myself. You're not upset, then?'

Sonya shook her head. 'Oh no! Hey, it's Oliver – I mean, it's

162

probably the nearest to phone sex he'll come in his life.' She laughed. 'Just imagine how he's going to feel in the morning.'

Gayle was laughing now too. 'He told me he'd changed his mother, and that she was eating ice cream and wearing high heels!'

'Oh my god, he's really lost it,' Sonya said, doubling up with laughter. 'He gets therapy, gets drunk, somehow changes his mother and makes a dirty phone call – a lifetime of repression and political correctness blown in one night!'

'He'll probably call back in a minute and do some heavy breathing,' Gayle said, getting up to fill the kettle. 'Do you want some tea?'

'Please. And let's make sure he doesn't.' Sonya took the receiver off the hook.

Gayle spluttered with laughter. 'What if he rings reception and asks to speak to Sonya with the magnifishent breasts? The concierge will have to come over here with a message.'

'Don't!' Sonya cried. 'Stop, I'm laughing so much it hurts.'

'Your fault,' Gayle said, setting out the cups. 'You siren, you, corrupting poor innocent Oliver.'

Sonya snorted with laughter and grabbed some tissues. 'Oh dear, we'll never let him forget this, that's for sure.'

They sat together on the sofa, drinking tea, watching the end of the movie.

'What a night,' Sonya murmured. 'Our first concert with the musicians, Oliver's first attempt at phone sex . . . '

'It's good, isn't it?' Gayle said. 'Doing this, I mean, the dancing, the trip, the three of us being together.'

'Very good,' Sonya said. 'Very good indeed.'

'You can't believe how incredibly daring all this is for me,' Gayle said, 'how totally transformed I feel since we started dancing.'

'I've got an idea,' Sonya said, smiling at her. 'After all, you're very different from the woman I met at Angie's hens' night.'

'Yes . . . scary, really. After a change like this, you feel . . . I mean, I feel, I can never go back.'

'Back home or back to the way you were?'

'Both really, and that's what's so hard, coping with all that, with Angie, and Brian. All those battles there'll have to be.'

'Angie'll be all right about it, surely?'

Gayle nodded. 'In the end she will, but it's sure to rebound on her. And then, I have no idea how to live, even how to get myself out of the house and into somewhere else – all that practical stuff.'

Sonya reached over and took her hand. 'It'll be okay, Gayle, really it will. You have friends, we'll help you. And I'm sure Oliver will too.'

'The entirely new Oliver?' Gayle said with a grin.

'Him and fragments of the old one, I suspect,' Sonya said. 'If you really want to leave, you can come and stay with me while you make up your mind what you want to do. You aren't alone, you know.'

'Thanks. I *will* need help. It's horrifying, really. I'm fifty-six years old, never lived alone, always . . . well, almost always stuck to the rules. Now I seem to be breaking every rule in the book.'

'Sounds good,' Sonya said, getting up. 'Sounds as though it's time you started breaking rules. And look, there's a long way to go yet. I mean, you haven't even started getting drunk and making dirty phone calls in the middle of the night.'

Gayle laughed. 'Does that come next, d'you think?'

'Almost certainly,' Sonya said. 'So start thinking about it. Imran maybe, or Ali?'

'Ah, that'll be the day.'

Back in her room, Gayle sat in an armchair by the open window watching the shadows in the garden. Oliver's call, as uncharacteristically funny as it was, had started more than just laughter. Alone in the dark she realised she had also felt a stab of jealousy.

Frank was struggling, the days passing in a blur. His usual forensic analysis of cases, the ability to think laterally and make the leap of imagination required to understand the workings of the criminal mind, were severely compromised by trauma and fatigue. Each night he returned home exhausted, knowing that he would get little sleep until a couple of hours before it was time to get up and go to work again. As always in this state he feared he might be a danger to those around him, that he would make the wrong decisions, overreact, miss something crucial, but, as always, he kept going because keeping going was all that he had.

There was no one to talk to, no fixed point of emotional safety. The counsellor he'd seen a few times had moved away and the prospect of finding another and going through all the background again seemed unbearable. He was caught like a mouse on a wheel, each time recycling the same old stuff in the same old way. The only thing he could hold on to was the knowledge that he would eventually reach the other end of this dark tunnel. He grasped at that prospect, returning again and again to thoughts of Marissa.

'You don't sound too good, Frank,' she'd said on the phone. 'Is everything okay?'

'Oh, busy, busy, and not sleeping too well,' he'd said, longing to unburden himself. Talking to her, even telling her nothing, felt like a lifeline. The last thing he wanted was to appear needy or, worse still, neurotic.

'I'm not sure you lead a particularly healthy life, you know,' Marissa said. 'Too much work stress, probably not a very good diet, no regular exercise, and definitely too much coffee.'

He attempted a laugh. 'I think it's that terrible dandelion coffee substitute that's to blame.'

'Rubbish,' she said, and he thought he could hear a smile in her voice. 'It's much better for you than all that caffeine. No wonder you can't sleep. And what did you eat today?'

They discussed his failure to eat breakfast, and his consumption of a pie and chips for lunch and a double burger with cheese and fries in the car on the way home. Her solicitousness, disguised as disapproval of his eating habits, warmed him.

'And exercise,' she went on. 'Walking, swimming, that's what you need to counter the stress.'

'No time,' he protested half-heartedly, and mainly so that she would keep talking.

'That's ridiculous. Even detectives are allowed to have a life. Walking at South Beach, and swimming – we'll do it together.'

'Will we?'

'Yes . . . well . . . if you want to, of course . . . sorry, I'm interfering.'

He could hear her backing off. 'No,' he said hurriedly, 'no, you're right, I need someone to help me get motivated. It's a deal – walking and swimming and a better diet – when you get back.'

There was an awkward pause, as though they had both retreated to their respective corners. 'Good,' he went on, to fill the silence. 'That'll be good. And how's it all going up there?'

She told him about the camel ride and their performance at the conference.

'So we're free today and then we have the closing thing tomorrow, and we're off to Port Hedland on Monday.'

'Hmm . . . Hedland,' he said. 'Not one of my favourite places.'

'Me neither,' she said.

'Your first touchdown in Australia all those years ago. Ever been back there since?'

'No,' she said, sounding different now. 'No, I've always managed to avoid it . . . I have bad memories of Port Hedland. I'd rather not be going at all.'

'Sometimes going back to a place helps,' he suggested. 'Like you said before about the bike – confronting it can make it less frightening . . . ' He was running out of words.

'Maybe,' she said. 'We'll see. Meantime, you take care of yourself, Frank, and I'll see you soon.'

It seemed silly that just hearing her say his name should have mattered so much, should have seemed so intimate, so affectionate, so much as if she cared.

'You too, Marissa,' he said. 'Take care in Port Hedland.' And he hung up feeling as though the crack of light at the end of the tunnel had widened ever so slightly.

SEVENTEEN

Gayle set off early in the morning while her resolve was still strong. She had checked the map and reckoned it would take her twenty minutes to walk to the landscape centre. Saturday morning was probably not the best time to try to corner someone in that business, but she had to make the best use of the time left to her.

The centre was on a corner with a parking area enclosed by a low limestone wall facing onto the street. She stopped on the opposite corner, looking beyond the car park and stacks of paving slabs to an area filled with fancy stonework, waterfalls, birdbaths, stone benches, large plant pots, and some statuary. *Hayes Peterson Landscaping. For all your paving and landscaping needs. Props: Dan Hayes and Josh Peterson* said a sign on the entrance. Taking a deep breath to calm herself, she crossed the street, heart beating fast in anticipation.

A young man in work shorts and heavy boots was stacking some plastic sacks of compost into the back of a white van and Gayle watched as he finished loading and called out that he was leaving to make the delivery. Was he calling to Josh, perhaps, or Dan? Gayle hesitated near the entrance, hidden from sight by a palm tree. She could see more now, past the slabs and the statuary to the single storey building that looked like an office, and then to the shade houses beyond.

Hayes Peterson Landscaping. It seemed extraordinary to Gayle that Josh could have been part of building this professional-looking business with its large premises, its staff and stock and vehicles. She'd expected something small and scruffy. But he'd always wanted manual work, building, or gardening, something in the open air, work he could do with his hands. It was Brian who had bullied and cajoled him into a business degree and Josh had hated every minute of it. Commerce, accounting, marketing – he loathed it all and abandoned it the day Brian drove him out of the house, but clearly some of it must have served him well.

Gayle took a deep breath and walked in through the car park, along the side of one of the shade houses where foliage glistened, still moist from the morning sprinklers, and towards the office.

'Can I help you, ma'am?' a voice said behind her, and she turned to see a tall, olive skinned man emerging from the shade house.

Gayle's mouth went dry. 'Dan?' she said. 'It is Dan, isn't it? We only met once . . . a long time . . . '

Shock, or perhaps embarrassment, crossed his face. 'Oh, it's, um . . . Mrs Peterson. Sorry, I didn't recognise you.'

They stared at each other, paralysed by awkwardness. Dan was older than Josh by five or six years. He looked strong and fit, and so much older than when she had last seen him. For the first time she wondered how his life had been changed by the events that had robbed her of her son.

'Yes,' she said. 'It's a lovely place you've got here. I didn't expect it to be such a big business.' She heard her voice sounding high and false. 'I'm sorry, this is probably not the best time. I was looking for Josh.'

Dan ran his hand through his hair. 'I'm afraid he's out. I don't think he was expecting you.' He glanced at his watch. 'He won't be long, though – fifteen, twenty minutes, maybe. Would you like to wait in the office?'

She hesitated. 'I don't want to get in the way. You must be very busy.'

Dan glanced around. 'It's not too bad for a Saturday morning, and we've plenty of staff on today. They can do without me for a bit. Come over to the office and I'll make some coffee.' He led the way behind the slabs past a forklift and in through glass doors to a large office where two desks were piled high with paperwork.

'Have a seat,' he said, indicating a couple of armchairs and a coffee table. 'How would you like your coffee?'

Gayle sat in one of the low chairs, looking around her at the trade certificates hanging on the walls, the photographs of land-scaping in different stages, some framed plans. She was fearful now of Josh's reaction if he found her sitting there. Her heart started to race and she stood up and made for the door just as Dan entered with two mugs of coffee on a tray.

'I think I should go,' she said, so nervous that she felt herself shaking. 'It was wrong of me to come, unfair, Josh won't want to see me.'

Dan put the tray on the table and straightened up. 'No,' he said. 'You must stay, really, Gayle – sorry, Mrs Peterson.'

'Gayle is fine.'

'Well then, Gayle, you have to stay. He *will* want to see you; it's just that he won't know how to handle it.'

'He knew how to handle it the other day,' she said. 'And he was clear then that he didn't want me interfering in his life, he doesn't . . . ' She paused, blushing. 'He doesn't trust me and I can't blame him for that. I'm sorry to have put you to the trouble, Dan, but I ought to go.'

He caught her arm. 'No,' he said, 'please don't. This is hard for both of you, it's been so long, but Josh needs this. He may not have let you see it the other day, he would have been protecting himself, but he needs to see you, to get to know you again.'

'He didn't call,' Gayle said, fighting back tears. 'He said he would but he didn't, and I'll only be here a couple more days. I thought . . . .I just couldn't wait any longer, couldn't leave without seeing him again.'

'Of course not and now you're here you must stay. Josh needs this, Gayle, really he does.'

'What exactly is it that I need, then?' said a voice from the doorway. Josh was standing there, the look in his eyes a contrast to the hostility of his tone.

Oliver woke to brilliant sunshine pouring from the study window onto his face, temporarily blinding him as he opened his eyes. For a moment he couldn't make out where he was until, turning away from the light, two empty wine bottles and a heavily

fingermarked glass on the desk reminded him of his book packing, photo sorting and pizza. He straightened up uncomfortably,
stretching his arms above his head, yawning and flexing his legs.
It was only when his foot connected with the telephone that he
remembered his call to Sonya. He picked up the phone, returned
it to the desk, sank his head in his hands and groaned audibly.
What had he said? And what about Gayle, hadn't he spoken to
her too? From her perch on the shelf the new Joan smiled down at
him, her peep-toe shoe dangling sexily.

Oliver was a respectful and orderly person. It was a terrible
shock to him to wake in a study that looked as though it had been
trashed, with the memory of what would certainly be construed as
an offensive phone call to a woman he liked and admired. Sick at
heart and also sick in his stomach, he made a dash to the bathroom
and spent the next few minutes with his head in the toilet bowl.

It was an hour or so later that he emerged from the house, showered, changed and feeling extremely hungover and in need of fresh
air and coffee. He thought a walk might do him good and he set off
cautiously towards the cappuccino strip, blinking in the sunlight,
cringing at the sounds of noisy car engines, and wondering how he
could redeem himself. By the time he was seated at a café table with
a very strong coffee and a plate of raisin toast, he was convinced he
had committed an act of total depravity. He would have been on
the phone to Andrew's rooms asking for an emergency consultation but fortunately it was Saturday – fortunate for Andrew, of
course. So Oliver was on his own with his shame and embarrassment on a bright Saturday morning when everyone else in
Fremantle seemed to be happy, lighthearted and free of guilt. On
his own, that is, until a large shadow fell across him.

'Oliver, isn't it?' a voice said, and Oliver looked up at a man
who had his back to the sun and his features in shadow. 'Aren't
you from the university, friend of Gayle's? You remember me,
don't you? Angie's dad. You were at the wedding. Brian, Brian
Peterson. Mind if I join you?' And without waiting for an answer
he drew up a chair.

Oliver opened his mouth and shut it again. Had he compiled a
list of all the people he would have preferred not to bump into

this morning, Brian would certainly have been at the top. On second thoughts he would not have been on the list at all, for in all the years he had known Gayle, Oliver had never run into her anywhere off campus, and the likelihood of meeting Brian had been nowhere on his radar.

'Can I get you a coffee?' Oliver asked with a generosity he did not feel.

'I've ordered, thanks, and it's on its way,' Brian said. 'A cooked breakfast. Gayle was supposed to be home this weekend but she changed her plans . . . no one to cook for me.'

'Sure,' Oliver nodded. 'Well, they do a good breakfast here.'

'Trouble is,' Brian continued, 'I'm not used to it – being alone in the house, I mean. Seems a bit odd.'

'Yes, it would, I suppose,' Oliver said.

'You married? Live with someone?'

Oliver shook his head. 'Divorced, years ago. I live alone.'

'I guess you get used to it,' Brian observed as his coffee and a large plate of bacon, eggs, sausages and tomatoes were delivered to the table accompanied by thick slices of toast.

Oliver breathed deeply and hoped he wasn't going to throw up again.

'Women,' Brian went on, unwrapping his cutlery from the paper napkin. 'Up and down like yo-yos. I don't understand them, never have. Take Gayle, for instance. You've known her a long time, haven't you? What do you think of this belly dancing caper?'

'Well,' Oliver began cautiously, 'I don't know, really –'

'Exactly! Nor do I. It's totally out of character. I told her to give it away but no, off she goes all over the place. Now that's not like her, is it?'

Oliver's heart sank. The last thing he needed this morning was to be drawn into some argument between Gayle and Brian about belly dancing. 'Well,' he began again, watching nervously as Brian stabbed an egg yolk with a piece of toast. 'I suppose it is a little out of character for Gayle, but then we all change as we get older, don't we?'

Brian looked at him in surprise. 'Do we? Can't say I do. I've been doing the same things for as long as I can remember: working hard mostly, used to play squash but gave that up some years ago, bit of golf from time to time. I don't feel the need to do anything different.'

'Women . . . women do, I think. I mean, I *suppose* they do. Empty nest, that sort of thing, you know.' Oliver knew he sounded like an idiot. His capacity for conversation with a man like Brian was limited at the best of times; this morning he was bordering on the inane.

Brian leaned back and looked at him. 'You reckon it's common then, with women, doing something like this? Midlife crisis, menopause, something like that?'

Oliver shrugged and looked around for an escape route. 'I'm not sure, really, but one hears about it. I think the desire to reinvent oneself in later life is not uncommon. Men too, of course, but particularly women.'

'So you mean I shouldn't worry? You don't think there's anything wrong with her?'

'Who can say?' Oliver replied, preparing to back off now that Brian seemed to be treating him as an authority on the subject. 'You'd know Gayle better than I do.'

'That's the thing, you see,' Brian said. 'That's what's worrying me. Hope you don't mind me confiding in you like this but I've been wondering how well I do know her. You'd know her pretty well, I should think. Did she say anything about it to you?'

Oliver moved his chair a few degrees away from Brian and crossed his legs. 'Not really. I mean, she told me she was going but we didn't discuss it.' He wasn't sure now if Brian were simply looking for help or interrogating him. 'In fact, I've only seen her a couple of times since Angie's wedding. I've been away myself, to Berlin – now there's a wonderful city. Have you ever been there?'

'Never. Can't stand the Germans. So you think it's all right, do you? Nothing to worry about?'

'I shouldn't think so,' Oliver said, abandoning his unsuccessful attempt to change the subject. 'Why don't you give her a call, talk to her?'

'Phone's always switched off,' Brian said through a mouthful of sausage. 'I've left messages but she hasn't called back. Have you spoken to her recently?'

A memory from the previous night flashed through Oliver's mind and he discarded it as irrelevant. 'No,' he lied, 'not for a while now. Might be best to give her some space, you know.'

'You think so? Someone else told me that.'

'There you are, then.'

'I s'pose you're right. I'd thought of flying up there, to Broome. There's a flight this afternoon, thought I might surprise her.'

Oliver hoped his sharp intake of breath hadn't been audible. 'I wouldn't do that. She might think you were interfering, see it as an intrusion.'

'Really? I thought she'd be pleased. I could liven things up a bit, take her and the other ladies out for a nice meal.'

'Not a good idea,' Oliver said, moving more enthusiastically now into his advisory role. 'I'd play it cool if I were you. Don't call for a while, back off.'

'That's what she said, the other person I asked. "Back off," she said.'

'There you are, then.' Oliver rose from his chair and stood up. 'Well, I'll leave you to it, Brian.'

'Sure,' Brian said, wiping his mouth with his serviette and reaching out to shake hands. 'Nice to meet you again. Thanks for the advice.'

Oliver shook the proffered hand, picked up his newspaper and headed off down the street, hoping that his efforts to dissuade Brian from racing up to Broome would go some way towards mitigating his earlier bad behaviour.

'You shouldn't have come,' Josh said when Dan had closed the door behind him. 'Not here, you shouldn't have come here.'

'Where then?' Gayle asked. 'Tell me where and when and I'll go there, but you didn't call and I have to talk to you before I leave.'

Josh dropped into a chair and looked at the coffee Dan had put on the table. He shrugged. 'You're here now, I suppose.'

Gayle sat down facing him, wishing she'd had the courage to tell him the last time they met. 'I'm sorry,' she said. 'I know I'm doing this all wrong but you're not making it very easy.'

He glanced away, irritated. 'Easy, no, why would I? It hasn't been easy, any of it, but it was okay, I'd come to terms with it. Now you're stirring it all up again.'

Gayle leaned forward. 'Look, Josh, what you said the other day was right. I let you down badly and you don't trust me anymore. I understand that, really I do. But I came here to try to explain to you –'

'Explain what? What is there to explain? Dad chucked me out, you let him. Oh, I know you said stuff and were upset and all that, but in the end you didn't do anything. You phoned, you sent me money, but you didn't fight for me. You had a choice, him or me, and you chose him. That's how it was – what's to explain?'

'It wasn't as simple as that,' Gayle said, her voice shaky with emotion. 'I thought I could make him change his mind.'

'But you didn't,' Josh cut in. 'You never made him change his mind about anything, not the colour of the wallpaper or what he ate for breakfast. He is an unchangeable person because he's always right. He's a pig-headed bigot, immoveable. You know that, you must've always known it. How could you believe you could change his mind about something as big as this?'

'I kept hoping,' Gayle said. 'It sounds stupid but I kept going back to the fact that he loved you. I thought he'd see sense and realise what he'd lost, that in the end the love would overcome the prejudice.'

'Well, it didn't, and whenever it was that you realised that, you still did nothing.'

Gayle sighed. 'What should I have done? Tell me.'

'You should've left him,' Josh said, looking straight at her, years of hurt and disappointment burning on his face. 'That's what I kept waiting for you to do. Leave him. Show him that I mattered more. I kept thinking you'd do it – it's not like he was such a great husband, after all.'

'He was a good provider, always generous, he looked after us in that way . . . ' She faltered as Josh rolled his eyes in exasperation.

'You might not think that's important but it was important to him. That's what he thought it was about. To Brian being a husband and a father is about being a provider, and being in control. It was his attempt to do the right thing.'

'It didn't work,' Josh said, surly now. 'He was never there, never at assemblies or prize givings, never even bothered to come when I played football. We never did anything together and when I asked him for the one thing that really mattered, acceptance of who I am, he couldn't even give me that.'

'Josh, I'm not here to defend your father. What he did was indefensible, and what I did was no better. I'm here to tell you something about the past. I can't explain Brian to you except to say that he's the product of his times and circumstances. You remember what his parents were like, you know what his brothers are like, but he's not all bad. I'm here to tell you something I should have told you years ago, something that might help you to understand why I am the way I am, or at least have been.'

Josh put his cup down on the table. 'It can't change anything,' he said. 'It happened. It's history and I've moved on.'

Gayle shook her head. 'In some ways, yes,' she said, 'but not in others. The anger and the hurt are still there and I guess they always will be, but please give me some time, listen to what I've come here to tell you.'

Josh shrugged and stood up.

'This is what I should have done a long time ago,' she said, watching him as he walked towards the window. 'Everything I'm doing now and will do when I get home I should have done years ago. I know it's all too late, that the damage is done, that I've hurt you beyond belief. But it's not as simple as you think, Josh, and although I know you can't forgive me, I hope you might begin to understand.'

On Monday morning Brian sat in the stream of commuter traffic crawling along the Kwinana Freeway into Perth feeling quite pleased with himself. Gayle's absence had been a blow but he'd coped all right. Spent the weekend alone and enjoyed it in a strange sort of way. Watched the footy and the soccer, cleaned the pool, read the papers from cover to cover, had a couple of siestas. Maybe this was what he needed, a bit more time to enjoy life, smell the roses. Perhaps he'd been too hung up on work all this time, and maybe Gayle really was trying to tell him something. Now that the regulation board drama had been put to bed he could relax a bit, they could have a holiday somewhere. And Oliver had surprised him. Nice bloke, really, not the sort of university wanker he'd expected, and he seemed to have a bit of common sense. Helpful too.

Brian took the left lane off the Narrows Bridge, turned right onto Mounts Bay Road up the Terrace past Parliament House and on to the office in West Perth. Kings Park was bathed in sunlight and as he drove down into the car park under the building he felt unusually peaceful and optimistic. All his life he had struggled: struggled to be tougher than the other boys at school, struggled to keep up with the schoolwork that had always been hard for him, struggled to succeed, to be on top.

As he switched off the engine and leaned back in the driver's seat he realised that he *was* on top, that he had been for some time, that he really didn't need to struggle any more. He had a good job, plenty of money, property, investments, his daughter was happily married, his son – well, he hadn't got a son. And Gayle – this weird patch was a pain in the arse, but they'd had a good run. Awareness of his good fortune filled him with pleasant warmth. Locking the car he set off up the back steps into the building. It was almost ten o'clock, more than an hour later than his usual time, but it would be a quiet day.

A large cardboard box sealed with brown tape stood slap in the middle of the reception area. Brian nudged it with his foot. 'Get this unpacked whatever it is, will you, Janice,' he said to the receptionist. 'Doesn't look good out here. Photocopy paper, is it?'

'It's not . . . er . . . it's not paper,' Janice said, glancing nervously over her shoulder.

'Whatever it is, get it out of the way, will you?'

'It's all right, Janice,' a voice said and, looking up from the offending box, Brian saw Mal's bulk, contained in a rather loud check suit, filling the doorway of the meeting room. 'Good morning, Brian. A little tardy this morning, but better late than never. I've been here since half after eight.'

'Mal? I didn't know you were coming to Perth,' Brian said, annoyed at being caught on the hop. 'To what do we owe the honour?'

'Things to discuss, Brian, things to discuss. I think we might talk in your office.'

'Sure,' said Brian. 'Could you organise us some coffee, please, Janice. Mal likes cream with his, I'll have the usual. Come on in, Mal,' he said, opening his office door. 'Sorry I've kept you waiting. If I'd known, of course I'd –' He stopped dead in his tracks. The office was empty. Everything personal had been removed. The papers had gone from the desk, the pictures from the walls, the books from the shelves. Brian actually felt himself grow pale. His mouth went dry and he struggled to swallow.

'What the . . . ?'

Mal pushed past him into the office and took Brian's old seat behind the desk. 'Gotta let you go, I'm afraid,' he said. 'Gotta let you go.' And he motioned him to the visitor's chair. 'A sad business, Brian, very sad, but that's what it is, of course – business. You know how it is.' And locking his hands behind his head he leaned back in Brian's chair and began to outline the terms of the severance package.

Gayle lay on the couch, her legs curled under her. On the television the Melbourne Symphony Orchestra was playing something she recognised but couldn't name, and she closed her eyes, letting the music soothe her and going over the events of the day once again.

'Gayle!' Marissa had cried as she opened the door. 'You've been gone for ages, we were worried about you. How did it go?'

Speechless with tiredness and thankful that she wouldn't have to dance that evening, Gayle sank onto the couch feeling her remaining energy ebb away.

'It was all right,' she said, her voice trembling. 'In the end I think . . . I really think it was all right.' And then she started to cry so hard that the sobs shook her whole body. Marissa sat beside her on the couch, an arm around her shoulders and Sonya, summoned from the bedroom, fetched tissues and joined them.

'I thought he wasn't going to listen,' Gayle managed to say as the sobs subsided, 'that he was just going to get up and walk out of the office any minute and that would be it. And, you know, for a moment I almost wished he would. I felt like chucking it in at that point, it all felt too hard. Once I'd told him, then I'd be honour bound to tell Angie and then there would be Brian to deal with. And there was this moment when I thought, why bother? You've lived with all this for so long, why not just go on? Be boring, useless Gayle again, spineless and pathetic, because this is just too hard.'

'Okay, okay,' Marissa said. 'Take your time, there's no rush. Do you need a glass of water, a drink?'

'Water, please. Sorry about the crying. It's all so sad but it's such a relief too.'

Sonya got up and filled a glass. 'So you talked for ages obviously . . . ?'

'Yes, ages. I found Dan first and he was lovely. He said Josh needed this as much as I did, and I kept thinking of that and thinking that even if he hated me for what I was going to tell him, even if it meant I never saw him again, I owed it to him, to let him know me, to help him understand . . . '

'Drink this, Gayle,' Sonya said, putting the water in front of her.

'Thanks, I'm so sorry to be like this –'

'There's nothing to apologise for,' Marissa cut in.

Gayle gripped Marissa's hand. 'It's so good to be able to talk about it.'

'Yes, yes,' Sonya said impatiently, 'but tell us what happened. We're dying to know.'

'Okay,' Gayle said, managing a laugh. 'Well, eventually he gave me a chance. He was standing looking out of the window, so I just started talking.'

She had begun by explaining about her father, the grandfather who'd died before Josh was born. 'A bully,' she'd told him. 'Not physically cruel, but threatening, always threatening, so you were never sure you were safe. Oh, I know that's not the picture you ever had of him. My mother always made him out to be some sort of saint and I wasn't game to spoil that for her. But he bullied us both, always kept us in line with threats – so much so that often he didn't have to say anything, threaten anything specific, because being frightened of him had become a way of life.'

'Why are you telling me this?' Josh asked irritably, turning round to face her. 'What's it got to do with you and me?'

'A lot,' she said. 'Honestly, Josh, an awful lot. I grew up terrified of putting a foot out of line, believing that if I got it wrong something terrible would happen to me or Mum or both of us. I lived in fear and anxiety. When Dad died, I thought I was free at last. I passed my exams, and with the money from his insurance Mum sent me to uni. I was going to have a new life, be free and independent, and then I met Brian. It felt good to be with someone who was strong enough to take care of me. I looked up to him, I suppose, tried to be what he wanted me to be.

'But it wasn't long before I realised I'd married my father. What I'd thought was caring was actually control by intimidation. I was back where I'd always been, trying to please someone because I was scared of what would happen if I didn't. He'd come from the same sort of family but he'd beaten it by becoming the perpetrator instead of the victim. I don't think he means to be unkind but he doesn't know how to be any other way. His ego relies on the same sort of emotional standover tactics as my father did.'

They were sitting down again by now, facing each other across the coffee table and she was shaking with cold in the warm, airless office.

'Go on,' Josh said.

She swallowed hard. 'So you see, I had got myself into a relationship that replicated the past. Dysfunctional, painful, but somehow almost comforting in its familiarity, and I didn't have the emotional wherewithal to get out of it. Then you came along and that made it all worthwhile. And Brian adored you – really,

Josh, he did. I know you feel he wasn't there for you and you're right, most of the time he wasn't, but that was how he was. He couldn't cope with domesticity, he just worked, worked, worked. But that was also part of his love for you. He wanted you always to have the best. It was the only way he knew how to show love.'

Josh looked down at the floor without responding.

'And then . . . ' She paused. 'And then I . . . I met someone else, another man.' This was the part she had been dreading most of all, this saga of deceit and pragmatism. Perhaps after this any remaining shred of respect he had for her would be gone, but at least he would know the truth. So she told him about the affair, about the lover who had begged her to leave, and promised to care for her and Josh, and promised to leave his wife so that they could be together. And who, when she finally agreed, changed his mind and backed off in panic. She had never seen him again.

'And then I realised I was pregnant,' she said, and Josh looked up, confused now, wondering what was coming next. 'I was pregnant and not by your father.'

Josh was staring at her, his hands trembling. He reached for the bottle of water on the table and gulped at it. 'So what did you do?'

'I had no option. I had to tell Brian. I was terrified. He hit me – he'd done that a few times before. I wanted to leave but I was still so unprepared to cope alone, to look after myself and you. And then he told me that if I left he'd make sure I lost you. He would sue for custody, and he might have got it because I was carrying another man's child. I couldn't lose you, Josh. You were almost four years old and you were so precious to me. I couldn't take that risk. And so . . . '

'And so . . . what happened?'

'And so we made a deal. He promised not to lay a finger on me again, and that he'd treat the baby as his own. His pride was terribly hurt and he didn't want anyone else to know that I'd had an affair and that Angie wasn't his. I was worried he'd treat her differently but he didn't. If Angie had been a boy I think it would have been harder for him not to favour you. I think he tried to be fair, to treat you both the same.'

'Well, he was equally absent for both of us,' Josh said. 'And so that time . . . that day when I told you about me, you . . . what did you feel?'

'Terrified. Absolutely terrified. I knew he wouldn't take it well, that's why I didn't want you to tell him straight away, but you wanted to, quite rightly, I suppose. But I thought if I had more time I might be able to bring him around and, of course, I kept on thinking that, even after he'd thrown you out.'

'And you stayed for Angie?'

She nodded. 'I'd stayed for you the first time, and the second time I stayed for Angie. He . . . ' She paused, wondering whether she should go on. Perhaps she had already said too much, but she had promised him the whole truth. 'There was a huge row about three weeks after he'd kicked you out. He wouldn't back down. I threatened to leave and take Angie with me and he went absolutely berserk. He threatened to tell Angie that he wasn't her father, tell her about the affair. She was just coming up to her exams and I thought it would be all too much for her, so I just backed off. You were nearly twenty by then; you had friends, a lover, an income, a life. I thought you'd be okay. I never thought it would go on and on as it has, with you as an outcast, and me crippled by my own inadequacy.'

The silence seemed deafening.

'And now?' Josh asked. 'What happens now? You tell me this and just go back, stay put, keep out of trouble?'

Gayle shook her head. 'No. Once Angie got married I knew I couldn't go on, being there with him, just the two of us, but I didn't know how to change it. I've been with him so long, Josh, that, miserable as I was, it still felt safer than trying to change it. And then . . . I drifted into this dancing. I didn't want to go at first, but once I started it felt good. At first it was just the music and the exercise but it's very grounded and it celebrates female power. I felt as though I was stepping into a part of me that I hadn't realised was there. And these two terrific women – Marissa, the teacher, and Sonya, who's a beginner like me – they're both so strong, that started to rub off on me.'

'Does Angie know all this?' Josh asked.

'No. But I'm going to tell her the truth when I get back. She's got her own life with Tony now. I'm telling you because I know I owe you both the truth.'

Josh looked at her across the table, his gaze unblinking, biting his lip.

Gayle stood up. 'Perhaps I should go . . . and give you some space . . . ' She picked up her bag. 'Thanks for listening –'

'Don't go,' he said. 'Please don't go.' He walked over to her. 'You did the right thing, coming here,' he said. 'You've given us a second chance.' He put his arms around her and, as they held each other, Gayle knew that this moment would last her all her life.

EIGHTEEN

'So you're still doing the dancing then?' Tessa said, and Sonya, shocked almost speechless at this first phone call from her sister in years, admitted that she was. 'When will you be back in Perth?'

'End of the month,' Sonya said. 'We're in Port Hedland now, then we're driving down to Geraldton for a week and then home from there. Why?'

'Just wondered. I thought you'd want to know Donna's had the baby, this morning. A little boy.'

'That's wonderful news,' Sonya said. 'Congratulations, Tess, you're a grandmother. And are they both doing well?'

'It was a bit traumatic. She ended up with a Caesar, but she's fine now and the baby too. We're all very happy about it.'

'Well, I'm thrilled for you, and for Donna and Ray. What've they called him?'

'Ned,' Tessa said. 'Just Ned, not Edward or anything else. Odd, really. Wouldn't be my choice but they like it.'

'Is she still in hospital?' Sonya asked. 'I'd like to send some flowers and a gift.'

'She'll probably be home in a couple of days,' Tessa answered. 'Best to send it to me, because she's coming here for a while before she goes home.'

'It's wonderful news,' Sonya said, wondering how to continue the conversation. 'And how's everyone else? David? Alannah?'

'All fine.'

'And Mum and Dad?'

'Oh yes. They're okay, delighted with their first great-grandchild. Anyway, I'll let you go. Just wanted you to know about the baby. And you'll be back in Perth at the end of the month?'

'Yes, should be, why?'

'Oh, just wondered,' Tessa said. 'Well, I'll let you get on.'

'Okay,' Sonya said. 'And thanks for telling me. It was good to talk –' but Tessa had hung up.

Sonya took the phone away from her ear and stared at it. The last time she had had a call from Tessa was when Alannah was staying with her in Perth. Tessa would call to speak to her daughter, and when Sonya answered there would be a brief and awkward exchange of information and Sonya would take a message.

They had been close as children. Tessa was five years her junior and Sonya had enjoyed alternately mothering and bullying her younger sister. She had graduated from university and was almost a year into her first job when Tessa moved up to Perth, ready to embrace the excitement of life in the city. That excitement rapidly found its focus in drugs, and she soon moved to a depressing flat with Gary, a drummer ten years older than her who spent more time trying to score heroin and pump it into his veins than he did on his music, and Tessa was soon shooting up as well.

For Sonya – ambitious, focused and genuinely fearful of putting a foot wrong in any direction – they were nightmare years in which she constantly rescued Tessa from one drug-related drama after another, taking her to hospital, to the methadone clinic, to counsellors, giving her money or sweet-talking her out of police stations, while fending off anxious calls from their parents. The turning point came the day Tessa found Gary dead from an overdose, blood trickling from his nose and mouth from an encounter with a corner of the table. Sonya had grasped the opportunity to get her sister into a detox clinic, from which she emerged some weeks later, scrawny and grey faced, to sit speechless in the front seat of Sonya's car as she drove her back to Kalgoorlie.

To Sonya there was something surprisingly admirable in the way that Vera and Lewis had taken in their errant daughter, nursed her back to health and supported her until she was physically and mentally able to take care of herself and get a job. They had been frantic with worry and strongly disapproved of Tessa's lifestyle, but there were no recriminations. Sonya respected and loved them for it. Back in Perth again she was relieved that she no longer had the responsibility of looking after her sister and could get on with her own life. But something had changed, something that in all the subsequent years Sonya had never been able to understand. It was as though Tessa had cut her off, as though in leaving behind the chaos of that time she had chosen to leave Sonya behind as well.

'She'll get over it, dear,' Vera had assured her the following year when Tessa, just starting a job as a receptionist in a doctor's surgery, had treated Sonya like a stranger all through a Christmas visit. 'It's been hard for her and she hasn't always been easy to get on with. It'll all sort itself out in time; you have to be gentle with her.'

'I was, Mum. Probably too gentle for too long,' Sonya said. 'So many times I rescued her, bailed her out financially, and now she's better she treats me with contempt.'

'I know,' Vera soothed. 'She's an emotional girl, always has been. Not practical like you, Sonya. Don't push her, give her time.'

'She can have all the time in the world,' said Sonya, 'but I'm sick of being treated like shit.'

By this time, Sonya was twenty-five and engaged to Alex, a recently graduated civil engineer. Later that year they were married and Sonya found she was playing rescuer again. The legendary capacity for drink that had made Alex a hero in the engineering faculty also made him a domestic nightmare, and Sonya had more to worry about than her sister's coldness. A couple of years later, Tessa had married one of the doctors in the practice where she worked and was fitting neatly into the role of perfect wife.

'He's a nice guy, your dad,' Sonya had once told Alannah. 'I always liked him, so it wasn't anything to do with that. Your mum and I just never got it together again. We drifted further and further apart to the point that when we do meet, we don't know what to say to each other.'

'She's weird,' Alannah had said. 'She talks a lot about when you were kids and how great it was to have you as a sister.'

'Well, she clearly doesn't think it's so great these days,' Sonya replied. 'She makes me feel I shouldn't exist.'

This phone call had come right out of the blue, any new information about Tessa's family usually reaching her through her mother or Alannah. Sonya, who had been sitting in the hotel lounge with a cup of coffee when Tessa called, longed to talk to the others. It was only ten o'clock but it was all feeling a bit like the first night of their tour, each disappearing into her own shell to reflect on her own problems. Since they arrived in Port Hedland they'd had large and enthusiastic audiences and that in turn had improved their performances. They were a younger crowd here, more of them in their thirties and forties, some of them bringing children who sat watching in boredom or snuck outside to avoid embarrassment while their mothers made their first attempts at dancing.

'Different entirely from all the other places,' Gayle had commented as they'd made their way back to the hotel that evening.

'That's Hedland,' Marissa said with some feeling. 'Different. Too bloody different.'

'It seems quite a nice town,' Sonya said. 'Much nicer than I expected.' And Marissa just grunted and disappeared into her room as soon as they reached the hotel.

'Whatever's bugging her?' Gayle asked.

'She doesn't like it here,' Sonya explained. 'She says she has bad memories and she doesn't want to open it all up, but my guess is that that's just what she needs to do.'

'Opening it up,' Gayle said with a wry smile. 'Now, that's where I'm the expert.' They had stopped in the bar for a cup of coffee before going upstairs and Gayle skimmed the froth off her cappuccino with a spoon. 'I've opened up the biggest can of worms imaginable. God knows what's going to happen when I get home.'

'But you did it,' Sonya said. 'You did it. You took control of the situation and now you'll be able to manage the next stage. Whatever it is you decide, you'll cope now, Gayle. You know that.'

Gayle had nodded. She paled suddenly as tiredness hit her. 'I suppose. Anyway, Sonya, I'm sorry but I'm wiped out. I'm off to bed.'

Alone now in the empty lounge, Sonya swallowed the remains of her coffee and ordered another. Tessa had ensured that it would be hours before she could sleep.

'What I'm not sure about is what it *means*,' Oliver said, fiddling nervously with his cuffs.

'It may not mean anything other than that you got drunk and made an inappropriate phone call,' Andrew said.

'But I've never done anything like it before. Surely it must mean something?'

'Not necessarily. But it's certainly part of this period of change, of loosening up, that you're going through.'

'But it could mean something significant, couldn't it?'

'Yes it could, and you seem to think it does, so what do *you* think it means?'

'You're the therapist.'

'Indeed,' Andrew said, 'and you're the client and it's your sub-conscious we're dealing with so let's kick off with your analysis first.'

Oliver sighed. 'Okay, well, I suppose it could mean that I have until now been suppressing an interest in large breasts.'

Andrew raised his eyebrows and gave a slight nod, waiting for Oliver to continue.

'Or it could just mean that without realising it I really do fancy Sonya although I told her I didn't . . . ' He paused. 'That's a possibility, isn't it?'

'Certainly,' Andrew said. 'Anything else?'

Oliver shook his head. 'What do you think?'

'I think that either of those is a possibility but there may be other, rather deeper issues here.'

'For example?'

'For example, it's possible that your decision to change your mother's photograph from one that symbolises intellect and aca-demic achievement to a more lighthearted one that reveals a sensuous side – the ice cream on the lip, the dangling shoe –

means you were acknowledging the sensuous side of your own nature, allowing it to surface, being prepared to risk exploring it.'

'So it could be about the change in me, but might be nothing directly to do with Sonya herself?'

'Possibly. She may simply be the focus. She's a woman you admire and feel at ease with and the partner in your most recent sexual encounter.'

'So I could be projecting something onto Sonya?'

'Quite possibly.'

'Like what?'

Andrew took a deep breath. 'This could be primal stuff, Oliver. Exploring our sexuality always brings us back to our primary relationships – in your case, of course, one primary relationship.'

'My mother!'

'Exactly. In choosing to ignore or perhaps forget that aspect of your mother's life, you have also chosen to suppress that side of yourself. Open up one and you open up your own sexual can of worms.'

'You mean I could be a raving sex maniac?'

'Unlikely, I think,' Andrew replied. 'More likely just a case of getting a little more balance into your life in this area and coming to terms with the Oedipus complex.'

'Couldn't it just be that I got drunk and made an inappropriate phone call, like you said in the first place?'

'It could indeed be that, alone or in combination with any or all of the other elements.'

Oliver groaned. 'So how will I know?'

'We'll need to do a bit more work around this,' Andrew said.

'I prefer the getting drunk or suppression of large breasts theory,' Oliver said, panic-stricken.

'Naturally,' Andrew answered, 'they're far less challenging explanations, but as you said yourself they're totally at odds with your nature. I mean, prior to this occasion when did you last have too much to drink?'

'At Gayle's daughter's wedding, the day I met Sonya. I started knocking back these very strong champagne cocktails and didn't stop.'

'And prior to that, when were you last drunk?'

Oliver shrugged. 'No idea, years ago . . . too long to remember. Ten years, maybe.'

'Aha!' Andrew said with a smile. 'Interesting, and why do you suppose you chose to get drunk at the wedding?'

'Did I choose it?' Oliver asked in confusion. 'Couldn't it just have happened?'

'In the light of what you've said it seems unlikely. Can you recall how you were feeling at the wedding? Before Sonya showed up, I mean. For example, how were you feeling about your friend Gayle, about being in her home?'

'Oh Christ,' Oliver said. 'Where the hell is this going next?'

Marissa took the long route. She'd avoided the town for nearly forty years; another hour or so wasn't going to matter. And in any case it wasn't Port Hedland, or that particular house, that haunted her but what had happened there; avoiding the place had simply been the focus to stop her thinking about the rest of it. It was much more complicated than conquering her fear of motorbikes by climbing on one. What had happened here had determined who she had become and had kept her in emotional isolation for decades.

The town formed the backdrop to the memories that stalked her: the roar of the iron ore crushing mill; the trains, some almost three kilometres long, that hissed and clattered back and forth to Mt Newman; the red dust that coated everything and worked its way into skin, hair and clothing. Days after that terrible night she had stood watching the huge ore carriers in the port and the vast rust-red equipment of the crushing mill, seeing so many opportunities to surrender to a physical mutilation as brutal as that which had already destroyed her spirit.

It would have been so easy to disappear. Who would have known or cared? Not Blue. Wendy and Mike maybe, but not her parents, or Roger, or any of the people who had made up the life she'd abandoned for . . . for what? Whenever Marissa remembered that day, she felt it was the salt that had saved her. She had walked for hours with no purpose and no sense of where she was heading, and ended up where the stockpiles stood, dazzling pyramids, their crystalline whiteness sparkling in the sunlight. Somehow they seemed a symbol of hope. Now, years later, it seemed extraordinary that those salt piles, their reflections sharp and clear against the glassy surface of the water, had given her the courage to go on.

They had been in Australia only a few days. The trek through Europe and the Middle East and on to South East Asia had been tougher and more challenging than she had expected, but she had no regrets. By the time they reached Australia their group had dwindled from eleven to seven and for six of them it was a homecoming.

'Well, here you are, Jean,' Blue had said as the small aircraft crossed the coast on its descent to the airport. 'Welcome to the wide brown land.'

Apart from the clear blue water bordered by white sand, it bore no resemblance to the sort of paradise Marissa had envisaged. The dusty red industrial landscape brooding on the coast had come as a shock and she longed to move on. She couldn't remember now how they all came to end up at the house, but they had pounced on it as a chance to draw breath before they separated to go their different ways. It was a dreary place, a sprawling bungalow of yellowish brick with a barren garden enclosed by asbestos fencing; depressing but cheap – free, in fact, for a few weeks.

The relationship with Blue had petered out over the months of travel, his interest in her waning consistently in every place where it was easy for him to find casual sex. And although they sometimes shared a bed for the sake of convenience, the burst of sexual chemistry that had initially brought them together was a thing of the past. Marissa found their present friendship preferable, as at times his possessiveness had been oppressive. And, even after fifteen months of travelling, of close living in tents, hostels and caravans where the group had squeezed together to save money, Marissa knew little more about him than she had at the start. He was a cagey, secretive man, rarely revealing anything more than trivial anecdotes about himself or his family, from whom he seemed happy to keep his distance. And while she still felt connected to him because he had sprung her from domestic confinement, Marissa thought the time had probably come for them to go their different ways. She was tossing up between heading to Cairns with a couple of the others in the group, or down to the south coast of Western Australia with Wendy and Mike, to whom she had become quite close.

'Come with us,' Wendy had urged. 'It's great down there – fantastic forests, and the beaches are so quiet. You'll love it, Jean.'

With a shiver of recognition, Marissa looked down the street which was much as she remembered it, just a little tidier and the houses showed signs of improvement, but it was still an ordinary street of single storey houses, a few cars parked on the road and in driveways, a couple of kids kicking a ball, two women talking on a front lawn, a blue heeler dozing on the pavement. She walked on slowly and was shocked as a soccer ball shot across her path almost tripping her. On the other side of the street, two boys, masking guilt with hostility, stared at her, daring her to say something. Ignoring them she walked on in silence, past the paved front yards, past scruffy lawns and dust-covered lantana, until she could see it, set back further from the road than the other houses, just in the curve of the turning head.

It looked better than she remembered, cleaner. The asbestos fence had been replaced with a low wall of similar yellow brick and someone had taken an interest in the garden. There was the old lemon tree and, beside it, neat beds of roses struggling to survive the climate and the clay. There was a shiny aluminium garden shed and a single room had been added onto one side of the house. So this was it, this ordinary house in this ordinary street. The place of nightmares, and she was standing right in front of it, almost inside the gate, feeling nothing but a little light-headed.

'G'day, love, looking for something?' An elderly man holding a pair of secateurs emerged from behind the lemon tree.

Marissa jumped and stepped back. 'Sorry, no,' she mumbled, blushing. 'Just . . . just admiring your garden.'

The man looked around proudly. 'It doesn't do too bad, considering. Takes too much water, though. The wife's always
grumbling about the water. Mind you, she likes the roses.'

'Have you lived here long?' Marissa asked.

'Bought it in eighty-four,' he said. 'Shocking state it was in
then. We've done a lot to it.'

Marissa nodded. 'I stayed here once,' she said. 'Long before
that, though, in the late sixties.'

'Did ya? Well, there's a coincidence. Family live here, did
they?'

She shook her head. 'I don't know who owned it. I was with a
group, travelling, and we ended up staying here.'

The man grinned. 'Dick Penfold, pleased to meet you,' he said,
holding out his hand. 'Come on in and have a look round. You'll
see a few changes.'

Marissa hesitated in the gateway, about to refuse, but he had
turned away from her and was already heading up the pathway
to the front door.

'I won't stay . . . ' she began, but he didn't hear her.

'Molly,' he called through the screen door, 'put the kettle on,
love. We've got a visitor.'

NINETEEN

Brian sat on the top deck of the Manly ferry looking out across the harbour where dozens of sailing boats raced across the choppy surface, their white sails plumped by the strong wind. Behind him the city and Circular Quay grew smaller and Manly beckoned. He'd always liked Manly: the wharf, the curving beach backed by Norfolk Pines and the lively atmosphere along The Corso. He'd always fancied owning an apartment near the waterfront, but he had no idea why he was here now, sitting on the ferry, no idea why he was in Sydney, except that he'd found it impossible to stay on in Perth, alone in the house.

He'd been due to fly to Sydney the day after his encounter with Mal in the Perth office. That day he'd driven slowly back home as though shell shocked and, not knowing what else to do with himself, he'd called Qantas to cancel his reservation, only to discover that it had been cancelled the previous week. It was the same with the hotel bookings in Sydney and Melbourne. And when he started on the client meetings he'd organised he found these too had been cancelled. Worse still, he couldn't get past the secretaries or receptionists to speak to his contacts. It seemed that everyone knew he'd been 'let go'.

He spent the next four days alone. There were no calls on his mobile, although Angie sent him a text message saying she hoped he'd managed all right at the weekend. The landline was also silent and he felt incapable of calling anyone to whom he might have to explain. Resisting the urge to think about what had happened, he also resisted the urge to think much about anything at all.

The televisions in the lounge, his study and the bedroom were left on all the time. He watched everything, from breakfast programs to *Bananas in Pyjamas*, from cooking shows, *Days of Our Lives*, *Oprah* and *Dr Phil* to current affairs; he watched good movies, bad movies, quiz shows, reality TV, American crime series, endless news bulletins, football, motor racing and home shopping. His attention span was annoyingly short but, terrified of turning a set off and being forced to think, he channel-surfed until his eyes hurt. His head buzzed with American accents, cheering crowds, images of Middle Eastern countries devastated by bombing, and scantily dressed young women with straight blonde hair and teeth so perfect they looked like dentures.

'Bit crook, are you?' asked the lawnmower man, who knocked at the front door to be paid on the morning of the fifth day.

'Yep,' Brian said, pulling notes out of his wallet and realising that he hadn't got out of his pyjamas for almost a week. 'Got a bit of a bug.'

'Lot of it about,' the man said, writing a receipt. 'Nasty one, gastro thing. My kids had it. Went through us all like a dose of salts.'

'That's it,' Brian said, rubbing the five days of stubble on his chin.

'You take care. Mrs Peterson'll soon be back to look after you, that's for sure.'

Brian closed the front door. 'If she even fucking remembers I'm alive,' he said to himself, slumping once again in front of the television. The lawnmower man's visit proved to be a wake-up call, though. He felt restless now and padded barefoot to the gate, collected the mail from the box and dumped it in the kitchen. The sink was full of dirty plastic containers from the food he'd microwaved, and the bin was overflowing with milk cartons and empty wine bottles. The time had come to do something. He made a negligible attempt to clear up the mess in the kitchen, and went upstairs to have a shower. And in the early afternoon, he drove across the Narrows Bridge and up to West Perth and sat outside the office for some time, staring up at the front of the building to the fourth floor window from which he had so often looked out across the park. Then he drove home and booked a business class flight to Sydney.

'They never did!' Collette said, sitting in one of the armchairs in the hotel room. 'What, just dumped you on the spot like that? No notice or anything?'

Brian shook his head. 'A decent payout, of course, that's how it works in these big companies. Somebody's head has to roll, and you're gone the same day – same hour, in my case.'

'That's terrible, so unfair. I mean, I thought there were laws about unfair dismissal and stuff like that.'

Brian just shrugged. It would have been incomprehensible to Collette that such considerations had no place in the sort of levels at which he'd been working. How could he begin to explain to her the long and complex saga of the regulation board case and the final decision, or the internal politics that had left him exposed? And he certainly didn't want to tell her about the last humiliation of Mal's sanctimonious homily on family values, the woman seen leaving his Chicago hotel room and the unacceptable nature of some of those charges on his credit card.

'So what did your wife say?' Collette asked.

'Haven't told her yet.'

'You what? I thought you said this happened on Monday – it's Saturday now.'

'She's away,' Brian said.

'Yes but –'

'You're the first person I've told and I'm not telling anyone else, not yet anyway, maybe not for a long time.'

Collette looked at him in amazement. 'You're kidding. How'll you hide it?'

'They're used to me being away, and Gayle's away too. I'll just keep shtum till it suits me, until I've decided what to do.'

'But what *will* you do?'

'Not sure yet. Might set up on my own,' Brian said.

'Management and marketing consultancy, something like that. Could be a godsend, really, my own business – decide what I want and when I want it. I won't have to put up with all the wankers trying to cover their own backs.'

Telling Collette was an experiment, an attempt to find out how it felt to talk about it, and now he knew it felt terrible; so bad that, to his horror, he began to cry. Tears ran down his cheeks and a lump in his throat broke into a series of shattering sobs. 'Shit,' he groaned, sinking his face into his hands. 'Shit and fuck. Fuck 'em all.'

Collette moved closer and put her arm around his shoulders, and he reached out, wrapping his arms around her, burying his face in her lap until he was able to stop crying.

'Sorry,' he said eventually, attempting to dry his eyes. 'Sorry . . . don't know where that came from. Haven't cried since I was a kid.'

'Oh, stop it, Brian,' she said, 'you're upset and so you should be. Nothing wrong with that.'

She stood up again, straightened her skirt and glanced at her watch. The hour that had been paid for by credit card when Brian booked her was almost up. She was no stranger to men's dramas, their pain, the confidences and the times when all they needed was to talk out their anger and sense of impotence, but she had never anticipated it with Brian.

'Look, love,' she said, 'time's nearly up and I've got another booking on the other side of town.'

Brian got up. 'Sure,' he said, 'sorry. Next time it'll be all right. Sorry.' He reached for his wallet. He always gave her an extra fifty dollars in cash but this time she shook her head.

'No, darl. I never even got my knickers off,' she said with a smile.

'Doesn't matter,' he said sheepishly. 'Go on, take it.'

But, pushing his hand away gently, she picked up her bag. 'Won't be seeing you so often from now on?'

He shrugged. 'I'll be back and forth, I reckon,' he said. 'And I'll be here for the next few days.'

'Okay then,' Collette said. 'Well, take care of yourself. And take my advice – tell your wife and your daughter as soon as possible.

The longer it goes on the harder it'll be.' And she kissed him lightly on the cheek and closed the door behind her.

'You all right?' said a woman sitting a little further along the wooden seat on the ferry. She was holding a packet of tissues out to him.

Brian put his hand up to his face and realised there were tears running down his cheeks. 'Thanks,' he said, taking the tissues. 'I'm fine . . . just the wind making my eyes water.'

'Sunglasses,' the woman said with a smile, nodding towards the pair that were tucked between the second and third buttons of his shirt. 'That'll stop it.'

Brian put on the glasses but the tears kept coming, and even after he had disembarked at Manly they didn't stop. They seemed to have a life of their own.

'I don't think this is a good idea,' Gayle said. 'It's almost nine hundred kilometres to Carnarvon. Why don't we aim for one of the roadhouses tonight and go on to Carnarvon tomorrow, then Geraldton the next day? We're already leaving a day ahead of schedule. Why is it so important that we do all this distance in one day?'

Marissa, tight-lipped at the wheel, shook her head. 'Look, I swapped the car for the camper so we can go further today, doing the driving in shifts and taking turns to sleep in the back. We can go through the night if we want.'

'And suppose we don't want?' Sonya asked, exchanging a look with Gayle in the mirror. 'Suppose we just want to check in somewhere, have a shower and something to eat, and sleep in a proper bed?'

Marissa shrugged. She knew they were angry with her and concerned about what was happening. Since her visit to the house the previous day she had disappeared into her shell, changed the car booking, cancelled what should have been a rest day at the motel, and hassled them into the journey south. Their final

197

performance the previous night had gone well, but no thanks to her. She had gone through the motions, and it was Gayle and Sonya who had carried it, challenged by her mood to infuse their own dancing with greater levels of energy. She'd been impressed by the flair of their performances, but she was incapable of telling them so.

'I'm sorry,' she managed to say now. 'I know you think I'm unreasonable but I just want to get as far away from Hedland as I can.'

Sonya shrugged and lay down on one of the bunks, strapping the seatbelt around her. 'Obviously,' she said, 'so, since you had us up before daylight, I'm going to catch up on lost sleep.'

In the front seat, Gayle fidgeted uncomfortably. 'Me too,' she said, reclining the seat slightly and closing her eyes. 'Wake me when it's my turn to drive.'

It was just before six and the open road stretched ahead of them, promising Marissa relief with every kilometre. She fixed her eyes on the middle distance and put her foot down; two hundred kilometres to Roebourne. With that behind her, the images that tortured her, the horrifically revived memory of the house, would soften . . .

'This lady,' Dick had said, holding open the screen door, waiting for her to follow him, 'she used to live here a while ago.'

Marissa hesitated on the step. 'I don't think . . . '

'Yeah,' Dick said. 'Come on, you came here to see the place, I'll bet. Funny business going back to places. I've done it meself a few times.'

The inside of the house was initially shocking in its familiarity, despite the changed décor. The central passage, once a grubby shade of ochre, had been painted a delicate duck-egg blue; the four doors that led off it were a darker shade of the same tone. She followed Dick Penfold through to the completely remodelled kitchen off which was a cosy breakfast room where there had once been a scruffy sleepout.

'You've transformed it,' she said with a sense of relief, looking around the sparkling kitchen and through the window to the well-tended vegetable garden beyond. 'It was a mess when I was here.'

Her tension eased a little. It was familiar but different; different people, different energy. The past had been exorcised. She sat at the table cautiously taking in her surroundings and drinking her tea while Molly and Dick described the state the house had been in when they bought it, and how he had done most of the repair work himself.

'So when were you here, dear?' Molly asked.

'The late sixties,' Marissa said. 'I was backpacking with a group of people.'

Molly nodded. 'All the young people were doing it then, backpacking. Could never see the attraction myself, but I was too old for it even then.' She smiled at Marissa and pushed a biscuit tin towards her. 'Help yourself. Stay here long, did you?'

Marissa felt the fear rising again and shook her head. 'Just a few weeks. People were going off in all directions. I managed to get a lift to Perth on a truck.'

'Dangerous,' Molly said. 'Hitchhiking, I mean. You never know whose car you're getting into. Dangerous.'

Marissa smiled. 'The driver was very nice,' she said, and restrained herself from adding that it didn't feel half as dangerous as spending another moment in the house. She set down her cup. 'I'll get out of your way,' she said, getting up from the table. 'It was lovely of you to invite me in, and thanks so much for the tea.'

Dick struggled to his feet. 'Before you go I want to show you what I did with one of the other rooms,' he said, guiding her gently in the one direction she really didn't want to go. 'You probably remember this used to be a bedroom.' He flung open the door and Marissa leapt back in shock.

She didn't see the vast model railway that filled the room, its tracks weaving through valleys and pastures of green plastic, the tiny houses and industrial buildings, the minute details of the trains and the stations, the rigid figures of passengers waiting on the platforms, and the miniature packing cases and sacks of coal. What she saw was what she remembered: dirty ochre walls, the ceiling stained by years of tobacco smoke, herself, the others and beyond them Blue's face in the doorway. She felt the bile rise in her throat and she turned away. 'I'm sorry,' she called as she reached the open front door. 'I'm sorry, I have to go.' And she ran out and up the street without looking back.

Gayle's eyelids were heavy and she was relieved to be able to lie back in silence and let the humming of the tyres on the bitumen lull her into relaxation. She had left Broome feeling at peace for the first time in years. Facing Josh, telling him her story, had made her stronger and although he hadn't put it into words, she felt his forgiveness. They had talked for hours that day, and in the days that followed. Watching the tenderness and affection that characterised Josh and Dan's relationship, Gayle wondered briefly whether, given time, Angie and Tony would mature in this way. Although Angie seemed happy, she and Tony appeared to lack the affectionate ease and companionship she could see in her son's home.

'How's Ange?' Josh had asked almost as though he could read her thoughts. 'Is he okay – Tony? I only met him once last year when they came up for a long weekend.'

'He's nice,' Gayle said. 'Not the person I'd have picked for Angie. He's pretty focused on work and very ambitious, but they seem happy. Maybe . . . ' she hesitated . . . 'maybe when I've sorted things out at home you'll come down to Perth? Both of you, so we can all get together?'

Josh turned away from the sandwiches he was preparing for lunch. 'Without Dad,' he said, 'after you've . . . when he's . . . .'

'Yes,' she said. 'When I've told him it's over. When I've found a place of my own.'

Josh looked surprised. 'Why should you move out? Make him go and you stay in the house.'

Gayle shook her head. 'I can't live there, Josh. I never liked the place, anyway, it's too big and pretentious. It never felt like home. Angie reckons that's my fault for not putting my own stamp on it but I couldn't, I didn't have the heart.'

'Where would you go, Gayle?' Dan asked. 'Will you stay in Perth or shift somewhere else? Come to Broome, perhaps?'

She was moved by his suggestion that made living near them suddenly seem the most natural thing in the world.

'I don't know yet,' she said. 'First I need to sort things out with Brian, and then find a place to rent for a while.'

There was a silence as Dan brought the sandwiches and plates to the table, and began to draw the cork on a bottle of white wine.

'I could help you if you want,' Josh said suddenly. 'With that move, I mean. If you feel you want some moral support.' He looked up at Dan. 'You could manage without me for a week or so if I went down to Perth, couldn't you?'

Dan smiled, resting his hand on Josh's shoulder. 'Of course – or I could come too. We could get Lawrence and Mike to take over, like they did when we went on holiday. Then we could both help.'

It was extraordinary to Gayle that just a few days had taken them from estrangement to this point. 'I couldn't ask you to do –' she began.

'You didn't ask,' Josh said. 'I offered, and so did Dan. Think about it. If we don't come for the move, then we could come a bit later.'

Gayle had thought the hardest part still lay ahead but now, heading south, aware that only one stop remained on the journey home, she realised that the hardest part, the fear of rejection, the challenge of risking it, was gone.

Sonya lay on the narrow bunk, her portable CD player resting on her chest, earphones pumping Placido Domingo into her ears.

'Placido is my favourite of the Three Tenors,' she had said earlier, in an effort to start a conversation. 'His interpretation is more sensitive. Don't you think?'

Gayle raised a hand sleepily, conveying nothing in particular, and Marissa favoured her with a grunt. 'Well, thanks for that, girls,' Sonya said in a voice audible only to herself, and replaced the earphones. 'I get the message.'

They wanted silence but it was such an awkward silence, with

Marissa hunching over the wheel, driving like a maniac. Sonya stared at her back, torn between sympathy and frustration. The previous afternoon, Marissa had returned from her walk drawn and silent and, brushing off their concern, had disappeared into her room until it was time to go to the community centre. Sonya was both hurt and irritated; the warmth and companionship they had shared now seemed to her to have been built by Gayle and herself. Marissa had always held back, disclosing very little of herself. Didn't she trust them? Perhaps she'd been wrong about the friendship, projected onto it what she wanted rather than what it really was.

Sonya tossed restlessly on the bunk. Everything seemed to be in a disturbing state of flux: Gayle was changing by the day, Marissa transformed from confidence to chaos, even Angie had stopped sending her cheery and encouraging text messages, and no one at the office had found it necessary to consult her about anything for at least the last couple of weeks. Even Oliver was changing. He had left it rather too long to call back with an apology and, despite being amused rather than offended by his call, she had started to feel that she might *become* offended if he didn't call back soon to apologise. Oliver sober would surely have assumed that his call *was* offensive, but was he just going to ignore it? Finally, after what had apparently been a grim period of soul searching, he had called a couple of nights after they arrived in Port Hedland.

'I hardly know what to say,' he'd begun and Sonya, deciding not to be too much of a pushover, let him struggle. 'What I did, what I said, it was appalling, insulting . . . ' he said eventually. 'I'm so very sorry, Sonya.'

'Thank you, Oliver,' she'd said, attempting not to burst out laughing. 'It was rather over the top and most unlike you.'

'Yes,' he said, clearly relieved that she was even speaking to him. 'Yes, I'm afraid that's how I am at present, most unlike myself, and it's pretty confusing. The therapy, you know . . . not that it's any excuse for what I did. That was really unforgivable.'

'You are forgiven,' Sonya said, enjoying the pleasure of magnanimity. 'It was an aberration. Therapy can do that to people. Besides, it was rather flattering to know that my breasts have made such a lasting impression on you.' She could imagine him blushing at the other end of the line, searching for an appropriate response, and she hoped he could handle it. If there was one thing Oliver needed to learn it was how to flirt harmlessly. But clearly he had a long way to go.

'Oh, yes, absolutely,' he said, 'it was entirely complimentary. Well, it was meant to be, I hope . . . '

'Yes,' she laughed. 'Yes, Oliver, it's okay. Don't take everything so seriously. What's a little phone sex between friends?'

'Phone sex! But I wasn't –'

'Stop right there,' she said. 'Relax, I'm joking, and I'm trying to get you to join in.' There was a long silence at the other end of the line; she could almost hear the cogs turning in his head. 'Are you still there, Oliver?'

'Yes,' he said eventually. 'Yes, I'm just thinking about what you said. Andrew, my therapist, said something similar about lightening up, learning how to play . . . I think that's how he put it.'

'Sounds like good advice,' Sonya said. 'Keep taking it. You don't need to be so intense, so serious and correct. Spontaneity, that's what you need.'

'That's what Andrew said: relax, play, be spontaneous, discover my sensuous inner self . . . '

'Exactly, and are you doing that?'

There was another longish pause. 'I'm trying but I really need a road map. It's hard to change, isn't it, Sonya? Hard to break the habits of a lifetime?'

'Of course, but you'll do it. I can sense it happening already.'

'Really?'

'Yep, really. And when I get back we can talk about it, how you might develop a sexy personality.'

'Sexy personality? You mean . . . flirting . . . '

'Yes, if you'd like to, that is.'

'I would, I'd really appreciate that, Sonya, because somehow Andrew expects me to manage that part on my own.'

'You're on,' Sonya said. 'Coaching in the game of life begins when I get back.'

'Good, good,' Oliver said. 'And how's Gayle, is she all right? I was thinking of giving her a call.'

'She's fine,' Sonya said, and updated him briefly on Gayle's reunion with Josh. 'She's a changed woman, you'll be amazed. There's no way she's going back to the way things were. There are big changes afoot chez Peterson.'

'Really?' Oliver's tone was thoughtful. 'Well, that's good, isn't it? So I'll phone her, I think, don't you, Sonya? Is that a good idea?'

It pulled Sonya up short. 'Yes, do that, I'm sure she'd like to hear from you.'

'Okay then, I will. Great, thanks. And apologies again. You're a good friend, Sonya, I'm so relieved that you're not . . . that you're still speaking to me.'

'I'm speaking to you, Oliver,' she said, 'and we'll speak more soon.'

'Yes, indeed. Flirting – that's very good.'

Thinking back on it now, with Placido serenading her through the headphones, Sonya puzzled once more over what had happened. One minute she was enjoying the conversation and the next they were talking about Gayle and she was feeling strange. Was it Oliver's sudden enthusiasm at the prospect of speaking to Gayle? She was, after all, a very old friend and their estrangement was brief and recent. It was perfectly reasonable that on hearing Gayle's good news, he would want to call her. Perfectly reasonable. So why, Sonya wondered, did she end up feeling disappointed – or was what she felt really more like a twinge of jealousy?

TWENTY

Frank sat in the bar of the Norfolk Hotel staring into his fourth Johnnie Walker. He'd had an appalling week. Every move they'd made on the drugs case had drawn a blank. The night he'd arrested Marissa's neighbour he'd been confident he would crack the case wide open within a few weeks but here he was, months later, the big operators still eluding him and the Deputy Commissioner increasingly impatient for a result.

His gloom about the case was compounded by the old depression and the fact that Marissa was neither answering her phone nor returning his calls. Her silence over the past week was deafening. Something had happened in Port Hedland and she clearly wanted to be left alone. He feared that whatever she was struggling with might end up changing things between them.

'Cheer up, Frank, it might never happen,' said a voice behind him, and before he could turn, there was a hand on his shoulder and warm breath in his ear.

'It already has, Gina,' he said. 'Haven't seen you for months. I didn't know you were back in Fremantle.'

She settled on the stool beside him. 'Been back a while now. Couldn't stand the southwest – too quiet. I'll have a Redback, if you're buying.'

He signalled the barmaid, and ordered her drink and another for himself.

'You look as though you might have had enough already,' Gina said, adjusting the plunging V-neck of her black dress. It was long and simple, made of some sort of T-shirt fabric that draped softly over her legs. 'You're a mean man when you're drunk.'

'You never complained before,' he said. 'In fact, I thought you got me drunk to take advantage of me.' How easy it was to fall back into playing the old games.

Gina grinned and raised her glass. 'You should be so lucky,' she said, and Frank knew that he could, if he chose, get lucky again right now.

'You're looking good,' he said. 'Are you working?'

She nodded, 'New Age shop down the road, weekends.'

Frank smiled. 'What are you reading this time? Classics?'

'Get off,' she said with another grin. 'The tarot, and palms, whatever people want. Like me to take a look at your palm, Frank? Want to know what's waiting round the corner?'

He shook his head. 'I can barely cope with the present, let alone the future,' he said. 'Are you living in the same place?'

Gina shook her head. 'That warehouse conversion on South Terrace. I moved in last week.'

Frank let out a low whistle. 'Going up in the world. Not your usual style.'

Gina took a long drink of her beer. 'A legacy. My dad died. It's all right, you don't need to do the sympathy thing. He was in his nineties and didn't know one day from the next. He was ready to go.'

'Just the same . . . '

'Yeah, just the same . . . It's sad, but he went peacefully.'

'And he left you something?'

'Everything. I knew he would, I'm an only child. What shook me was finding out how much there was. He'd been living like he was hard up but it turned out he'd got a whole lot of investments. He had one of his mates in the RSL looking after them.'

'So you rented a fancy apartment.'

'Bought it. I knew I'd fritter that money away if I didn't put it into bricks and mortar. I'm fifty-three and it's the first time I've owned my own home.'

Frank raised his glass. 'Impressive starter home,' he said. 'Well, here's to you, Gina, a good decision.'

Gina nodded. 'Two bedrooms, state-of-the-art kitchen, white marble bathroom, spa bath,' she paused. 'And a jacuzzi in the courtyard with jets in all the right places. You should come and have a look, Frank, help me christen it.'

He paused, looking hard at her. She had the complexion of a much younger woman; only when he got as close as this were the tiny lines visible around her eyes. The once-blonde hair was streaked with grey, and it brought a lump to his throat.

'How long have we known each other?' he asked suddenly.

Gina shrugged. 'Twenty years? More maybe, on and off –' she laughed – 'literally! What d'you reckon? You look like you need something to take your mind off your troubles. What is it this time, the Vietcong or the crims?'

'Bit of both,' he said, 'and more. A Jacuzzi, eh?'

'Big enough for four but more fun for two.'

'Sounds like just what I need,' he said, finishing his drink and signalling again to the barman. 'Better take a couple of bottles of decent champagne with us so we can do it properly.'

Gina threw back her head and laughed again. 'Ah, dear Frank,' she said. 'As long as I can remember, you've always known how to do it properly.'

Oliver was feeling rather as he had done at the age of ten, on his first visit to the Royal Show. He'd been looking forward to seeing the animals, to throwing balls into the open mouths of plastic clown heads as they turned from side to side, and he'd pictured success at the shooting ranges. But Janet, who was a year younger, had dared him to go on the Big Wheel. Even at ten the prospect of being suspended hundreds of feet above the ground in a perilously swaying wooden box was not Oliver's idea of fun, but he felt bound to rise to the challenge.

Having survived the Wheel, and even almost enjoyed it, he had foolishly dared Janet to go with him on the roller coaster, confident that the prospect would reduce her to tears. But Janet was made of sterner stuff, and they were soon careering at breakneck speed up and terrifyingly down the steep slopes and wild curves of the track, grasping a metal bar that shuddered in his grip. Oliver had emerged white faced and shaken, and for the next hour at least was at severe risk of bringing up his lunch. That was exactly how he felt now as he left the centre of the floor and headed for the plastic chairs lined up along one side of the studio.

What madness had induced him to inflict this torture on himself? One minute he was chatting to Gayle on the phone, feeling happy, positive and inspired, and now here he was, three days later, wondering what on earth he was doing. Gayle had a lot to answer for – she, after all, had suggested it. It had been so good to talk to her again he'd been completely carried away by the relief of finding their friendship intact. She told him all about Josh and her own past and he, in turn, told her about his therapy. No apology, no going over what had happened seemed necessary; it was a conversation like they used to have, only better, because now she was telling him things about herself, and he was remembering to ask.

'I do admire you for sticking with the therapy, Oliver,' Gayle said. 'I tried once and it was so confronting I couldn't face going back.'

'But look what you've done now, Gayle,' he answered. 'Going on this tour, finding your son and telling him everything, and now you're telling me. That's huge and really brave.'

'It's the dancing,' she said. 'It got me out of my head and into my body, made me see everything more clearly. Come to think of it, Oliver, something physical might be good for you too.'

So a couple of hours later he'd found himself standing in front of the noticeboard in the Fremantle Public Library, staring at the advertisements for tennis clubs and gyms, yoga classes, Pilates, fitball and pleas for members to join the soccer team. But Oliver was the least sporty person imaginable. He had once joined the university gym only to set the treadmill running so fast that his glasses steamed up and he couldn't see how to stop it. He'd been rescued by a student whom he'd recently failed for plagiarism, so it was embarrassing as well as scary.

There was a walking group wanting members, someone looking for a golf partner, and a sponsorship form you could fill in to pledge that you would run the city-to-surf in aid of the Heart Foundation. Oliver's own heart missed a beat at the mere prospect. And then he saw it, a scarlet postcard with the black silhouette of a couple dancing.

> *It Takes Two to Tango!*
> *Get fit, meet people.*
> *Learn the tango, the rumba, the salsa.*
> *Beginners welcome.*

It had seemed like a good idea at the time – after all, look what dancing had done for Gayle, and Sonya too was insisting that she was fitter and more in touch with her body. That was obviously what he needed and so here he was, sweating profusely from exertion and embarrassment, and clearly the only person in the room totally incompetent when it came to Latin American dance.

'No, no, Oliver,' Ramon called when he spotted him slinking way into a corner. 'More practice, come back here, try again. Judy will help you this time, won't you, darling?'

Oliver's heart sank. Ramon was a slavedriver with gleaming gelled hair, olive skin and a body like a rod of iron. In a scarlet satin shirt and tight black flared pants he might as well have had a whip in his hand given the authority with which he dominated the dancers.

Oliver lurched against the wall as Judy came towards him smiling, hands outstretched. 'Come on, darl,' she said kindly. 'Just go through the moves with me and then he'll pick on someone else.'

Oliver was relieved to see someone he knew at his first class. Judy was married to his doctor and he was staggered to discover that this plump, grey-haired, sixtyish woman, normally seated behind the reception desk at the surgery, was a tigress on the dance floor.

'I may not have any moves left in me,' he groaned as she put his hand on her waist and hers on his shoulder. 'Are you sure I should be doing so much my first time?'

'No half-measures with Ramon,' she said with a smile. 'He's a great believer in the deep-end theory. He tortures everyone the first week, so we've all been through it. Now we'll have a go and that'll keep him happy. Let's do the promenade, seven steps, a turn and then the corte and the quebrada – that's where you bend me backwards and lean over as though you're going to ravish me. Don't worry, you'll be fine. I'm a trained nurse.'

'I saw Angie the other day,' Trish said, 'in David Jones. She was buying a wok.'

'She told me,' Gayle said. 'An electric one. She said she'd seen you.'

'I'm surprised she didn't get one as a wedding present. So you've spoken to her, then?'

'This morning,' Gayle said towelling her hair with her free hand. Trish had called just as she was coming out of the shower.

'Is everything okay?'

'Great. Really. I mean, I've told you about Josh – it's made such a difference to me, Trish. He might come down, he and Dan, when I've sorted things out. You won't recognise him.'

'Yes, yes, I know, that's wonderful, Gayle. But I meant Angie. Is everything okay with Angie?'

'As far as I know. Why wouldn't it be?'

There was a pause. 'I don't know . . . ' Trish began. 'It's just that she didn't quite seem herself. I mean, she's normally so bubbly but I thought she was rather down.'

'She didn't say anything to me,' Gayle said. 'Is it Brian, d'you think?'

'No, I don't think so. Angie said she hadn't heard from him for more than a week now. He's away. When did you last speak to him?'

Gayle hesitated. 'A couple of weeks ago. I suppose I should find out when he's coming back to Perth.'

'Does it feel odd, being away so long, having all this happening? Fronting up to Josh and not being on the end of the phone for Brian whenever he chooses to call?'

'It feels fantastic. Like I've been let out of a cage. I still have to talk to Angie and Brian, though, and, Trish . . . I'll tell you more when I get home. More about me, and the past.'

'Yeah yeah,' Trish said. 'I know, all the secrets are coming out. Plenty of time for that. But Angie, you're sure she's okay?'

'I think she'd quickly be on the phone to me if she wasn't. Anyway, I'll be home soon.'

She sat down on the edge of the bed, dropped the phone back into her bag and stared at the concentric patterns on the carpet. Trisha's call had dampened her spirits. It was a reminder of what was ahead, that this particular adventure was coming to an end and a new and difficult one was about to begin. Three days left in Geraldton, and then a day's drive back to Perth. Perhaps she should find out where Brian was and when he'd be home. Reluctantly she got the phone out again and sent him a text.

Brian, with a sheaf of real estate agents' papers in his hands, was viewing a three-bedroom apartment in Manly, with a view across the water. He could just see himself here, sitting out on the balcony in the mornings in his dressing gown, morning papers, pot of coffee. It was small, of course, a third the size of the house, but Gayle had always complained that the house was too big. A mausoleum, she'd called it, which was hurtful really, considering he'd only been trying to do his best for her and Angie. Somewhere like this ought to keep her happy, though: sell the house, make a move over here, set up a consultancy business. On the other hand, he could afford to retire. Play the stock market a bit, some golf, get into a wine club, things he'd always wished he'd had time to do. Plenty of men younger than him were taking early retirement and plenty more wished they could afford it.

The agent was having a long and loud conversation on his mobile phone, and Brian went out onto the balcony and watched the ferry pulling in to the wharf. A week earlier he'd moved out of the Sydney CBD hotel into one in Manly to see if he liked it. He did. He felt better here, and when he thought of Perth he realised it was over for him. It reeked of failure and he didn't need that.

Ruminating on the past he recognised that he had got a few

things wrong. He should have spent more time with Gayle, for a start. It couldn't have been much fun for her stuck at home while he was travelling around the country and back and forth to Chicago. Well, he could put that right, they could do plenty together from now on. She could ditch the job and the study thing that she'd probably only been doing because she missed having him around. With a place like this, they'd have a great time, travel a bit – take a cruise, maybe – and he could buy a boat, one of those motor launch things.

'Top class location, isn't it?' said the agent, joining him on the balcony. 'It won't be around for long at this price, Mr Peterson. Someone'll snap it up in the next couple of days.'

'Give it a rest, mate,' Brian said. 'I wasn't born yesterday. This place has been on the market for a couple of months because the vendor is demanding an exorbitant price and won't look at a lesser offer. I've done my homework. Now, if you really want to sell me this joint you'd better stop playing silly buggers. Let's go and have a drink and talk about a deal.'

Gayle's message buzzed into Brian's phone several glasses of wine later, just as he was shaking hands with the agent. He stood in the shade of the palms in The Corso to read it. When was he going to be home? Perhaps her going away had been a good thing. Maybe now she was looking forward to getting back to normal again. He smiled at the text, wondering whether he should play her own game for a while, let her wait for an answer. Overnight, perhaps? Maybe a few days? He wasn't ready to go home yet, he had to feel right about it. He needed a bit more time and then, when he went home, he could tell it his way, make it seem more as though he'd been part of the decision. And there'd be the sweetener: a place in Manly, a whole new life. Perhaps it was turning out to be a blessing after all, a new start. That was what he needed, what they both needed: a new start.

Getting away from Port Hedland hadn't proved to be all that Marissa had hoped, but it was an improvement. Despite the way she felt, she was pretty sure she was giving the impression of normality, but she knew she could unravel at the slightest provocation. Part of her longed to be home, safe in the cocoon of her house, wind chimes singing on the verandah, the scent of lavender in the garden. But each time she imagined herself there she knew that something had changed. The isolation she had treasured was now much less appealing. The intimacy of this shared journey had given her a taste for the company of friends and, much as she wanted to be home, she didn't want this time to end.

'The day you trust someone, Marissa, is the day you're going to crack wide open,' Gina had once said, slipping the cards back into a pile after a reading. 'That day all hell's going to break loose and whatever it is you're hiding is going to hit the fan like the proverbial –'

'I'm not hiding anything,' Marissa had said.

'Maybe hiding's the wrong word, but whatever's festering away in there will burst out one day and, if it doesn't kill you, it'll set you free.'

'Good lord, Gina, you're even starting to *sound* like some wise old gypsy now.'

'I'm a wise old gypsy's granddaughter and another's great-granddaughter,' Gina said. 'I know what I'm talking about, believe me. One day, Marissa, you'll let down your guard and someone will sneak in. They'll get under your skin, may even love you, and when they do, you'll face your biggest ever battle.'

'I don't have battles,' Marissa had said, putting on her sunglasses despite the rather dark interior of Gina's rented cottage. 'I don't need to.'

Gina laughed and stood up, taking the money Marissa held out to her. 'Your battle is with yourself, Marissa, yourself and the past. As soon as you let someone in, you'll have to face the fact that they can see who you are and they might actually like what they see.'

Marissa had slipped her wallet back into her bag and headed for the door. 'The reading was good, Gina, the psychology was shonky. See you next time.' She hadn't, though, because next time she wanted her cards read she went to another tarot reader, who didn't know her.

Marissa picked out her costume for tonight, checked that the fastenings were okay and slipped it into her bag. Two more performances, two more days to go, and they'd be on the home stretch. Then what? Would these new friendships last, or was it just an element of the journey that would evaporate once they were home again? She knew that while a part of her desperately wanted the friendship, another part was terrified of breaking out of her emotional isolation.

There was a tap on her bedroom door. 'You ready?' Sonya called.

'Almost,' Marissa said. 'Come in.'

Sonya flopped backwards onto the bed. 'I'm exhausted,' she said. 'We're in our fifties, for god's sake – actually our late fifties. Aren't we supposed to take life easy, get our hair permed, wear fluffy slippers and have a rest in the afternoons?'

'Wrong generation,' Marissa said. 'You and Gayle are baby boomers, the generation that changed the world. You're still changing it now.'

'Why just us?' asked Gayle, who had followed Sonya in and was sitting on the other side of the bed. 'You too.'

Marissa shook her head. 'Too old to be a baby boomer. I'm a war baby.'

Sonya sat bolt upright. 'Get off, you're not. How old *are* you, Marissa?'

'Sixty-one, but don't tell anyone.'

'You mean don't tell Frank,' Sonya said.

'Not even him.'

'You're a great advertisement for belly dancing,' Gayle said. 'Hope I look as good as you in five years' time.'

'Will we still be dancing in five years' time?' Marissa asked, not looking up for fear of revealing her vulnerability.

'Of course we bloody will,' Sonya said, getting up. 'We'll be dancing, talking, listening to Normie Rowe, guzzling wine round your kitchen table, won't we, Gayle?'

'Obviously,' Gayle said, heading for the door. 'Why wouldn't we? Now, get a move on or we'll be late for our own performance.'

The chaos of Marissa's emotions made her weak and dizzy.

'You lead tonight, Gayle,' she said, trying to keep her voice calm as they went down the stairs. 'Right out in front. This is your night. And you tomorrow, Sonya.'

Gayle turned to her in shock. 'I couldn't,' she said, 'no way.'

'You did it the last night in Hedland, when I was a zombie.'

'I wasn't out in front.'

'No,' Marissa agreed, 'but you led. You drove that performance. Of course you can do it again, only this time you'll be leading from the front.'

'Yes,' Sonya said. 'You can, Gayle. You'll be great. Do it, and I'll do it tomorrow. Our last two nights, let's give it a go.'

Gayle took a deep breath. 'If you really think so . . . '

'I know so,' said Marissa, knowing too that she did not have it in herself to lead them tonight. 'This is the new you, the woman you've become – let's see her on the stage.'

'Hurricane Gayle,' Sonya said with a grin. 'Come on then, whip us up a storm.'

Frank could barely believe his luck. Just a few days earlier he'd been crying into his drink in the Norfolk, feeling a failure at every level, and then, suddenly, everything had changed. An informant he'd been cultivating for months had finally come good with a tip-off, and not just any ordinary tip-off but the ultimate one. By next morning, along with half a dozen other officers, he was on an unmarked launch heading up the coast towards a large yacht moored a kilometre from the coast off Dongara. As they drew closer, giving a convincing impression of a handful of blokes enjoying a few days' fishing and drinking, the police helicopter was on standby in Geraldton and a couple of patrol boats were positioning north and west of the target.

It was the most satisfying moment of Frank's years in the force when, pleading for a can of fuel to get them back to shore, they had pulled alongside with the grudging agreement of the skipper. As he leapt from the prow of the launch onto the deck of the yacht, Frank felt a shot of the old adrenaline course through his veins. Seconds later, in the cabin, the syndicate boss who had eluded him for months was his, caught literally with his pants down, staring shocked and helpless into the barrel of Frank's police revolver.

It was a coup and Frank knew it, planned at short notice and executed like clockwork. The long months of detective work, of waiting and near misses, had at last paid off. Not only did they have the big man, they had his girlfriend, clutching a sheet around her and blabbing everything she knew before the hand-cuffs were on. That and the drugs they found on board assured him they had evidence that would stand up in court. The operation had recruited and run teenagers as mules carrying heroin into the country through Bali, as well as trafficking in cocaine and crystal meth through a network of small boats moored off Fremantle and Geraldton.

Elated despite several hours of interviews, Frank dealt with the paperwork and walked out of the Geraldton police station, pausing to inhale the fresh night air. The adrenaline was still pumping: not only was the case stitched up but fate, or rather, the drug trade, had brought him to Geraldton at just the right time. Marissa and the others had arrived earlier in the week and were staying nearby. He needed to go to the pub, buy drinks for his team and join in the post mortem, but by the time he'd be able to get away, Marissa and the others would be back at the hotel.

The pub was crowded and noisy. News of the arrest had spread and the bar was packed with locals and off-duty police. As the drinks kept coming, the story was acquiring wilder and more heroic dimensions and it was building up to a long night of cele-bration, but Frank had other plans. He left a message on Marissa's phone and then joined the throng, accepted the plaudits, the slaps on the back, listened to the tall tales and bought a few rounds, and when he was sure he'd talked to everyone who'd played a part in the operation, he slipped quietly away.

It was ten o'clock when he got to the hotel, later than he'd intended, but when he glanced into the bar he saw Gayle and Sonya in a booth tucking into an enormous plate of sandwiches.

'Normie!' Sonya said. 'What a surprise. Come and join us.'

'Was it you who arrested those guys on the boat, Frank?' Gayle asked, pushing the sandwiches towards him. 'I heard it on the early news.'

He nodded and took a sandwich. 'Me and others. At bloody last, we've been after them for long enough. I thought I'd be retired or dead before we pinned this lot.'

'Well done, Frank, congratulations,' Sonya said, thumping his shoulder. 'Let's get you a drink. What'll it be?'

He hadn't realised how hungry he was – he hadn't eaten since breakfast – and he wolfed down the sandwich.

Gayle pushed a bowl of fries towards him. 'You look exhausted,' she said, 'and hungry. Dig in. Does Marissa know you're here?'

'I left a message on her phone,' he said. 'Where is she, anyway?'

'She went up to her room,' Gayle replied, glancing at her watch. 'Said she'd just be a minute. We've not been back long, but Sonya and I were ravenous so we didn't wait to order.'

He nodded and started on another sandwich as Sonya returned with the drinks.

'To the conquering hero!' she said, raising her glass. 'So, tell us all about it. Were you incredibly brave and commanding?'

'Naturally,' he said with a grin. 'Cheers!' He took a swig of his drink. 'There's a lot of stories circulating in the pub but, to be honest, it went like a dream.'

'Come on then,' Sonya urged, 'how did you get them –'

'Hang on,' Gayle said, 'Marissa should be here, she'll want to know too. What's she up to?' She pushed her plate aside. 'I'll go and get her. Don't start the story yet.'

'Why don't I go?' Frank said, getting up. 'What's the room number?'

'Twenty-five,' Sonya said. 'Hurry up, I want to hear all about it.'

Frank took the stairs two at a time and made his way along the passage. Whisky, exhaustion and adrenaline had pumped up his heart rate. Suddenly he remembered his first date, arriving at the girl's house to pick her up for the school dance. The same heady mix of excitement and nerves buzzed through him now as he tapped on the door. There was no answer.

'Marissa,' he called, knocking again. In the next room a television played softly, but there was no sound from twenty-five. Perhaps she'd decided to go to bed. But there was light shining under the door, strong light, so she couldn't have been asleep.

He knocked again, louder this time. 'Marissa, it's Frank,' he said, but there was no response. Perhaps she just wanted to be left alone. Disappointment shaved the edge off his mood, but as he turned away he thought he heard a sound, a moan from inside.

He knocked loudly with both hands and then, pressing his ear to the door, he heard the sound of water running. 'Marissa, Marissa, let me in,' he called, fear prickling his skin.

He turned the handle and the door swung open. There was no sign of her in the room but the shower was running, and steam drifted out through the open bathroom door. Frank was there in an instant and, wrenching back the shower curtain, he saw her, slumped in a corner of the cubicle, the water pounding down on her and swirling into the drain stained pink with her blood.

'But why?' Sonya said, fidgeting under the bright lights of the waiting room. 'Why didn't she say something? She seemed okay this evening.'

'Search me,' Gayle said. 'She'd seemed better since we got away from Port Hedland. Whatever it is, she's very good at hiding it.'

'I feel like such a lousy friend,' Sonya said. 'I was cross with her when she raced us off that morning. I should have been a bit more understanding, tried to draw her out, then she might have talked to us.'

Frank, elbows on his knees, hands clasped, shook his head. 'Don't blame yourself,' he said. 'Something like this was always going to happen.'

'You know, then?' Sonya said, turning to him. 'Whatever it is, you know about it?'

'No, but I know the signs. Post-traumatic stress – takes one to know one. Something happened in Port Hedland years ago, that's all I know, that and the fact that I don't think she's ever even talked about it, let alone got any help.'

'So why did we go there?' Gayle said. 'We didn't have to.'

Frank shrugged. 'Maybe she thought she could lay a few ghosts.' He rubbed his hands over his face, pushing down a wave of nausea. 'I've gotta get some air. Call me if anything happens, will you, I'll be just outside the door.'

He dropped some coins in the drink machine, took a bottle of water and wandered out. The night was crystal clear, the stars so much brighter than they ever seemed in the city. A couple of hours earlier he had stood outside the police station high on success and the anticipation of seeing Marissa. And now? He shook his head and took some deep breaths. Physically she would be fine. There was a vicious cut across her wrist, but the angle meant that it had missed the most vulnerable point. He was convinced that the cry he'd heard had come the moment before she fainted. It was a nasty injury and she was in shock, but it wasn't disastrous. It was the psychological effect that worried him. Gayle had mentioned her apparent calm and he knew it well: the sudden and unusual detachment alongside the recognition of being at the brink of collapse, then the chaos and the dizziness, and finally the mindless panic in response to some trigger. And in this case, Frank was in no doubt that he'd been the trigger – he who, above all people, should have known better. Marissa's recovery was assured but what would it mean for her, and would there be a place in it for him?

'Frank?' He jumped as Sonya materialised out of the shadows. 'They say we can go in and see her now, but only two at a time. We . . . Gayle and I . . . we think you should go in first – on your own.'

TWENTY-ONE

Gayle stared at the uncharacteristic evidence of Brian's last days in the house. Each room had its own collection of dirty glasses, plates, cups and empty wine and beer bottles. A pair of food- and wine-stained pyjamas lay on the bedroom floor alongside a pair of grey suit trousers and a blue shirt; several weeks' worth of unopened mail was spread across the study desk in an untidy pile and the smell from the kitchen had greeted her as soon as she opened the front door. The rubbish had been bagged but left standing in the corner and the aroma of old curry and rotting meat made her gag. It was two weeks old at least and she could barely bring herself to pick it up, dump it in a larger bag and take it outside.

Her irritation was mixed with confusion; Brian was not domesticated but neither was he a slob. He liked things clean and tidy, and while he preferred to have someone else cleaning up after him he was not one to leave a place in a mess. And he was really neurotic about taking out the garbage every day. Clearly something very strange had been going on. He'd sent a vague reply to her text message saying he was busy but would let her know which day he'd be back. Presumably she had a few days to sort herself out before facing him, but right now she had to face his mess.

Angie had called to say she was on her way over. 'I'm dying to hear all about it,' she'd said. 'I'll be over by four and then maybe we can go out later and eat.'

Gayle found an apron, collected up the crockery, bagged up the empty wine bottles and some out-of-date milk and smoked salmon she'd found in the fridge, and chucked the dirty washing into the laundry. With every task, her anger increased. Had Brian deliberately left the place like this so she'd have to clean it up? Deciding to tackle him about it and to get a firm date for his return, she dialled his number, but it diverted to message bank.

'What *is* that smell?' Angie asked from the front door. 'It's like dead rats.'

'Garbage. Specifically, some ageing curry,' Gayle said, wiping her hands on her apron. 'Dad left it on the kitchen bench when he went away; it's going to take a while to get rid of the stink.'

Angie screwed up her face. 'Good thing you're back now or it would've walked out the door on its own. Did you try some air freshener?'

Gayle nodded. 'Lemon and lavender is no match for it. I've opened all the windows. Anyway, darling, how are you?'

'Okay,' Angie said, hugging her. 'I really missed you, Mum. I'm so glad you're back. Is Marissa okay?'

'Not too bad,' Gayle said, looking away. 'It was a minor accident, she'll be fine.'

'Good. I got you some milk, shall I make some tea?'

Gayle thought Angie looked a bit pale, perhaps tired. She was struck by a sudden awkwardness. For several weeks she'd been planning what she would say to Angie, thinking about how, when and where to do it. Now the prospect overshadowed everything: it seemed unnatural, unfair almost, not to tell her straight away.

'Please,' she said, 'I'm just going to take my bags upstairs and have a wash.'

She dumped her bags in the bedroom, and stared at herself in the long mirror. The enormity of what she was about to do descended on her; at a distance she'd been able to consider it in a practical, almost detached way. She had felt strong, and capable of anything. Now her reflection showed a small, pale figure dwarfed by the task ahead. Had she always looked so small and insignificant in this mirror? The sense of inertia and powerlessness that had characterised her life in this house returned with a force that made her dizzy. She was stronger, she knew she was. She just had to remember how she had felt when she'd led the dancing. The old Gayle could never have done that. Where was the power and energy of the dance now, when she most needed it?

'Are you coming down,' Angie called, 'or do you want me to bring the tea up there while you unpack?'

'Unpack,' Gayle thought, 'what's the point? I'll tell her now, and tomorrow I'll find a place to go. I have to get out of here as soon as I can.'

'Mum?'

'I'm coming down,' she called, and with the flat of her hand she patted the top of the vanity unit in the familiar drum rhythm. 'It's just another performance, a different sort of dance,' she told herself. 'Another performance straight from the heart,' and, straightening her shoulders, she made her way down the stairs as the phone rang.

'He's not here,' Angie said. 'No, I don't think Mum knows, but don't you have a copy of his diary?'

'Who is it?' Gayle asked quietly.

Angie's face was white with shock as she held out the phone. 'It's Dad's office. They need to talk to him about the corporate credit card. He should have handed it over on the twenty-fourth, the day they let him go.'

'I don't understand why he didn't just tell us,' Angie said later, sitting cross-legged on the lounge and tucking into a large slice of the pizza that had just been delivered. 'It's so unlike him. You'd think he'd be raging around like a wounded bull, expecting us all to run after him, tell him how unfair it is, all that – like he did when you went away.'

Gayle shook her head. 'No,' she said, 'not really. It was different with me because, angry as he was, he would have felt he was still in control, that this was an aberration on my part, but a temporary one. So he could make a big fuss with as many people as possible, and then it dies down and everything returns to normal, but this – this is different.'

'Makes no sense to me,' Angie said. 'Just buggering off like that without saying a word. It's not Dad's way.'

'Look, what's happened to him is huge. His whole identity is based on his work, and now the ground's been cut from under him. He's worked hard and the money and the status have been hugely important to him.'

'I can understand the money,' Angie interrupted, 'but what status is there in marketing cigarettes? People think it's indefensible.'

'Some people,' Gayle answered.

'Well, you and I do for a start.'

'Sure, but we're not everyone. We're probably not even the majority. Tobacco is a legal substance, and growing it is a valuable industry in Australia. And we shouldn't forget that, despite our objections, we've lived very comfortably on the profits. No, status in the circles Brian moves in is really important to him. That's why it makes sense to me that he would keep quiet, go off somewhere and give himself time to construct his own version of what happened, and what happens next.'

Angie shrugged. 'I still think it's weird. Where d'you think he's gone?'

'Sydney. I'd bet on it,' Gayle said. 'He calls it his natural home. He'll be somewhere in Sydney, writing his own story. And it'll be a story that gives him some say in this decision. It'll be about him being offered something unacceptable and turning it down, or him being placed in an untenable situation and choosing to go rather than do whatever it was they wanted. By the time we hear it, the humiliation will have become a choice and a new opportunity.'

'You don't know that,' Angie said. 'He might just be very upset, depressed, drinking himself under the table somewhere.'

'He'll be doing the latter, that's for sure,' Gayle said. 'But depressed? No, he's done that. That's what I saw when I came home: the mess. That was the initial shock and depression, but the fact that he's gone means he's moved on, he's rebuilding himself somewhere.'

'You don't sound very worried about him,' Angie said.

'Brian's tough,' Gayle replied. 'He's also quite vulnerable but in a way that builds his toughness. He can always rewrite what happens so that he's in the right.'

'Whoo hoo, cynical Mum!'

'You know it's true,' Gayle said, looking straight at her. 'You've seen it often enough.'

'Yeah, but all the same . . . and anyway, if you're right, what do we do? Tell him we know or pretend to believe his version?'

Gayle hesitated. 'It's not as straightforward as that,' she said. 'Angie, there's something I have to tell you – several things, in fact – about Brian and about me and . . . well, about you. None of it's easy and I've been agonising over how and when to tell you, but in view of what's happened I need to do it now.'

When he woke on the morning after his first dance lesson, Oliver had the distinct impression that he'd been run over by a truck. Everything ached and, being something of a hypochondriac, he lay there wondering if he had flu, or perhaps glandular fever. As he emerged slowly from the fug of sleep, however, he remembered the previous evening's torture at the hands of Ramon. The physical pain detracted somewhat from the satisfaction of his eventual triumph, but not enough to spoil his pleasure. At the end of the class, Ramon had pronounced him the main man and, surprisingly, found it necessary to kiss him on both cheeks.

'You will be a fine dancer, Oliver,' he said. 'You have the lightness of a panther and the speed of a leopard – magnificent.'

Oliver had smiled in spite of his embarrassment. 'I'm surprised he can tell all that after just one lesson,' he whispered to Judy.

'He can't, dear,' she said. 'Take no notice. He says it to everyone, however much they clodhopped around the room. Torture then praise, that's Ramon's recipe for success. Not that *you* clodhopped, of course, but you know what I mean.'

Oliver was pretty sure he *had* clodhopped for most of the evening and that any hint of leopard or panther in his performance would have been too fleeting to be noticeable. But he had enjoyed the praise, which, he felt, was an acknowledgement of his endurance, and an admission to the fellowship of Latin American dancers. The morning after, though, he realised how appallingly unfit he'd become. It was months – years, probably – since he'd done any exercise; not since his run-in with the treadmill had he done anything more energetic than walk from the car park to his office, or stroll down to the cappuccino strip. No wonder he felt so rough after a bit of dancing. It was a warning that he needed to do something more than once-weekly dance classes – indeed, he needed to do something in order to *survive* the dance classes. And so, moving cautiously at first, he got himself out of bed and into a very hot shower, where bits of him began to soften and loosen a bit.

'Must keep moving,' he told himself, and painfully he donned his tracksuit and headed for the Leisure Centre, where he began some slow and rather ragged laps of the warm, shallow, twenty-five metre pool. Since then he had swum almost every day, slowly increasing the distance, and after the first week he graduated to the open air fifty-metre pool and felt his coordination and stamina improving as he ploughed up and down in the medium speed lane.

How quickly one built a habit, he thought, and how quickly one could feel the beneficial effects of regular exercise. By the fourth class, even Judy was commenting on how much more flexible he was, how he had loosened up and started to use his hips. Hips: a part of his body with which he had long ago lost contact. Loosened-up hips, Oliver thought, might be very handy if he ever got to have sex again – which, at the moment, seemed highly unlikely, but then you never knew what might happen. And that was the other thing – he was feeling more optimistic.

'Exercise is a great tonic,' Andrew said. 'It'll help you shift some of your emotional blocks.'

Oliver had heard about the potential problems in client/therapist relations; how, for the first few visits, the client would often be resistant, hostile even, to the therapist, and then there would be a breakthrough in the therapeutic process at which point the patient may well imagine himself in love with the therapist. There was no way that Oliver thought he was in love with Andrew, but he did admire him and find him interesting and wished they could have a drink or dinner together.

'Socialising is not part of the therapeutic relationship, Oliver,' Andrew explained. 'It's important that we stay within the boundaries for both our sakes, yours in particular.'

'But there are things I'd like to discuss with you,' Oliver said. 'Things about my research which I think would be interesting to you, and I'd value your opinion.' And he explained about the book he was writing and the research and interviews he'd recorded in Berlin.

'Fascinating,' Andrew said, chewing one of the arms of his glasses. 'I suppose we could perhaps have a professional, research-based relationship, as long as we're both clear about its nature.'

'Oh, absolutely clear,' Oliver said. And so on the following Sunday morning, after his swim, Oliver prepared with enthusiasm for Andrew's arrival. He was feeling loose limbed and positively rejuvenated. On a tray he set out the coffee plunger, mugs, a small jug of cream and some almond croissants he'd picked up on his way home from the pool. Then he set up his cassette player on the table on the deck.

'Now, this is Helga's tape,' he said, slipping it into the cassette player when Andrew had done with admiring the house and the wisteria that rambled over the pergola. 'This is the one I find most fascinating. Why don't you start with this while I make the coffee?'

He stood in the kitchen, waiting for the kettle to boil, leaning against the sink and whistling contentedly through his teeth, half listening to the slow drone of Helga's voice drifting in through the open window. And then he stopped whistling. He didn't notice the kettle switching itself off as he moved closer to the window. As he listened again to Helga's story, he realised for the first time he was hearing a much larger story, his own story and Gayle's, and that of millions of other people; a universal story of people trapped in the prisons of their past, their upbringing. He realised that he was listening again to the women's stories that Joan had told him, stories of the sexual politics of fear and intimidation, of love and duty, of powerlessness and inertia even in the face of moral and ethical dilemmas. He was overcome with a desire to bang his head against the wall in frustration at his own blindness, for now he understood his fascination with Helga's tape.

He walked out onto the deck and sat down opposite Andrew. 'I think I'm a complete fool,' he said, reaching out to stop the tape. 'Somehow, while I read about those women, while I talked to them and then listened to the tapes, I thought that to stay silent, effectively to collude with their husbands through their silence, must mean that they somehow lacked moral fibre, must be in some way evil.'

Andrew smiled at him. 'And now you think differently?'

Oliver dropped his head into his hands. 'I suppose it's that we are all the products of our upbringing, not just our parents' but the circumstances and societies in which we're born and grow.'

'But you're a historian, Oliver, a *social* historian. You must always have known that.'

'Of course, this is ridiculous. Of course I've always known it – but in my head, only in my head. As I was listening to Helga then, for the umpteenth time, I knew it in my heart, and in my gut. I knew it at a personal level, not just a theoretical, intellectual level. I felt myself in there, and my friend Gayle, and then fragments of lots of other people –' He stopped suddenly, embarrassed to find himself choked with emotion.

'I was so judgemental, expecting women to be morally and ethically perfect. Suddenly it all seems so sad and confusing. My mother – she wasn't perfect by any means, and she certainly didn't expect it of others. She never intended that I would become such a narrow, boring prig.' He pulled out his handkerchief and blew his nose noisily. 'I'm sorry, Andrew – boundaries, I know you said boundaries, I didn't mean to . . . .'

Andrew reached across the table and patted Oliver's arm. 'Don't worry, Oliver,' he said, 'these things happen. Why don't you sit there and I'll go inside and make the coffee?'

'Yes,' Oliver said, nodding. 'Thank you. I'm such a late developer, aren't I? Everyone understands this messy, human, personal stuff except me.'

Andrew laughed and got up from the table. 'No, Oliver, by no means, but you've lived a long time in your head. You survived on intellect and now you're gaining a new and more complex understanding of the human condition. The journey from the head to the heart is the longest journey in the world and some never make it.'

'But I've wasted so much time with my stupidity and blindness.'

'It's not unusual. Midlife is the turning point for many of us. You tried to fit your relationships with women into one particular box, but sexual attraction, love and relationships are chaotic and, as Helga points out, much that's shameful or inexplicable is done in their name.'

TWENTY-TWO

'There is no way I'm leaving you on your own tonight, Marissa,' Sonya said, dumping her bag on the floor. 'We agreed this in the car, with Gayle. You promised to stay with me. Okay, you changed your mind, you want to be in your own place and I can well understand that, but, that being so, I'm sleeping in your spare room and I'm not leaving until I'm confident that you're okay.'

'I won't do anything silly, Sonya,' Marissa said. 'Honestly. I totally lost it, I know that, I went right over the top, but I'll be fine now. Look at me, I'm fine.'

Sonya looked at her across the kitchen table. 'I look at you, Marissa, and I see someone who's shattered and a bit spacey; a woman who looks rather worse than the night she started to play with razor blades. Sorry – I'm not subtle. Probably I should be dancing round you not referring to any of this, but then, I've never been in this situation before.'

Marissa nodded and looked away. 'I'll make some tea.'

'Good idea.'

They stood in awkward silence on opposite sides of the kitchen table, not looking at each other. Marissa switched on the kettle and, unlocking the back door, walked out onto the deck. Her neighbour Alberto had kept the lawn mowed for her and pulled out the worst of the weeds, but everything needed attention. The sunflowers, just bursting into bloom, had grown tall and bushy; nasturtiums roamed wildly, wrapping themselves around the

229

foot of the orange tree, and crowding the daisies. The table on the deck was coated with garden dust; dead leaves had blown in and settled around the ceramic dish painted with lemons that always stood in its centre. She blew away the worst of the dust and pulled out her favourite chair. Its cushion was covered in cat's hair; clearly there'd been a regular feline visitor in her absence. It all looked tired and a little neglected, but it was hers, her sanctuary, and she was thankful to be back.

A madness had overtaken her that night. She could remember feeling shaky and light-headed as they left the hotel, feeling that she needed one of the others to lead the dance or she might not make it. Autopilot had got her through the dancing but back at the hotel, in the noise and harsh lighting of the foyer, panic overtook her. If she were alone she'd be all right, she could calm down, get through it, she thought.

'Just need to run up to the room,' she'd said. 'I won't be long.'

'Okay, but hurry up,' Gayle responded. 'We need you.'

'Yeah,' Sonya added. 'The sisterhood is incomplete without you.'

Sisterhood: the word buzzed in her head. What she longed for was reaching out to her but now, having sought it, she wanted to run from it. The long passage to the room seemed to sway ahead of her, and she fumbled for her key and sank onto the bed. She couldn't go back downstairs. Sleep might help. She must stay here, stay calm, try to breathe.

The phone startled her; it was the answering service callback. Try to be normal, try to be calm, play the message, she told herself. She listened to Frank's voice and her head started to spin. The message kept repeating itself and there was a painful drumming in her ears. It seemed as though the bed, the very room, was shaking. She dropped the phone and grasped her head, it seemed gripped by an iron belt.

That was when the coldness hit her, a terrible cold that made her teeth chatter. Hot water, that would help, hot water . . . She staggered to her feet and stumbled across the room, hitting her head on the bathroom doorjamb. Dragging her clothes off, she fumbled with the taps and that was when she saw the razor. It seemed so logical, so right, the answer to the cold, the shaking and, better still, the answer to the fear and to the great scar, silent and brooding for so long, that had now reopened into a livid wound.

'Chamomile,' Sonya said, carrying the pot in one hand and two mugs in the other. 'Chamomile, I think that's what you like.'

Marissa looked up, jolted from her reverie. 'But *you* don't.'

Sonya shrugged. 'I can get used to it, as long as my supply of caffeine isn't completely cut off.'

'You must have things you want to do at home,' Marissa said.

'Oh, you don't get rid of me that easily,' Sonya said, pouring the tea.

'That's not what I meant. It's just that, well . . . what I said . . . we've been away a while, you must have heaps of things of your own you want to do, and I'm stuffing that up.'

Sonya pushed a mug towards her and sat at the other end of the table with her own, looking out onto the garden. 'You know, Marissa,' she said, 'you're right. There's heaps of things to do, always are when you've been away. Opening the mail, airing the house, checking what's grown in the garden, unpacking, catching up with people . . . but right now none of it seems more important than being with a friend who's going through a crisis. Right now, that seems the most important, most special thing, the thing I most want to do.'

She looked across at Marissa. 'If these last weeks have meant to you what they've meant to me you'll know why I want to be . . . *have* to be here now. It's called friendship; it's not a new concept, although my guess is that it's a scary one for you despite the fact that you show signs of being very good at it.'

She paused before continuing: 'Sorry. Sorry I'm being patronising and facetious. It's because I feel so inadequate. Look, Marissa, the other night Gayle and I thought we'd lost you. We were both really frightened and, frankly, pretty pissed off, and we don't want it to happen again. Nor does poor bloody Frank, who doesn't know what's hit him –'

'It's not about Frank,' Marissa cut in.

'No, but you might want to explain that to him. Obviously it's not about Frank, but he *is* a factor.' She stopped suddenly and leaned across the table to take Marissa's hand. 'Don't make it harder on any of us, darl. You asked us to dance with you and we did, and a whole lot more happened as a result, so now you're stuck with us. Get used to it. Practise feeling what it's like to have people who care about you, because we're not going anywhere and we're not going to let you down.'

The last time Brian had shaved was on the morning of the day he got the sack. For the next four days while his life stood still, his beard had grown; when he decided it was time to act, he soaped up his shaving brush, got out his razor and then put it away again and ran his hand over his chin. Who'd care if he shaved or not? Why bother?

By the time he was ready to fly back to Perth, he thought the beard was shaping up rather nicely. His hair had grown too. Normally he'd have had it cut by now but it seemed to go well with the beard, so, rather than get his usual once-over from the barber, he went instead to a unisex hair salon and, for the first time in his life, had his hair styled and his beard trimmed and shaped. As he put his jacket on and stood at the desk while the receptionist swiped his card, he thought he looked pretty good. He hadn't had a beard since the seventies and it had suited him then too. His hair had been redder in those days but it had faded over the years and was now streaked with grey. He thought it looked distinguished. He no longer appeared the company man, but his own man. He wondered what Angie and Gayle would say when they saw him.

'Hardly recognised you, Mr Peterson,' said the clerk on duty in the Qantas Club. 'The beard suits you, if you don't mind me saying so.'

It was reassuring to be recognised, to be greeted in at least some of the places to which he'd been so accustomed.

Once on board he opened his briefcase and went through the paperwork again. In the Manly hotel he'd made a full assessment of his assets, superannuation, investments on and off shore, cash in the bank accounts, a rough valuation on the house and a couple of small commercial premises in Perth's northern suburbs. He'd also drawn up a financial plan for the future. There was the house to be sold, some investments could be shifted around and the nature of some of them changed, but on the whole there was plenty of scope. A lot of what they owned was in Gayle's name and there was no reason to change that. He just might need her to sign off a release on one portfolio if he decided he wanted business premises, but he was shifting closer to the prospect of a life of leisure. The last few weeks had made him realise how totally his time and energy had been focused on work; suddenly liberated, he was discovering what he'd missed. The real estate agent introduced him to the golf club and he enjoyed long, leisurely games with interesting new acquaintances. He was invited to a wine club, and to a day's fishing on a luxurious launch.

There was life beyond tobacco marketing, and he was glad that particular episode was over. Gayle would be pleased too – she'd always objected to it. Now that she'd got the damn fool dancing business out of her system they could concentrate on the future. It had briefly occurred to him that he should let her know about the Manly apartment, check that she liked the idea, but he had always made the big decisions, organised their life together, and she could hardly complain about this the way she had about the house. It was time to go back to Perth and get things going from that end.

Brian leaned back in his seat watching the bed of cloud beneath the aircraft wings and reflecting on his own ability to move forward, in this case at great speed. Three weeks ago he was in the pits. Now he owned a new home and had opened the door to a fresh start.

'So what do you think?' he asked, dropping his bag on the floor and smiling at the look of surprise on Gayle's face. 'Improvement, eh?'

'It suits you,' she said, but without the enthusiasm he felt was warranted. 'Makes you look thinner – yes, an improvement.'

She'd only been home a few days but Brian didn't think she

looked any better for her weeks away. In fact, he thought she looked quite pale and strained. But then she was probably worried about having upset him and so she should be. He had a right to be angry, but equally he could now afford to be generous . . . magnanimous – that was the word. He would add it to his repertoire of negotiating options. It was only when he went upstairs to the bedroom that he sensed something was different. He wasn't a particularly observant person at the best of times and couldn't for the life of him make out what it was. The bedroom and bathroom were exceptionally tidy, and the vanity unit was pleasantly free of Gayle's various creams and potions.

Brian washed his face and hands and studied his hair. It seemed that having one's hair styled rather than just cut required rather more maintenance than he was used to. Was this the time to apply more gel or not? How did one tell? It looked okay, he thought. Gayle could probably advise him, and Angie would definitely know. He stepped back, satisfied with his appearance, and made his way downstairs, and that was when he became aware that the strangeness he'd detected in the bedroom seemed to have seeped into the other rooms. There was an uneasy atmosphere which was a little disturbing. Perhaps it was just Gayle's long absence and the awkwardness she must be feeling about her shoddy behaviour.

'Good to see you back,' he said, rubbing his hands. 'All went well, did it?'

Gayle nodded. 'Yes thanks, very well,' she said. 'And you? Good trip to Sydney?'

'Excellent. Lots to tell you, got some interesting new ideas. I fancy a drink. Usual for you?'

They sat, for some reason, at the kitchen table. Later when Brian reflected on it he didn't know why they hadn't sat somewhere comfortable. He wondered if she'd done it deliberately. The kitchen was her domain, the only area she never complained about; perhaps she'd wanted to drop her bombshell in her own territory. It was a beautiful evening, clear and mild, and the view out through the open glass doors, over the terrace and across the river to the city, was spectacular at dusk.

'Well – big news,' he began. 'There's going to be a few changes. I've left the company.'

'I know,' Gayle said. 'The office called. They need you to return the corporate credit card, and sort out payment for anything charged since they . . . since you left.'

'Damn,' he said, suddenly and unnervingly wrong footed, 'I forgot about that. I'll sort it out tomorrow. That bastard Mal put me in an impossible situation. Moral dilemma, really, something I couldn't go along with. I'll tell you about that later.' He took a swig of his drink. 'I've no doubt bloody Rod Campbell in Chicago was behind it.'

'I thought it might be something like that,' Gayle said. 'I thought that's what you'd say.'

She sounded a bit weird and Brian felt as though he'd lost ground. It was a damn nuisance she'd got that call, but still, no turning back.

'One can only go along so far with things that one doesn't think are right,' he said.

She nodded without looking at him. 'I'm sorry, it must have been hard for you.'

Brian swallowed the remains of his drink and got up to pour another. 'It hasn't been easy but, you know, Gayle, I'm starting to feel it's all for the best. All those years I kept my head down, worked hard, gave it all I'd got, and in the end they don't appreciate you. So, I thought, I'm sixty next month, this is the time for a new start, time to enjoy the good life. Refill?'

Gayle shook her head. 'Brian, I –'

He held up his hand to stop her. 'Hang on, haven't finished. It's a gift, really, you know. It takes a bit of a crisis to make you sit up and take notice, take stock, and that's what I've done.' He reached for his briefcase. 'First of all, I thought we'd make a move. I've bought a place in Manly –'

'Brian, look,' she cut in, 'before you go any further there is something I need to tell you.'

'Can't it wait?' he said. 'This is big stuff, Gayle.'

'So is mine,' she said, and there was an unfamiliar sharp edge to her voice.

Magnanimous, he reminded himself. 'Okay, go ahead, but I can promise you you're going to like this.' And he leaned back and folded his arms.

'You're probably not going to like what I'm going to say. The first thing is that it's over, Brian. We're finished, our marriage is over. I'm leaving you and I want a divorce –'

'Ah, bloody hell!' he said, throwing his hands in the air. 'What is this? Some claptrap from those dancing women? Divorce, indeed! Don't play silly buggers with me, Gayle.'

'I'm serious,' she said. 'It's over, I'm leaving – in fact, I've already left. I've moved my things out of the house. I've just come back to talk to you.'

'But you've only been back a few days.'

'There's more,' she said. 'I saw Josh in Broome. I told him everything. I've also told Angie. They both know that you aren't Angie's father and they know about the deal we made, about my affair, everything.'

Brian felt the colour drain from his face. 'You what –' he began, but again she stopped him.

'I haven't finished yet. I went to see Josh to put right what I did all those years ago. I should never have allowed you to throw him out. I should have left with him. That was what I wanted to do. I stayed for Angie, and then because I was too scared to do anything else. But that's all changed now, and Josh and Angie are adults and have a right to know the truth.'

Rage consumed him. He could feel the pressure pounding in his temples, his heart racing. He clenched his hands into fists and smashed them down on the table, making her flinch.

'You had no right, Gayle, no fucking right. What the hell do you think you're doing? That dancing's sent you right off your stupid bloody head . . . I don't believe this . . . '

'I still haven't finished.'

'Oh really?' he yelled. 'What? I suppose you told fucking Mal as well, did you, and put a notice in the newspaper?'

'I've found a lawyer and he'll be writing to you. I think it's best if we let the lawyers work out some sort of settlement.'

'*Lawyers*?' he roared. '*Settlement*? You have no idea what you're talking about, woman. There won't be any divorce, or any settlement. We're selling the house, like you always wanted, and moving to Manly. No divorce, you hear me? No fucking divorce. But Christ knows what damage you've done, Gayle. We had a deal, you promised me. I kept my side of the bargain. Jeez, what about Angie . . . ?'

'You didn't keep to the bargain, Brian –'

'I bloody well did. It wasn't me who shot my mouth off.'

'Part of the bargain was that you would lay off me –'

'I did,' he said, knocking his chair backwards onto the floor as he stood up. 'I never laid a finger on you since, so don't start saying I did . . . .'

The extraordinary thing, he thought later, was that she kept going, kept arguing with him. She didn't back down, didn't suddenly go quiet like she always did. She kept going, trying to shoot him down every time.

'No, you didn't bash me again, but it was more than that, Brian. You promised the bullying would stop but it didn't. In fact, absolutely nothing changed. You still bullied me whenever I didn't agree with you. You ignored what I said, overruled me, intimidated me about everything.' She paused and seemed to be swallowing hard. 'You even bullied me into sex when I didn't want –'

'You never wanted it,' he spat. 'Not for years.'

'No,' she said, standing up. 'I didn't. You know why? I couldn't bear the thought of it with someone who just made use of me, who never listened to me, who never had any respect for me or interest in who I was or what I cared about.'

Brian felt as though his head were going to burst, and it was hard for him to breathe. He kicked another chair away from the table and sat down abruptly, taking deep breaths.

'What about Angie?' he said. 'My girl . . . I treated her like my daughter. She *is* my daughter. I love that girl.'

'I know you do,' Gayle said, softening, 'and she loves you. It's me she's angry with. She's refused to speak to me since I told her. As far as Angie's concerned, you're the victim and I'm the villain. She wants to see you as soon as possible.' She got up and took her handbag off the workbench.

'Where the hell are you –' he began.

'I think it's best you have time to think about this and calm down,' she said. 'But there's probably not much more that we can say to each other that's productive. You never listened to me, anyway, so it's best to let the lawyers sort it out.'

'But you can't . . . I'm your husband, this is your home . . . '

'I've told you, Brian. I've left,' Gayle said. 'I don't live here anymore.'

TWENTY-THREE

Frank had been flat out since he got back from Geraldton: interrogating prisoners, interviewing witnesses, dealing with the media, meeting with the police prosecutor, and generally doing everything possible to build a watertight case. Thankful that he had something so demanding to focus on, he'd worked long hours and fallen into bed each night mentally and physically exhausted. Now, in the passenger seat of a squad car heading back to the station after interviewing another possible witness, he was in an emotional and psychological no-go zone in which he operated mechanically, feeling nothing but detachment. He was numbed by what had happened with Marissa, by his own stupidity and the role it had played in that awful night. Whatever had overwhelmed her, he knew that his message had been the catalyst, and if he needed any confirmation of that, it was in Marissa's reaction to him at the hospital.

Accident and Emergency was busy with the usual Friday night parade of injured drunks, road accidents and suspected heart attacks. Frank was used to hospitals, particularly emergency wards, used to facing the injured victims and perpetrators of crimes, their faces a mass of wounds and stitching, or heavily bandaged, tubes and masks connecting them to drips and oxygen. He was used to the smell of fear, to weary, stricken relatives and overworked medical staff, and he had learned to manage it all by focusing on the situation and what needed to be done, leaving his emotions at the door. But that night it was different.

Objectivity and detachment had evaporated the moment he opened the door of Marissa's room – he'd been a seething mass of raw nerves and chaotic feelings.

'She's in here, Inspector,' the nurse said, opening the curtains. 'Not too long now, please.'

Marissa, propped up on pillows, eyes closed, was attached to a drip and her wounded wrist was heavily bandaged.

'Marissa,' Frank said softly. 'Marissa, how're you doing?'

Her eyes shot open and he could see that it took her a few seconds to focus.

'Hi,' he tried again, moving to take her hand. 'So you *are* awake.'

Her eyes were black with fear – or was it anger? 'Go away, Frank,' she said, turning her head away from him. 'I don't want to see you. Please go away.'

He shifted his weight and drew back his hand. 'I just wanted to see if you were okay . . . I . . . '

'Well, you've seen me, and I'm okay. So now you can go.'

Frank hesitated. Nothing in his life until now had felt like this, the yearning to make it right, the agony of understanding some of what had happened, along with the pain that neither logic nor understanding could dispel.

'Sure,' he said. 'Sure, okay. I understand. If that's what you want. I'll . . . I'll come back tomorrow –'

'No,' she said. 'Don't come back.' She paused and turned to face him again. 'You probably saved my life . . . '

'I don't think so.'

'I ought to be grateful but gratitude isn't what I feel.'

'I don't want gratitude –' he began.

'Fine. So just go,' she'd said. 'Just go, Frank, and don't come back. Please don't come back.'

Frank brought his mind back to the present as the uniformed constable slowed the car at the traffic lights, and slipped into the left hand lane to wait for the green arrow.

'We were down here last night,' he commented as the lights changed. 'Great big house along here on the left.'

Frank straightened up and glanced at where the officer was

pointing. 'That place?' he asked. 'Slow down, constable.' Letting down the window he peered in through the open gates of the property. It was Gayle's place. He'd driven in and around that circular rose bed the morning he'd given her a lift to the airport. 'So what was the trouble?'

'Odd, really,' the constable said. 'Got a call from the lady, a Mrs . . . er . . . '

'Peterson?' Frank supplied.

'Peterson, that's it. Know them do you, sir?'

'Just get on with it.'

'Yes, sir. Well, we got this call saying that she and her husband had had a bit of an argument. She was outside the house and he was inside smashing the place up. She was afraid he might do himself some damage. We were the nearest car so we came in and had a chat with him.'

'And?'

'It seems that she'd told him she was leaving him and he wasn't real keen on the idea, so he was laying into the furniture. Anyway, we calmed him down. He's a big bloke and he'd done quite a bit of damage – hurled a few chairs through the windows, thrown a lot of stuff in the swimming pool, cut his foot on some broken glass, but nothing serious. He was all right when we left.'

'And Mrs Peterson?'

'She went off to wherever she was staying.'

'Which was?'

Constable Ng screwed up his face. 'Como, I think. She did give us the address.'

Frank took his organiser from his inside pocket and keyed in Sonya's name. 'Twenty-three Antrim Street?'

'That's right, Antrim Street.'

'Okay, constable. Just take the next left, will you, and run me over there now.'

'Ah, you heard about last night,' Sonya said. 'Gayle's just gone down to Fremantle to see Marissa. She's fine, though – Gayle, I mean. I think she feels the worst is over now she's told Brian.

From this point on it's just a matter of hanging in there and getting the legal stuff sorted out as soon as possible.'

'Must have been pretty hard for her, though,' Frank said. 'From my brief encounter with Brian Peterson he's not a bloke I'd want to take on too often. If she'd let me know I could have hung around in the background in case it got nasty.'

Sonya smiled. 'Aren't you a knight in shining armour? Oh, get off with you, I'm only taking the piss. Why don't you come in? Gayle'll be back soon. Have a glass of wine. I'm making risotto, there'll be plenty for three. Oh . . . ' she had just looked past him to the car. 'What about the young bloke?'

Frank hesitated, then said, 'Well, if you're sure, I can send him back to the station.'

'What'll you have?' Sonya asked, opening a packet of rice when he came back.

'A beer, please,' Frank said, looking around the kitchen. 'Nice place.'

'In the fridge, help yourself,' she said, reaching up to a high cupboard and lifting out a salad bowl. 'Yes, it's nice. I was thinking of moving somewhere a bit fancier but now I'm not. Getting away for a while helps sort out the priorities. Anyway, you're probably dying to know how Marissa is.'

Frank walked to the other side of the workbench and pulled out a stool. 'Obviously. Subtlety is not my thing, and I clearly don't know when to leave well alone.' He twisted the top off a VB stubby.

'I'm not so sure about that,' Sonya said, sitting down opposite him and reaching for her own glass. 'Quite subtle, I think, and sensitive. Maybe too sensitive for your own good at the moment.'

Frank shrugged and looked away. 'So how is she?'

'Fragile, I'd say. Still fragile, but improving. Physically she's fine, her wrist is healing well, but emotionally it's going to take a while. Do you think it was a real attempt to kill herself? If so, she wasn't very good at it.'

Frank took a swig of his beer. 'I think it's hard to tell. She was in a bad way and she had a panic attack. Sometimes people freeze. They become totally detached and cut off from everything around them. Others harm themselves and it's not really clear whether it's suicidal in intent or something to do with the belief – conscious or otherwise – that physical pain will kill the emotional pain. My feeling is that it was the latter, and I don't think she'd done it before – but then, what would I know?'

'Quite a lot, it would seem,' Sonya said. 'Anyway, I stayed there with her for a couple of nights and despite her protests I think she was glad of it. I've been down to see her every day since then and so has Gayle, and we'll keep doing that for a while. That house means a lot to her – it's almost like a cocoon and she feels safe there. We've talked to her about counselling but she's resisting that pretty strongly at the moment.'

Frank nodded, tracing patterns in the condensation on the beer bottle.

'Would you like a glass for that?'

He shook his head.

'So what about you, hon?' Sonya asked quietly.

He shook his head again, swallowing down the great wave of self-pity that her sympathetic tone had triggered. 'Not the best,' he said. 'I mean, I'm used to seeing a lot worse than that, but I'm . . . I guess I'm not used to caring.'

'And you care quite a lot, don't you?'

'Yeah! Yeah, I do, a helluva lot. More than I realised. Not that it's going to do me much good now, I suspect.'

'Hey, come on,' Sonya said. 'It's early days. She freaked out, you were the one who found her. She doesn't know how she feels about that yet. You have to give it time.'

Frank nodded. 'Maybe.'

'Definitely. Look, Frank, none of us knows what Marissa's demons actually are. She doesn't give much away but until that night she had a lot riding on you. It was obvious in the way she talked about you, the way she looked for your calls even if she didn't return them.'

'Maybe. But I stuffed that up, and at the hospital . . . '

'At the hospital she was in crisis. She needed a scapegoat and it's hard luck it was you. I know you think it was your fault with some message you left –'

'I'd had a few drinks, I was high on tying up the case . . . I was over the moon and I didn't stop to think,' Frank said, the words tumbling out of control. 'All these months I've been so careful, both of us have, sort of feeling our way. We both knew the other was a mess, screwed up by things from the past, and then I go and blow it.'

'So you'd had a few drinks and you didn't leave the most appropriate message. And then at the pub you had a few more, but there's no way you were drunk or crude or anything. I can't imagine what you think you could have said to –'

'I said I was in Geraldton and wanted to see her. I told her . . . I told her I loved her.' He looked straight at Sonya, aware that his eyes were full of tears. 'I love you, Marissa, that's what I said. I love you.'

There had been days in the past when Oliver had seen a semester, a week, a day – even a single lecture – stretching ahead of him as prolonged torture. Teaching, although he was apparently quite good at it, was the price he paid for the framework in which he could do his research and writing. Before each lecture and class he had always suffered from bursts of crippling performance anxiety, unable to sleep the night before a morning lecture, unable to eat lunch before an afternoon class. The fact that he knew many of his colleagues suffered the same anxiety did nothing to alleviate it.

Now, as he parked in a shady corner of the university car park, he marvelled at his new enthusiasm for his work. Was it exercise, or therapy, or a combination of the two? Whatever it was, he rose earlier and went to bed later, he slept better and his daytime hours seemed more rewarding than they had for years. Students of whom he had despaired seemed to be responding to him better – somehow he was managing to challenge them, spark their curiosity, even laugh with them. So it seemed almost obscenely unfair that he should be enjoying this personal and professional rebirth while his dearest friend was tunnelling through the slough of despond.

'Don't be so silly, Oliver,' Gayle had said when he mentioned this dilemma at their first breakfast on campus after many months. 'It's wonderful to see the change in you. In fact, it's wonderful to see you, and to be back at work. And I'm not in the slough of despond. I won't say it's not difficult at the moment, especially Angie's reaction, but, frankly, the relief of leaving Brian is enormous, and I've got my son back.' She fished a package of photographs out of her bag, pulled two off the top and handed them to him. 'Josh and Dan,' she said. 'And that's the three of us together.'

'He's so like you,' Oliver said, genuinely surprised. 'And you all look so happy.'

'I was. You can't imagine what it was like to see him, to feel forgiven. I know forgiveness is supposed to be best for the forgiver, but I've got to say it's pretty amazing to be on the receiving end.'

Oliver smiled. 'I'm sure. But what about Angie? Any sign of a truce?'

Gayle shook her head and took back the photos. 'Afraid not. She's very angry, and very hurt, and of course she has every right to be. It's a bit hard to see her canonising Brian, though. She's grumbled about him as much as I have in the past. And now she's even taking it out on Sonya for being a bad influence on me.'

Oliver raised his eyebrows. 'How extraordinary. You didn't even know Sonya when . . . well, when you . . . .'

'When I had the affair and got pregnant – no, of course not. There's no logic to it. I guess she just needs to lash out and I know that I have to cop that, but it seems unfair on Sonya. Angie's even asked for a transfer out of her section. Anyway, what about you? The dancing, the swimming – you look so much better.'

Oliver smiled. 'I'm ready to bore you with my new routine,' he said. 'Less caffeine, lots of raw food and less red wine.'

'A little is supposed to be good for you.'

'But almost two bottles over the course of an evening and resultant embarrassing phone calls are not,' he said sheepishly. 'I guess you heard – of course, you answered the phone.' He was moved, quite suddenly, by the ease of their conversation and the feeling that their friendship now had a depth that it had previously lacked. 'I haven't been a good friend to you, Gayle,' he said. 'If I had, you'd have been able to talk like this before. I'm sorry. I was so much up my own bum. I seem to have spent my life trying to reach some higher plane of political correctness and being totally unaware of the dilemmas of the people I cared about.'

She put her hand on his arm. 'There were two of us, Oliver. Both cut off, both struggling. Perhaps that's what drew us together, even though we couldn't talk about it.'

'And now?' He wasn't sure why he'd said it, or what he expected.

'Now there's still two of us and we're still struggling, but we understand each other much better, and we can talk about it. That means a lot,' she said. And to his enormous surprise she leaned across and kissed him on the check. 'An awful lot, Oliver, really.'

TWENTY-FOUR

Marissa looked at her costumes spread across the spare bed. The trip had been hard on them, frequent packing and unpacking along with the usual wear and tear of dancing meant small rips, trimmings pulled from the fabric, broken fastenings that needed repairing and she needed to fix one for tonight's class, the first one since she'd got back. She'd taken a risk closing them for twelve weeks and knew she might have lost people to other classes. Tonight she could well find herself staring at an empty room, having to start all over again drumming up business. All she could do was turn up and hope for the best.

She threaded a very fine needle with a purple silk thread and began to repair the hem of her favourite skirt. She'd worn this costume the night she danced at Gayle's house, more than a year ago. Gayle had changed so much in that time she was barely recognisable as the mousy, intimidated woman who had thought that no one would join in the dance.

Marissa had never met Brian, but she had heard enough about him to piece together a picture. And while she understood why Gayle had chosen to stay with him, she couldn't begin to imagine how she had survived it and remained such a rational and generous person. To Marissa, who felt she had boldly shaken off her past and taken control of her own life, it was incomprehensible.

Pricking her finger she jumped and sucked quickly at the bulging spot of blood. Since that night at the hotel, tiny shocks sent her into a panic and it took a huge effort to pull herself back.

She wondered if it would get better, fade away in time, if she would go back to normal, or at least as she had been before, able to control it, able to recognise small hurts, shocks, irritations for what they were without overreacting. She kept trying to quash the memory of that night but it wouldn't let her go.

She ruffled up the fabric of the skirt and held it softly against her face. The smell was her own and the feel of it brought her back to what it meant to her to wear it, and the strength and congruence that she experienced when she danced. Leaning back against the wall, her feet up on her bed, she picked up the needle again. The tour had brought her a whole lot more than she had bargained for: offers to teach in different places, bookings for private functions, and she had completely sold out of the practice video and needed to order more. But the most important thing she had gained was friends. During those weeks of travel, so unlike the travel of her youth, she had learned something about friendship, with two women as different from her and from each other as she could ever have imagined.

'We've got you in our clutches now, Marissa,' Sonya had said the previous day. 'No escape. Scary, isn't it? You have friends who don't just like you, they love you.'

'Mmm,' Gayle agreed. 'More fool us. We pick a friend who can't even make a decent cup of coffee and wants us to drink herbal tea. That's a pretty rugged test of friendship.'

So, that morning, Marissa had bought a plunger and some coffee. She hoped they would understand that doing it was a way of saying how she felt even if she couldn't trust herself to say it with words.

She drew her thread and started to stitch some sequins back onto the purple skirt. Tonight would be the first night she had danced since . . . there it was again. She'd missed the last night in Geraldton because they wouldn't let her out of the hospital, and Sonya and Gayle had danced alone. She owed them a lot, them and Frank . . . but she'd ruined that, of course, and at the thought of it sadness overwhelmed her again, sadness and the uneasy feeling that what had begun that night in Geraldton was not complete, that there was more to come before she would be free of it.

Sighing, she broke off her thread and shook out the skirt. Concentrate on tonight and what she'd do if no one turned up, concentrate on how to cope if people *did* turn up, because since Geraldton she felt as though she'd lost her nerve.

The group of women waiting outside the hall let out a whoop of delight as Marissa rode up on the Harley, and by the time they were in the hall, the number had doubled. They clamoured around her, asking about the tour. Slowly, carefully, trying to stay calm, Marissa set up the CD player and got out her cash box and registration book.

'We missed you,' said a woman in her seventies who had started dancing with her four years earlier to keep herself on the go. 'You're not allowed to go away again, Marissa.'

'No, and you missed Emma's baby being born,' said another. 'A little girl, she's called her Marissa, and Emma's mum is making this tiny belly dancing costume. Emma's bringing her round later to show you.'

There seemed to be more women than there had been at any previous class, old faces and plenty of new ones. She was surrounded, and panic was creeping up on her, making it hard to breathe.

'Hey, girls, give this dame some space,' Sonya said, and Marissa swung round in relief. 'Now, I'll take the money and sign you up.'

'And anyone who's new can come and talk to me,' Gayle said, drawing them to one side. 'I'll tell you about getting started.'

They hadn't told her they were coming but here they were in full costume, no leotards or T-shirts, the full thing: sequinned belts, headbands, made up to the nines as though for a performance. Sonya was even wearing the red hairpiece.

Marissa breathed freely as the reassuring drumbeat began to relax her, then the sounds of the kanoun and the oud, on the haunting Eastern scale. Gayle was standing ready on one side, one arm raised high holding the corner of her veil, the other arm holding the opposite corner out at right angles. Sonya, fluffing up her emerald skirt, slipped into place on the other side.

'Right,' Marissa said, and her voice sounded strong and confident even to her own ears. 'On four . . . one, two, three . . . ' Energy surged through her and she was back again in the rhythm and spirit of the dance, the magic that had sustained her so many times before.

Brian's foot was giving him hell. The night of the furniture smashing he was in his socks and had trodden on some glass. It seemed to be taking ages to heal. He was furious with himself for the damage he'd done that night, although he knew his anger was justified. He'd never seen Gayle like that before and he didn't like what he saw.

After she'd gone, and he'd got rid of the police, he'd sat out on the terrace in the darkness with another bottle of wine, staring at the television set bobbing around in the swimming pool. What a bloody waste, he thought, perfectly good television set, perfectly good windows, chairs, glasses. What a bloody waste, all of it. All those years and where had it got him? Here, alone, in the dark, surrounded by broken glass and a pool full of floating furniture. He had no idea how long he sat there, with his cut foot wrapped in a towel, but at some point he'd gone inside, been violently sick in the downstairs toilet and staggered up to bed, leaving everything as it was: doors open, lights on, spilt wine still dripping off the edge of the table.

He woke just after nine with a blinding headache, his foot throbbing painfully. The towel was now stuck to his wound with dried blood and he had to soak it in the bath to loosen it. When he was finally able to see the damage, it was clear he needed stitches so his first job was a trip to the hospital, followed by a visit to Angie to try to repair some of the damage that Gayle had done by deciding to blab after all these years. His old optimism had returned: Gayle would certainly be back, if not today then in a few days, maybe even a month. The main thing was to sort out the mess in the house, get it valued and put it on the market. Things would go ahead as he'd planned, there would just be a minor delay and he could rise above that.

Angie, who had taken a sickie, fell on him when he arrived. 'Oh, Dad! Everything's so awful. How could she do this? And your job . . . ' He steered her inside and sat her down on the couch.

'It's okay, Princess,' he said awkwardly, stroking her hair. 'Makes no difference, you know, never has, never will, makes no difference to you and me.' Although moved by her distress he was still able to enjoy a certain degree of satisfaction at the fact that Gayle was obviously cast as the villain of the piece. The trouble was he had no idea how to handle Angie when she wouldn't stop crying and wailing. In the end he had to tell her quite gruffly to pull herself together.

'Sorry,' she mumbled into another handful of tissues. 'But it's all been such a shock . . . like my whole life has been based on a lie.'

To his surprise, Brian managed to find some words that seemed to comfort her, although when he thought about it later he couldn't for the life of him remember what he had said. Eventually she stopped crying, and he suggested she make some coffee. He sat on a stool in the kitchen and told her about his foot, and about the television and the chairs that were still floating in the pool. He almost got a laugh out of her then, and together they took their mugs out into the small courtyard that was decorated with bright blue flower pots filled with white geraniums.

'Your mother'll see sense very shortly,' he said, stirring his coffee. 'She'll be back home, same as ever, and I've got big plans.'

'I don't know, Dad,' Angie said, shaking her head. 'I think she's serious. I think you're going to have to accept that she means what she says.'

'I'm sure it sounded that way when she spoke to you but, remember, she's never been on her own, never had to look after herself.' He leaned back in his chair and clasped his hands behind his head. 'Take it from me, Princess, it's this dancing thing that's ruined everything. Give it a bit of time, a week, maybe two, and she'll be back.'

Angie shrugged. 'Well, I don't care what she does. I don't want to talk to her. How could she do that to you, Dad? And making it so that neither of you would tell me, that is just so wrong.' The tears looked like starting again, and Brian once more summoned his magic words, but managed not to mention that it was he who had been the architect of the deal that he and Gayle had struck. No point in scoring an own goal at this stage of the game.

'So,' Brian said eventually, 'd'you like my new look?'

'Oh, yeah,' she said distractedly. 'Yeah, it's good, it suits you. Cool.'

He smiled. 'Thought I'd have a bit of a change.' He rubbed his chin. 'Feels good. And the hair – you noticed the hair? Styled properly, like you kept telling me.'

'Oh sure,' she said. 'Nice. Anyway, the most important thing now is to get started on looking for him. I'm applying for a transfer out of Sonya's department – I certainly don't want to work with her anymore. I'm taking annual leave while I wait for that to come through. It'll give me heaps of time to get going on a search, but the first thing I need is his name and whatever else you can tell me.'

Brian, confused and a tad disappointed that his makeover had not received more attention, finished his coffee and put his mug down on the table. 'You've lost me,' he said. 'Who are we talking about now?'

'My real father, of course.'

'Your what?'

'I need to know who he is, see if I can find him.' She paused suddenly after seeing Brian's face. 'Oh, don't be upset, Dad, you're my dad, always will be, but I need to find my biological father.'

'Why? What the –'

'Mum wouldn't help me. She wouldn't tell me his name,' Angie went on. 'She said it was too soon, I needed to think about it. I don't need her. You know who he is, don't you? You'll help me, I know I can rely on you.'

The prospect of Angie wanting to make contact with her biological father had never occurred to Brian, and it was as shocking as the news that Gayle, albeit due to some temporary insanity, might want to leave him. His immediate reaction was to lie and say that he didn't know the man's name. Angie meant the world to him and was obviously still very upset. He didn't want to make the situation worse, but at the same time there was no way he was going to do anything to help her find the bastard he'd spent the last twenty-seven years trying to forget.

'Your mother never told me who he was,' he lied. 'And anyway, it might be smart to wait a while until things calm down a bit. Leave it a week or two and I'll see what I can do.'

Delay was the answer: delay and plenty of fatherly attention might drive the idea out of her head. But now she was still hassling him. She'd thought about it, she said; in fact, she'd thought of nothing else, and she was relying on him to get the name from Gayle, to whom she herself refused to speak.

It was one thing on top of another. He'd had the window reglazed but his foot was still painful and slowed him down and, worse still, he would have to have a conversation with Gayle, possibly even ask her to cooperate with him in preventing Angie from starting on this ridiculous quest to find her father. The solicitor's letter that had arrived a couple of days after Gayle left had come as a shock, but he still hadn't taken it seriously. It requested a response within seven days, but he threw it in the bin, and then on the ninth day a letter was hand delivered, requiring a signature as proof of receipt. Perhaps she was serious after all. Brian went to see his own lawyer and it came as a further shock to discover that if Gayle went ahead with this divorce, she would be entitled to half of everything.

'But I earned it all,' Brian protested. 'I worked my arse off for years.'

'Gayle also worked, Brian,' Bob Tremlett, the lawyer, said in an infuriatingly calm voice. 'For most of the years of your marriage, Gayle has worked part or full time. She also raised your children, ran the family home, and entertained your business guests.'

'So what?' Brian said. 'She never earned much in that library job, and the other stuff doesn't count.'

Tremlett sighed. 'You seem to be a little out of touch with the law on these matters, Brian,' he said. 'Income is not the only contribution which is measured. Now, stop pacing around, sit down and we'll go through this one step at a time.'

Brian listened with a mix of anger and frustration. 'It's outrageous,' he said when Tremlett had finished outlining the sort of settlement that was likely to be awarded if they went to court. 'Bloody outrageous. Look, I even raised her child – I should get some compensation for that. I read in the paper the other day that some bloke got compensation for maintenance he'd paid for kids that weren't his. He got a DNA test.'

'Look, Brian,' Bob Tremlett said, 'as I understand it, you took responsibility for Gayle's daughter. It was your choice. Gayle didn't lie about it and, according to what she's told her lawyer and you've told me, you suggested that Angie should be registered as your child. In fact, you registered the birth yourself, and it was your suggestion that the matter should be kept confidential between the two of you. Are you now saying you want to disown Angie, because that's what it'll mean.'

Brian caught his breath. 'No, no, of course not,' he said, irritably tapping his fingers on the edge of the desk. 'No. But I want you to go in as hard as you can. If you screw Gayle financially, she's more likely to change her mind.'

'You do realise, don't you, that at present more than half of what you own is solely in Gayle's name? Attempting to screw her, as you so elegantly put it, is not only extremely complicated, it's also extremely unwise and most unlikely to work.'

TWENTY-FIVE

Sonya, wrapped in a towel, stood shivering in the queue for the showers in the women's changing room. Around her teenagers chattered about *Australian Idol*, and harassed mothers shepherded wriggling toddlers over the duckboards and into the cubicles. Finally scoring a berth herself, she turned the taps on full and stood in the torrent of hot water, sighing with relief. Getting up early on a Sunday morning to go swimming had not been her idea.

'But you'll love it, Sonya,' Oliver had insisted. 'Honestly, you've no idea how it'll set you up for the day. And I'll buy you a thundering good breakfast afterwards. Come on, give it go. Live dangerously.'

'*Live dangerously*?' Sonya had said. 'Are you sure you haven't had a brain transplant? Or maybe it's not the real Oliver I'm talking to, maybe you're a replacement; a cunning lookalike planted by the government to infiltrate the university system.'

'Go on,' he said.

'Oh, all right – just once, though.'

It had not been as bad as she'd expected, it had been much worse. After a week of gloriously warm days, Sunday had dawned dull and cold. It was at least ten years since Sonya had done any serious swimming, and the sheer length and depth of the pool looked horribly challenging. She'd hoped to escape to the small, covered pool but it was closed for repairs.

'You wait – once you get in there you'll love it. There'll be no stopping you,' Oliver had said, dumping his tracksuit on the benches by the poolside. And Sonya noticed that he was actually developing muscles. He gave her a wave, pulled on his goggles and, with a reasonably neat dive, was off, swimming competent laps in the medium lane.

Despite all her recent exercise on the dance floor, Sonya had difficulty staying afloat for a full lap. The slow lanes were full of children and teenagers weaving over and under the ropes and attempting to drown each other, and there was no way she was going to venture into the medium or fast lanes, where a lot of blokes in very tight Speedos and silly hats were ploughing along at a rate of knots scattering slower swimmers in their wake. Sonya made a valiant effort but soon abandoned the attempt and headed for the shower.

'Swimming is not my thing,' she said later as they made their way out through the revolving gate. 'And no thank you, I *don't* want to walk. I want you to drive us to the nearest breakfast place and park as close as possible. Meanwhile, I shall think up some horrible activity I can subject *you* to.'

'So how's it been having Gayle stay with you,' Oliver asked once they were seated and waiting for the eggs and bacon to arrive. 'It's been quite a while now, hasn't it?'

'Six weeks. And it's fine, we get on really well. I'd never share on a permanent basis, I like my own space too much, but it's made sense while Gayle sorts herself out. You know she's found somewhere now? She's moving in next week; a lovely townhouse.'

'She told me,' Oliver said, 'and apparently Brian's given way on some of the furniture.'

'That which he didn't dump in the pool,' Sonya said with a grin. 'He really is an extraordinary bloke, you know. Did she tell you he thought she wasn't entitled to anything and then he remembered a whole lot of it was in her name?'

Oliver nodded. 'He does seem to be a bit of a dinosaur. And Gayle's such a wonderful woman, isn't she? I do so admire the way she's done all this. And she's looking so lovely these days, since the dancing and everything, don't you think?'

Sonya looked at him curiously. 'She is indeed,' she said,

wondering just exactly how wonderful Oliver thought Gayle was. 'Very lovely.'

'There's something I want to tell you, Sonya,' Oliver began as their breakfast arrived.

'About Gayle?' she asked, bracing herself for the possibility of confidences similar to those she had heard from Frank.

'Not directly but about this whole situation, you know, Angie being so upset and hostile and the whole Brian thing.'

'Ah, that,' she said. 'Excellent breakfast, by the way. Well, go on.'

Oliver lowered his voice and leaned a little closer. 'Between you and me, at this stage at any rate, because it's really pure sup-position, but Andrew, my therapist – I think I told you he and I are doing some work together, he's interested in my book and we were discussing the tapes, and –'

'Oliver, I know all that, get on with it. Why are you being so conspiratorial?'

'The thing is, Andrew and I were talking about the Nazi wives, and I said it had made me realise how women's condi-tioning sets them up for some of these awful moral dilemmas, you know, love and duty, being intimidated, bullied, unable to speak out –'

'So? What is this? Feminism 101?'

'No, no, of course not. But, you know, it made me think about Gayle, because when I was pissed off with her after the wedding I couldn't understand how she had gone along with all that stuff of Brian's, you know . . . '

'Yes, I know. And frankly, Oliver, you must have known that and your mother would be horrified that you didn't make use of what she taught you. You could have been a bit more under-standing. Man cannot live by theory alone, she'd probably have said. Eat your breakfast, it's getting cold.'

'Yes . . . the long and short of it is, Sonya, that Andrew started talking about how women inherit this sort of submissiveness, and he told me about a client of his, a young woman – no names, of course – whose mother has always been intimidated by her father, and now she, this young woman, finds herself in the same situation. She's married, recently, mind you, a man just like her father . . . not exactly like him, but you know what I mean.'

'Oliver, where *are* you going with this? We know this is a repeating pattern, we know women often marry their fathers – Gayle's a good example – just like some men marry their mothers. What are you getting at?'

'Well,' he glanced nervously over his shoulder.

'Stop behaving like Austin Powers.'

'Shh, listen. Andrew said that this woman had only been married about a year and it was all extra complicated because now her parents were splitting up and there were other complications and . . . .'

'And?'

'A week later, when I went for my appointment with Andrew, I was in the car park and I saw Angie coming out of his rooms, and she was looking pretty upset.'

'You mean . . . ?'

'Yes, I think she might be.'

'Shit,' said Sonya. 'It does look a bit that way, doesn't it? What do you think we should do?'

'There's nothing we *can* do,' Oliver said, starting on his breakfast at last. 'It just strikes me that this is the worst time ever for Angie to be refusing to talk to Gayle and, for that matter, to you.'

Frank was on leave. In a spur of the moment decision he'd applied to take some of the time owing to him and now he was packing a few clothes. A break down south might help – anything, to get him out of this miserable state. The accused in the drugs case had been committed for trial but that was a few months away, and he was low in energy and motivation, still battling the old demons. So often he had got himself through the dark times with those intense bursts of booze and sex, but the night he'd headed home from the pub with Gina he'd known things were different. He'd grasped at the chance to blot out his feelings, but by the time he'd made all the right noises about

Gina's new home and poured the first glass of champagne, he realised it wasn't going to work this time.

'Here's to you,' he'd said, raising his glass. 'Great place, Gina. I hope you enjoy it.'

'I will,' she said. 'No doubt about that. I've had it with crummy rented accommodation. I've moved on.'

'You said it. And you know, babe, I think I have too. This is not going to work for me.'

She looked at him in surprise. 'You're not running scared, Frank?'

'Not scared, exactly. More tired, I suppose.'

'Tired of champagne and sex in the spa? You've gotta be kidding.'

He swallowed some champagne. 'You know what I mean.'

Gina sighed. 'Yes, I do know what you mean. It all gets a bit meaningless after a time, doesn't it? The booze, the sex, just to kill off the loneliness for a few hours or days.'

He put his arms around her. 'You deserve better, Gina,' he said. 'You've got the good place, now you need a good bloke to go with it.'

Gina hugged him in return. 'Too right – but good blokes are an endangered species.'

He picked up his phone and wallet from the coffee table. 'You'll find one eventually,' he said. 'As soon as you can convince yourself you deserve it. Maybe living here will help with that.'

'And what about you, Frank? Convinced yourself you deserve a good woman yet?'

'That's a bit more complicated,' he said.

The question was, having exhausted one coping behaviour, what would he use from now on? Perhaps getting away would help.

He rolled two pairs of socks into a ball, tossed them into the bag, and then added some T-shirts and a thick sweater. The wind from the ocean could suddenly take you by surprise even in summer. His phone rang and he had to rummage under the mess of clothes on the bed to find it.

'We need a man, Frank,' Sonya said, 'and we think you're it.'

'Only if you need a mere shell.'

'Don't be a wanker,' she said. 'Gayle's moving on Saturday. She's got proper movers, of course, but we need a man with power tools and we think you might be a power tool sort of bloke.'

'Is that supposed to be a compliment?'

'Naturally!'

'Okay, I do have power tools and, better still, I know how to use them.'

'Brilliant,' Sonya said. 'How about a fun-filled day putting up shelves, hanging pictures, fixing curtain rails and so on? Our friend Oliver is coming but I wouldn't let him within a mile of a power tool. We'll reward you with takeaway and a couple of bottles of good red. What do you say?'

'I was planning to drive down to Yallingup on Saturday for a bit of a break –'

'How selfish –'

'Exactly, but I was about to say that as a man who rarely gets a chance to use his tools in the service of the fairer sex, I could go on Sunday instead.'

'You're a star, Frank. We'll make it worth your while, honestly.'

'Yeah, yeah! Promises, promises . . . the only thing is, Sonya, is Marissa . . . ?'

'No, she's not coming. She has a longstanding booking to dance at a wedding.'

'Okay,' he said. 'What time and where?' And he took down the address, and wandered out to the shed to find his toolbox and drill.

Sonya wasn't looking forward to this conversation. She was flying blind on the strength of Oliver's gut feeling and who could tell how reliable that was?

'Come in, Angie, have a seat,' she said, indicating the armchairs either side of the coffee table. She hoped she had managed to hide her shock at Angie's appearance. She had lost weight, certainly, but with it she seemed to have lost her vitality. 'Thanks for coming in,' Sonya began, trying to strike the right sort of balance between head of department and someone who was once also considered a friend. 'I know you're on leave but I thought it was important that we have a chat before I sign off on your application for a transfer.'

Angie nodded and fiddled with the strap of her handbag. 'It'll go through all right, won't it?' she asked. 'You don't envisage any problems?'

'Oh, you know the process, it's all pretty straightforward,' Sonya said, 'but I have to write a short report to accompany it and, of course, make a recommendation. My problem is that you made this application just days before I came back from leave, so I'm not clear about the reasons for the move and what you feel it has to offer you in terms of professional development.'

Angie flushed. She'd obviously not been expecting this and didn't know where to start. 'Well,' she began, 'I thought it'd be good, you know, to do some stuff on the home schooling issue.' She paused, looked up at Sonya, then away again.

'You realise it's a step backwards in career terms, don't you?' Sonya said. 'I'm interested to know why you made the decision. I couldn't help wondering if you'd done this rather opportunistically.'

'Opportunistically? What do you mean?'

'I mean that there was an obvious vacancy in home schooling policy, and that if you had any problems in this section, then a move there might look like a solution. I was concerned that this might be a decision taken in the emotional heat of a particular moment rather than a carefully considered choice.'

There was an uncomfortable silence. Sonya lowered her voice. 'Angie, I know things are very difficult for you at the moment, but a move like this may not be the best way to deal with personal problems.'

'It would get me away from you,' Angie shot back.

'Yes it would,' Sonya said, 'but there are other, more constructive ways of achieving that if it's what you want – ways that wouldn't disadvantage you career-wise.'

'You changed everything,' Angie said accusingly, her face suddenly dissolving into tears. 'I trusted you. I thought you were my friend. I asked you to my party, my wedding, and then everything changed. It's all falling apart, Mum going off like that, and now she and Dad splitting up, and . . . and everything else, it's all falling apart.' She was sobbing now, and Sonya fetched a box of tissues from the desk.

'I understand how you must feel, Angie,' she said, 'but I think you're rewriting it all rather simplistically. Remember that day we went to look at the apartment? What you said to Gayle then was pretty tough. She took it to heart; it was hurtful for her to hear that, especially in front of Trish and me. It's partly what led her to make this huge decision. No one put a spell on your mother. Various things happened that made her decide to take control of her life.'

'So you're saying it's my fault?'

'No, I'm saying it's not *anybody's* fault. It's life, Angie. Shit happens and it happens to good people. Gayle's made some changes that are really important to her and you're caught in the fallout. She's been there for you for years, hanging on, waiting until a time when she thought you could handle the truth, but obviously it was never going to be easy.'

Angie dried her eyes. 'It's all so hard,' she said quietly. 'There's too much to cope with and I don't know what to do.'

Sonya thought she looked about twelve sitting there, her eyes red from crying, her face pinched and pale. 'Talking to Gayle is one thing you could do. She's your mother, she loves you dearly, and you've always talked to her in the past.'

'But what about Dad?' Angie protested. 'It's so awful for him . . .'

'Of course,' Sonya said, leaning forward, her elbows on her knees. 'But no one's asking you to choose between them. They're two very different people who made some decisions that don't look so good all these years later, so now they're going in different directions. But you don't have to pick one, you can have them both. In their own, very different ways they've both tried to do the best for you. You might not like some of what's happened, you might think they should have done it differently, but they did the best they could for you. That's the most you can ask of any parent.'

Angie was silent, shredding tissues between her fingers.

'There's other stuff,' she said eventually. 'With Tony. And I want to find my real dad.'

'Naturally, and Gayle's the person who can help you with all of that. You just need to call her. That's all it'll take.'

Angie nodded. 'I suppose . . . you won't tell her . . . '

'About this conversation? Of course not.'

' . . . and the transfer . . . ?'

Sonya raised her eyebrows.

'I did like working with you,' Angie said grudgingly.

'Mmm. I liked it too, and you're very good at your job.'

'And I'm not really interested in home schooling.'

'That's what I thought.'

'So what should I do?'

'Do you really want to know what I think?'

Angie nodded.

'I think you should tear it up. Take your leave, take more if you need it, have a rest, talk to your mum, and then, when you come back, we'll talk again. If you want to move, there are always opportunities in other areas. If you decide to stay here, I'll be delighted.'

Gayle took a last look around the house wondering if she should have been feeling nostalgic, or even guilty. In fact, all she felt was relief and satisfaction that another stage in the process of separating herself from Brian would soon be complete. They had finally come to a financial agreement that left her very comfortable although, according to her lawyer, it was considerably less than she would have got if she'd wanted to fight it. She didn't. She just wanted it to be over. The papers had been signed and the house put on the market. Now Brian had finally agreed to give her time alone in the house to organise and label what she wanted to take. Tomorrow she would be in a place of her own.

Angie's car pulled into the drive. She had called a couple of days earlier and this would be the first time they'd seen each other since Gayle had broken the news to her.

'We could meet at the house,' Gayle had suggested. 'I'd like to be sure that you don't particularly want any of the things I was planning to take.'

As Angie walked in the door, Gayle had difficulty concealing her shock at the change in her daughter. The pale, tense look that she'd noticed on her first night home was nothing compared to the strained expression in Angie's eyes now, and the hollows beneath them.

'You've lost weight,' Gayle commented, feeling that an emotional reunion was not on Angie's agenda. 'You must be pleased.'

'Yes. Four kilos.'

They stood in the entrance, not touching, not speaking. Gayle was overcome by the longing to leave. She'd wanted to see Angie, to talk to her, but suddenly it all seemed too hard. The last six weeks of battle with Brian, the decisions, the job of finding a place to rent had drained her. This felt like one battle too many.

'Maybe you can just go through and see what you think,' she said in what she hoped was a calm, unemotional tone. If it were going to be awkward, then they might as well be done with it as quickly as possible. 'Everything I'd like has been labelled, but none of it is essential. If you want something, just say. Then, when that's all out of the way, you can sort out the rest of it with your father.'

Angie swung round, looked accusingly at her and then looked away again. Gayle, flushing slightly, wished she hadn't used that term but she wasn't going to watch every word.

'I spoke to Josh,' Angie said.

'Really?'

'He says he and Dan are coming down to stay when you've moved.'

Gayle nodded. 'They offered to come and help but I thought I'd prefer to get straight first.'

'Josh thinks I'm being stupid. Stupid and selfish, but I suppose he's told you that.'

'He hasn't mentioned it to me.'

'Anyway, it's what he thinks, and I guess it's what everyone else thinks – except for Dad, of course.'

'Well, it's not what I think,' Gayle said.

Turning away from her, Angie went down the steps into the

family room, and fingered the pleated silk shade on one of a pair of table lamps. 'I always liked those lamps,' she said, 'but I don't want them. So what *do* you think?'

'About you? I think you're hurting badly. You feel I've lied to you and betrayed you, and that I lied to and betrayed Brian too, all those years ago, and you're right. I think you're angry with him as well, but you feel he's the aggrieved party because of my infidelity and my deciding to leave, especially now when he's just lost his job.'

'He *chose* to leave the job,' Angie cut in.

Gayle looked straight back at her without responding, and Angie looked away again. 'I think that anyone suddenly finding out that one of their parents is not their biological parent would be in a state of deep shock and hurt,' Gayle said. 'So I suppose I feel that your reaction is perfectly understandable, but, of course, it's also pretty painful for me.'

'So why aren't you bothering to tell me what a good mother you've been? How you stayed in a marriage that didn't work, a home you didn't like, and hung on after Josh was kicked out, just for my sake?'

Gayle shrugged and sat down on the top step. 'Whatever sort of mother I've been you know about – you were on the receiving end. I explained everything else to you and you've obviously discussed that with Josh. I'm not about to give myself a testimonial. I love you, Angie, more than I can ever tell you. More than you can ever begin to understand until you have children of your own. But I think you already know that.' To her surprise, Angie walked back and sat near her on the step, her hostile body language softening.

'Yes,' she said. 'I do know that, but it's hard, finding out something like this, and then you and Dad splitting up. I feel as though the ground has been cut from under me, as though nothing's safe anymore.'

Gayle nodded. 'I know, and I'm sorry, really sorry. I made some awful mistakes and now you're paying for it and there doesn't seem to be much I can do to help. Except perhaps help you trace your biological father if that's what you want.'

'You said you wouldn't.'

'I said I wouldn't give you his name straight away. I wanted you to think about it, talk to Tony, and, of course, to Brian. It's a big thing, not just for you, but for . . . for Brian, and for your biological father. I wanted to be sure you gave yourself enough time to think it through, but if you still want to . . . '

'I still want to,' Angie said.

'Okay then, I'll help you in any way I can.'

'The thing is,' Angie said, 'there's something else . . . something you don't know. No one knows, really.' She hesitated, looking around the room, looking everywhere but at her mother. 'Tony and me . . . it's not working.'

'Not working? What do you mean?'

'It's not like I thought . . . he's changed. I mean, I always knew he liked his own way, but it's different now. He just takes it for granted that what he says goes, and if I disagree he takes it badly.'

'How badly?'

'Very badly.'

'So what happens?' Gayle asked, moving a little closer.

Angie sat up straighter and brushed a strand of hair back from her face. 'Well, first off he goes very cold and hostile, and he starts talking down to me as though I'm stupid, as though I don't understand anything. So sometimes I shut up, give in and let him have it his way. It's not just stuff about what we should do or buying stuff for the house, it's other things too. Like, this row that's going on about outcomes-based education – he knows nothing about it and I do, it's my job, after all, but he just dismisses what I say as though my opinion's not worth anything. And you know the asylum seekers' action group where I was volunteering? He made me give it up. He's very anti the whole thing so I had to stop going, it was just too hard.'

Gayle swallowed and reached out to take her hand. 'And what happens if you don't give in, Angie? If you don't shut up?'

'It varies,' she said, returning Gayle's grip but still not able to make eye contact. 'Sometimes he'll just ignore me, behave like I don't exist, or he'll be really contemptuous. He does other things too, like refusing to do anything in the house. In fact, sometimes he'll deliberately create a mess, leave his stuff all over the place. Then I've either got to clear it up or, if I leave it, he somehow turns it on me, somehow he makes it my fault.'

'Anything else?'

'Sometimes he'll come up really close and grab my arm and shout right in my face. It's . . . it's really intimidating.'

'So how long has this been going on?'

'Since we got married. At first when we had an argument or something he'd be really horrible and then we'd end up having a laugh and it'd be all right. But now he never backs down. I'm not allowed to have an opinion that's different to his. And it's a bit like . . . well . . . '

'Like me and Brian.'

'Yep. Like you and Dad.'

'And you think it's my fault?'

'No, not your fault, it's just that I can see what he's doing, what I'm doing . . . '

'You're right, of course. Have you talked to anyone else?'

'I've been seeing a therapist.'

'Good, and?'

'It's helped me to see it more clearly, understand why it happens. He told me some things to do and it all makes sense when I'm in his office, but it's like trying to batter Tony with a lettuce leaf when I actually try to do it.'

Gayle felt physically sick. The desire to protect her daughter was more fierce and painful than the desire to protect herself had ever been. 'So what do you want to do?' she asked.

Angie shrugged. 'I thought counselling together might help but he won't go. Even suggesting it made him furious. What do you think?'

'I think it's great you went to a therapist. It's the first step in finding a solution, and looking after yourself – something I was never able to face doing. But in the end you're just going to have to make up your mind whether you think this is fixable, or even worth fixing. Believing you can change someone is traditionally a losing wicket. But if you want to try –'

'I don't think so,' Angie cut in. 'You see, the thing is that he wants a baby, he wants me to get pregnant *now*. And I can't, I can't bring a child into this relationship, Mum, I really can't, and he won't take no for an answer.'

TWENTY-SIX

'You've all been perfectly wonderful,' Gayle said, drawing the cork on a bottle of Margaret River Shiraz. 'Time to knock off now – anything else can wait for another day.'

'One more minute,' Frank said from the top of the ladder, 'and this will be completely finished.'

'I am totally and utterly stuffed,' Sonya said, sinking down onto Gayle's cream sofa. 'I can't believe how exhausting it is even when you have proper removalists doing the heavy stuff. All that unpacking, cutlery, crockery, books . . . '

'Now, if you'd just swim regularly, Sonya . . . ' Oliver began, sitting down beside her.

'One more word about that, Oliver, and you're a dead man. Today's labour was your punishment for making me go swimming.'

'Now, now, children,' Frank said, stepping down from the ladder, 'no fighting. And if Oliver was being punished for making you go swimming, what was I being punished for?'

'I don't know,' Sonya said. 'But give me a minute and I'll think of something.'

'I'm hanging out for this,' Oliver said, taking a glass of wine from Gayle.

'I'd still be surrounded by unpacked boxes without you guys,' Gayle said. 'The curtains would still be packed instead of hanging, and without you, Frank, I'd have no shelves and no pictures on the walls.'

'There's nothing like a man with a power tool,' Sonya said.

'You should take note, Oliver, get Frank to give you some lessons with the drill. It could improve your chances with women.'

'It's never done *me* much good,' Frank said, sitting on the floor. 'We're a couple of burnt-out cases, Oliver, you and I, totally uncool and past our use-by date.'

'I fear so,' Oliver said, joining him on the floor. 'But you never know; where there's life, there's hope. Some woman with insight may one day toss us a glance and recognise our true worth.'

'Looking at you both sitting there with a patina of dust, sawdust and sweat, I'd say it's pretty unlikely,' Sonya said.

'In the meantime,' Gayle said, 'we could think about ordering some food.'

'And then,' Oliver said, a couple of hours, two family size pizzas and a few bottles of wine later, 'you have to do this lunge thing – it's called a corte – followed by a quebrada – where the woman thrusts her pelvis forward and leans back and you lunge over, as though you're going to ravish her.' He straightened up rather precariously. 'No daylight should be seen between the two bodies. Not easy, and pretty – well, pretty . . . '

'Pretty raunchy,' Sonya interjected. 'This seems so out of character, Oliver, this twice-a-week ravishing at the community centre.'

'It's not *actual* ravishing, Sonya,' Oliver said, looking around for his glass and treading on a pizza box. 'Oh dear, I don't think I was supposed to do that. No, we don't exactly ravish anyone, we just lunge.' He pushed his glasses further up his nose and wished the room would keep still.

'You practise being raunchy.'

'That's what I need,' Frank said. 'Practice.'

'It's difficult to explain, really,' Oliver said. 'I think I may have had too much wine.'

'Perhaps you could just dance it for us, Oliver,' Gayle suggested, smothering the laughter that was threatening to erupt. 'Rather than just talking us through it, I mean.'

'I'd need music . . . '

'I've got music,' she said. 'I've got tango music, and you've already connected the stereo.' She scrambled to her feet and looked through the stack of CDs she'd rescued from the house. 'Here,' she said triumphantly, 'Los Reyes del Tango.'

'I'll need a partner,' Oliver said, searching for the correct button on the stereo. 'Sonya?'

'No way, darl.'

'You did a rather good jive with me at Angie's wedding, if I remember right.'

'But I've never attempted the tango.'

'Well ... er ... Gayle, perhaps?'

Gayle held up both hands. 'Not me, I've never danced the tango in my life.'

Oliver sighed. 'That's pretty disappointing. I thought this might help me meet people, but no one will dance with me.'

'You don't need to meet us, Oliver, you already know us.'

'I can tango,' Frank said. 'In fact, in my heyday I used to be shit hot on the dance floor.'

Sonya clapped her hands. 'Brilliant. There, you see, Oliver, perfect. Keep doing the tango and you'll meet people like Frank.'

'I meant women, actually.'

'Yes, but in the absence of them, Frank can partner you. I take it you *were* volunteering, Frank?'

'Yes,' Gayle joined in. 'Come on, Frank, let's see what you're made of.'

'I don't know ... ' Oliver began.

'Come on, Oliver,' Frank said, getting to his feet and smoothing down his shirt. 'These dames need to see how it's done. I'm your man. Will you ravish or will I?'

'I definitely want to be the man,' Oliver said, grasping Frank's hand. 'I haven't got those steps right yet so there's no way I'm going to try doing it all backwards. So okay, Frank, remember: slow, intense, passionate. Now, this is how Ramon counts it – "Walk, Walk, Tan – Go – Close", so we'll start on a promenade. I'm leading with the right foot. Ready? On three. One, two, three ... '

Side by side on the sofa, Gayle and Sonya, smothering their laughter, watched as the two men, shoulders square and torsos upright, executed an elegant promenade across the room, finishing with a spectacular corte and quebrada as the music ended.

It's surprising the effect that one unexpected and sober person can have on a room full of people who've drunk too much. Marissa's slow handclap startled them. 'That was quite extraordinary,' she said from the doorway. 'The sort of thing one sees only once in a lifetime.'

'No, no,' Oliver protested, in the swing of it now. 'We're just getting started. We can do it for you again if you like.'

'No,' Frank said firmly. 'No we can't.'

'I think you were both fabulous,' Sonya said, clapping. 'So what are you doing here, Marissa? Aren't you supposed to be performing at the wedding?'

Marissa dropped her keys on the coffee table. 'I was, but I finished earlier than I expected, so I thought I'd pop over and see how you were getting on. I rang the bell but you didn't seem to hear and the door wasn't locked, so I . . . '

'It's great that you're here,' Gayle said, handing her a glass of wine. 'There's some leftover pizza – can I warm it up for you?'

Marissa shook her head. 'I'm fine, thanks. Cheers, everyone – looks as though you've all done a great job with the moving.'

Oliver extended his hand. 'We haven't met but I'm Oliver,' he said. 'Can you tango?'

Marissa grinned and glanced at Frank, who was poised awkwardly on the arm of the sofa. 'I can but –'

'Splendid. Put the music on again, Gayle,' Oliver cut in.

'Another time maybe, Oliver,' she said, 'not this evening. This is just a flying visit, I'm not stopping.'

'You have to come and see how lovely the bedroom looks,' Gayle said, and she led Marissa off upstairs.

'I think I'll call it a day,' Frank said, collecting up his tools.

'It's early,' Oliver said. 'The night is young.'

'You don't have to leave just because Marissa's come,' Sonya whispered. 'Have another drink.'

He put up his hand to stop her. 'I've had enough, thanks, Sonya. I want to get off early tomorrow, be in Yallingup before lunch. Good to meet you, Oliver, happy to tango with you anytime.' He felt ridiculous. His pleasure in the camaraderie of the day and the relaxed, boozy evening had been destroyed by Marissa's unexpected arrival. If there were one person in the world he'd rather not have seen him dancing with another bloke, especially that particular move in the tango, it was Marissa. Oliver helped him carry his tools out to the car and as they came back up the path, Frank saw Gayle through the kitchen window stuffing pizza boxes into a rubbish bag.

'Just came to say goodnight,' he said, putting his hand on her shoulder.

She turned and hugged him. 'Thank you, Frank, for everything.'

'Even the tango?'

'Most especially the tango. And, Frank, about Marissa–'

He held up his hand. 'A lost cause, Gayle, I know that.'

'Don't be so quick to write it off.'

He leaned forward and kissed her on the cheek. 'I know when I'm beaten,' he said, 'and I'm dealing with it.'

'Are you really?'

'Sure!' He smiled. 'Off on holiday tomorrow. I'll see you when I get back.'

Walking to the car he paused briefly alongside the Harley, running his hand over the black leather seat.

'Have you ever ridden one?'

He jumped and swung round. Marissa was standing right behind him.

'Years ago,' he said. 'But not a Harley. Goodnight, Marissa.'

'You shouldn't drive, Frank,' she said. 'You've had a lot to drink.'

He bowed slightly. 'You're right, your honour, but I'm going to drive anyway.'

'That's pretty stupid. I thought you had better judgement.'

He fished his keys out of his pocket. 'Judgement? Me? No, Marissa, I have lousy judgement. You of all people should know that.'

'Frank, leave the car here. I'll run you home. I've got a second helmet.'

'I'll be fine.'

'You're way over the limit.'

'Story of my life.'

'Why don't you cut the clichés,' she said, unlocking the top box behind the pillion and taking out a second helmet. 'Just lock your car and put the helmet on.'

Frank hesitated and then flicked the remote control to lock his vehicle.

'How long since you rode pillion?' Marissa asked.

'Decades, and never on a Harley.'

'Okay, well, it's the same thing. Nice and loose, like a sack of potatoes, but try to remember that Harleys don't like sharp corners. Don't start anticipating the turns.'

It was quiet for a Saturday night, and as they reached the top of the hill ahead of them, the booze bus was waiting. Marissa slowed and followed the traffic officer's direction into the left hand lane and they sat, engine idling, waiting for their turn. Frank's embarrassment grew. He'd be on his way for a urine sample by now if she hadn't persuaded him not to drive. He felt awkward sitting behind her on the bike, and the delay made it worse. She already thought him crass and insensitive, and tonight's little performance would have convinced her that he was stupid and drank too much as well. This Good Samaritan business of getting him home must be really pissing her off.

'Thanks,' he said, getting off the Harley outside his house and removing his helmet. 'You saved me from a very embarrassing incident.'

Marissa switched off the engine. 'Can we talk?'

He shrugged. 'Here? Now?'

'You could ask me in,' she said, taking off her helmet. 'If it's not too late.'

Gayle turned off the lights and stood listening to the unfamiliar night-time silence of her new home.

'It's very different, very much cosier,' Trisha had said that afternoon as she unpacked crockery. 'I can see that it's much more you than the old house ever was.' She'd hugged Gayle as she hurried off to go to a family dinner with Graham. 'I really admire you, Gayle. I thought you'd be stuck in that house and that marriage forever. Now look at you starting again, a new woman with a new life.'

Starting again, becoming a single woman at this time of life, would have its challenges, but all Gayle could feel now was a sense of joyful anticipation. She remembered the night of the first belly dancing class, the sudden and surprising sense of competence, and the feeling of her body loosening and extending, feelings that had strengthened each time she danced.

She went upstairs in the darkness and looked down onto the street below, where Frank's car stood. She wondered what was happening right now between him and Marissa, who had disappeared as suddenly as she had arrived. And then she wondered about Sonya and Oliver, whose cars were also lined up on the street after sharing a taxi home, and she smiled to herself at the thought of Oliver, the anxious, cautious man whom she'd known for so long now shedding skins and actually developing some sex appeal. Gayle closed the blinds in the bedroom, slipped out of her jeans and T-shirt and wandered into the bathroom, wondering, rather wistfully, about Sonya, and what *she* really felt about Oliver and whether she realised that he was so obviously in love with her.

Getting out of the taxi, Sonya leaned back inside and kissed Oliver on the cheek. ''night, Oliver. Thanks for all you did. And, by the way, that tango? Better than power tools, I reckon.'

He grasped her hand and kissed it. 'Thank *you*, Sonya, for grabbing me by the throat and shaking me into doing something about myself.'

She let herself in, dropped her bag on the floor, walked through to the bathroom and switched on the light. 'Grabbed by the throat – it makes you sound so powerful,' she said to her reflection in the mirror. 'So how come you're the only one who hasn't changed? Letting your family see who you are for once is such a drop in the ocean compared to what's happening around you. And, anyway, what good did it do?'

She thought about Marissa and Frank and wondered what they were doing right now, and about the new Oliver, astonishing them with his humour and the tango. And she thought about Gayle, who had gained so much strength and revealed so much wisdom, and she wondered what Gayle really thought about Oliver, and whether she realised that he was so obviously in love with her.

Oliver stood in his front garden and stared up at the stars. He picked out the Southern Cross and Orion, which were the only two constellations he knew, and breathed in the honeysuckle-scented night air. He wondered what had caused the unease between Frank and Marissa. Gayle and Sonya obviously hadn't told him the full story. He thought about himself and how thrilling it was to tangle with the shifting demands and messages of head, heart and gut, instead of responding just to his head. And alone in the front garden he clasped an imaginary partner and for the second time that night executed a slow and sensuous promenade finishing with a lunge at the front door.

TWENTY-SEVEN

Marissa paced small nervous circles around the lounge room while Frank made a big deal of boiling the kettle and clattering cups and saucers in the kitchen. Why had she done this? Why was she here? She held a hand out in front of her and was amazed to see that it was absolutely still, for she felt as though every part of her were trembling. Staring at the closed front door she momentarily contemplated slipping quietly out and away into the night.

Frank masked his own discomfort by searching for herbal tea. 'I've got green or chamomile,' he called, 'both, amazingly, still within their use-by date.'

'Chamomile, please,' she said, overcoming that sudden urge to flee. But what next? 'Can we talk?' she'd said, but talk about what? About the fact that his message had touched a nerve so raw it sent her crazy? *Can we talk?* A line from a soap opera, the line before the commercial break that made sure you wouldn't change channels. *Can we talk?* Not an invitation to a chat about the cricket or the weather, but a question charged with meaning: about us, about what happened, about why I'm a nut case, about why I treated you like shit, about why this could never work.

'There you are,' Frank said, 'you probably need to leave the tea bag in for a bit.'

'Thanks,' she said, taking it from him. 'Are you drinking coffee at this time of night?'

He nodded, switching on a couple of table lamps and turning

off the harsh central light. 'I need it, and it's things other than caffeine that keep me awake. Sit down, Marissa.'

She sat awkwardly at one end of the sofa and they looked at each other in silence; a silence charged with embarrassment and anxiety.

'This is a nice place,' she said. 'First time I've been here.'

He managed a smile but his face looked crushed. It was a look she'd seen only once before, at the hospital, when she'd told him to leave.

'I want to apologise for the way I treated you at –' she began.

'No apology necessary,' he cut in. 'My fault, I was way out of line and –'

'And about what I did –'

'Marissa –'

She held up her hand. 'You have to let me say some things without interrupting.'

He nodded and leaned forward, elbows on his knees. 'Sorry, go on.'

'I said I wasn't grateful to you; well, that's not true. I just couldn't say so at the time.' She paused and dropped her head, closing her eyes and then inhaling deeply. 'You and I . . . I felt we understood each other. I thought I understood about Vietnam, about how it must have been for you. After all, I've read about it, the things you'd have been through, the things you saw and probably still see. I suppose I felt I understood but, of course, I don't. I can't. Only someone who's been there can know what it was like then and how it affects you now, and only you know what triggers it for you. Am I right?'

'Exactly right.'

'But it's different for you. You see, I felt you understood that I . . . well, that I was also haunted by something, and I lost sight of the fact that while you recognised trauma you had no idea what my demons were, while I could tread carefully around areas that would obviously be hard for you. You had absolutely no signposts. *Anything* you said, *anything* you did, had the potential to blow up in your face.'

Frank nodded. 'Yes,' he said again. 'That's right, that's how it felt. I was being so careful and then . . . ' His voice trailed away.

'And then you left your message. Just once, you stopped walking on eggshells and it *did* blow up in your face.'

'I'm sorry,' he said. 'Marissa, I'm so sorry . . . I didn't want . . . '

'No,' she said. 'No, please don't apologise.' Her hands *were* shaking now, very obviously shaking, and her teeth were starting to chatter just like they had that night. 'Let me go on, I didn't mean to tell you this now but . . . '

Frank got up to move towards her but she held up her hand. 'Don't! Please don't touch me.'

He dropped back into his chair.

'I told you I was worried about going to Port Hedland. I was on a tightrope, and part of me thought going back there might settle something. I needed to make something happen to either get to the end of the tightrope or fall off. So I went back to the house where I . . . where we stayed, the people I was travelling with. I'd had this on–off thing with that guy I told you about.'

'Blue?'

'Yes. He was strange, a real macho bloke, and sex to him was like a way to constantly keep proving himself. He was young, younger than me, and perhaps that explains some of it, but he didn't seem to have any sense of how anyone else might feel. And he was really only interested in me when he couldn't pull anyone new. So I was over it, and waiting to get away, trying to make up my mind where to go next.' She paused again; talking about it was making it hard to breathe.

'Are you sure you want to go on?' Frank asked.

'Then there was a party,' she said, ignoring him. 'A lot of people around, people from the pub, the backpackers' hostel, from god knows where else. Lots of booze, hash, LSD – probably other stuff too, I don't know. Well, you can imagine how it was: music, noise, smoke, people groping each other . . . I'd had a few drinks more than usual and Blue rolled a joint. He had a lot of good quality hash, really strong. I couldn't handle it, and I thought this roll-up was just leaf, but I think he'd souped it up. Anyway, you must know how it is, a few draws and everything begins to feel soft and floaty and . . . sort of safe, as though the world's backed off to a safe distance. And then he started to get very affectionate, which was unlike him – he couldn't really relate to women other than through sex. So I was in this dopey state and he was stroking my face, kissing me and then he said he'd had enough of the party.'

Her breath was coming in short bursts now, and she struggled to slow it down. Frank was looking at her but she could no longer look at him, and she stared down at the floor, twisting her hands together in an effort to stop them shaking.

'So, he said, "I just want to be with you, Marissa. I love you, I really love you." Any other time I think I would have laughed at him but the drink and the dope . . . it was all so seductive, and although I'd felt it was all over between us, in a way I was still connected to him because of how we'd met and what all that meant. We were out in the garden, everyone was out there drinking and dancing, it was a lovely warm night and I was really stoned and it suddenly all seemed quite romantic. Anyway, he said, "Let's get away from the others and go to bed." We went inside and were heading for the room he was sharing with a couple of other guys and then he said, "I'll just get us a couple of beers, you go on in, I'll be there in a minute." So . . . so, I went into the bedroom and I didn't put the light on, just pulled off my gear and got into bed. And then someone switched the lights on.

'At first I didn't realise what was happening, but then they were on me, dragging off the bedclothes, holding me down, one of them's unzipping his fly and they're cheering him, egging him on, and I started yelling, but the music was so loud. I tried to kick him off but they were holding my legs . . . and he . . . he . . . he . . . climbs on top of me and he's yelling out, "Come on, line up, who's next . . . ?"' She stopped, unable to repeat the words.

'And then the door opens and there's Blue standing there in the doorway, and I think, thank god, thank god he's going to stop them, and I yelled for Blue to help me, to stop them, but he just stood there watching . . . And then he climbed on the bed and hit me across the face and put his hand over my mouth and held me down . . . and . . . and they all . . . they all . . . ' The tears were pouring down her face now, and her throat was burning. 'And Blue, him too . . . ' She was gasping for breath, she could feel them closing in on her again, feel the hands gripping her, holding her down, smell the sweat and the booze, feel Blue's hand over her mouth, her teeth biting into his flesh and the salty taste of blood and sweat.

'He set me up,' she finally cried, 'he told me he loved me, then set me up . . . ' Violent tremors racked her body, and she gulped for air and began to tear at her inner wrists with her nails, scoring red weals onto her skin.

Frank moved to sit beside her but she recoiled, drawing back into the corner of the sofa, turning her face away from him. He paused and waited before reaching out to put his hand on her shoulder.

'It's okay, Marissa,' he said softly, 'it's okay. It's over now, it's over.' He slid his arm very slowly around her shoulders and drew her to him, and then he was holding her, rocking her very gently.

'He set me up,' she said again. 'He told me he loved me, he planned it all . . . he set me up and he . . . they . . . all of them raped me.'

TWENTY-EIGHT

Brian walked around the house checking every room. The removalists had collected Gayle's things a few days earlier but she didn't seem to have taken much. The house was up for sale and he was trying to do a deal with the buyer over the remains of the furnishings. Now it was clear that Gayle was not coming back, he just wanted it sold as soon as possible.

Once his initial anger and disbelief had passed he'd spent a few days simply feeling winded, as though the breath had been knocked out of him, and then he'd started to feel hurt, to see himself as a victim of his own good nature. All he'd tried to do for the best had been ignored or misunderstood. But Brian's essentially self-serving emotions had always enabled him to make over events in a way that reflected well on him, and they did not let him down now.

It didn't take him long to decide that this new situation suited him, that it was what he wanted and that he had so frequently chosen loyalty and responsibility to his family over his own desires. He was to be a single man; a single man with a classy bachelor pad in Manly; a member of a prestigious golf club, and an even more prestigious wine club; a single man running his own small marketing consultancy with an elite clientele. He didn't waste time wondering about living alone. It seemed entirely reasonable to expect that he would be able to take his pick of female company – social, sexual, whatever. There was never any shortage of women on the lookout for cashed-up men to give them a good time.

'Don't you think you'll get lonely in Manly?' Angie had asked him.

'No way,' he said, telling her about the clubs he'd join, 'and I'm going to get myself a boat, a motor launch, I think – yachting's not my line but I like being on the water.'

'But what about at home,' she persisted. 'You're used to being looked after at home.'

'So I'll get a cleaner, and I'll eat out a lot. Plenty of places close by. Breakfast on the waterfront reading the papers . . . you know the sort of thing. It's the way of the future, you know, Ange, eating out. Very European. Asian too.'

Angie shrugged. 'Well, if that's what you want, but I'm worried about you.'

'Don't be,' he'd said, putting an arm around her shoulders, 'I'll be fine. Worry about yourself, darling girl. I can look after me. And I've got plenty of space, and a nice room with an ensuite for when you come to visit.'

Brian had been both shocked and furious when Angie and Gayle together had confronted him with Angie's situation. His first instinct had been to go straight around to the house and king-hit Tony, let him know that no one messed with his daughter like that. But that had sent Angie into more floods of tears and Gayle had restrained him.

'This is not helping, Brian,' she said in that new, stroppy tone she'd got from her dancing friends. Brian felt he hardly knew Gayle anymore; she was so damned bossy and confrontational now. 'Just listen to Angie, hear what she's saying. She needs our support. What she doesn't need is you barging round there and making things worse.'

What Angie was saying was that she wanted Tony to move out for a while to give her some space. Gayle's view, as she told him while Angie was in the bathroom repairing her make-up, was that Angie wanted a separation and a divorce but couldn't confront Tony with that in her present emotional state. Time apart was, in fact, the first step towards ending the marriage.

'Then if that's the way you want it, okay,' he said, taking Angie's hand. She was calmer now. 'But I won't put up with that bastard bullying you. If he won't move out, you just get straight on the phone and I'll be –'

'Brian, stop!' Gayle had said, glaring at him. And he'd stopped.

Stopping didn't, of course, stop the overwhelming urge to protect his daughter. The thought that any man could bully her like that chewed away at him like a swarm of termites. But he was able to draw some satisfaction from the fact that Gayle now had an example of what bullying really was. He hoped that she was contemplating her own unfair complaints and accusations about him. Anyway, it was water under the bridge. The new, harsh Gayle wasn't someone he wanted to be around.

'There's something else you need to know, Dad,' Angie had said. 'Mum's told me who my real . . . I mean, my biological father is.'

Brian's stomach did a sickening somersault. Somehow this was the one thing that he had not been able to remake to his own liking. Having always done the right thing – indeed, what he had often thought of as the positively noble thing in the circumstances – the very thought of Angie somehow connecting with that man got to him in a way that nothing else could. Gayle had stitched him up completely over this, firstly by making a cuckold of him years ago, and now by spilling the beans. He was cornered. His only option was to grin and bear it, to be magnanimous. There it was, that word again. It hadn't done him much good the last time, but it was the only tactic now left to him.

He forced a smile and a shrug which he hoped looked self-deprecating. 'If that's what you want, Angie, of course I won't be the one to stand in your way. But you've gotta remember that he's probably got a family too.'

She leaned over and kissed him then and slipped her arm through his. 'Thanks, Dad, I knew you'd help. And I don't want to rock the boat for him. I just want to meet him once. I'll be discreet.'

Gayle got up to leave then, and he followed her to the front door.

'You know, Brian,' she said, turning around to him before she opened the door. 'You do have a child of your own. In view of the way things have turned out, you might want to give some thought to that. Josh and Dan will be down here in a couple of weeks – maybe you feel you have something to say to your son?'

There it was, that winded feeling again. It made him stop in the middle of the hall and gasp for breath. Was there no end to this?

'I have nothing to say to him.' Brian had said, moving forward to open the door. 'Absolutely nothing at all.'

Sonya walked around the house savouring the solitude. After weeks on the road, and then having Gayle live with her, the still-ness and the sense of being alone were strange, but life was returning to normal. She went down the three steps from the back door into the garden and sat on the bench under the jacaranda, brushing aside the flowers that had fallen like a purple puddle onto the garden table. What instinct was it that had made her want to move from this place? Whatever it was it had gone now. She loved the house and the garden; they were full of precious memories. Maybe it wasn't the house that had created that nig-gling restlessness – perhaps she had just needed a change.

She pulled some weeds out of the rockery which she'd built a few years ago and which now looked as though it was nature's own idea. Small patches of moss, clumps of baby's tears and some tiny pink star-shaped flowers that she couldn't name rambled over the rocks; it bore her stamp, a stamp that would be totally out of character in a glitzy apartment building. The phone rang as she walked back into the kitchen.

'I'm ringing from the station,' Tessa said.

'Oh, good, that's nice,' Sonya replied, wondering why she needed to know that Tessa was at the station. 'Where are you off to?'

'Nowhere,' Tessa said. 'I've just arrived. I'm here, in Perth, at the East Perth terminal. Are you at home?'

'Obviously.'

'I mean, are you going to be there if I grab a cab and come over?'

Sonya put down the phone. 'Weird,' she said aloud, 'totally

weird. What the hell's she doing here? Should've asked her,' and she looked around to see if there were anything she wanted to put away or rearrange before Tessa paid her first ever visit to the house.

'Nice place,' Tessa said when Sonya opened the door a short time later. She leaned forward to kiss her, and Sonya, totally taken aback at this sudden and unexpected gesture of affection, almost moved away – almost, but not quite. She patted Tessa awkwardly on the shoulder to compensate for any apparent lack of warmth.

'I think so. Well, come on in. Coffee? Tea? Glass of wine?'

'Wine would be nice.' Tessa followed her through to the kitchen. 'So this is how smart senior bureaucrats live.'

Sonya gave a sharp intake of breath and felt her hackles rise.

'Sorry,' Tessa said, blushing deeply. 'Shit! I'm sorry, Son, I didn't mean that like it sounded. It was a joke, a stupid one. Honestly, I'm sorry.'

'That's a relief. I thought we were off to a pretty bad start there.'

Tessa pulled out a chair and sat down. 'Just when I'm trying to do it right, I go and stuff it up completely.'

Sonya took two glasses from the cupboard and found a corkscrew. 'So what exactly is it you're trying to do, Tess? You've barely acknowledged my existence for the past couple of decades, and then I get a phone call about your new grandchild and now a surprise visit. Why are you here? I'm confused. Have I some-how missed an important chapter of the family history?'

Tessa fiddled with her gold chain-link bracelet, a habit she reverted to under pressure. Even in the days when there had been no gold, but a couple of narrow black leather strips woven through some coloured beads, the twisting had always been a sign of her anxiety. The memory of that bracelet and the times she had watched Tessa's fingers tugging and twisting at the leather returned to Sonya with astonishing clarity.

'I hoped we wouldn't start off like this,' Tessa said. 'That we could sort of work up to it.'

Sonya raised her eyebrows. 'Really? We barely speak for twenty-odd years and then you roll up at the door and we have a nice glass of wine together and chat about the weather, or that very elegant suit you're wearing? Shit, I'm doing it now – sorry. Why don't we call it quits and start again? Why've you come to Perth?'

Tessa reached out for her wine glass. 'To see you.'

'You came all the way from Kal to see me? Is there something wrong at home? Mum and Dad, are they sick?'

'No, Son, everything's fine at home. Mum and Dad are fine, they sent their love.'

'They did? I thought I'd been disowned. They sent their *love*?'

'Of course, why not? You didn't really think that stuff about the belly dancing would last, did you? Look, by the end of that week Mum was accepting compliments about you at the CWA, and she and Dad were telling everyone how proud they were.'

'You're kidding.'

'No. They think the sun shines out of your bum, for heaven's sake. It's just that you took them by surprise, you should have told them before you arrived. All they needed was time, and in the end it was done for them because the women at the CWA couldn't stop talking about how wonderful the belly dancing was. Sometimes Mum and Dad forget that they're not living in the fifties, and that we're not teenagers. You take it all too seriously – they always come round. They *were* disappointed that you didn't call in before you left, though, but there you go.'

'I see,' said Sonya, who didn't really.

'So, no, there's absolutely nothing wrong at home. It was . . . ' Tessa hesitated. 'It was just that I wanted to see you, and to talk to you . . . I wanted to apologise.'

Sonya's suspicion returned. 'For what in particular?'

'Lots of things, but most of all for treating you like shit all these years.'

Sonya sighed. 'But *why*, Tessa? Why? I never understood. And why is it different now?'

Tessa twisted her bracelet so tight that the catch snapped, suddenly making them both jump. She laid it on the kitchen table, fiddling with it still, pushing the flat chain into different shapes. 'I was jealous, just so unbearably jealous.'

'Of what?'

'Of you, of course, you and your perfect life in the city. Your independence, the prestigious job, jealous of the sort of person you were, something I could never be. And most jealous of all about you being the favourite, the trophy daughter who gets boasted about all the time.'

'Me?' Sonya said. 'Since when?'

'Since always. Well, at least since I went off the rails.'

'But you got back on the rails. You married a *doctor*, you produced the perfect grandchildren for them, Tessa, how prestigious . . . how much *on* the rails is that?'

'Oh, I know it should be,' Tessa said. 'But, you see, it never *seemed* like it, because you were out there in the bigger world, doing important things, being successful, achieving. I felt like second best. A basket case who'd had to come home in disgrace, had to be rescued from her own stupidity by her big sister.'

Sonya stared at her. 'It wasn't like that, Tess.'

'It was to me. That's just how it felt. Call it paranoia, if you like. Put it down to the drugs. But that was how it was, and nothing I did seemed to make it go away. You think Mum and Dad disapprove of you? Heavens, they forgave me and took me back after my episode as a junkie – belly dancing's nothing. They huffed and puffed that night but it doesn't stop them thinking you're the bee's knees. David reckons it's you and me that are stuck in the past, not Mum and Dad. He says that in our own ways we're still reacting to what used to be, with them and with each other.' She shrugged. 'Who knows? But it was my jealousy, you see, I just couldn't let it go.'

'And now?' Sonya said. 'What's different now?'

'I saw you dance,' Tessa said. 'Alannah made me go. She came back after she'd dropped you off at the hotel. David and I were home by then. And she just got stuck into me. She said I had my head in the sand and was being stupid. That I kept talking about how wonderful it was when we were kids, and I was missing out on having a great sister. She said I was being childish. And then she said she wanted me to do one thing for her, and that she'd be deeply disappointed if I didn't agree.'

'What?'

'She wanted me to go and see you dance.'

'And?'

'Well, of course, I said no, and I could tell she *was* really disappointed in me, so I hung on all week and then, on the day of your last performance, I called her and said I'd go.'

'So you *were* there,' Sonya said. 'Marissa and Gayle both said they thought saw you, but I didn't. At least I didn't *think* I did. Maybe it just seemed so improbable that I wasn't *able* to see you.'

Tessa shrugged. 'Maybe. But I was there and *I* did see *you*.' A tear slid down Tessa's cheek and she brushed it away. 'And you know what? I looked at you up there dancing, and you looked so beautiful, and so confident. You were doing something I'd never dreamed you might do, and quite suddenly – I felt proud. Incredibly proud that you were my sister. I felt proud instead of jealous. And then I . . . I realised how terribly I'd missed you.'

TWENTY-NINE

Frank was grating cheese for a moussaka. He was finding it hard to keep his mind on the task at hand but he persevered, making a roux, adding milk, white wine and cheese and then folding it between the layers of potato and vegetarian filling. Finally he put it in the oven, set the timer, poured himself a glass of wine, went out to the verandah and sat gazing into the shadows of the garden. So much had happened since the night Marissa had told him her secret. He'd sat with her until she finally stopped crying, then he'd poured her a brandy, and when she protested, he'd been able to persuade her to drink it in some warm milk with honey.

'I'd better go after this,' she'd said, sipping it cautiously.

And he'd laughed and said: 'The only place you're going, Marissa, is to sleep. You can have my bed and I'll sleep down here. I'm not leaving you alone tonight.' He thought she might protest, but she just looked at him and nodded, and he could see that she was so exhausted she hadn't the strength to argue.

He helped her up the stairs and into the bedroom, where she climbed fully dressed into the bed. She was asleep within minutes. Downstairs again he poured himself a very large brandy and sank into his chair to drink it before looking for the spare pillows and a blanket. But the next thing he knew there was sunlight pouring in the window, and the brandy was still on the coffee table.

'I'm sorry I woke you,' Marissa said. 'I feel very bad about taking your bed. You must have been really uncomfortable.' She was stepping into her leathers as he sat up, rubbing his eyes.

'Where are you going?' he asked stupidly.

'Home, of course,' she said. 'Aren't you going away today – Yallingup, was it?'

'Yes,' he said, waking up fully now, 'yes, I was, but –'

'I don't want to hold you up.' She picked up her helmet. 'I don't really know how to thank you for . . . well, for listening, for taking care of me. When you get back –'

'Don't go yet,' he said. 'I'll make us some breakfast, or at least let me make you some coffee, or tea, you prefer tea . . . '

'I could have some tea, I suppose,' she said, hesitating by the door.

'Have some tea and then come with me,' Frank said.

'Sorry?'

'Come to Yallingup. Come today. The place has two bedrooms, it's right near the beach. You can rest, relax, read books, swim – that's what I'm going to do. You don't have to talk about anything or be sociable.'

She looked at him for what seemed ages. 'I couldn't,' she said. 'It's Sunday and I've got classes next week. I was away for ages and I've only just got going again. I can't stop now.'

'What about Sonya or Gayle, wouldn't they do it for you?'

Marissa hesitated. 'I suppose . . . no, they couldn't teach.'

'No, but they're pretty experienced now. Couldn't they just get the others practising?'

She shook her head. 'I couldn't ask them, they've already been so good. Anyway, what would I tell them?'

'The truth?'

'The truth? All of it?'

'You told me.'

'I didn't mean to. I didn't know I would . . . '

'But you did, and that was brave, and it was also a huge step and you're going to feel shattered for the next few days at least. Even if you stay home you need to rest, you may not be able to teach your classes.'

She swayed slightly, steadying herself with her hand on the doorjamb.

'See – you're wiped out. You certainly shouldn't get on the bike. Come and sit down.' He led her back to the couch.

'I will tell them,' she said. 'I want them to know, but I don't think I can cope with going through it all again yet.'

'I could tell them for you,' he said, taking her hand. 'Or we could go together. They'll understand, Marissa.' His longing for her to agree made his chest ache.

'Do you really want me to go with you?'

'I wouldn't ask if I didn't.'

Frank checked his watch now by the light of the kitchen window. Another fifteen minutes and the moussaka would be done to a turn. He sat back in contentment, remembering his own conflicting emotions as they had driven out of Fremantle and headed for the southwest. His delight at having her there beside him in the car was woven through with anxiety about her state of mind and whether he had done the right thing in persuading her to come with him. Perhaps in his desire to be the one who supported her through this crisis, he had been more concerned with his own interests than Marissa's. Maybe this was a time that she needed to be in her own place, surrounded by familiar things, close to her other friends.

Marissa slept most of the way to Yallingup and later they walked to the restaurant for a meal and back along the moonlit beach. Next morning before six he heard her moving around in the kitchen and got up to find her waiting for the kettle to boil, pacing up and down, her face drained of colour, hands shaking.

'Hey,' he said, 'I'll do that. You come and look at the view.' Out on the balcony there was a stiff breeze off the ocean, and he wrapped a blanket around her shoulders as they stood watching the small black-clad figures of the surfers clustering in wait for the next wave. Then he set her up in a reclining chair, with her feet on a stool.

'I'm not an invalid, you know,' she said, mustering a weak smile.

'I know,' he said, handing her a mug of tea. 'But just indulge me for a day or two.'

'Frank,' she said, not looking at him, 'there's something I've wanted to ask you. The plants – my plants, you brought them back.'

'Yes.'

'Why?'

'Why not?'

'It seemed odd. You could have charged me.'

'Would you rather I had?'

'Of course not, but I wondered why you didn't.'

'Waste of time. The kids that pinched them told us where they got them. We were around your street a lot that week but we had bigger fish to fry than you growing a bit of weed in the back garden.'

'I kept wondering,' she said. 'I thought perhaps there was some sort of hidden agenda.'

'Of course there was,' he said, sitting down beside her. 'I wanted to ask you out.'

She smiled and sipped her tea. 'For a while, I thought you were playing some sort of power game with me. So I dumped the plants.'

He laughed. 'But you didn't give up, I'll bet. You do still have a smoke?'

'Only other people's,' she said. 'What about you? When are you going to give up tobacco?'

He thought she sounded as though she cared what he did but he knew that he should not attach too much meaning to anything she said or did over the next few days.

He fetched shopping and the papers that morning, and she watched as he pottered around the house and later took himself off for a swim. When he got back, she was crying again, just quietly crying, and he made no attempt to stop her. He knew there must be a lot of crying still to come. Being with her had seemed perfectly natural: he gave her the same space he needed for himself, and felt entirely at ease.

'Twice you saved my life now,' Marissa had said when he finally dropped her at home in Fremantle the following Saturday afternoon.

He laughed. 'You're worth saving.'

'I owe you.'

'No,' he'd said. 'This is what friends do – you just have to get used to it.'

The timer pinged, and Frank swallowed the last of his wine and went inside. The moussaka was golden and bubbling. He wrapped a tea towel around his hands and lifted it out of the oven.

'That looks good and smells even better,' Marissa said, appearing at the kitchen door. 'What is it?'

'Moussaka.'

'Your speciality. Very Greek, very seventies.'

He smiled. 'That's me,' he said. 'Very seventies. It's actually vegetarian moussaka – please note the major concession to your dietary preferences. And, by the way, you have a very poor collection of cooking equipment. How did your class go?'

'Fine, really good,' she said, dropping her keys on the table. 'That smells and looks absolutely delicious. Will it keep?'

Frank's face fell slightly. 'It's ready to eat now,' he said. 'Timed to perfection. How long?'

Marissa shrugged. 'Half an hour, an hour . . . maybe more?'

He tried to hide his disappointment with a shrug. 'Well, if it has to, I suppose. You won't get it at its best, of course. What did you want to do?'

She stepped up to him and put her arms around his neck. 'This,' she said, and she kissed him, gently at first and then passionately, her tongue finding his.

Frank had imagined it so often but now she took him by surprise. 'Just this?' he asked, kissing her again, sliding his fingers into her hair.

'Well, quite a lot of this,' she said, 'and some other things.'

'Are you absolutely sure about this, Marissa?'

'I'm absolutely sure.'

'Moussaka keeps for ages,' he said. 'In fact, I always feel it benefits from standing overnight.'

'This is beautiful, Marissa,' Gayle said, shaking the sequin-embroidered scarf from the tissue paper and holding it up. 'Thank you so much.'

'And look at mine,' Sonya said, 'it's the same green as my

favourite costume. Did you make them, draw the pattern and sew on all those sequins by hand?'

Marissa nodded. 'I just wanted to thank you for . . . for everything – coming on the tour, helping me so much, looking after the classes the other week –'

'Teasing you about Frank,' Sonya cut in.

'That too,' Marissa said with a smile. 'But most of all for showing me what it's like to have friends, and for making it safe for me to talk about the past.'

'Friendship isn't a one-way thing, Marissa,' Gayle replied. 'Without you and the dancing, without being with you and Sonya all those weeks, I doubt I'd have had the courage to do what I've done.'

'Gayle's right,' Sonya said. 'Me too. And look what it's done – taught me something about my family, and most of all myself. Heavens – you guys even made my sister like me again.'

'I think that's overstating our role somewhat,' Gayle said. 'Just the same, Marissa, it's an indication that next time you ask someone to dance their way around Western Australia with you, you can never be sure what will happen.'

Marissa laughed. 'I can't imagine doing it with anyone else.'

'I should hope not,' Sonya said. 'Thank you, Marissa, this is beautiful.'

'They're rather selfish gifts, really. After all, they're only of any use if you go on dancing. So they're my way of saying I hope you're not going to stop now.'

'*Stop*? You're joking.' Sonya replied.

'Me neither,' Gayle said. 'So it seems you're stuck with us and with Frank, I suspect.'

'Yes,' Marissa said, 'and Frank.'

'And there's Oliver too,' Gayle said. She had been thinking about him a lot, about the fact that in all the years she had known him she had seen occasional flashes of the hidden Oliver: a remark here, a gesture there, the discussion of an idea, that had all been evidence of the man who was now, so rapidly, emerging from his shell. 'Is it a domino effect, do you think? Or has it nothing at all to do with us?'

'I'd like to think that by bonking Oliver I played a seminal role in his transformation,' Sonya said with a grin. 'But, actually, I think that it's more complicated than that. Lots of things came together at the same time.'

'I think you're right.' Gayle said. 'Not, of course, that I want to undermine the important and entirely selfless nature of that contribution of yours.' She paused, wondering whether she should say anything or just shut up. 'But as we're having this very frank discussion, Sonya, you do realise, don't you, that Oliver is in love with you?'

Sonya, who had just picked up a couple of dried apricots from a dish on the table, nearly choked. 'You've got to be joking,' she managed to say when she'd finished coughing. 'Oliver? In love with me?'

'Of course, that's why he's learning the tango.'

'But I don't dance the tango.'

'No, but he wants to show you he can be what the tango represents – dramatic, passionate, sensuous, because that's how he sees you.'

Sonya held up her hand. 'Hang on, Gayle, you've got this all wrong. Oliver is in love, certainly, but with you. Can't you see that? The way he looks at you, the way he is when he's around you. Big mistake, Gayle. Oliver sees me as his mate – you are his object of desire.'

Marissa drew the cork from a bottle of chilled white wine and poured it into three glasses. 'You're both wrong,' she said. 'I've only met Oliver a few times but I can tell that Oliver is, very clearly, a man in love with himself.'

'That's a bit unkind,' Sonya said.

'I don't mean it unkindly. It's just that Oliver is like a butterfly crawling from its chrysalis, and he's surprised, stunned probably, by his own transformation. He's marvelling at the size and colour of his wings and that with them he can fly. He won't really be able to fall in love with anyone until he's done more flying practice.' There was a silence and Marissa wondered briefly if she'd offended them. 'Sorry,' she murmured, 'that was pretty insensitive, especially if one, or even possibly both, of you are in love with Oliver.'

'In love with him? Of course not,' Gayle said, looking away. 'I mean, I love him to bits, but I'm not in love . . . anyway, I'm too busy flying myself. Although –' she looked across at Sonya – 'I did feel a bit jealous when he admired your breasts so much. Isn't that silly?'

Sonya laughed. 'I know what you mean. I am definitely not in love with Oliver, but I'm very fond of him and I think he's becoming more attractive by the minute – or maybe by the tango class. Even so, I felt a bit jealous of you, Gayle, when he started talking about how wonderful you are.'

Marissa raised her glass. 'This is all very interesting,' she said, 'and it's far from resolved. My guess is that all this leaves room for possibilities and I may yet be counselling one or both of you about Oliver in the future.'

'Well, look who's the relationship expert now,' Sonya said. 'I notice there are two toothbrushes in your bathroom.'

'Is nothing sacred?'

'No. Did you give Frank a present too?'

'I have one planned,' Marissa said. 'But it's more complicated.'

'Not a sequinned scarf?'

'Not his style, I think,' she said. She took some folded papers from the pocket of her jeans. 'But have a look at these emails.'

'The thing is, Ma,' Oliver said under his breath, addressing the headstone, 'I got it all wrong, even you. I even got you wrong. Trying to be what I thought you wanted, I forgot to be myself. In fact, I don't think I ever knew who myself was.' He emptied a plastic bottle of water into the stoneware vase, stripped the cellophane off the bronze and white chrysanthemums, pressed the stems into the oasis and straightened up. He'd been in the habit of coming here at least once a month, but now three months had passed since his last visit, since the day that Andrew had asked him why he continued to visit so often.

'I owe it to her,' Oliver had said, suddenly bewildered by both the question and the answer. 'Why? Do you think that's odd?'

'I think the frequency is unusual,' Andrew said. 'Commendable, of course, but unusual, especially after . . . what . . . twelve years?'

'Thirteen.'

'So that's it, is it? You go because you feel you owe it to your mother? And would she think you owe her that?'

Oliver wavered. 'I don't know. I've never really thought about it like that. But I suppose, knowing her . . . no, she'd think it was a waste of time.'

'Well, then?'

'Now that you've asked, I think I haven't been going there for her, but for myself. I have a chat with her, you see.'

'You mean she communicates with you?'

'I talk to her.'

'Or to yourself?'

'Yes, to myself, really, but I think . . . well, I suppose I pretend to myself that I'm talking to her.'

Andrew nodded.

'It *is* odd, isn't it?' It had shocked him to realise that he'd set off, time after time, with a strong sense of duty and responsibility, often when he didn't feel like going there at all, thinking he was doing it for Joan. Once again he'd been using her, just as he had hidden behind her ideology and made her the excuse for so many things. If she had indeed communicated with him, she would doubtless have said, 'For heaven's sake, Oliver, get a life! Just get a life!'

Oliver brushed grass clippings from the knees of his jeans and stared down at the stone. 'Okay,' he said. 'It will be different from now on. It's already different.' He glanced at his watch and gave a mock bow to the grave. 'Gotta go now, Ma. Getting a life is pretty demanding.' And, blowing a kiss in the direction of the grave, he strode off down the path and back to his car.

His appointment was the last one of the afternoon and Andrew's previous client was obviously running late. In the waiting room, Oliver thumbed through a copy of *Wellbeing*, reading advertisements for herbal remedies, meditation, visualisation, cranio-sacral rebalancing, and Feldenkrais practitioners. He was attempting to follow a five minute guide to the Alexander Technique when a woman emerged from Andrew's consulting room looking shell shocked. She stumbled along the corridor and paused, seeming to realise she was going in the wrong direction, then she turned, clutched the wall and made her way to the front door and out into the sunlit forecourt.

Oliver watched her, remembering his first visit, and the shock of insights that had left him stunned and confused. It all seemed much longer ago than it really was, and he wanted to run after the woman and tell her it would be all right, that it was worth entering the dark tunnel, because emerging at the other end was simply brilliant. These days he wondered how he could have worn blinkers for so long, and he still blushed with embarrassment that he had had the temerity to criticise Gayle for hiding from the truth of her life when he could now see that he had spent all his life hiding from himself.

'You'd be proud of me, Andrew,' Oliver said, settling into the chair. 'I flirted with a woman at the dance class, and I did it so successfully that she asked me to go and have a drink with her.'

'And?'

'And I went, and it was fun.'

'And you didn't talk politics or feminism to her?'

'Not a word. Not any sort of politics. I didn't even ask her if she liked Leonard Cohen, because she was probably too young to have ever heard of him.'

Andrew smiled. 'Well done. Are you planning to see her again?'

Oliver shook his head. 'Oh no, although I guess I'll see her at the class. She's nice but she's very young and we have very little in common other than the tango and the salsa. I felt as though I was out with one of the students.'

'And your friend? You said last time that once the rift between you had been mended, you were confused about your own feelings for her.'

'I'm still confused,' Oliver said. 'We're similar in so many ways, and now, here we are, both of us going through these

299

incredible changes in our lives at the same time. Maybe I just think I love her because all the boundaries are moving – maybe I just love what's happening to her.'

'That could be the same thing,' Andrew said. 'Do you think she has any idea of this? Any chance that she might feel the same?'

Oliver shrugged. 'I just don't know. I think it's too soon. She's got so much happening at the moment, I doubt she knows what she wants yet.'

'I hate to sound like a cliché,' Andrew said. 'But time really will help. "Wait and see" is a tedious technique but in this case it seems to be the best course.'

'Yes, and it was time that I wanted to talk to you about,' Oliver replied. 'I think it's time I stopped coming. I know it hasn't been very long but I've made a lot of progress thanks to you.'

Andrew smiled. 'Some people don't need very long,' he said. 'Once they get a few things clear they can strike out on their own, and of course you can always come back if you wish.'

'Well, that's the thing,' Oliver said. 'Frankly, Andrew, I'd just like us to be able to go and have a drink together when we feel like it and talk about all sorts of things, not just my weird hang-ups. Couldn't we just be friends?'

Andrew chewed one arm of his glasses. 'I'd like that immensely,' he said, 'but suppose you feel the need to return to therapy?'

'Then I'd have to find someone else, wouldn't I? You could suggest someone.'

'You're becoming positively assertive, Oliver,' Andrew said, looking hard at him.

Oliver stood up. 'Yes. Good, isn't it? Anyway, I'm your last client today, so come on, let's go.'

'Go where?'

'Over to the pub. We're going to celebrate the transition from therapist and client to mates. And we could have a meal as well. If you haven't got anything else on, that is.'

'I never have anything else on,' Andrew replied. 'Since my divorce, I haven't had a life – I simply encourage other people to talk about theirs. Just give me a minute to lock up.'

'You know,' Oliver said as they walked across the park to the pub a few minutes later, 'maybe you should see a therapist yourself, Andrew. On the other hand, I could introduce you to my friend Sonya.'

THIRTY

'I still don't understand why we had to come on the bike,' Frank said as Marissa pulled into a parking space. 'Why couldn't we have come in my car?'

'Because it's a surprise,' she said. 'Come on, put your helmet in here so I can lock it up.'

Frank, feeling somewhat uneasy, handed over the helmet and undid the top buttons of his leather jacket. It wasn't that he had any objection to the Harley; in fact, he was learning to love it, although not with quite the same degree of passion that Marissa obviously felt. No, his unease was about the surprise, about not knowing where they were going or why. He was used to being in control, to determining how and when things would be done. Letting someone else plan for him was a leap of faith. He knew he needed to learn to trust, but knowing didn't actually make it easier.

Marissa had trusted him, not only by telling him about her past, but letting him help her through the aftermath of that revelation. She had let him take over, put her in his car, drive her to a place she didn't know, and look after her for a whole week when she was at her most vulnerable. And then she had let him into her home, her secrets, her life, in the most intimate way. Frank felt churlish that he seemed to be finding the whole letting go and trusting thing so hard. Tonight, for instance, she said she had a surprise for him, and she wanted him to come with her and not ask questions.

'So when we've done whatever this is shall we go and have a

meal somewhere?' he'd asked, trying to get some clue about the evening ahead.

'Maybe,' she'd said. 'Stop trying to find out by stealth. It's a surprise, Frank. Try to trust me.' And he *was* trying, really hard.

They headed south out of Fremantle and three-quarters of an hour later she pulled into a busy car park behind a large building.

'This is totally off my patch,' Frank said.

'It's quite safe,' Marissa grinned. 'It's only Mandurah. I haven't exactly abducted you.'

'Sorry,' he said, smiling and taking her hand. 'I'm such a control freak.'

She leaned over and kissed him. 'It's okay, but now you have to be really brave and close your eyes for a minute. Promise me you won't look until I tell you?'

He closed his eyes and they started walking, her arm in his. 'What if I trip?'

'You won't,' she said. 'I won't let you.'

Frank swallowed hard and kept his eyes closed as their feet crunched across the gravel.

'Not yet,' she said, and he felt an increase in the noise level. They were near other people, quite a lot of other people, and even with his eyes shut he knew they had gone from the dark of the car park to somewhere that was brightly lit. He wondered how many people were looking at him walking along with his eyes closed.

'Okay, you can open your eyes now.'

He blinked in the light. They were in the crowded foyer of a theatre, and right in front of him was a poster with a photograph of a face he knew almost as well as he knew his own. Goosebumps pricked his flesh and he turned to Marissa, finding it hard to speak.

'Normie Rowe in concert. I didn't even know he was over here,' he said eventually.

'That's because you never read the arts and entertainment pages,' she said. 'So can you relax now? We've got the best seats in the house.'

'I can relax,' he said. 'And thank you, Marissa. It's the best surprise imaginable.'

She shook her head. 'No,' she said with a smile. 'The best is yet to come. Let's go in.'

Brian was ready to go. Tomorrow morning he'd be on a flight to Sydney, the car and the rest of his possessions on the way by road and rail. There was a great sense of relief in leaving, he thought, in walking away from the past and starting again. For years he'd been hamstrung by responsibilities, the job, Gayle, Angie, the house – all the things that other people expected of him. Now he was free to please himself, take life one day at a time. Carefully he folded the remainder of his clothes and put them into the suitcase that contained all he'd need until the rest of his stuff arrived in Manly.

'Seems like it might be for the best after all,' he'd said to Gayle a few days earlier. 'Nice place you got yourself.' He was feeling quite warmly towards her again now. He still reckoned she'd got far too much out of him, although Tremlett had told him that she could have got a whole lot more if she'd decided to push it. The law seemed pretty unfair to him, but what could you do but grin and bear it?

'I hope it all works out for you,' he'd said. 'And you know where I am if you need me, or if you're ever in Sydney . . . '

'Yes,' she said. 'And we'll keep in touch about Angie. It's a difficult time for her.' They'd stood there for a few minutes, a chasm of awkward silence separating them.

'Well, I suppose this is it, then,' he'd said, moving to kiss her on the cheek. She let him but she hadn't returned the kiss. It seemed a strange way to part, to end a marriage after all those years together.

Brian made a tour of the house, checking cupboards, putting his toiletries into his bag. Nothing left to do. Tomorrow the Flying Domestics would be in to clean up and the following day the new owners would move in. It looked awfully bare now, despite the fact that some of the furniture was staying. Gayle, of course, had never liked it and now he wondered how he felt. He'd been proud of it certainly, but perhaps . . . perhaps he had been a bit too concerned about how it all looked to outsiders rather than how it felt to live in.

He closed his bag and walked out of the bedroom, down the stairs and out of the house. He'd booked a hotel near the airport for the night. In the morning he'd deliver the car to the transporters and be on his flight by eight. He stretched uncomfortably. There was an unpleasant feeling in his chest. The curry he'd had for dinner had left him with indigestion. Dropping his bag into the boot he got into the driver's seat, started the engine and looked back one last time across the darkened garden to the empty house; then he drove the Saab out through the gates for the last time.

'So was it worth trusting me?' Marissa asked as they made their way out of the theatre.

Frank put his arm around her shoulders. 'Absolutely,' he said. 'It was brilliant. It's twenty years since I actually saw him perform. He's still terrific, isn't he?'

'He's really good,' Marissa said. 'And I guess I most enjoyed thinking about him and you back then.'

He pulled her closer and kissed her. 'Me too,' he said. 'Thank you, Marissa, it's the best present I ever had. Thank you so much.'

'Good,' she said, 'because now you have to trust me again.'

'Ah!' he said. 'So we *are* allowed to eat, and you know some strange place where the moussaka is better than mine.'

'No moussaka is better than yours,' she said, taking his arm as they made their way out through the jumble of people by the exit.

'Are we walking or biking to the restaurant?' Frank asked.

'We're walking this way,' Marissa said, leading him to an alley at the side of the building.

'But we can't get out that way,' Frank protested, pulling her back.

'We're not going out,' she said, 'at least, you're not.' She pointed down the alley. 'Look down there – someone's waiting for you.'

Frank stopped to look. In the light from an open doorway someone was waving.

'Frank?' a voice called, and Frank held up his hand to shield his eyes from the light. 'Frank Owen?'

The man began to walk towards him. Goosebumps prickled Frank's skin and a huge lump swelled in his throat. 'Norm?' he said. 'Is that you, Norm?'

'The same. It's been a long time, mate.'

Frank shook his head, unable to speak.

'Go on, Frank,' Marissa said. But he was frozen to the spot.

'Jeez, mate, you haven't changed,' Normie said, and they stared at each other in the half-light, finally stumbling together, hugging, tears bright in their eyes.

'You must be Marissa,' Normie said eventually, taking her hands. 'Thank you so much for this.'

She smiled. 'It's a very great pleasure. Off you go then, Frank.'

'Aren't you coming?' he asked.

She put her hand on his cheek and kissed him. 'No, not tonight. Another time maybe, but tonight is secret men's business.'

As she rocked the Harley off its stand and started the engine, Marissa couldn't stop smiling. It was a new feeling for her, this immense satisfaction of planning something special for someone she loved and having it work to perfection. It had amused her to see Frank trying to resist the desire to take control, to trust what she wanted to do for him. She would probably have been the same herself if she hadn't been so emotionally exhausted by breaking her silence that she hadn't had the strength to resist his effort to care for her.

'So you think he's the one, do you?' Sonya had asked her a few days ago.

'I do,' Marissa said. 'The one I was waiting for without knowing I was waiting.'

'I guess we're all doing that,' Sonya said. 'But you get to a stage where the waiting is unconscious, and there's no longer any real expectation attached to it. And then it's really comfortable.'

Marissa, who had been driving Sonya's car at the time, taking her to the airport for a flight to Kalgoorlie, had turned to her in surprise. 'I thought you were radically single and totally over the idea of meeting anyone.'

'I am,' Sonya said. 'But that doesn't mean that it will never happen – after all, look at you. You know, Marissa, I've learned a lot about myself in the last few months, part of which is that I tend to lock myself into certain positions. For years I thought I was locked out of my family, only required to appear and perform in a particular way from time to time. Now I'm chatting often to my sister, going to my great-nephew's christening, and actually staying with Mum and Dad. How different is that?'

'I'm so pleased for you. And what about Gayle?'

'Well, I'm sure she wouldn't marry again, but she'll probably have other relationships.'

'Plural?'

'Who knows, she might enjoy things being less than permanent, but on the other hand there's always Oliver.'

Marissa slowed the Harley and took the slip road off the freeway. She needed fuel and some milk and, remembering that there was a 24-hour petrol station on the northern side of Canning Highway, she made the slight detour and drew into the forecourt. She'd always liked being out on her bike at night. Maybe she could persuade Frank to get a bike. They could ride side by side, independence and proximity. She filled the tank and walked into the brightly lit store. A man was standing at the register, his back to her, grumbling about the shop's lack of indigestion tablets.

'D'you mean you haven't even got a packet of Rennies?' he said, and the guy on the cash register mumbled something and shook his head.

Marissa glanced around looking for milk; the fridges were at the far end of the store. She strolled down half listening to the conversation and, as she opened the fridge door, something made her look back. The man's back was turned, but there was something familiar . . . She tensed, looking up at the closed circuit screen above her head. He was fatter, much fatter, and older, but then he would be, and there was something about the set of the shoulders, his voice, the reddish hair, the way he held his head. She was dizzy with the sense of recognition.

As she turned from the screen he was heading for the automatic doors. The hair on Marissa's neck stood on end. Was it really him? Her breath seemed caught in her chest.

'Blue?' she said. 'Blue?' but he was outside now, getting into a black car. She dropped the milk carton and stumbled over it as she ran to the door and out onto the forecourt. 'Blue?' she cried, looking around, but he was gone, the Saab accelerating up the hill to the freeway, its tail lights disappearing amid the other traffic. It was him, she was sure of it.

Marissa walked back inside.

'Everything all right, love?' the attendant asked. 'You look as though you've seen a ghost.'

'Yes,' she said, nodding her head, 'yes, I really think I did.'

ACKNOWLEDGMENTS

To Jo Culbertson, Lisa Resch, Val Flowers and Jan O'Meara, thank you for that Sunday morning hens' breakfast that was the inspiration for this book. Special thanks to Pete and Ray, the Vietnam veterans who talked to me about post-traumatic stress disorder and who prefer to remain anonymous; and to Normie Rowe for allowing me to put words in his mouth. And many thanks to my belly dancing friend Christine Nagel for advice and information on all the right moves.

As always, Cate Paterson, Sarina Rowell and Jo Jarrah have used their sensitivity and professionalism to make this a better book than it would otherwise have been and I am very grateful. Thanks too to the indomitable Jane Novak, and my agent Sheila Drummond for also being a special friend and sounding board.

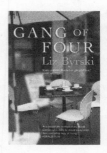

Liz Byrski
Food, Sex & Money

It's almost forty years since the three ex-convent girls left school and went their separate ways, but finally they meet again.

Bonnie, rocked by the death of her husband, is back in Australia after decades in Europe, and is discovering that financial security doesn't guarantee a fulfilling life. Fran, long divorced, is a freelance food writer, battling with her diet, her bank balance and her relationship with her adult children. And Sylvia, marooned in a passionless marriage, is facing a crisis that will crack her world wide open.

Together again, Bonnie, Fran and Sylvia embark on a venture that will challenge everything they thought they knew about themselves – and give them more second chances than they could ever have imagined.

'*Food, Sex & Money* is an entertaining, ultimately optimistic, novel'
WEST AUSTRALIAN

'The issues of financial security, emotional independence, career, diet, motherhood and sexuality transcend age, making this a relevant, enjoyable read for all women, and for men who seek to understand them.'
GOOD READING

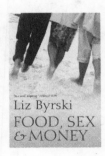